D1487143

Bardwell's Folly

A LOVE STORY

Bardwell's Folly

A LOVE STORY

Sandra Hutchison

SHEER HUBRIS PRESS

Troy, New York

SHEER HUBRIS PRESS
37 Bolivar Ave.
Troy, New York 12180
SheerHubris.com

Publisher's Note: This is a work of fiction. Names, characters, places, and incidents are a product of the author's imagination. Locales and public names are sometimes used for atmospheric purposes. Any resemblance to actual people, living or dead, or to businesses, companies, events, institutions, or locales is completely coincidental.

Book Layout © 2015 BookDesignTemplates.com
Cover typography layout by Tugboat Design

Library of Congress Control Number: 2016918978

Bardwell's Folly / Sandra Hutchison -- 1st Ed.
ISBN 978-0-9911869-5-2

For my parents, Southerners
who taught us to love justice.

Chapter 1

It wasn't long into the May meeting of the Friends of the Bedford Bardwell House when Dori Bardwell, age twenty-six, began to fantasize about running away from it.

She poured cups of tea from one of the three porcelain teapots pressed into service in the front parlor and saw her escape in her mind's eye, like a movie: It would be a beautiful spring evening. She, a sturdy, petite woman in jeans and t-shirt – still young, still shapely, still conceivably attractive to someone somewhere – would quickly stuff a few boxes into her little Subaru and drive away before any of the old ladies noticed she'd left the room.

There'd be a perky soundtrack in a major key to signal it was going to end well. Nothing bleak or tragic – or worse, dull.

"Eudora?"

"Hmm?"

"There's no more tea in that pot."

"Sorry," she said, and switched to the next one.

"Where's Salinger today?" one of the ladies asked.

"No idea," Dori said. "I told him about the meeting, but I guess he couldn't make it."

"He hasn't made the last eight," said the lady with the thinnest, sharpest face – Marjorie Haight, President of the Friends and also one of the trustees in charge of her parents' estate.

"I believe Salinger has moved on in his interests," Dori said. "He just informed me he's not attending classes anymore either."

Marjorie shook her head. "Another semester's tuition wasted."

"I know. I've decided not to wait for him anymore. It's my turn now."

Marjorie's smile was tight, as usual. "Best to take that up at a meeting of the trustees, dear. These ladies are here about the festival."

Of course. Dori decided she would focus on the tea and the

meeting in order to savor its full horror. She needed any extra motivation she could find to finally get the hell out.

Although it was impossible to tell without looking closely, the Bedford Bardwell House had been built just thirty years earlier when her father, rich after the publication and hit movie of his Pulitzer Prize-winning novel, *Tea and Slavery*, had left the South to settle in Jasper, Massachusetts with his wife. If anybody knew why they had chosen an economically depressed rural village in that unfashionable part of Western Massachusetts that was not quite in the Berkshires, not associated with any colleges, and nowhere near any friends or relatives, they hadn't told Dori.

Perhaps it was the cheap real estate. Perhaps it was an instinct for seclusion. Or perhaps her parents had realized they were less likely to be criticized for erecting a grand Southern plantation house, complete with giant white pillars, in downtrodden Jasper than they would be in a New England village with prouder traditions.

It was true, few residents of Jasper ever criticized the house for being out of place. Instead, they criticized it as a foolish and vulgar waste of money. The house was known to most people in town as "Bardwell's Folly," which irritated the trustees and the Friends, who preferred it be called "The Bedford Bardwell House."

The trustees – per her father's will – administered the estate to protect the house as a home of literary note not only because Bedford Bardwell lived and wrote there, but because he had modeled it after the plantation house in *Tea and Slavery*. Of course, this one did not have a working plantation attached to it, and certainly no slave quarters. Just a nice two-acre lot on Main Street.

She had suggested the ladies might prefer coffee to tea because she'd hoped what was left over might supply some of her morning coffee at the Friends' expense. But Marjorie Haight was having none of that. "We wouldn't want to get the dears all riled up over a simple beverage change, Eudora, dear, when we have so much more substantive issues to discuss."

Substantive issues? The annual Bedford Bardwell Days followed exactly the same pattern year after year: tours of the house, tours of the garden, cake and tea under a tent on the expansive front lawn, a used book sale, a plant sale, a decorated hat competition (one bold year of experimenting with full costume hadn't been deemed a success), a little genteel music from any halfway-capable musician who could be pressed into playing for free, and – in the one sop to the presence of children – a sack race.

Listening to the ladies earnestly check these items off one by one, discussing each fully as if they might do something different that year, made Dori want to scream. She asked, "Have you ever thought about renting a bounce house? The kids love them."

Marjorie said, "I'm quite sure you will not find a bounce house in *Tea and Slavery*."

"And thank heavens for that!" another member added.

Dori said, "If it's historical accuracy you're aiming for, don't we need some slaves? I'd be willing to wear a little blackface. Anyone else?"

The horrified silence that followed was by far the longest she'd ever provoked.

Marjorie Haight shared a look with her vice president before pinning Dori with a much sterner one. "As I suspect you realize, that would hardly be appropriate. We're not trying to recreate the antebellum period religiously. And I'd hate to do anything that might disrupt attendance or reduce contributions. This event is quite critical to our budget."

Depend on Marjorie to put it in dire financial terms. The fact Dori relied on the efforts of these women to keep the taxes paid was inescapable. On the other hand, they also prevented her from doing anything that might allow her to make enough income to pay the taxes herself – like subdividing the place into apartments or just plain selling it off.

Not that it was their fault. It was her parents who'd set up this fucking trust.

"Moving on," Marjorie said. "Is there a problem with the lawn mower we should know about?"

"Not that I know of," Dori said. "Why?"

"The grass, dear. It's getting so long."

"That's Salinger's job. You pay him for it, don't you?" They didn't pay her for keeping the interior of the house clean and picked up. Instead, twice a year, before the Christmas Open House and the summer's Bedford Bardwell Days, they showed up and did everything Dori failed to do: the floors, the windows, the ceilings, the curtains, the polishing of wood and silver and brass. Another contingent showed up early each spring to tend the garden and pot up divisions to sell.

"Yes, dear, but obviously... it isn't happening."

Dori said, "I guess you'd better talk to him, then."

The newest member, Madeleine Fourier, leaned forward eagerly. She was a recently-retired social worker. "Are you two not getting along?"

Dori stuck her tongue in her cheek while she decided how best to answer. Madeleine probably had a bunch of fine, upstanding siblings who'd graduated college and gone on to careers with distinction. She and Salinger had not. "We get along fine as long as I don't depend on him to do anything."

Marjorie shook her head sadly. "With no parents left, somebody needs to remind the poor boy that adults must accept their share of responsibility."

Dori said, "Some adults seem willing to accept a lot more responsibility than others. You, for example, are an absolute paragon."

Marjorie smiled uncertainly. "You know I feel I owe it to your dear mother."

"And I'm sure she'd feel you're extremely dedicated to it," Dori said.

There was an uncomfortable silence.

"What about the lawn, then?" one of the other ladies said.

"I guess we'd better hire someone," Marjorie said. "We'll just pay whoever that is instead of Salinger. Maybe that will teach him to value the opportunity to earn a little spending money."

Wait a minute. Dori could use more spending money herself. Could she fit the job in?

But if they paid her, Marjorie would feel more entitled than ever to call her up every time she drove by and felt the grass was getting too long. Besides, they probably wouldn't want to pay her enough to make it worth her while. Over the years she'd learned it was smarter not to volunteer for anything.

One of the other ladies said, "I hear Joe Gagnon does a good job at a fair price."

Dori froze. Was it just her imagination every head in the room had immediately swiveled towards her?

But perhaps it was to be expected after that horrifyingly public marriage proposal. Followed by her horrifyingly public refusal.

Madeleine Fourier said, "Perhaps we should give Eudora a say."

Dori felt her face burning. It was the curse of her red hair and pale skin: her complexion never let her hide strong feelings. "It doesn't matter to me."

And it didn't, not really. Eight long years had passed since Joe had last spoken to her. And what was an angry ex-boyfriend when she had more immediate worries, like whether her food budget would stretch to the end of the month?

She decided she wouldn't pass the cookie tray unless someone asked about it. There might just be leftovers.

Chapter 2

Shortly after she'd gotten home from work the next day the front door bell rang. She pulled the heavy, creaking door open and there he was. Joe Gagnon.

"I'm here about the lawn," he said.

He looked so respectable. No pony tail; no scraggly dishwater-blond attempt at a Che Guevara beard; no earrings; no defiant messages of any kind on his thoroughly ordinary polo shirt. She had seen his trucks around town but not him. Now she wondered if she had actually seen him and just not realized who he was. He was still attractive, but in a completely ordinary-guy-next-door kind of way. No wedding ring, but then she was certain she would have heard about that. "Joe?"

He smiled stiffly and stuck out his hand for a formal handshake. "Hello."

"How are you?"

His eyes met hers briefly, then slid past, down the hall. "I need to go over this contract with you."

She swallowed. Still not forgiven. "Why?"

His eyes flickered back to hers in surprise. "It's your lawn."

Not really, but the trust was complicated enough she didn't bother to try to explain. "It's not my contract. Who made the arrangements?"

"Marjorie Haight."

"You'd better discuss it with her, then."

"I did. She asked me to go over the expectations with you, so you could make sure we were meeting them."

"Oh, I see. She wants me to be the bad cop if you screw up." She was hoping for a smile, for some tiny spark of something, but there was nothing. She felt the dull stab of an old, familiar pain. "Won't you come in?"

He took two steps into the grand foyer, enough for her to pull the door closed behind him, then held out the contract.

"Do you want to sit down?" Dori asked. "Can I get you a cup of coffee or something?"

"No, thank you," he said. "I was asked to go over the contract with you. If you don't want to read it, perhaps I could just quickly run down the particulars of our service." He was refusing to make eye contact.

She sighed. "Shouldn't you have warned Marjorie you'd rather die than have a civil conversation with me?"

That finally earned her a sour glance. "I assumed we could manage a simple business relationship."

"I would have thought so, too. It's been eight years. That's a lot of water under the bridge. Why don't you tell me how you're doing?" She knew a lot of it already, of course, but it would be nice to hear it from his mouth.

"If you don't mind, I'd prefer to keep this purely professional," he said. A flush was climbing up his neck. "First of all, we provide mowing as needed, which can vary depending on the season and other factors, such as –"

"How much are they paying you?"

He shifted on his feet. "Seventy dollars per visit."

Damn. That would have made it worth her while.

"You have a big lawn," he said, apparently feeling some justification was necessary. He gazed stiffly at some point just over her right shoulder. "And we provide the kind of expertise a fine lawn demands. In addition to mowing, we perform regular dethatching and aerating, fertilization, grub control, weed control ... whatever is required to keep it looking great."

She stared at him, trying to calibrate the scruffy, radical-minded Joe she'd loved with this angry, buttoned-up lawn service salesman guy. People said he was doing well, so presumably he treated other clients better than he was treating her. "Okay. I got it. Maybe I'll see you out on the front lawn one of these days."

His eyes met hers again, this time with just a hint of triumph in them. "That's unlikely unless there's a problem. I have a crew that handles the actual work."

"How splendid. I won't expect to see you at all, then." Her throat closed up unexpectedly, and she swung the door open for him before turning and fleeing down the hall. He could close the door himself; he was good at that.

She walked into the kitchen later and found Salinger sitting at the long kitchen table, wolfing down the cookies she'd managed to save from the Friends tea.

"Planning to leave me any of those?" she asked.

"Help yourself." He gestured magnanimously at the nearly empty package.

"Did you already eat dinner?"

"Yeah, I had the chicken." He saw her face. "You wanted that too? Sorry. It was really good. Some of the best you've made."

She sat down at the table, disgusted with herself. She'd known she needed to hide the chicken better if she wanted to get any more of it.

So, dinner. What could it be? Scrambled eggs? Maybe a frozen waffle?

"You might want to grab some of these now before I eat them all," he suggested.

"Thanks, I will." She quickly squirreled them away behind a cereal box in one of the lower cabinets. Salinger usually only ate things stored at or near eye-level. "You missed the Friends meeting again," she told him. His idiotic ginger dreadlocks were looking distinctly dusty, but she had resolved never to say anything about them. Best to save her nagging for more important stuff.

"I can't believe you actually show up for those things," he said.

"The funds they raise pay our taxes, you know. Without that, the house would belong to the town and you and I would be out on the street."

Salinger picked at something in his teeth, apparently already bored with the topic.

She sighed. "I'm supposed to let you know they hired someone else to mow the lawn."

"Oh, good. I wasn't into it anymore. Every time I'd go out to get started I'd realize I needed to get some gas and that just always seemed like too much trouble."

So many things in his life seemed to fall into that category. "How much were they paying you?" she asked.

He looked vague. "Twenty-five?"

Just as well she hadn't asked, then. They probably would have expected her to do it for peanuts, too. "So what are you going to do, now?"

"Oh, you know. My needs are not great."

"Yeah, well, now you're not in college anymore, my needs include half the phone, electric, and heating oil. And half the groceries. You haven't been pitching in the way we discussed."

"Actually, I'm moving out."

"To where?"

"Jenna's."

"Jenna won't mind supporting you?"

"It's not supporting me. She's my *girlfriend*."

Dori snorted.

"What?" he said. "I do my part."

"What's your part? Buying the weed?"

"Who buys? I've got a little patch out in the woods." He grinned. "Even brings in a little money once in a while. You want some?"

"I've told you before, dealing could land you in jail."

"This is why I don't offer more often. You always jump to the worst-case scenario."

Supposedly, the reason her brother hadn't died with the rest of the family was that he'd been grounded for pot-smoking at school, not allowed to go on the trip to Martha's Vineyard, though Dori had long suspected he simply hadn't fit on the plane. Why her parents thought leaving a fifteen-year-old alone at home all weekend would do anything to inhibit further pot-smoking was beyond her. Certainly nothing had slowed him down since.

"Who got you started on that stuff, anyway?" she asked. "Chuckie?"

"No. Dad. He thought it would help me relax."

"Dad?" She stared at him.

"You know, back in ninth grade when I was freaking out because Angie Clausen dumped me? He said, 'Come on, man, we need some father-son time.' And he had a bag in his fishing box.

What, are you saying he never smoked with you?"

"No, he never smoked with me!"

"Wow. Bummer. I know why, though. He probably figured you'd give him a big lecture about how it was illegal and addictive and supporting the lifestyle of violent crime lords in Mexico or whatever. Or it would land him in jail."

Was it crazy that she felt jealous of Salinger for being turned into a pothead by their father? At least they'd gotten to share a few laughs. Though it was also true she'd sneered at just about anything her father had said in those days. Once she'd smelled liquor on his breath she'd wanted nothing to do with him and by then he was usually having his first bourbon over breakfast. Well, except towards the end, when he was suddenly, obnoxiously sober.

Joe was the only person Dori had ever smoked pot with. And her father had never seemed to like Joe. "Do they have running water at that kid's place?" he'd asked once. "Should I buy him a razor? Or is there some deep philosophical reason he insists on looking like a homeless person?"

"He doesn't think physical appearance is important," she'd said.

"Bullshit. It takes effort to look that unkempt. He probably washes his new clothes with rocks until they get holes in them."

Some of the kids at school did do things like that to age their jeans, but Joe had come by his scrappy look honestly – almost everything he wore came from the thrift shop. His struggling single mother considered it a point of honor to never, ever pay full price for any item of clothing, and he'd always preferred to sock most of his own earnings away in savings. Not that his pants came from the thrift shop with holes in them – and it was certainly true he preferred them after they got ragged.

So maybe it had been his appearance he cared about.

Maybe Joe Gagnon *had* been a big fat hypocrite all along.

"So who's going to mow the lawn?" Salinger asked.

"*Joseph Gagnon Landscaping LLC.*" She'd found the card on the floor of the foyer when she went back to lock the door. Joe's way of saying *here's my number, don't call me.*

"Joseph Gagnon? As in Joe Gagnon? *Your* Joe Gagnon?"

"He looks pretty different now."

"That must have been kind of weird, huh?"

She recognized this as the closest Salinger was likely to come to offering brotherly support. And she'd take anything she could get. "Yes, very weird." She got up and pulled the egg carton out of the refrigerator. Oh, thank God. There were still two eggs left.

Chapter 3

After dinner Dori sat at the kitchen table, feeling stubborn about the dishes Salinger had left in the sink even though she knew it was stupid. Hadn't she rewarded him for doing just that by cleaning up after him again and again? No wonder he still acted like the same fifteen-year-old she'd suddenly been responsible for after her parents' death.

Joe Gagnon, meanwhile, had morphed into somebody all but unrecognizable.

But perhaps he wasn't the only one. She might as well be a grandmother for all the fun she had anymore. She couldn't remember the last time she'd gone to a party, or even just gone up to the ledges, something she and Joe had done at least once a month once he had a car.

It was stupid, avoiding a place she loved just because she thought of it as *their* place. And yes, it was scarier going places on her own, but how many rapists or homicidal maniacs were likely to be lurking in a bird sanctuary?

So she traded her flip flops for sneakers and got in the car.

The ledges were the most prominent feature of a mountainside overlooking Jasper and the Deerfield River. Hiking trails led to patches of lady slipper orchids along shady woodland paths. There were birds, too, but Dori was no bird watcher. She was not surprised when she drove up to find only one other car in the visitor's parking lot; it was a place that was tricky to find if you didn't already know where it was, and it closed at sunset, which was not far off.

She took the short walk to the ledges, brooding over the presence of that one other car, because she'd done something she'd never done before: accepted a joint from Salinger. He'd offered, and he had, after all, taken the last of the chicken. But she didn't have the nerve to pull out an illegal substance and smoke it when someone else might come along at any moment.

When they were teenagers, she and Joe had been shy with their pot-smoking, too, only indulging when they were absolutely sure they were alone, often on these same ledges. How she'd loved giggling with him, setting aside any concerns about high school or what might come after, forgetting their adolescent outrage at whatever in the world was offending them.

She wanted to smoke a joint in honor of that fond memory – and erase, if possible, everything that came after. But first she needed the people who owned that car to leave.

"I think I see my car. Yay, we can go!" she heard a young woman's voice say. Dori almost laughed. How often was the universe so obliging?

"You haven't seen the view yet," answered a deeper voice she recognized all too well: Joe.

Not so obliging after all, the universe. Perhaps even spiteful.

"Come on," the woman said. "I took your hike like you wanted. I looked at the lady slippers. I still don't see why they're such a big deal."

"I told you, they're an endangered species. And it's an awesome view. Right there. Come on, Lisa! You barely have to walk ten feet."

There was a heavy sigh, and approaching footsteps. Dori hunkered down as far as she could, hoping she'd blend into one of the little islands of low-bush blueberries and ferns and rhododendrons that screened the great rock ledge from the parking area. Maybe they wouldn't notice her and she could quietly slip away.

They didn't notice her – but Dori stayed, overcome by curiosity, as well as dark satisfaction that Joe's companion was giving him a hard time. Lisa – tall and lithe with long blonde hair – walked out onto the broad lip of the ledge and stood looking down at the valley, her hands on her hips. She shifted her flawless ass to one side. "Okay, you're right, it's a great view." She took a device out of her rear pocket and snapped a couple of pictures. Then she turned around, fiddling with it, and raised it up, smiling in a constipated sort of way and trying different angles. "Come here," she told him. "Get in the picture."

"No thanks."

"I promise I'll set it to private."

He made a face, but scooted up next to her.

"Smile," she said, and tilted her head towards his.

He didn't reciprocate on the head tilt. Dori recognized his fake smile from days of old. He still glowered the same, too, she discovered, when his eyes dropped from the woman's device and landed on her still sitting quietly next to the bushes. "What the hell are *you* doing here?" he said.

She wanted to say "None of your damned business," but her throat closed up.

"Oh!" Lisa said. "Sorry, we didn't know you were here!" She turned to Joe. "You guys know each other?"

"Yeah," Joe said, and sighed. "Lisa Summers, meet Eudora Bardwell."

"Oh my God! Eudora Bardwell! I know you! Clem was in my class."

Dori smiled stiffly. "A pleasure."

"I went to the memorial service and everything. I shook your hand, do you remember? I was, like, only fourteen, though."

"There were a lot of people there," Dori said. She gave Joe a sidelong look – he hadn't been. He scowled and looked away.

"I don't know how you could stand it! I would have completely lost it. I mean, *God,* your whole family, *bam,* just like that."

Dori winced. "Actually, one of my brothers..."

"Oh, yeah, I know! Salinger. Everybody knows Salinger."

It was true. Everyone knew Salinger.

"So how do you know Joe?" Lisa asked, and sat herself down on the stone next to Dori.

Dori looked at Joe, who folded his arms. "We were in high school together," she said.

"Really?"

"Class of 2007," Dori supplied.

Joe walked further out on the ledge and looked down towards Jasper.

Lisa looked back and forth. "Wait a minute," she said. "Aren't you the one who turned him down? Like, it's even on video?"

That turned Joe around. His hands landed on his hips.

"Not a very good one," Dori said. Thankfully. They had been some distance from the camera, and it was impossible to hear what they said to each other, especially over the excited whooping and hollering in the crowd. Not that it mattered, with body language so brutally clear: Dori had literally taken a step back as Joe kneeled in front of her. There had been that long moment of delayed comprehension from him, and that slight protective curl over his belly. Then the leap to his feet, the angry strides away while Dori stared after him. The crowd, after a brief moment of shocked silence, erupted. "Are you *shitting* me?" somebody said, close to the camera, before the video ended.

"Lisa!" he said. "Could you *not?*"

"Yeah, he never talks about it," Lisa said. "But it's kind of legendary. I just can't figure out why he'd do that if he didn't already know what answer he was going to get. Did you change your mind on him?"

"Nope," Dori said. She'd *already* told him that she preferred to wait until after college. "But it's old news now, isn't it? I thought I'd come out here to smoke a joint for old time's sake, in honor of the days when we were young and stupid and Joe was still speaking to me. Care to join me?"

"Young and stupid is right," he said. "I don't do that kind of thing anymore."

"I'd love a few puffs," Lisa said. "Tell me about Joe when he was in high school."

Dori carefully unwrapped the single joint and the matches she'd packed. "You want to do the honors?"

"Sure," Lisa said, and got it started. "Maybe it will keep the bugs away." She inhaled deeply. "Oh man. This is good stuff."

Dori said, "You know your stuff?"

Lisa giggled. "Not really."

"Lisa is a clerk at the trooper station," Joe said, possibly to remind Lisa.

Lisa grinned. "What, you think those guys never smoke a little weed?"

Joe said, "I sure hoped they didn't."

Dori said, "Sorry, Joe. I didn't come out here to corrupt a minor, I swear."

Lisa giggled. "I'm not a minor! I'm twenty-one!"

Joe shook his head and put some distance between them and him. Dori smiled at Lisa and wondered what Clem would look like if he were still alive. He'd been in the middle of a gawky, pimply stage when he died.

She reached out and took the joint from Lisa. She inhaled, then coughed and gasped. But she persisted, taking another long drag, then another. Yes, there it was, that spreading feeling of lightness, except that it wasn't as pleasant as she remembered. There was a hint of vertigo about it. "Did you like Clem?" she asked thickly.

Lisa giggled again. "Oh yeah. He was a wicked funny guy, you know? Real class clown."

"Yeah," Dori said. "He was the most appropriately named of all of us."

Lisa looked blank.

"We were all named after authors," Dori explained. "Clemens for Samuel Clemens. You know, Mark Twain?"

"Uh huh," Lisa said, still looking vague. "Who were you named after?"

"Eudora Welty."

"Who?"

"She's not that popular anymore," Dori said. "Salinger for J.D. Salinger. Flannery for Flannery O'Connor. Carson for Carson McCullers. And Harper..."

"I know! For Harper Lee."

"Yes, very good."

"Did your dad expect you all to become famous writers too?"

Did he? "I doubt he would have welcomed the competition."

"So you're not a writer?"

"Me? No. I work in a nursing home."

Joe turned sharply. "What?"

"I work in a nursing home. Shady Grove Rest Home – over in Greenfield."

"You have a job?" He looked stunned.

She stared at him, puzzled. "I have *two* jobs. I also just started working at a grocery store, part-time."

"I don't believe it," Joe said, and shook his head. "She's pulling your leg," he told Lisa.

Dori grabbed the joint back from Lisa and took a few deep drags. It didn't work; she was still boiling mad. "You know what's funny, Lisa? Even people who ought to know better think I'm rolling in money just because I'm a Bardwell and I live in that house."

Joe frowned. "But your dad..."

"My dad left behind a will designed to make sure that our only real asset will remain a monument to his everlasting literary genius. Otherwise, believe me, I'd have sold it years ago."

"My big sister's an LPN," Lisa said. "She works over at the VA hospital in Holyoke."

Dori smiled. "Good for her. I'm afraid I'm just a CNA."

"This is total bullshit," Joe said. "You are not an aide at a nursing home."

"And you do not provide comprehensive lawn services."

"This is all a game to her," he told Lisa.

"Fuck you, Joe," Dori said. "You don't know anything about me."

"I heard you never finished college," he said.

"I got landed with a brother to take care of, in case you didn't notice. Oh wait a minute – that's right – you didn't."

Lisa stood up. "Maybe we should get going."

"I wasn't even in this country when all that happened," he said. "I was overseas. I didn't have enough money to come back even if I'd wanted to."

He hadn't even sent a condolence card. He could have done *that* from Europe. Dori lay back flat on the sun-warmed rock; she needed the anchor. "Here, take it." She offered Lisa what was left of the joint. "I don't want any more."

Lisa took it, looking uncomfortable.

"You know what's funny?" Joe said. "*I'm* the one who got my degree."

"Yeah, I know. And you majored in lawn mowing."

"Landscape design."

She didn't respond. She knew what he'd majored in. She knew where he'd gone to school: SUNY Cobleskill. She knew he'd taken a year off to travel around Europe before he went – she'd had that straight from his mother. Joe's mother had always been kind to her. From her, she also knew he'd started a business in upstate New York. It was from others that she knew he'd returned a couple years back, a few months before his mother died in hospice care, and had started up a local landscaping service.

It was hard to believe they'd never run into each other since, even if she did transact most of the business of her daily life in Greenfield, where gas and groceries were cheaper and the library was open for many more hours.

Unless she hadn't recognized him with his new look? Or he'd been actively avoiding her? Which he obviously had. Even so, how could he not know where she worked, or that she had a job? Didn't he ever talk to anybody about anything?

Maybe it was just her he never talked about.

"Well, Lisa," she said. "You've got yourself a real up-and-comer there. Don't let him get away, now."

Lisa smiled uncertainly. "We're just dating."

"*Shhh*, careful. He's probably thinking of it as a lifetime commitment."

"Time to go, Lisa," Joe said.

Lisa leaned over her and asked, "Are you going to be all right?"

It comforted Dori that even a gorgeous twenty-one-year-old had a double chin from that angle. But she was a sweet girl. "I'm fine. It was nice to meet you." She affected her mother's Southern drawl. "Y'all take care, now."

"Good bye, Dori," Joe said, in a tone of disapproving sobriety.

She didn't answer. She just lay there and let the mountain hold her.

Chapter 4

When Dori got home from work Monday afternoon there was a message on the ancient answering machine from her best friend, Ruth.

"I'm home, I'm an official J.D., and I need to party. How's tonight? And when are you going to get a normal phone so we can text like normal people?"

Dori smiled. How long would Ruth be home? She always made life in Jasper more interesting, even if she apparently thought cell phones were paid for by special cell phone fairies. Dori had shut hers and Salinger's down years earlier after Salinger had somehow managed to rack up thousands of dollars of expenses on their account in just a couple of weeks by doing something called "tethering" between his phone and his laptop that she still didn't entirely understand. All she knew was that she was still paying it off on her credit card bill, along with a raft of other expenses she'd accumulated before she'd realized what a trap that minimum required payment was.

She'd already cut expenses to the bone. She'd given up cable and broadband. If she needed to type something or send an email or look something up on the Internet, she went to the library. At first, she'd always taken her laptop. Then her laptop died, so she started relying on the library's computers. But that could get tense if people were waiting for a spot on the machines. She'd begun to use them less and less.

As time passed, she realized how little she missed all that. She sometimes watched people glued to their phones, staring down at those little rectangles no matter where they were, and thought there was something sad about it. Also, she'd noticed that the friendships she'd maintained online seldom seemed to cross over into real life. Ruth had been her best friend before the accident and she still was; the others were just people she knew and occasionally ran into, and it didn't help that they all seemed to be forging ahead with degrees and jobs and marriages and children and other accomplishments, all happily shared on Facebook, while she stayed exactly where she was. Her newer freshman college friends had faded away as if they'd never existed, not that she blamed them. She hadn't even finished the first year with them. And all that death made things awkward.

Over time, she'd decided her life was better without the virtual hugs or the virtual pity. She also didn't miss the occasional resurrection of that proposal video, or seeing what got posted involving Salinger leisure activities. Nor did she miss the occasional weird friendship request from strange men who always seemed to work for oil companies or the military. Ruth had warned her they were con men looking to steal identities or sweet talk lonely women out of their money.

As if she had any.

Yet even Joe apparently thought she had inherited a fortune. If he thought that, perhaps the whole town did.

While it was true crashing a small plane into the sea with most of his family aboard had boosted her father's dwindling royalties significantly – if temporarily – it had all gone into the trust. A good chunk had disappeared into the pockets of a consultant whose plans the trustees soon discovered they could not afford to implement. So while her father had envisioned a museum and library devoted to the study of his papers and memorabilia, they were, in fact, still in the same old drawers and file cabinets and cardboard boxes in the attic where they had been stored during his life.

It didn't help that her father's literary reputation had begun to fade even before his death. His second novel, *The Measured Marriage,* had received mixed reviews and enjoyed little commercial success. The third and last novel, *The Buried Prince,* had been roundly panned and was already out of print.

Of course, also complicating her father's dream for the house was that Dori and Salinger still lived there.

Or, apparently, just Dori.

"Dori!" Ruth's mother said, when she answered the door, and gave her a big hug. "How are you? Why is it we never see you?"

"I'm working in Greenfield, so I'm not around as much."

"Oh dear. That can't be a fun commute in the winter."

"It's fine."

There was a shriek, and Ruth came running down the hall. "Girlfriend!"

Dori laughed and hugged her friend, who had more curly black hair and less body mass than ever.

"How long are you here?" Dori asked.

"The whole summer!" Ruth said. "I decided I need a good rest before I even think about studying for the bar exam."

Dori looked at Mrs. Moscatiello, who smiled grimly. Ruth's last breakdown, a year earlier, had landed her in a hospital for a month in the middle of midterms and cost her another whole semester.

"I'm really glad you're home," Dori said, and she meant it, for herself. She wasn't so sure it was a good sign for Ruth. "You ready to go?"

"Let me just get my purse," Ruth said, and ran down the hall.

"Get her to eat something," Mrs. Moscatiello murmured.

"So you want to party?" Dori said, a little apprehensively. She wasn't sure exactly how to meet that request.

"Oh I don't really care," Ruth said. "I just thought it sounded appropriately fun and carefree."

Should she ask her brother for another joint? Not that she had found her own personal reunion with marijuana all that fun. "So what are you in the mood for?"

"Pizza?"

Oh, that was easy. "Sure, pizza." She drove down the hill and parked in front of the only pizza joint in town, which had survived for decades while every other restaurant except the diner had changed hands repeatedly or just gone out of business. It was a tiny place, but they snagged one of the four booths without difficulty. The same photograph of Greek fishing boats in an island harbor that had been there when they were twelve hung on the wall over the table, its original colors faded to blues and pinks.

Anthony grinned at Ruth. "You're back!" His comb-over had gotten thinner and suspiciously black.

"I'm back," Ruth agreed, grinning. "And you know what, Anthony? There's no pizza as good as yours in all of Boston."

"You always make Anthony happy," he said. He turned his attention to Dori and his tone turned reproachful. "And where have you been?"

"Sorry," Dori said. Clearly, she didn't always make Anthony happy. "You want to share a small pie?" she asked Ruth.

"I just need a slice," Ruth said.

"That works," Dori said. "One veggie slice for me, and a glass of iced water."

"One mushroom slice for me and a diet Coke," Ruth said.

"You girls need to eat more!" Anthony said, with a glower. "Look at you!" He pointed at Ruth. "You look sick! You starve to death!"

"Anthony, Anthony," Ruth said. "Don't bully the customers."

He shook his head and left. When he brought their drinks over he put a basket of hot garlic rolls in the middle of the table. "On the house! Now eat!"

"Thank you!" Dori said, and reached for one immediately. She took a bite and moaned in appreciation, partly because she was trying to entice Ruth to partake and partly because it was so good – yeasty, hot, and dripping with olive oil and garlic.

A man leaned around from the booth behind Dori. "Sorry, but I really have to know what you're finding so delicious."

Dori blushed and chewed desperately so she could answer without her mouth full. The young man smiling at her was just plain pretty: perfectly tanned skin, perfectly-coiffed long brown hair, beautiful brown eyes. Even his teeth were straight and white – and he was actually wearing a shirt and tie. He wasn't as tall as Joe, but that wasn't his fault.

"Garlic rolls," she finally managed.

"You must rate," he said. "He's never given me garlic rolls on the house."

Ruth said, "You can have mine."

"Don't mind if I do," he said, and Dori felt a pang of loss as the free food passed to someone else. Was that how pathetic her life had gotten? That she would rather hoard a garlic roll than flirt with a beautiful man?

"*Ohhh*," he said, lightly mocking Dori's earlier moan. "They are good." He smiled. "I haven't seen either of you in here before," he said.

Ruth said, "We haven't seen you either." She gave Dori a look Dori recognized from many years and many boys past: Ruth was putting in her dibs.

"She was away at law school," Dori said, content to let her have him. He was out of Dori's league, anyway – that much was clear.

But he asked Dori "And where were you?"

"I don't eat out much."

"Because you enjoy it too much?" He raised his eyebrows suggestively.

Dori laughed.

Ruth said, "Would you like to join us?"

"I thought you'd never ask." He stood up and looked expectantly at Dori, so she made room for him to slide in next to her. It seemed to her he got a little closer than was strictly required; she could feel the heat of his body next to hers.

She inhaled nervously. It had been a long time since she'd sat next to a guy who wasn't her brother or at the end of his life. "You didn't eat yet?" she asked.

"No, I'm still waiting."

Anthony brought over their slices. "You sit here now?" he said to the young man, looking irritated. "Five minutes more for your pie!" His eyes narrowed. "These are nice girls."

"Yes, I can tell," the man said, and smiled blandly at Anthony.

Anthony harrumphed and left.

"So," Ruth said.

"Robert Putney-Lewis," he said, holding out his hand to shake hers, then Dori's. The name sounded familiar. Was she failing to recognize somebody she should know?

Ruth introduced herself and Dori.

"Dori Bardwell?" he asked her. "Is that by any chance short for

Eudora? Eldest daughter of Bedford Bardwell?"

"Yes," Dori said, disheartened.

"I knew your father."

"Really? How?" He didn't look old enough.

"He and my dad were friends. You mom and dad used to visit our summer camp quite often. It's not far from here. You've heard of Robert Putney?"

"Robert Putney is your dad?" No wonder his name sounded familiar. It was Robert Putney's plane her father had crashed, in fact. Did this Robert know that? "What's the Lewis for?"

"My mother, of course."

Ruth said, "You mean the Putneys who own all those newspapers and radio stations?"

"Yep."

Ruth's eyes narrowed. "And you're Robert Jr.? Scion of an incredibly wealthy family?"

Robert looked nonplussed. "I don't know about the 'incredibly' part. Dori here is a bit of a scion herself, isn't she?"

"More like a sucker," Dori said. She looked over at Anthony, who looked away quickly as if he hadn't been leaning on the counter watching them. She hoped Robert's pizza wasn't burning.

Robert and Ruth were exchanging puzzled looks.

"Sorry. Horticultural joke," Dori said. She'd taken an interest, back when Joe was her boyfriend. Plants were his thing.

Robert said, "I'm embarrassed to admit this, but I'm not really up on the great horticultural jokes."

She smiled. "When you're grafting apples, the *scion* is the cutting you graft onto the hardy rootstock. It's the variety you want to grow, the valuable part of the tree." Joe had taught her that. "*Suckers* come up from the root. You cut them off because they'll never bear the fruit you want, they drain resources, and they can end up taking over the whole tree."

He said, "Oh, I see. So if you're a sucker, you're quite terrifying, really. In a very slow, horticultural kind of way. Ah, my pizza. At last."

Anthony put down the pizza with a frown and stalked off.

"Go for it, ladies," Robert said, grabbing a slice.

Dori had already finished her own slice and was still hungry, so she helped herself eagerly. "Thanks."

Ruth picked a mushroom off her own slice and popped it in her mouth.

Robert said, "Why didn't your parents ever bring you over? My sister and I would have welcomed another kid to play with."

"There were six of us. It would have been more like a riot."

"Nonsense, it's a huge place. You would have loved the lake."

Perhaps her parents had just been delighted to leave the kids behind in her care and go drink other people's booze. But it might also have been the lake. She'd noticed her parents preferred to keep their distance from large bodies of water. All the kids had been marched off to the YMCA in Greenfield in turn to be drown-proofed, never just for the joy of swimming. Once when they'd nagged for an above-ground pool like some of their friends had, her mother had given them the garden hose and said, "Here, go to town."

Ruth said, "So what's a Putney doing at a place like this?"

Dori, who knew the feeling well herself, could see he was irritated at being called *a Putney*.

He said, "Eating dinner."

Ruth said, "And I guess Putneys dress for dinner even when it's at Anthony's."

That earned Ruth an outright glare. "I just got off work. I'm a reporter."

"In *Jasper?*" Dori said.

"I cover the west county for *The Recorder*. Why not Jasper?"

Dori snorted. "Nothing ever happens here."

"Sure it does," he said.

"People die," Ruth said, a bit sourly.

No kidding, Dori thought, but Robert smiled. "Yes. Then there's the 4-H club, milk prices, bitter controversy over whose roads get new gravel, the cow that ended up in someone's swimming pool. And of course the annual Bedford Bardwell Days. I'd like to do a feature about that, actually."

Dori said, "Excellent. The old ladies will pee themselves over the free publicity."

Ruth kicked her under the table.

Dori looked at her, annoyed. "What?"

"You're talking to a reporter," Ruth said between clinched teeth, as if Robert wouldn't hear her if her lips didn't move.

Dori sighed. "Excuse me, Robert. What I meant to say was I'm sure the Friends of the Bedford Bardwell House would be extremely pleased to see the Bedford Bardwell Days mentioned favorably in the press."

He grinned at her. "I'm not on the job right now. I promise."

"You hear that, Ruth? Eat your slice," Dori said. She knew Ruth was right, that she should watch her mouth, but it was irritating to be reined in when she was having a good time.

"So, you both grew up here? What would you say most people do for fun?" Robert asked.

Dori said, "Abuse substances."

Robert laughed.

Ruth just shook her head.

"It's true!" Dori said to Ruth. "What else is there to do? Cow tipping?"

"Gossiping online," Ruth said. "Watching porn. Hooking up. Getting pregnant. The eternal pursuits of humanity."

"Oh, yeah," Dori said. "Sex. I do have a vague memory of it." How long had it been? At least three years since she'd briefly dated a guy who'd worked in the nursing home's kitchen. She turned to Robert. "My family is still considered newcomers, so it's not a big deal for me, but there's a limited gene pool up here in the hill towns. If people rule out their relatives – not that everybody does – the pickings can get pretty slim."

Robert said, "They should be happy to see a new face in town, then."

Ruth said, "Why do you think I asked you to join us?"

To break the sudden awkward silence in the conversation, Dori said, "Also, sometimes we go out for Anthony's fabulous pizza."

He smiled pityingly at her; apparently he did not share her enthusiasm for it. "But seriously," he said. "Other than sex and substance abuse and eating the odd slice of Greek pizza, what do people do?"

Dori said, "I'm sure you've read the brochures. Hiking, swimming, skiing, boating, fishing, and hunting. Bird watching. A contra dance at the Odd Fellows hall once a month. Polka is big if you're Polish. Or, you can join the Friends of the Bedford Bardwell House and enjoy tea and cookies at really exciting monthly meetings. And if all that's not enough, the library is open three days a week." She gave him a big fake grin and held up the corresponding three fingers.

Ruth said, "Most people get in the car and drive somewhere."

"Is that what *you* do?" he asked, turning to face Dori.

Dori knew she should try to make herself sound more appealing, but instead she just told him the truth. "I do a lot of reading. Tonight I'm having pizza with my friend Ruth."

"How about writing?"

She'd already declared an English major her freshman year, actually, but she hadn't had the desire to write a single word since the crash. "I think one writer in the family is more than enough."

Robert said, "Even though he's not here anymore?"

Like hell he wasn't. Her father's career had been all-enveloping and still was. She smiled apologetically, aware her mood had turned grim. She didn't ask Robert if he wrote. As a reporter, he obviously did. And Dori didn't want to have to rule him out as a new friend – not yet.

Chapter 5

"Speaking of substance abuse," Robert said, after dinner, as they stood awkwardly on the sidewalk in front of Anthony's Pizza, "Would you care to join me for a drink at The Mill?"

Dori and Ruth looked at each other.

"Sure," Ruth said.

Dori raised her eyebrows in surprise. "But –"

"But nothing." Ruth tugged on her arm. "I told you I needed to party, didn't I?"

"At *The Mill*?"

Robert looked from one to the other. "We could drive to Charlemont."

"The Mill is fine," Ruth said. "The Mill is perfect."

They walked two blocks down Main Street to the low-slung, tiny-windowed bar that had, like Anthony's Pizza, survived every economic vagary of the last fifty years and a couple of floods, too.

Dori felt her shoes start sticking to the floor as she walked in. She stopped to let her eyes adjust to the gloom. It seemed to her people turned to stare, but just as quickly turned back to whatever they were doing. The bottles arrayed behind the bar glowed in backlit splendor, a beacon in the perpetual gloom of the interior. The bartender, a burly guy she didn't recognize, was handing a customer a drink. He looked up at them and nodded familiarly at Robert.

Robert was probably a regular, then. But reporters were always hanging out in bars, weren't they? She tried to remember whether it was because it was part of the job – keeping their ears to the ground – or because they were all drunks. Maybe both.

Ruth had her arms folded across her chest and was looking towards the back hall.

"Let's get a booth," Robert said, and led them to the corner farthest away from the jukebox, which was caterwauling country music that sounded pretty much the same as what had been play-ing the last time Dori had been in here, eight years earlier – before she'd reached legal drinking age, but that had never been an issue at The Mill.

She had been in a post-Joe funk and had accepted a beer from an older man she didn't know. He hadn't appreciated it when she'd removed his hand from her ass during the slow dance he'd insisted on. "Don't be a fucking tease, Red," he'd said, breathing angrily into her face and clamping down hard on her wrist.

"Sorry," she'd said, and pulled free of him. Heart pounding, she'd run for the door, then all of the six blocks home, raising a surprised look from her mother as she ran past her and up the stairs. She hadn't been back since.

Robert once again chose to sit on Dori's side of the booth, his thigh in close proximity to hers. He looked from Dori to Ruth and back again. "Why do I get the feeling I put my foot in it by sug-gesting this place?"

Dori looked at Ruth. It was up to her to tell or not.

"My dad got stabbed to death in the men's room here when I was sixteen," Ruth said.

Robert's eyes widened. "Seriously? I'm so sorry. Let's go someplace else." He started to get up.

"No, let's not," Ruth said. "I was sixteen. This is my life, not his. It's not my fault my mom sued the bar."

There was a moment of silence as Robert digested that. Sound-ing just a little squeaky, he asked, "Did she win?"

"Yeah, but it got reduced a lot on appeal. And of course the lawyers took a huge chunk."

"Still, it must have cost the bar something."

"Oh, no doubt," Ruth said. "Supposedly Mom drove it out of business. It seems to be hanging on pretty well if you ask me, though."

"Same owners?"

She shrugged. "I have no idea."

"Same owners," Dori said. "They declared bankruptcy, and then they sold it to their brother, but they kept running it. A few years ago he moved to Florida and they bought it back for a dollar or something like that."

"Aren't you a little font of information?" Ruth said. "How come I never heard any of this?"

"You never asked."

A waitress in what looked like painfully tight jeans appeared at their table. "What'll it be?" she said to Robert, ignoring Dori and Ruth. She flipped her hair back and smiled encouragingly at him.

"Ladies?" Robert asked.

The waitress turned to them, frowning slightly.

"You want to split a beer?" Dori asked Ruth. She wasn't just trying to save money – she got buzzed off any more than that, and she still had to drive Ruth back up the hill.

"Double vodka straight up, twist of lime," Ruth said to the waitress, ignoring Dori.

"I guess a seltzer," Dori said.

"Jesus, Dori," Ruth said. "If you can't drink a whole beer, just leave some of it."

"I'd rather not."

"Please, don't worry about it. I'm buying," Robert said.

"Thanks, but I have to drive her home, and I have an early morning tomorrow."

He looked thoughtfully at her for a moment and Dori imagined he was pegging her as something: responsible, cheap, or just no fun. He ordered himself the only dark beer The Mill had on tap. "Maybe you'd like to have a taste of mine," he said. He made it sound intimate.

"Maybe," Dori said. Would she like a taste? It was becoming clear, even to her – and she tended to be slow on the uptake in these matters – that a taste of Robert Putney-Lewis himself was on offer. And it had been a very long time since she'd had a taste of anyone, let alone a good-looking, filthy-rich guy.

Their drinks arrived. Ruth tasted hers and closed her eyes in apparent bliss. Dori removed her straw and sipped her seltzer. Drinking with a straw just emphasized that it wasn't a real drink. Just to be sociable, she sampled Robert's and nodded and smiled at him over it. It was good.

Robert sat back and folded his arms. "Your father literally died here?" he asked Ruth. For the first time Dori thought she saw the reporter in him.

"Yeah. Of course, he probably started it," Ruth said. "He loved to argue, and he was drunk as a skunk. So was the guy who nailed him."

"Shouldn't your mom have sued *that* guy?"

"It would have been pointless. He didn't have a penny."

Robert looked interested and waited.

Ruth shrugged expressively, raising both hands. "What are you gonna do? Dad had let his life insurance lapse. The guy who did it went to jail for a while, but that sure wasn't going to provide for us. It didn't make my mother popular, but it's not like people loved us to begin with."

"Anthony loves you," Dori said.

"Anthony loves any woman who will flirt with him. You should try it sometime, you'd get more free rolls."

"So you would say you're not popular?" Robert said. He looked at Dori as if he expected her to contradict this, but Dori didn't say anything. It was true. It was part of the reason she and Ruth were such good friends. They were both unpopular, had both done too well in high school, had both appeared to be rolling in money they didn't actually have – or so Dori assumed, because she wasn't sure what the story was with Ruth – and had both had drunks for fathers.

Ironically, though, Dori's father had died during one of his occasional bouts of sobriety. She sometimes wondered if this was why he'd felt so confident he could handle flying conditions that should have kept them on the ground. Just the weekend before, her dad had crowed to her about the new sense of clarity he had, the amazing productivity he was experiencing in his writing, and she'd said *that's wonderful, Dad*. She hadn't told him what she was really thinking: that it wouldn't last.

"You know that was your dad's plane, right?" she said to Robert.

He didn't skip a beat. "Yeah, I know."

Ruth said, "Excuse me?"

"It was his dad's plane," Dori said. "The one Dad crashed."

"He'd asked to borrow it," Robert said to Ruth, before turning his attention back to Dori. "I'm sure my dad must have talked to you about it."

Yes, Robert's father had come up to her at the memorial service, offering to help her and her brother in any way they needed, though she hadn't heard from him since then. "Dad hadn't been able to keep his own plane anymore. Too expensive. We wouldn't have all fit into one, anyway." She stared at him. "What are the chances I'd just run into you like this?"

He looked a little self-conscious. "Pretty high in a town this size."

"Huh," Dori said, chewing this over. Even as small as Jasper was, she mostly knew her immediate neighbors and people she'd gone to school with or done business with over the years.

"I think we all feel a little guilty about what happened to your family," he said.

"Do you?" Ruth said, suddenly looking keen. She raised her hand to signal the waitress she wanted another drink.

"I don't see why," Dori said.

"Dad never replaced the plane. He decided they're just too risky."

It hadn't been mechanical error, according to the official investigation. Weather had perhaps contributed to pilot error, for the evidence suggested her father, probably disoriented by an ocean haze, had ignored his instruments and flown into the sea.

"I hope we can still be friends," he added.

Dori shrugged. "It's not your fault my dad mooched off your dad."

He said, "I wouldn't call it mooching. My dad thinks of himself as a patron of the arts. He felt strongly your father had another great book in him. And at that point, according to my dad, your father also felt strongly he had another great book in him."

"He always thought that," Dori said. "I guess we'll never know."

"But he was writing something when he died, wasn't he?"

"Yeah, he was."

"Was it any good?"

She shrugged. "It was far from finished. His agent didn't think anything could be made of it."

"Where is it now?" Robert asked.

"I don't know," she said. "Probably the attic."

"I'd love to read it."

"Really?" She supposed she ought to try to sound more enthusiastic about her own father's work.

"Are you a patron of the arts, too?" Ruth said, a little thickly. She had swallowed down a fair amount of her second drink. Maybe being skinny made the alcohol more potent. Or maybe she'd started drinking before Dori had picked her up. It wouldn't be the first time.

Robert snorted. "On a reporter's salary? I'm lucky I can be a patron of this bar."

Dori began to worry about the tab. And the time. And what a drunk Ruth might say. "We should probably get going," she said.

"Yeah, me too," Robert said.

"Oh come on," Ruth said. "There's time for one more."

"No, there isn't," Dori said. "I have to be at work at seven tomorrow." She stood up and caught the waitress's eye and made the universal sign for check, please. The waitress lifted a finger with another universal sign: wait a minute.

"Come on," Ruth whined.

Dori had forgotten that whine, which only came out when Ruth wanted more alcohol.

"I'll take care of it – you go ahead," Robert said to Dori.

"Her tab is going to be pretty steep."

"Oh please," Ruth said. "He's a Putney. He can wipe his ass with hundred dollar bills if he wants."

Robert said, "Actually, my parents believe children need to learn how to make their own way in the world."

Another person who looked wealthier than he actually was? Maybe they should form a club. She said, "Don't worry, we can wait for the bill."

"That's not what I meant," Robert said. "I said I was buying. Anyway, at thirty the trust fund kicks in no matter what my parents think, at which time I suppose I can start wiping my ass with hundred dollar bills if I want to. In the meantime, I'm sure I can spot you a few drinks."

"Well, thank you," Dori said. "Come on, Ruth. Let's go."

"Party pooper," Ruth said, but she got up. "A Putney wants to ply you with drinks and all you can think about is getting to work the next day so you can empty more bedpans."

Dori grimaced an apology at Robert and pulled Ruth to the door.

She got them into the car – she had to argue with Ruth to put her seatbelt on – and drove up the hill silently, fuming that her friend had mentioned the bedpans. Added to the remark about Putney ass-wiping, it could hardly have left a pleasant impression. Dori knew she hadn't been particularly sweet and charming either, but at least she wasn't a loud drunk with a possible anal fixation.

Ruth suddenly burst out, "You realize all your problems are solved, don't you?"

Dori glanced at her. "How's that?"

"You just need to sue Robert Putney's ass for lending that plane to your dad. It hasn't been ten years yet. So you still could."

Dori wished she could believe that was a joke. She pulled up in front of Ruth's and set the emergency brake. "Are you going to be all right to get in?" The slope was pretty intense.

"I'm serious," Ruth said. "He's obscenely rich. His lawyers will settle just to shut you up. You could be sitting pretty for the rest of your life. He knew your father had a drinking problem and yet he still encouraged him to use his plane!"

"Dad wasn't actually drinking at the time."

"That's neither here nor there. Your father was always drink-ing. Your father was a well-known drunk."

This was true, of course, but somehow Dori didn't enjoy her best friend pointing it out so bluntly. "So was yours."

"Exactly. You'd have no trouble finding plenty of witnesses to testify to the general level of intoxication your father exhibited on a routine basis."

"There wouldn't be any point. They did a blood test. He was clean."

"I thought it was a plane crash. Into the ocean."

"It was."

"And there weren't even enough remains to –"

"Could you please just drop it?"

"I'm just saying, an expert witness could tear that blood test apart. This guy owes you, Dori."

"No, he doesn't. If anything, we owe him a plane."

"He knew your father. He had to know he was an alcoholic–"

"Damn it, Ruth, the only alcoholic we should be talking about right now is you!"

Ruth blinked at Dori. Then she got out of the car and slammed the door.

Dori watched her stalk up the front path.

"Damn it," she said to the empty car. She'd been so happy to have Ruth back in town.

Chapter 6

The next day Dori had just guided Mrs. Frankowski out of the shower when her boss knocked on the bathroom door and leaned in. The old woman gave a tiny shriek and clamped her bony hands over her bare chest.

"I need to talk to you before you go home today," Bonnie said.

Dori raised the towel to cover her patient's nudity as best she could without letting her go. "Okay, I'll stop by later."

Bonnie left. Mrs. Frankowski's head shook with more than the usual tremors.

"Sorry," Dori said, fumbling with the old woman's bra. "Bonnie must not have realized you were just in the shower. Let's get you all nice and pretty for the afternoon, okay?"

Mrs. Frankowski's head continued to shake. "Just get me dressed before somebody else barges in!"

"I know. I'm going as fast as I can." Dori helped her thread her wasted arms into her sleeves. "There, all decent." She helped her sink down into her wheelchair and reached for the brush. "We might as well try for nice and pretty too, as long as we're here."

"Honey, I gave up on those a long time ago." Still, she closed her eyes and leaned into the brush. "At my age you just aim for warm and dry."

"Oh, I don't know about that," Dori said. "It seems to me you're the reason half those old guys out there still make it to the TV room."

Mrs. Frankowski cackled. "Silly girl!" But she didn't stop smiling.

"You wanted to see me?" Dori asked Bonnie. She stifled a yawn. She hadn't slept well the night before. She had awakened in the middle of the night from a recurring nightmare about the crash.

She was on the plane with the rest of her family, arguing fruit-lessly with her father to read his instruments. In her dreams the worst part was never the crash itself, but the way the water came pouring in afterwards and her seat belt wouldn't release. That wasn't realistic, of course; the plane had disintegrated on impact, scattering body parts and wreckage.

"Are you leaving us?" Bonnie demanded. Her face was red, and a red-faced Bonnie was not a good thing.

"No," Dori said, confused.

"I got a call this afternoon from someone who said they needed to confirm your employment."

"Was it the grocery store? Maybe they only just got around to it." Bonnie already knew she'd taken the second job.

"No, it wasn't them. It was some landscaping service. I don't see why you would even be interested in that kind of job."

Dori went still. "Did you say landscaping?"

"Yeah," Bonnie said, looking down at the pad on the desk in front of her. "Joseph Gagnon Landscaping. He wanted to know if you were a good worker!"

Her heart began to thump in a full adrenaline rush of fury. "I can't believe this! I have definitely NOT applied to work for him, and he knows it!"

"Then you're not looking to leave?" Bonnie was beginning to look better.

Bad enough he'd called in the first place, but to ask if she was a good worker? "No."

Bonnie was apparently unimpressed by the force of that no; her eyes narrowed. "Aren't you happy here?"

"It's fine," Dori said. She enjoyed working with some of the patients, not with others. She liked some of the charge nurses, not others. Some of her fellow aides were vulgar-mouthed gossips, but others worked hard and kept their heads down. And Bonnie was far from the worst boss she'd ever had – tight with money and supplies, yes, and a little scary when she was angry – but she struck Dori as essentially fair and sometimes even maternal, which was something Dori didn't get from anyone else in her life.

"You are leaving, aren't you," Bonnie said gloomily. "Do you have any idea how hard it is to find good CNAs?"

Maybe you should try paying them better, Dori thought, but didn't say. Bonnie was prone to long diatribes about how nursing homes were being squeezed out of existence.

"What if I upped your pay?" Bonnie said.

Dori just looked at her, surprised.

"Fifty cents an hour," Bonnie said.

That only worked out to an extra fifteen dollars or so a week. But it was a hell of a lot better than nothing. "I wouldn't turn it down."

"Okay, fine," Bonnie said, looking irritated again. "A dollar an hour. That's as much as I can do and a lot more than I usually do."

"Thank you. That's great."

Bonnie raised a finger to point at her. "If it ever comes right down to it, Dori, you talk to me first. There's more to a job than how much you get paid for it. I love my girls, and I look out for them too. And don't think for a moment your contributions here aren't appreciated."

Dori nodded over the sudden lump in her throat. It was a little pathetic, how grateful she was to hear that.

When she got home the grass had been neatly mowed and the bushes trimmed. Her heart started pounding all over again in fury that Bardwell money was contributing to Joe Gagnon's success while he was busy trying to ruin her life. She should call Marjorie right now and tell her to fire the bastard.

But first there was a message from Robert. "Hey, it was really nice meeting you, Dori. Thought I'd follow up. Call me when you get a chance." Dori took a few deep, calming breaths and wrote his number down. She decided to put off getting Joe fired, especially since it would require Marjorie's agreement. Besides, she needed to find a reason she could give Marjorie that wouldn't make it sound like she was too eager for it herself – Marjorie, she felt, instinctively looked for reasons to reject anything Dori wanted.

There was no message from Ruth. Apparently she could expect at least a day or two of sulking there, if not more.

How many times had she hung in there, supporting Ruth

through this crisis and that, listening patiently on the phone, making the trek to the hospital to sit at her side during visiting hours? Meanwhile, if Dori tried to tell her about Salinger, or the nursing home, or the Friends meeting, Ruth would cut her off with something like, "You really need to get out of that town."

It hadn't always been that way, had it? In Jasper Elementary and Jasper Middle Senior High School she and Ruth had created their own tight little refuge from the popularity wars and their dysfunctional families. It was after Ruth's father died that things got a little out of whack, and then just kept getting more and more so. When Dori lost everyone, Ruth had come home for the memorial service, but that was about it. Dori's loss reminded her of her own, she'd said, sniffling. In fact, she'd ended up hospitalized not long after, so Dori had added her grief to the list of topics she shouldn't bring up with Ruth.

And now she was being punished for bringing up the drinking.

Was it possible all the affection and loyalty she'd invested in the people she loved up to that point in her life had been for nothing? Of her own family, there was only Salinger left. She loved him, but she'd postponed her own education to help him obtain his and eight years later he had utterly failed to get it done. He couldn't care less what it had cost her. It wasn't like he'd *asked* her to drop out of school. He probably didn't even consider it a sacrifice.

And then there was Joe's inexplicable desire to screw up her livelihood a full eight years after she'd declined to marry him until she'd finished college. She'd simply wanted more time to grow up, to experience life outside of Jasper. It wasn't her fault he'd forced her to reject him in front of the entire class of 2007! How could he be so intent on revenge so many years later?

Was it something she was supposed to understand by now – something she should have learned in college if she'd gone, perhaps – that all adult relations were conducted in an unwritten economy of self-interest? Had she somehow failed to realize the *quid pro quo* of companionship had to be carefully and constantly monitored for fairness and potential future vendettas?

Dori held up the slip of paper on which she'd written Robert's numbers. She hoped this wasn't going to be just another great big pointless expenditure of *quid.*

He picked up the phone immediately, and seemed happy she'd called.

"Why don't you come see the house," she suggested, because she knew he wanted that. "I'll be home by three Saturday afternoon if that's a good time for you."

"Why don't I just stop by now? We could grab some dinner afterwards."

She hadn't expected him to want to come so soon. "Is this for the story?"

There was a hesitation on his end. "Is that what you want?"

"No, it's just – well, I just got home. The place is a mess." *She* was a mess.

"There's a nice little Pan-Asian fusion café on the Trail, just opened a couple of months ago. I reviewed it just last week, actually. Perhaps you saw it?"

There was an eagerness there she found all too familiar. *Writers.*

"That's probably beyond my budget."

"Don't worry, it's my treat."

"On a reporter's salary?"

He laughed a little self-consciously. "Yeah, well. I left out the part where I live over at the family camp rent-free."

"Oh." So his parents' concept of having their children learn to make their own way included free housing. Not that this was necessarily such a big favor, of course; she of all people should know that.

"Tell you what," he said. "I'll be there in an hour, never mind any mess in the house, and we can talk about what to do. But just in case, why don't you dress for dinner?"

She agreed. Too late, she wondered what dressing for dinner meant to a Putney.

"Oh my goodness gracious," he said an hour later, with a truly terrible attempt at a Southern accent. He'd rung the front door bell, so she'd ushered him into the foyer. He gazed up the grand staircase. "We could be at Tara."

"It's sure humid enough for it," Dori said. She had made an attempt to blow-dry her hair into some semblance of order, but it was already frizzing and curling. She peered out onto Main Street, where heat rippled over the asphalt and a muggy haze hung in the still air. "I hope we get some Canadian air soon."

"No central air, huh?"

"No AC at all, just fans. You sure you want the full tour?"

"What I'd really love to see is where your father worked."

He must really love her father's stuff. Well, there were lots of people who did, at least the first novel. She led him down the hall towards the study with its full French doors that opened onto the shady, neglected back patio. Books lined two walls; a giant mahogany desk sat in front of one of them, facing forward.

"He used a typewriter?" Robert sounded surprised, as well he should.

"No, that's actually somebody's antique. He used a computer, but it was a big old ugly one and the old ladies thought it ruined the look of the room."

"Are you kidding?"

"Nope."

He turned to the bookshelves, tilting his head as he read titles. Dori watched, bemused.

"This is quite an impressive collection," he said.

"They aren't all his. The Friends didn't like the look of the paperbacks or some of the more popular titles, so they switched in a bunch of hard covers. I remember they particularly objected to *Jaws* and *Fear of Flying*."

His shook his head. "That's just criminal."

"It's the house most of them love, and maybe the movie. Not the writing. But they didn't throw his books out. They're either up in the attic or back in the family room, or Salinger and I have them."

"And the manuscripts, the correspondence?"

"Some in the attic, some in the desk and the file cabinets here."

"That stuff is worth something, you know."

"Yeah, I know. I get calls. But in the trust he set up, Dad said they should be kept here, so scholars could access them in the place where they were created. Which actually only really applies to the later books, which nobody cares about. But whatever."

"Who can access anything if it's all in boxes in the attic?"

Dori shrugged. "Honestly? I try not to get involved."

"Maybe you should. If they're not managing it properly, maybe you could petition the court to appoint different trustees, or even revoke the trust."

He obviously assumed she could afford a lawyer. "Are you hungry?"

"Always," he said. "Are you, um, ready?"

"I'm afraid this was the best I could do on short notice," Dori said, embarrassed. She'd tried a pair of brand-new leggings and decided they were too tight and sending a signal she wasn't ready to send yet, which was undoubtedly why they were still brand new. She'd ended up in her best pair of jeans and one of her prettier shirts. "Am I not sufficiently dressed for dinner?"

"No, of course you are." He gave her a frankly predatory grin. "You look good enough to eat."

Chapter 7

"Would you prefer the diner?" he asked, after she'd buckled herself into his sporty little Mazda.

"Yeah, I kinda would," she said. Normally she'd suggest they just walk the five blocks, but it was hot enough she didn't want to exert herself any more than necessary.

"I mostly alternate between there and Anthony's Pizza, myself."

"No home-cooked meals?"

"My parents lent me the place, not the cook." He looked over at her. "Do you cook?"

Was he angling for a meal? At least he hadn't asked her if she had a cook. "I do. Mom taught me all the Southern dishes, and then when I figured out how bad they are for you, I learned some other stuff. I still cook Southern for special occasions."

"Southern being what? Ham hocks and black-eyed peas?"

"Yep. And collard greens, if I can find them. Usually have to make do with mustard or kale." She affected her mother's drawl: "Buttermilk biscuits. Green beans with mayonnaise and bacon. Fried catfish. Lima bean soup. Grits."

He pulled into a parking spot on Main Street near the diner. "That all sounds pretty scary. I wouldn't mind a biscuit, though."

"Mama always said you Yankees was cowards."

"I believe *you* just got intimidated by Pan Asian."

"I'm not really sure what it is."

He chuckled. "The prices do run a bit high for this community. I think they're hoping the summer people will have enough money to keep them in business."

"And another restaurant bites the dust," Dori declared as they walked in the door. The waitress behind the counter looked startled. "Not this one!" she added, but the woman's mouth didn't relax into a smile. The Jasper Diner was one of the narrow, old-fashioned metal kinds, still polished to a gleam. The owners had never expanded into a larger dining room or a longer menu, and they ran the exact same specials every week. Tuesday was meatloaf.

They were lucky not to have to wait for a seat, but Dori was aghast to realize the empty booth they were heading for would put them right behind Lisa Summers and someone with the exact same height and hunch as Joe Gagnon.

For almost eight years she hadn't seen the guy, and suddenly he was turning up everywhere.

Lisa looked up and gave Dori a little smile and a wave.

Dori leaned close to Robert's ear. "Maybe we should try Pan-Asian after all."

"Why?" Robert slid into the booth, apparently not interested in any last-minute course changes. Dori saw Joe turn and recognize her as she hovered in the aisle, unwilling to sit down. He gave her a stiff little nod.

Her anger blossomed. "Because the guy behind us just tried to get me fired," she said loudly, for Joe's benefit, but a few other people turned around and looked, too.

Joe got out of his seat quickly. "I wasn't trying to get you fired!" he said, keeping his voice low.

She didn't lower hers to match. "Like hell you weren't!"

Joe gave Robert a quick glance and then a double-take before turning back to Dori. "Look, I'm sorry, and I'd like to explain – but can we talk about this outside? Please?" He turned to Robert. "Would you mind?"

Robert held up his hands as if to say it wasn't up to him.

Dori told him, "Excuse me." She stalked after Joe, who went out the front door and kept going half a block until they were out of view of the diner windows.

Then he wheeled around and faced her. "I have every right to check the credit-worthiness of my clients. It's right there in the contract you declined to read."

"I didn't sign that contract, as you well know. I'm not your client, the trust is. So you had no right at all. My boss hauled me in today to ask me if I was leaving!"

He winced. "Did it work out all right? I could tell she was a little freaked out."

"Why did you do it? And don't give me any more bullshit about the contract."

"I just couldn't believe you were working there."

"And that gave you the right to call my boss?"

"Like I said, I was sure you wouldn't be there."

"You could have just asked someone around town!"

Finally he had the grace to look a little embarrassed. "Yeah, well. I kind of made it clear to folks for a long time that I didn't want to hear anything about you."

She clenched her jaw, pushing away the older pain to focus on the injury at hand. "I can't believe you would stoop to something so malicious!"

He looked startled. "It wasn't malicious! I just wanted to know. I guess I just wanted to be able to keep thinking you were living on Easy Street. I see Salinger around, you know. He seems to be doing just fine without ever working a day. I assumed you were both just ... you know ... trust fund babies."

"Is that why you asked if I was a hard worker?"

He turned red. "That was just kind of automatic. It's hard to find good workers. And I mean – come on, Dori. An aide in a nursing home? A job in a *grocery store*? You can do better than that. *I* could probably pay you better than that. In fact, if you got fired because of this, I would be happy to give you a job."

She felt her face flush hot. "You're trying to humiliate me in every way possible, aren't you?" She turned to walk back to the diner.

"I swear I'm not!" he said, and grabbed her shoulder to slow her down. When she shook him off, he ran ahead and blocked her way. "*Did* you get fired?"

"No." She straightened up, trying to gather a little dignity. "She gave me a raise."

He began to smirk. "Well, then ... technically I did you a favor, didn't I?"

"You're just lucky it worked out that way. And don't you ever, ever think of pulling any crap like that ever again." With a final glare, she brushed past him.

"There's something else, Eudora."

She stopped, arrested by the sound of his voice saying her name.

He leaned towards her. "How well do you know that guy in there?"

"Why?"

"It's just — from what I hear he's already worked his way through half the women in town. They've been calling him Robert the Dick."

She searched his face for signs of more triumph, or malice. The thing was, Joe had never been a liar. "Look, do me a favor," she said.

"What?"

"*Don't* call him up tomorrow and ask him if I'm good in bed."

She enjoyed watching the emotions parade across his face: shock, amusement, consternation. She smiled triumphantly and strutted away.

It definitely reduced Dori's sense of having gotten the last word to return to the diner and discover Robert had switched to the other side of the booth and was deeply engaged in friendly discussion over the back of it with Joe's beautiful girlfriend.

It took him a moment to notice she'd returned. "Oh, there you are. I'm told you've met Lisa here."

"Yep."

"Hi, Dori!" Lisa said. "Robert was just telling me how his parents' camp is on a private lake."

"Is that so?" Dori said, and slid into the opposite seat.

"I don't believe we've formally met," Joe said to Robert. He stood fairly aggressively at their table, using every inch of the height advantage he held over the slighter man.

Robert held out his hand. "Robert Putney-Lewis."

"Joe Gagnon," Joe said, and shook the hand.

"Of *Joseph Gagnon Landscaping LLC*," Dori added. "He's my lawn guy. Robert here is a reporter. Does your father own the Greenfield paper, too, Robert?"

"Actually, no," Robert said. "Working for your own family

isn't exactly the way to build credibility in this business. Nice to meet you, Joe."

The waitress approached with their food.

"Enjoy your meal," Joe said, and sat down, but not before flashing an irritated look at Dori. She smiled sweetly at him. She was glad she hadn't gotten him fired yet– it had felt great to say he mowed her lawn.

Robert said, "So did you chew his head off?"

"Yeah, I'd say it's fully masticated."

"Since you were outside I took the liberty of ordering us both the special," Robert said.

"Oh. Okay. Thanks." Dori surveyed her plate; there was enough food there for three meals. Meatloaf wouldn't have been her first choice – Robert had been a bit presumptuous ordering it for her when he didn't even know if she ate meat. But at least it was free.

"Lisa is rather fascinating," Robert said. "Did you know she's studying to become an Emergency Medical Technician?"

"No."

"Her father is the fire chief in town. I've dealt with him a few times. Seems like a nice guy."

She smiled politely.

"Here's a thought," Robert said, raising his voice and twisting to include Lisa and Joe. "Why don't we all go over to the camp after dinner? We could take out the canoes, enjoy a paddle around the lake."

"Oh my God, that sounds fabulous!" Lisa said. "I love canoeing!"

Dori said, "I have a pretty early morning tomorrow."

"Me, too," Joe said. "Maybe another time would be better."

Robert said, "Oh, we'll be done before it gets dark. It's just ten minutes from here. I'd love for you to see the place."

Lisa was practically squealing. "I want to go! Imagine having your own private lake!"

Dori said, "Well, maybe just a quick stop after dinner." She'd decided it was worth it just to annoy Joe.

Chapter 8

"You don't really mind, do you?" Robert asked her, as they drove up tiny curving roads into hills lush with summer greenery. Joe was following behind them in his truck.

"I'm sure it will be interesting."

He glanced at her. "I would think you might enjoy a dip in the lake before you head back to that sweltering house."

Who'd said anything about a dip in the lake? She didn't even have a suit with her. For that matter, when was the last time she'd shaved her legs, or anything else? But there was nothing she could do about that now. "Just promise me you're going to be the one to give me a ride home."

He looked surprised. "You know them both, don't you?"

"In case you don't remember, I just had a fairly intense dispute with Joe."

"I had the impression it was resolved."

"Doesn't mean I want to spend more time with him than I have to."

He gave her a piercing look. "Don't tell me. He's your ex."

She pursed her lips.

He shook his head. "Must be one of those hazards of dating in a small town. Are you still hung up on him?"

"No!"

"Good."

Wow. Dori looked up and around the great room with its soaring ceiling, rough-hewn beams, and huge, sparkling windows that looked out on a respectable-sized lake.

And on a night like this the air conditioning alone counted as a plus.

Robert dropped his keys on one of the expansive granite counters and went to the refrigerator, pulling out and opening four

Bass ales without pausing to ask if anyone actually wanted one. "Glass or bottle?" he said, finally offering a choice of some kind.

"Bottle," Dori said.

"That's my girl." It was condescending, but she saw Joe grimace and that made it worth it.

"I'm a bottle girl, too!" Lisa said.

Joe swiped his bottle off the counter without saying anything and walked towards the giant fireplace, which was set in a high wall of natural stone.

Robert raised his bottle. "To a nice cool lake on a hot summer day."

Lisa clinked her bottle with his.

Dori raised hers in another toast. "To air conditioning."

"To air conditioning," Robert and Lisa agreed. They clinked bottles and drank.

"Nice place," Joe said. He had ignored the toasts and was running his hand across a row of stones. "Do you know who did this stonework?"

"Haven't the faintest," Robert said. "Let's go figure out the canoes, shall we?" He turned to Dori. "One of the most vivid memories I have of your father is him insisting everybody wear life jackets."

"Yeah, he had a thing about that," Dori said. She exchanged a glance with Joe. She'd gotten in big trouble once, at the dinner table, when she'd casually mentioned canoeing with him. "What gave you the idea you could just go canoeing without asking our permission?" her father had demanded. "You could have drowned!"

So she'd stopped telling them where she'd been when they went canoeing. But she also wore a life jacket. He'd made her promise.

Dori sat in the bow of Robert's canoe and paddled hard in the inevitable race, but the two crews were well-matched. Eventually the humidity won and both canoes drifted into a spreading mat of water lilies. Dori dipped her hand down and yanked one out of the water, then held it up to her nose. When she looked up, she caught Joe watching her with an odd expression and thought perhaps he was remembering old times; she'd always been one to stop and smell the flowers. She raised her eyebrows at him and he looked away.

"Look at them all, would you?" Robert said. "They grow like weeds. And yet my mother pays big money to grow things identical to this in a tiny pond down at the main house. She even over-winters them in the basement in giant tubs."

"Where's the main house?" she asked.

"Chappaqua."

"Where's that?"

"In Westchester County. A suburb north of the city."

From the other canoe, Joe said, "It's where the Clintons moved after they left the White House." Perhaps he had become a Republican in addition to looking like one.

"Yes, we've had them over for dinner once or twice," Robert said. "He'd enjoy your Southern food, Dori, or he would have before he turned vegan."

"You've had a president to your house for dinner?" Lisa was staring open-mouthed.

"Former president," Robert said. "And Hillary was our Senator at the time. Politicians like to 'keep in touch' with media people, you know; it's part of the job."

"Wow," Lisa breathed.

"If your father can dine with presidents, I wonder why he bothered with my dad," Dori said.

"Oh, he loves authors. He's published a couple of histories himself. I think in his heart he wishes he could write the great American novel. He tried once and everyone hated it. We don't mention it now. At least, not to his face."

Dori didn't say anything. When she was growing up it had seemed to her just about everyone not only *could* write a novel, but *did,* and they were always asking her father to read them. They didn't realize he would either delight in ridiculing them if they were bad, or sink into jealousy and despair if they were good. He particularly resented the bound galleys that arrived with requests for cover quotes. These he usually ignored or farmed out to her mother. He'd even farmed some out to her, once she was in high school, but once the novelty had worn off she'd begun to refuse most of them, preferring to wait and see what looked good in the library.

"My dad's also a bit of an expert on the antebellum period," Robert said. "I suspect that's why he first sought out your father."

Dori stared out across the lake, brooding over the question that had just occurred to her: If the Putney camp was really this close to home, why hadn't she ever been here before?

"Something wrong?" Robert asked.

"What? No, not really. So how often did my parents come here?" Dori asked.

"Pretty often. I remember my dad once said I should call them Uncle Nat and Aunt Ellen. Not that we did."

Nat? That meant they really knew him, for Nathaniel was his actual first name and Nat was what her mother called her father. But uncle and aunt? She hadn't even known Robert existed.

"Let's head back," Robert said, raising his voice to include Joe and Lisa. "Maybe we could have a quick dip just to cool off."

"Super!" Lisa said.

Back at the dock, Robert announced he was going to get more beers.

Joe said, "I don't know, Lisa. Let's make this quick, okay?"

"Sure," she said, and pulled her shirt off over her head.

Dori watched Joe's eyes widen. He said, "What the hell are you doing?"

"Making it quick," Lisa said. "Aren't you coming in?" She un-hooked her bra, then shimmied out of her jeans and her tiny little thong.

Such youthful skin, such perfect muscle tone. And no hair. At all.

Lisa smiled at Dori without embarrassment and approached the side of the dock with the obvious intention of diving in.

Dori yelled, "Hey, wait!"

Lisa looked over.

"You don't know how deep that water is."

Lisa stared at her a moment. "Oh. Right." She trotted past them down the dock to the beach and waded in instead.

Joe had just stood there on the dock, watching it all – how could he not watch? Even Dori was transfixed by Lisa's nudity. Robert came out shirtless with the beers and grinned broadly at Lisa standing in water up to her thighs. "Nice ass!" he called. "Want a beer?"

Lisa giggled and headed back to shore. Joe watched, shaking his head slightly.

"Kids these days," Dori said to him.

"Beer?" Robert called to them. "And are you going in?"

"No thanks," she called back. "But you go right ahead."

Joe asked in an undertone, "Did you really think she might have hurt herself?"

"It happens. You don't want to be one of those patients."

They watched Lisa take a beer from Robert and bump bottles with him in some kind of toast. Then she waded back into the lake and swam out to them, beer raised high above the water, and placed it on the dock. "Come on in, guys!" she said. "The water's great!"

Dori just smiled and shook her head, while Joe glowered.

"Suit yourself," Lisa said, and slid underwater.

"I guess I should thank you for stopping her," he said. "She can be a little impulsive."

Dori smiled. He returned it stiffly and walked back down the dock to the beach. It felt as if they'd achieved some sort of truce. She couldn't say the same for Joe and Robert; Joe pointedly refused the beer he was offered and sat down in one of the Adirondack chairs on the beach, his folded arms screaming I'm Ready to Go Home Now.

Dori decided to stay where she was. She took off her sandals, rolled up her jeans, and dipped her feet into the water. Robert could come to her, or he could hang out with Naked Girl. It would be interesting to see which he chose.

After trying one more time to get Joe to take a beer, Robert walked down to her, holding out the beer she had already refused. "Aren't you going in?"

She took the beer and shook her head. "No, thanks."

"You're not against nudity in principal, are you?" he said. "Not one of those women who have to get undressed in the dark and then crawl under the covers?"

"Do you run into a lot of women like that?"

His mouth started to form the word *no*. Then he stopped and looked at her suspiciously.

She smiled and looked out across the lake. "I heard you have a large pool of experience to draw on."

"Someone's been talking about me?" He looked back at Joe, then downed a slug. "All I can say is, consider the source. I'm sure I could find you a suit in the house if that's what's stopping you."

"Thanks anyway, but I really do need to get back pretty soon. As I said, my day starts very early."

"Then why not get him to take you back? You're both itching to go."

She looked at him, surprised and disappointed. "I already explained that."

He frowned. "Then how about staying here? It's air-conditioned. I could run you back in the morning. You could have a guest room, no problem."

"I have to be in Greenfield at seven."

"Oh. Ouch." He sighed. "Still, I guess I could get up at an ungodly hour. Especially if you made it worth my while." He gave her a frankly leering look.

Dori shook her head, smiling. For some reason she felt more amused by him than harassed.

Robert leaned into her and murmured in her ear. "Don't I tempt you at all?"

"Your air conditioning tempts me."

"Just the air conditioning? Maybe you don't realize what you're missing." He put his beer down and dropped his own shorts and underwear to the dock, then assumed a catalog pose front and back. "Not bad, right?"

No, not bad. Robert was rather startlingly well-endowed for a fairly slight guy, in fact. She smiled and lifted her beer in salute. "No, not bad at all."

He grinned, then yelled, "Ollie Ollie Oxinfray!" and ran down the dock, diving into the water with a splash.

"Water's great," he called, when he appeared at the surface. "It's not too late to change your mind," he said. "About any of it!" He ducked under again.

"You see?" Lisa called to her, from where she was bobbing in the water. "It *was* deep enough!" Then she gave a shriek. Apparently Robert was tickling her under the water.

Dori walked back to the beach and dropped into the chair next to Joe. "If he cops out on me can I have a ride home from you?"

Joe didn't take his eyes off the lake. "Yep. If you're smart you'll take one from me anyway."

Dori folded her arms. "Those two seem to be getting along awfully well."

He didn't respond, just watched the couple playing in the water. Eventually, he got up. "Lisa!" he called. "Come on, babe. We got to go."

Lisa popped up and squinted back at him. "Yeah, okay." She started wading back to shore. Robert swam to the dock.

"At least she takes direction well," Dori said. "That must make you happy."

He shot her a glare.

Lisa walked up, still utterly naked, squeezing water out of her long hair. She looked like a Barbie doll.

"Wax job?" Dori asked, looking at Lisa's hairless crotch.

Lisa grinned. "Yes."

Dori winced involuntarily. "Doesn't it itch?"

"No, not at all. You've never had one?"

"I've never even had a manicure."

Joe sighed. "Do you think maybe you could get some clothes on, Lisa?"

"Oh!" She smiled sheepishly and looked around her. "Where'd I leave them?"

Robert, back in his shorts, walked down the dock and held out a handful of her clothing and a half-empty beer. "I believe these are yours."

"Oh, thanks!" she said. "Do you think I could use a bathroom?"

"Sure, let me show you," Robert said, and walked back into the house with her. Joe and Dori followed behind.

Dori said, "Maybe she needs some privacy for changing."

That finally made Joe laugh.

Chapter 9

Joe and Dori stood awkwardly in the great room, listening to distant squeals of admiration from Lisa. Robert returned quickly. "She said she wanted to grab a quick shower."

"Great," Joe said. "That'll be at least another twenty minutes."

"Anyone want another beer?" Robert asked.

"No thanks," Joe and Dori said in unison. Joe gave her an annoyed look. He didn't want them to suddenly get along too well, Dori concluded. She withdrew to peer out of the giant bank of windows.

"Something else?" Robert said, head in the refrigerator. "I have water, soda, iced tea. White wine. Red wine."

Neither she nor Joe responded.

Dori looked at her watch. Now that it was finally growing dark outside, the windows were reflecting the yellow-lit interior of the house. In the reflection she watched Robert open an iced tea, check his phone, then flounce down on the massive sofa that sat in front of the fireplace. "Anyone want a fire?" he asked.

Joe said, "Don't you have the air on?"

Robert shrugged. "I can keep it low." He picked up a remote and flames leapt up, quickly dialed down to embers.

Joe frowned. "So where's the mood music?"

Robert cocked an eyebrow at him. "You want me to get you in the mood?"

Dori asked, "Do you have another bathroom?"

Robert said, "You'll find a couple of bathrooms just down the other hall there, between the bedrooms." He pointed towards the other side of the house. Dori couldn't help noticing that while he'd escorted Lisa, she was on her own.

"Thanks," she said, and took off. But as she passed the kitchen and front door she noticed a tiny half bath that was closer and ducked in. She sat down, noting the funky wallpaper with its rainbow trout motif, and realized she could hear the two guys talking quite clearly.

Which meant they could hear her, too. She'd have to try to pee softly. There were some drawbacks to the great room concept. She stealthily unrolled toilet paper, reluctant even to broadcast the clunk-clunk of the roll turning.

She heard Joe say, "You've got quite a reputation."

"Hey, it's not my fault women throw themselves at me. I don't know if it's my stunning good looks, my charming personality, or all that money. And, frankly, I don't care. I enjoy the ladies, and I make sure they enjoy me. I make no apologies for any of it."

Damn. Joe was right, Robert was a skank. That was the vibe she'd been getting from him all along, of course, but it was a little disheartening to hear him own it so wholeheartedly.

On the other hand that part about ensuring the ladies enjoyed it intrigued her a bit. No doubt there was something to be said for all that practice.

Also, the size of his instrument bore consideration.

Joe didn't sound impressed. "Have you shared this philosophy with Dori?"

"I follow a don't ask, don't tell policy in regards to my philosophy. But you've already warned her off, haven't you?"

Joe didn't answer, unless it was some visual response Dori couldn't see.

Robert continued: "What I like about Dori is that she clearly has a mind of her own. She's more than capable of making her own decisions about what might be fun. I find her very appealing, actually. She might even be a keeper."

As opposed to the old catch and release? Dori eyed the trout motif on the wallpaper and decided she felt vaguely flattered. She knew she could not compete with Lisa or half the other eligible young women in the world in terms of physical attraction, but apparently all a woman really had to do to fascinate Robert was be unusually uncooperative. She could do that.

Joe said, "If you really think that, why are you flirting with Lisa?"

"Because she's flirting with me. What am I supposed to do, tell her to bugger off?"

"Stick with the one you brought, that's what you're supposed to do."

Robert groaned. "Has anyone ever told you that you have a narrow, constipated vision of life?"

Joe took a moment before replying. "Perhaps I should just give you a friendly warning, then. Lisa's dad is very protective, and so are all of his colleagues."

"How kind of you to let me know. But aren't you supposed to be threatening me with your *own* brute strength?"

"Hey, if a girl decides she prefers someone like you, I won't stand in her way."

That was Joe, all right. And if a girl loved him but it wasn't on his precise terms she could go to hell, too. Suddenly furious, she dropped the toilet lid with a loud bam.

Silence fell.

She flushed the toilet and washed her hands and stalked out. "You're both assholes as far as I'm concerned."

"What did I do?" Joe said. "I'll go see if I can hurry Lisa up." He was smirking as he walked past her.

Robert had turned a bit pale. "I take it you heard me singing your praises?"

"I heard everything."

"Look, Dori –"

"Just give me a ride home, please, Robert."

"If you're never going to speak to me again, why not just go with Joe?"

"Who said I wasn't going to speak to you again? You have that article to write, don't you?"

He looked as if he was trying to decide whether she was just toying with him. She stared back at him and tried to decide whether, in fact, she was.

Joe came back with Lisa in tow. "God, it's the most fabulous bathroom!" she told Dori. "The whole master suite is just so gorgeous. It should be in a magazine!"

"It was, once," Robert said. "I actually sleep in one of the smaller bedrooms. This is my parents' place, you know. They're just letting me use it."

"Oh." Lisa looked confused. "I thought it was yours."

"He's not obscenely wealthy yet, Lisa," Dori said helpfully. "You'll have to give him a few years."

Robert threw her an irritated look. "I guess we can all go, then. Do you need to follow me back, Joe?"

"No, I got it," Joe said. Outside, he edged close to Dori as they waited for Robert to lock up. "Sure you don't need a ride?"

"I'll be fine," she said, mostly to irritate him. "Good night, Lisa," she added.

"Good night," Lisa said. Her brow was furrowed. Was she still trying to nail down Robert's economic status? Or had she just realized she was about to drive home with an angry Joe?

"Feel free to invite me in," Robert said, after he pulled up under the portico on the side of the house. In the original plantation house it had been constructed as the entrance for tradesmen and their goods; for Dori it meant easy access to the kitchen. She almost never used the ostentatious front door.

"Not tonight," Dori said.

"Or any night."

Dori smiled. "You're a nice enough guy, Robert. I'm just not sure how I feel about all those other people you've slept with."

"I'm very careful," he said. "I take every precaution."

"I'm sure you do." She put her hand on the door handle. "Thanks for dinner."

"It's not as bad as it sounded, anyway. There was quite possibly some exaggeration involved. I couldn't help wanting to depress that fellow a little, you know?"

She laughed. "Yes, I do know. Good night."

"Good night." He waited, still pouting, while she got out of the car and opened the side door with her key. He rolled down the passenger window and leaned over. "What if I got a doctor's note? Squeaky-clean test results?"

She laughed again and went inside.

There were two messages waiting on the old machine.

The first was from Marjorie Haight. "I need to talk to you, Eudora. Give me a call as soon as possible, please." She sounded stern, but then she usually did. Dori decided she could wait.

The second one was somebody sobbing. Ruth. Dori tried to understand what she was saying, but even after playing it over three times she had caught little more than a "sorry" and "I didn't mean to." Didn't mean to *what?* She tried one more time, but still couldn't decipher it.

It was after nine and she didn't want to talk to Ruth when she was ... whatever it was. Drunk or despairing or both. But she was a little worried she couldn't even figure out what she was trying to say. She sighed and moved to the phone in the tiny TV room behind the kitchen, so she could flop down on the sofa to dial back.

No answer.

"Goddammit," she said to the phone, suddenly exhausted, and hung up. She'd done all she could do, hadn't she? Ruth's mother hadn't picked up either – so either they were not home or they were intentionally not answering the phone.

That night Dori lay almost naked on top of her sheets under the fan, which barely made the sultry night tolerable, wondering if her comment about alcoholism had propelled Ruth into another self-destructive spiral. Cross another thing off the list of what she was allowed to say. What were they supposed to talk about any-more with so many subjects off limits?

Stop thinking about Ruth, she told herself, fearing she might never get to sleep. Think about something else. Anything else. Like how miserably hot it was. Maybe she should have taken a dip in that lake while she had the chance. Of course, she'd never looked as good as Lisa even when she had been Lisa's age, and she was looking less and less good with every passing year. In a Jane Austen novel she'd probably already be a confirmed spinster in a lace cap, a pitiable woman with no fortune who had lost her "bloom" and could only hope to be invited over to the neighbor's grand estate for gruel and tea.

So maybe it was worth contracting a social disease to have a good time with an entertaining lout like Robert, before all the louts of the world stopped looking.

It wasn't what she'd expected when she'd asked Joe to wait until they were finished with college.

Of course, if she had married him and then hadn't been able to meet his exacting expectations, she'd probably just be a bitter divorced single mother right now with the same crappy job prospects and even less chance of having sex.

Thinking about Joe wasn't helping her get to sleep, either. Air conditioning. That's what she should think about. How expensive could a single window air conditioner be? What if she put it on layaway?

Someone was in bed with her. Someone was *inside* her in bed with her. Not hurrying. Slow and steady, as if there was all the time in the world. *Mmm, nice.* She opened her eyes.

Joe was looking down at her.

The new Joe, of *Joseph Gagnon Landscaping LLC.*

She woke with a start. Outside rain was pouring down hard and thunder was rumbling, but the air was no cooler. She knew she should get up and lower the window to protect the sill, but she didn't want to move.

Oh, man. Joseph Gagnon, local lawn magnate, in a sex dream.

There was only one explanation for this: She really, really needed to get laid.

By anyone but him.

Chapter 10

She tried Ruth again in the morning, even though it was early. There was no answer. The hospital in Greenfield would be the first stop if Ruth had done something stupid. She called and asked for Ruth Moscatiello's room.

"She can't take any calls," the operator told her, after a pause. Damn. "Is she okay?"

There was another pause. "Her condition is listed as stable."

She would call Ruth's mother later in the day to find out what that meant. Probably. Dori was getting really tired of these episodes. Of course, so was Ruth's mother. And so, no doubt, was Ruth.

At work three cups of coffee were not enough to get her up to her usual speed.

"What's the matter with you?" Bonnie asked.

"I didn't sleep well."

"Still angry at that landscaper guy?"

"Yeah." Though her subconscious apparently wasn't. She thought about mentioning he'd said something about being able to pay her more, but decided she'd better not press her luck. "And my best friend is in the hospital again."

"That girl is a mess," Bonnie said. "What'd she do this time?"

"I don't know yet." Dori was planning to drive over after work and see if she could find out what happened. She was planning to, but she wasn't entirely certain that once she was in the car she would actually make the turns necessary to get there.

Bonnie cleared her throat. "Speaking of messes, somebody's got to attend to Kevin."

"Me? Who's going to help me?"

"Sorry, nobody. We're short. Antoine's out today. Probably because he always gets stuck with Kevin."

"You know I can't get him up by myself."

"I know. Just do the best you can."

"I should call out more often," Dori said.

"Go right ahead," Bonnie said, apparently not nearly as concerned as she had been the day before.

"You better not fire me if I curse him out."

"Just don't kill him. That's all anyone can ask with that guy."

Kevin Mackelroy greeted her with fart noises. He was the maestro of rude sounds, perhaps because his lips were one of the only parts of his body that still functioned properly. At 55 he was the youngest resident they had. Multiple Sclerosis had stolen his strength and coordination, but not his ability to hurl insults. Nor had it much reduced his weight. She'd be lucky to even get him on his side if he wasn't able or willing to help.

"Hey, sweet cheeks," he greeted her. "Come to clean my ass?"

"I'll try, Mr. Mackelroy. Do you need a bedpan first?"

"You tell me."

She sighed and looked at his chart. He'd had a movement the day before. Her resentment towards Antoine lessened slightly. Getting Kevin to shit successfully could take hours. "It doesn't look like it, unless you really want to."

"When do I get what I want? Did you come in here to give me a blow job?"

She'd learned not to engage with patients' vulgarities. It just made things worse. "I'll just get my supplies."

He said, "I'm pretty sure Raquel Welch isn't going to show up to give me a sponge bath, either."

She didn't bother asking who Raquel Welch was. One privacy blanket, two bath towels, eight wash cloths. No, ten. Warm water. Cleanser.

"I used to have her poster hanging above the bed in my bedroom when I was a teenager," he said. "She probably saw my dick hard more than any other woman in the universe. Though if I'm stuck in here long enough you might catch up with her."

She desperately wished to say something insulting about the unlikeliness of his dick ever being hard again, but managed not to. She laid out her towels and asked him to check the water in the basin. "That temperature all right for you?"

"Whatever. Raquel is probably some old hag now. But I'd still take a blow job from her. Or from you. From anybody. Well, anybody female."

"I'm going to wash your face now, Mr. Mackelroy, unless you would prefer to give it a try."

"Nah." Until recently Kevin had been capable of wiping his own face, but those days were gone, unless recent months were just a bad spell. As she cleaned his face, his eyes shut and he actually looked a bit soothed. The television blared in the background, some talk show with people blaming each other for various things she couldn't imagine anyone ever wanting to become public, let alone discussed in minute detail. "And now I'll clean your arm," she said. She laid her hand on his arm for a long moment, then lifted it slowly so she could slip the towel underneath. It was best to move slowly with Kevin; he was prone to muscle spasms.

When she got to it – thankfully, he'd managed to help her get him turned onto his side -- Kevin's flaccid white butt was interrupted by one big, red, angry-looking pressure ulcer. "Did Antoine shift your position yesterday?" she asked.

"Hell, no. Lately he's as shiftless as all the rest of them. Get it? Shiftless."

If Kevin was as abusively racist to Antoine as he was abusively sexist to her, no wonder the man had called out. Antoine was one of the most patient men Dori had ever met, but everyone had their limits. "Did the doctor check you over completely yesterday?"

"The doctor looks at me with his eyes down while he writes out his fucking bill."

"Mr. Mackelroy, I'm serious. Did he see your backside?"

Kevin hesitated, and then his voice sounded a little scared. "Why?"

"This ulcer on your behind. Did he say anything about it?"

"Oh Jesus, a bed sore! You want to get me all worked up over a fucking bed sore?"

"No, sir," Dori said, but she decided she'd have to document this one anyway. Kevin's ulcers were chronic, but this one even smelled bad.

He snorted. "*You're* the bed sore."

Kevin Mackelroy's mother had left him at the nursing home a couple of years earlier. She'd been sobbing uncontrollably, and on the way home she'd driven her car straight into an oncoming truck. He got visits once a month or so by one reluctant sibling or another. He usually spent the day watching television. He was so unpleasant to the other residents that the staff had plenty of incentive to keep him out of the common areas, though they really should have been getting him out of bed more often than they did. It didn't help that he was so big.

At the commercial he went back to his fart noises. She finished washing him and then making the bed under him. She knew the man's hatefulness was really just his way of howling at the universe. He was not unlike a fair number of the senile patients in this, although they were thankfully not as proficient as he was at landing their insults. And she supposed having words hurled at her was better than a fist in the face. Some of the most decrepit old folks still had surprising strength.

She finished the work she could handle on her own with him. She would need help and a lift to get him into a new position that might put less pressure on that ulcer.

"Do you need anything before I go?"

"That blow job."

"In your dreams, Mr. Mackelroy," she said, and walked out.

At the hospital, they said Ruth couldn't have visitors. Dori was relieved. She just wanted to go home and crash. But at home there was a clipped message from Ruth's mother to call her back.

"Hello, Dori," Mrs. Moscatiello said. Her voice was even tighter than usual.

"Is Ruth okay?"

"She tried to overdose on one of my prescriptions. Luckily it didn't work."

"I'm so sorry. I got home late Tuesday night. There was a message from her but I couldn't get through."

"She was very upset after your dinner," Mrs. Moscatiello said.

"I know – I said something to her about her drinking and she didn't like it."

Silence. Wrong answer, Dori concluded. "Well, I know they aren't allowing her any visitors yet because I tried to stop by to-day. Do you know when she'll be getting out?"

Ruth's mother erupted. "How could you even think of taking her to that place?"

Dori stood dumbstruck for a moment. "Ruth was the one who wanted to go. Well, somebody else suggested it but Ruth agreed. She insisted. I was pretty surprised."

"You should have known better! What kind of friend *are* you?"

Dori's heart began to beat fast, as if she'd been caught doing something wrong. How had this become her fault?

Mrs. Moscatiello wasn't finished. "I don't see how someone like you can be any good for Ruth right now, and I can't take any more of this. So do me a favor and leave her alone. You hear me? Keep the hell away from my daughter!" She hung up.

Dori stood there with the phone in her hand, heart still pound-ing.

She looked down the long, empty hallway.

"Salinger!" she yelled, experimentally.

Silence. At Jenna's, no doubt.

Dori sat down right on the floor, her back against the kitchen wall, phone still in her hand. She knew it wasn't her fault. She knew Mrs. Moscatiello had simply turned frantic and ugly in her anxiety about Ruth. But she felt she would give almost anything to hear any other person in the world agree with her about that.

Still feeling oddly shaky, as if she had survived a near-miss in the car, Dori opened a can of soup to boil and put two slices of frozen bread in the toaster oven. It was a pathetic meal even by her usual summer standards – she didn't like to heat up the kitchen – but she was trying to wait until after her Saturday morning shift at the store to buy any more groceries. If Salinger really was living at Jenna's she might just make it.

Just as she'd finished spreading the butter on her toast, the phone rang.

Let it ring, she told herself, but then she answered it anyway. She couldn't help hoping it was Ruth, or even Mrs. Moscatiello calling to apologize.

"Eudora! I thought I was going to have to leave another message."

"Hi, Marjorie," Dori said. She looked at her cooling toast.

"The Trustees met last night, Eudora, dear. I'm calling because we have two trustee vacancies that we need to fill as soon as possible."

"Are you retiring?"

"Oh no, not me. But Tom Shaftsbury and Bernie Cohen have both tendered their resignations. Poor Tom has serious health issues, and Bernie is moving to Florida."

"I'm sorry to hear that," Dori said. It was a formality. She barely knew either of them.

"Charlie thought I should ask you if you, um, have any recommendations."

They were actually asking her opinion about something?

"I told him you wouldn't," Marjorie continued. "But he insisted we should ask. He even suggested that you might be interested." She laughed in that insincere way she had.

"I can be a trustee?"

"The remaining trustees can select anyone of legal age to fill the vacancies that come up. You'd still be only one vote out of five, of course." There was a hint of sharpness there.

"But I thought..."

"What, dear?"

"I thought it was supposed to be a conflict of interest? I seem to recall, the last time I asked about attending the meetings..."

Marjorie coughed. "Well, you know, apparently that was a little error on my part."

"Then Salinger could be a trustee too, couldn't he?"

"Heavens, can you imagine? No, I don't think we could approve that. We need someone with a solid reputation, fiscal prudence, preferably someone who has achieved some success in the business world. Ideally, it would be someone who might have some money they'd be willing to donate to the cause. We've already approached a fair number of local business people but there hasn't been much interest. Which is why we thought of you. We agreed that you are a responsible young lady and you do, presumably, have some concern for your father's legacy. But we were also thinking that perhaps you've met some philanthropic-minded doctors through your work. Or their wives, even."

"Actually, I'd like to do it."

"You would?" Marjorie sounded stunned.

"Absolutely."

"It means regular meetings and quite a bit of responsibility."

"You just said you thought I was essentially responsible."

There was silence for a moment. "I'll let the others know, then," Marjorie said, her voice higher than normal. "In the meantime, we'll continue our inquiries, of course. By the way, the lawn looks lovely. That young man seems to be doing a good job, don't you think?"

"Mmm." Dori's desire to get Joe fired had faded, but she wasn't ready to sing his praises, or his workmen's. "Did you mention my college plans to the other trustees?"

"I had no idea they had reached the level of actual plans, Eudora. You're going to have to give us a little bit more to go on than what I've heard from you so far. And if that's what you want, there's really no point in becoming a trustee, is there?"

Well, there was that. But it was hard to make any plans when she had no idea what kind of money might be available to her. If she were a trustee, she'd know for certain.

Also, Marjorie clearly hoped she wouldn't do it. That alone made her want it.

But would it really help her accomplish her escape, or would it tie her to this house more firmly than ever?

Once again, she just wished there was someone, anyone, to talk it over with.

Chapter 11

"A drink?" Robert said, on the other end of the line. "I'd love to. But I'm covering the selectman's meeting tonight, and they often don't finish until after nine. I know you start work early."

"Yeah, I do. Well, maybe some other time."

"Have you eaten dinner yet?"

She looked at the kitchen table with its bowl of cold soup, its half-eaten toast. "Not really."

"How about I pick you up and we'll have a drink over dinner? I was just about to go grab something to eat anyway. We'll just have to hurry a bit, that's all."

"I'm not –" She stopped. She'd called him in the first place because she needed someone to talk to. "Okay. That would be great. Thank you."

She had barely managed to change and was already beginning to regret the impulse to call him when he knocked on the kitchen door.

"I wasn't really expecting to hear from you again," he said, as they walked out to his car. "Unless it was about the article. Is that what this is about?"

She said, "No, not that," and belted herself in.

He looked as if he was waiting for more of an explanation, so she added, "Ruth's in the hospital. Her mother says it's my fault. Because I took her to The Mill."

He frowned. "That was my idea. But she didn't protest."

"I know. I think I just really needed to hear somebody tell me that." Maybe she should tell him she didn't need dinner or a drink after all. Save him the trouble, and save herself any confusion about how she felt about him. But she didn't say anything as he pulled out and headed up Main Street away from town.

"Where are we going?"

"There's a place on the way to Charlemont that has both food and drink."

"Oh." If she didn't have enough to cover it, she decided, she would put it on her emergency credit card. She would willingly invest in having someone else to talk to.

"So what exactly happened to Ruth?" he asked.

Unfortunately, the person she had chosen to talk to was also a reporter. "Is there any chance this will turn up in the paper?"

"She didn't do anything criminal, did she?"

"Is attempted suicide against the law?"

He raised his eyebrows. "Actually, yes, but it's seldom prosecuted. Is she okay?"

She hesitated. Had she really just blabbed about her friend's suicide attempt to a reporter?

"I don't see any reason for this to end up in the paper," he said. "At least not yet. If she dies, it will end up there anyway."

"She isn't dead. That's all I know. Her mom just told me to stay the hell away from her."

"Nice. But Ruth is an adult. It's up to her who she sees or not."

"Yeah, I guess," Dori said. She didn't like to think of Ruth as grown up. It was more comforting to think of her as just hitting another one of her rough patches on the way to adulthood. It was shocking to think Ruth, at twenty-six, might be essentially the same screwed-up person she was now for the rest of her life.

Especially since that would mean Dori, at the same age, was already an adult, too. And that was far too depressing. Ruth had at least moved ahead and gotten her education. Did Dori really have to think of herself as grown up simply because of her age?

But maybe she did. Maybe this was who she was. Even if she did get a move on, she would never get back the last seven years of her life.

At the restaurant, a modestly comfortable place she had never been to before, she ordered a beer and a chicken sandwich, something simple and therapeutic-sounding. He ordered a hamburger.

"No beer?" she asked him.

"Not until I'm done for the night."

"How often do you have to work nights?"

"Two or three times a week, usually."

"Do you get overtime?"

"They try to avoid having to pay us overtime. Today I just started later."

"No wonder you didn't fancy driving me home at six in the morning."

"But I would have." He waggled his eyebrows suggestively.

She smiled back uncomfortably and took a swallow of her beer. Robert was charming in a predatory kind of way, and she could use a little romance in her life. Of course, 'romance' wasn't exactly the right word for what Robert was offering. If she drank enough, she could probably sleep with him without thinking about the consequences. Unfortunately, that didn't mean they wouldn't be there the next day when the buzz wore off. And while they'd be there, she doubted Robert would be.

"Do you know much about trusts?" she asked, partly to change the subject and partly because she figured if anybody knew about trusts it would be a Putney.

"A bit. Why do you ask?"

"There are two vacancies on my father's trust," she said. "I'm going to take one opening, and they asked if I could recommend somebody for the other. I just wish I knew more about what I might be getting into."

"You should ask my dad."

"Because he knows about trusts?"

"No, you should ask him to be a trustee."

She stared at him. "I don't even know your dad."

"But he knew your father, *and* cared about his work. And he serves on boards all over the place. He'd be perfect for it. I could ask him right now." He reached for his phone.

"Wait! No, no – I'm sure he's too busy for something like this," Dori said. "It's not paid or anything." She wished she hadn't brought it up.

Robert shrugged and put his phone away. "I think he'd be very keen. I don't think you realize how much he revered your father's work."

She looked up as the server delivered their sandwiches. Hers was so large she couldn't see how she was expected to get her mouth around it. "It's true, I don't get it. Why would anyone revere it that much, that they'd be willing to travel to Jasper and sit through regular meetings about a house and some papers? Especially someone as busy and successful as your father?"

Robert looked puzzled. "Don't you see any value in your father's legacy?"

"His legacy?" She swallowed hard. "I wake up every day in that ridiculous house and remember I'll never see the rest of my family again. *That's* my father's legacy. My father..." She took a breath. "My father was a self-centered, alcoholic asshole!"

She took another breath, trying to keep a helpless rush of angry, embarrassed tears at bay, but failed. Crying into her napkin, she was aware Robert was patting her ineffectually on her shoulder. She hid her face until her tears subsided into little hiccups. "Sorry," she sniffed.

"You okay?"

She nodded, her face still tucked into the napkin. She sniffed again, then tried to blow her nose on the napkin without making loud honking noises. Her face was probably all blotchy and mascara-ridden. "Don't you hate it when people start bawling on you?" Ruth had done it to her often enough.

"Oh, don't worry. I've seen my fair share of tears. Once I accidentally beat the police to a family who'd lost their son."

"I'll just..." She pointed towards the bathroom and took off so she could wash her face.

"Have I made you late yet?" she asked, when she got back to the table. She'd seen him check his phone.

"Not quite yet," he said. "Are you going to eat any of that?"

She looked down at her untouched food. "I'll take it with me."

He signaled to the waitress. "I hope you'll be okay. I'd suggest you hang out at the camp until I'm done, but I really don't have time to drive you up there. But if you'd like to drive yourself up —"

"Thanks, but I'll be fine. I'm sorry I dumped all that on you."

"What else are friends for?"

She smiled gratefully at him. That was exactly what she

needed: a friend. "Thank you."

"But I will call Dad about that trust thing if you don't mind," Robert said, as he drove her back. "If nothing else I'm sure he can give you some good advice."

Dori acquiesced with a touch of queasiness. But there were two openings, after all. Perhaps she and Robert Putney could form a voting bloc. With just one other trustee voting with them, they could overpower Marjorie on anything, even lawn care and window air conditioners.

Robert dropped her off without ceremony – he was definitely running late by the time they'd reached her door – and zoomed off. Dori hadn't even managed to unlock the kitchen door when she heard another vehicle pull up.

Surprised, she turned and saw Joe Gagnon's truck coming up the driveway. Reminded of her dream, she blushed.

He got out of it and walked over. "Your boyfriend nearly hit me on his way out."

"He's not my boyfriend, he's my friend."

Joe rolled his eyes. "Yeah, I'm sure that's all he has in mind."

"Why are you here?"

"I just got a call from Marjorie Haight."

"Complaining about the lawn?" Dori could imagine her doing it just for form's sake.

"No. She wanted to know if I'd be interested in becoming a trustee."

"What?"

"I thought it was strange. I mean, I do the lawn. I did it *once*."

"I know what this is! She hasn't had any luck getting one of her cronies in town to say yes. Now she's afraid I might become a trustee myself, so she's looking for an ally. Someone else who doesn't particularly like me."

He grimaced. "I thought perhaps she was hoping to get the lawn mowed for free."

Oh. "Yeah, I suppose that could be it, too. Why are you telling me this?"

"Because I thought you'd want to know."

"You're right. I do. Thanks." She gave him a smile.

"Are you going to be upset if I accept?"

What? "Why would you even consider it?"

He shifted uncomfortably. "Seems like maybe you could use someone in there who would look after your interests."

From sneering at her for being a spoiled rich kid just days earlier, he seemed to have become awfully damned solicitous about her economic well-being. Was he feeling guilty, or was it just some weird escalation of what he'd started by calling her boss?

"I want to be a trustee myself. I think I'd be the best judge of my own interest."

"She said there are two positions open."

He was actually willing to serve with her? "It's possible Robert Putney will be interested in the other opening."

"You'd offer a position of trust to Robert the Dick?"

"Not him. His father."

"You know his father?"

"Not personally, but he was close to my dad. At the memorial service he offered to help."

"And did he?"

No, she'd never heard from him again. "I never asked him to."

"Then for all you know he's a total dick."

True, but at least Robert Putney had been *at* the memorial service. "He has money and contacts and experience, he respects my father's work, and he was my father's friend. You couldn't stand my father, you think his books suck, you haven't talked to me for eight years, and you did something really nasty to me just a couple of days ago. So any choice between the two of you seems pretty obvious to me." She turned back to jiggling the key in the lock, but it refused to turn. She was using the wrong one. `She put the doggy bag down on the ground and cycled through her keys again, looking for the right one.

Joe hadn't left. "You want some help with that?"

"No! I don't want any help from you!" She banged her forehead against the door. The day was beginning to feel like one long nightmare.

"Fine," he muttered. "But just for the record, the last time we discussed this you thought your father's books sucked, too."

She stayed leaning against the door until she heard him get back into his creaking truck, slam the door, and take off.

After a few deep, calming breaths, she found the right key and got the door open. A wave of pent-up heat greeted her. Fuck. She'd be better off sleeping in the driveway.

Chapter 12

Robert called her the next evening. "How are you?" he asked. "I didn't want to call last night. I got out pretty late and figured you might be sleeping."

"I'm fine," Dori said, though she'd tossed and turned long into the night. "Thanks for asking."

"Would you like to come up to the camp tonight? We could take out a canoe."

"To be honest, I'm dead tired. I don't think I'd be good company. Some other time?"

"What if I promise not to jump your bones?"

She chuckled. "But then I wouldn't recognize you."

"Ha ha. There was another reason I called, actually. Dad says he can help."

Dori didn't say anything. She hadn't exactly requested his dad's help, unless bursting into tears could be interpreted that way. Probably it could.

He added, "He'd like to come up this weekend. Would you be available Saturday afternoon or evening? He suggested a barbecue or something up at the camp, a chance to get acquainted."

"All right," Dori said. It would give her a chance to assess what kind of guy Robert's father was. "I get off work at two, so I guess I could be there by three or so. Is that okay?"

"Yeah, that's fine." He hesitated a moment. "Don't you get any days off?"

"If I ask for them. Generally I prefer to get paid."

"Oh. Well, no wonder you're tired."

Yeah. It was kind of nice someone had noticed.

She remembered the way to the camp, though she had some misgivings when the private road in seemed to go on forever. To her surprise, the large gravel circle in front of the house was jammed with vehicles, and she could hear what sounded like live jazz coming from the back. Apparently this wasn't the intimate gathering she had assumed it would be. She was glad she'd taken a little effort to make herself look presentable, in a pair of cropped pants and one of her nicer blouses. She'd also brought along a pie from the bakery, and tucked a bathing suit in her bag.

At the door a chic young woman in a white blouse and black pants smiled and said, "Are you Eudora? They're waiting for you out back."

"Yes, I'm Dori." She held out her hand. "And you are?"

The woman shook it with an amused smile. "Samantha Rowe," she said. "I'm one of the caterers."

"Oh." Dori blushed; she'd assumed she was one of Robert's relations. "I brought a pie," she said, and held it out.

Samantha accepted it with a slightly strained smile. "How sweet of you. I don't think we'll need it today, but I'll put it aside for the family to enjoy later."

"Thanks," Dori said, wishing she'd saved her money. "Are you from around here?"

"We're out of Connecticut, actually. Fairfield County."

"That's a hike."

"I suppose." The woman gave her another small, condescending smile, and Dori realized she'd managed to label herself a hick in just about every way possible. She headed for the French doors onto the back deck. If she was doing this badly with the caterer, she hated to think how she was going to do with Robert's dad. On the other hand, she'd had no reason to expect this big of an affair. Why hadn't Robert warned her? Or was this what "getting acquainted" entailed when one of the people was a media baron?

The deck and adjoining beach were busy with tables and three musicians playing soft jazz. Her eyes narrowed as she recognized Karl Schreiner, with a female companion; Charlie Perrault, her father's lawyer and another trustee; and Marjorie Haight, who was talking to Joe Gagnon. So he'd somehow managed to get all three of the remaining trustees there and all the potential candidates.

Then there was Robert, leaning in to flirt with another young woman in black pants and a white shirt. Off to the side stood the man who must be Robert's father, because he looked so much like him, except that his brown curls were touched by grey and he had the beginnings of a middle-aged gut. A tall, distinguished-looking black man in wire-rim glasses stood next to him, chatting.

She took a deep breath and stepped out onto the deck.

"Dori," Robert said, going straight up to her. "I'm so glad you could make it. Dad's very eager to meet you."

"I didn't realize this was going to be such a big event," she said.

"I didn't either. Sorry. When Dad gets excited about something he can get a little carried away. I guess he decided to get the whole group together at once, while he had the time."

"How did he even know who to invite?"

Robert didn't answer, just escorted her to his father, who took her hand in both of his. "Eudora! You look so much better than the last time I saw you. But then that was a horribly sad occasion, wasn't it? Just terrible." He turned to the black man standing next to him, "This is Arthur Churchill Davis, Professor of English at Brooke College. Are you familiar with his work? He's considered quite the Bardwell scholar."

"I'm afraid not," Dori said, smiling stiffly and shaking the man's hand. "Call me Dori, please."

"And you may call me Arthur," he said, and smiled down at her.

Putney laughed. "Call me Robin. It's a useful way to distinguish between me and my son, especially now that we're in the same profession."

Dori thought Robert's answering smile was a little faint. He looked at his father as if awaiting dismissal, which apparently he received because he withdrew after nodding briefly at her. She watched him head for a nearby table and pick up a beer and wished she could go with him and pretend it was simply a summer party.

"I wasn't expecting to see all the trustees here," she said.

Putney smiled warmly. "I got so fired up I just couldn't wait to meet them. Your father's reputation has been sadly neglected in recent years. Hopefully we can do something about that."

"It happens to far too many deserving writers," Davis said. "Literary fashion is fickle. Look at your own namesake. I trust you've read her work?"

Dori smiled. "A fair amount of it. She's a bit Southern for my taste."

Davis looked intrigued. "Meaning?"

"Oh, you know," she said. "The claustrophobic little towns. The way somebody's always coming along and stealing some-body's man or artificial leg or whatever." Since she was talking to a black man, she decided not to mention the inevitable tortured race relations. "Reading that stuff always makes me want to take a nice long shower afterwards."

Both men laughed. "Robert did warn me you weren't lacking in opinions," Putney said.

"I diagnose too much Flannery O'Connor at one sitting," Davis said.

"Could be," Dori agreed. "It was bedtime reading for us. But the other thing is, I was born and raised here, where life just doesn't seem so – I don't know – gothic."

"A hometown girl?" Putney couldn't entirely hide his con-tempt for that idea.

"Yes, though I was nearing the end of my freshman year at NYU when my parents died."

"Well, there you go!" Putney said. "It's high time you got out into the world again, don't you think?"

"I would like to go back to school, actually."

"Yes, you definitely should," Putney said. "Hopefully we can help make that happen."

Davis smiled. "You should consider Brooke. Much smaller than NYU, of course. Will you study literature?"

"Maybe," Dori said, uncomfortable. It was embarrassing to ad-mit, at twenty-six, she still hadn't decided exactly what she wanted to study. She knew English would be easy for her, but nursing struck her as more practical.

"Or writing, perhaps?" Putney asked.

"No, not writing," she said. "If you'll forgive me, I'd like to get something to drink."

"Yes, of course," Putney said. "We'll talk later."

Dori resisted the powerful urge to grab one of the cold beers and asked the bartender for a seltzer instead. Then she moved to the first food table, which was laid out with an elaborate platter of sushi, something she hadn't really seen close up before except in little plastic trays at the grocery store. She stared at it in slightly repelled fascination, wondering if the Connecticut caterers had arranged it into the florid shape of a dragon themselves, or just bought it that way.

Joe came up. "Pretty wild spread, huh?"

"What are you doing here?"

"Marjorie said Robert Putney wanted to meet me."

Dori felt her face get hot. "You already know how I feel about that."

"Yep." He plopped a piece of sushi into his mouth and chewed it. "But I figured it might be about the lawn. Also, I never miss a chance to network with potential clients. This is good. Try some."

"Isn't it raw fish?"

"Not your thing? Then try the *unagi*, it's cooked. Or here, California roll. That's cooked, too."

Dori thought the *unagi*, whatever that was, looked a little more appetizing and nibbled a bit. It was good, so she ate the rest of it. Next she tried the California roll. She didn't particularly savor the mix of textures but she was pleased she'd managed to diminish her level of provincialism by at least a tiny degree. "Not bad," she said. "Thanks."

"You can get some decent sushi in Greenfield, you know."

Why was he telling her that? "Where's Lisa today?"

"She was busy." He stuffed another piece in his mouth.

"Sure you weren't just scared she'd take all her clothes off again?"

"You know," he said abruptly. "I'm tired of being enemies. I'd like to be friends, if that's at all possible."

He had a slightly mulish expression on his face as if he expected her to rebuff him. "I never asked to be your enemy," she said, surprised to hear her own voice so hoarse with resentment. Why was he extending the olive branch now?

"I realize that. In hindsight, you know, I think you were right." He looked across the lake. "I'm glad I got to go away and see some of the world before I settled down, and I'm glad I got to date different women. If we had actually married that young, we probably would have split up by now."

For someone who claimed he wanted to be a friend, he sure knew how to depress the hell out of her. She said, "I'm going to go say hi to the others."

"Isn't this a lovely party?" Marjorie Haight said, her face flushed with excitement, or perhaps drink. "I hadn't realized your father was such close friends with Robert Putney. Tom would have been happy to step aside earlier, you know. He was just hanging in because we didn't have anyone else to take his place."

"I would have been happy to step in," Dori said.

"But it's so much better if we can get someone who has a good strong track record in the financial world. And we certainly couldn't do any better than Robert Putney. I'm impressed that you were able to get him."

"Actually, he just sort of showed up," Dori said.

"What do you mean?" Marjorie said, looking confused.

"It doesn't matter," Dori said. It seemed clear only a steamroller could stop Robert Putney from becoming a trustee now. "I just want to be sure that other opening goes to me."

Marjorie looked sour. "I'm certain we'll discuss it fully at the next meeting."

"Which is when? I'd like to be there."

"Well, that's going to follow this little party, actually, but I'm pretty sure – we can confirm this with Charles if you'd like – that any election of new trustees would have to be in executive session. Behind closed doors. So we could all feel free to discuss it."

"Yes, let's confirm that with Charlie," Dori said. "He's here, isn't he?"

Charlie Perrault was a plump, balding man who had dressed like a lawyer even for this event, although he had removed his jacket and rolled up the sleeves of his dress shirt. "Eudora! It's been too long. How are you, my dear?"

Marjorie quickly explained what Dori wanted and how they couldn't allow that, now, could they?

"You want to be a trustee?" he asked Dori.

"Very much."

"Excellent," he said. "Marjorie is correct that the vote needs to be taken in executive session, but I don't see why you wouldn't be selected."

Marjorie frowned at him. "While it's wonderful to see Eudora so interested, Charles, we do have another candidate for the position whose business background is much more extensive, and who isn't planning to go off to college."

Charlie smiled at Dori. "Are you going off to college? That's great! Where?"

"Nowhere yet," she said. "I need to know how much tuition money I have available."

"Oh," he said, and that *oh* didn't sound good. "Well, to tell you the truth, I would have preferred to have a member of the family involved in this trust from the beginning. I think it would be particularly helpful now, given some of the challenges we face."

"Challenges?" Dori said.

"Financial challenges," he said. "Quite serious ones."

She stared at him. Just how serious was he talking?

"This is hardly the time or place to discuss it," Marjorie said. "Really, Charles."

"It could be very good timing, though," Charlie said. "If Eudora wants to go to college, dissolving the trust could give her the funds she'd need to do it. At least we could send her off with something."

Marjorie glared at him. "I hardly think we need to talk about dissolving the trust, especially with Robert Putney joining our group."

"He does seem to think it can all be fixed," Charlie said. "And perhaps it can if he's willing to pitch some money in. I guess we'll find out." He reached out and patted Eudora's shoulder. "I wouldn't worry. You're a very capable young lady. I'm more concerned about your brother." He nodded towards the lake, and Dori followed his gaze to a canoe with two people in it.

"Is that Salinger?" she said, shocked.

"And his friend," he said. "Jenna, isn't it?"

"What's he doing here?"

Marjorie smiled stiffly. "Mr. Putney asked for him, so I tracked him down. I take it he's not really living in the house anymore?"

"He claims to have moved in with Jenna," Dori said. "I have no idea how permanent that will be. Mr. Putney doesn't waste any time, does he?"

"The smart money never does," Charlie said. Dori thought he sounded a bit grim.

Chapter 13

Dori decided she really needed that beer, but she poured half of it into the large lined trash can behind the table so she couldn't accidentally overdo it.

"Is that the half-beer diet or something?" Robert asked, coming up behind her.

"Are you suggesting I need to lose weight?"

"God, no, woman," Robert said. "Why am I always getting into trouble with you?"

"Maybe it's the way you invite me to a casual get-acquainted barbecue and it turns out to be a catered event complete with all the trustees."

His face turned red. "I swear, I didn't find out how extensive this was going to be myself until this morning."

"I have an answering machine."

"If I gave you a heads up you might not have come. I didn't know he'd swoop in quite like this. But it'll be a good thing in the end, you'll see. He's done amazing things for Brooke College."

Dori shook her head, unconvinced, and turned to survey the rest of the party. Putney was talking to Karl Schreiner and a woman she assumed was Karl's wife.

Karl was a mortician. Dori had no idea why her father had chosen him as a trustee, unless it was the aura of dour solidity he exuded. He had always scared her with his dismal expression and dark clothing, and the natural association between him and death didn't help, either. Marjorie had taken the lead in arranging the details of the family's burial and memorial service, which Dori had appreciated at the time, not least because it meant less interaction with Karl.

But now it appeared she had Charlie's vote, but not Marjorie's. Tom and Bernie were already gone. So Karl would cast the deciding vote.

"What's the matter?" Robert said. "You've gone a bit pale."

"I have to talk to the angel of death," Dori said.

"Mr. Schreiner," she said. "How nice to see you again."

"Eudora," he said gravely. "You remember my wife, Thalassa?"

Dori smiled. "Hi." She did not, in fact, remember Thalassa, who looked artistic in her long silver hair and dangly earrings and smiled serenely at Dori. Karl was not wearing his usual dark suit, but somehow managed to look somber even in a patterned polo shirt.

Putney said, "I've just been telling Karl here about your college hopes, Dori."

She smiled stiffly. "Mr. Schreiner, do you think I could speak to you privately for a moment?"

"Of course," he murmured. His loafers were eerily silent as he padded alongside her clomping sandals to a corner of the deck.

She stopped and took a deep breath. "I'm not sure whether you're aware I'd like to be elected to one of the open trustee positions?"

He looked pained. "I see we've suddenly gone from not having enough candidates to having to turn someone down."

"I think it would be ideal to have a member of the family involved, don't you?"

"I would hope you would always want to be involved."

Was that a reproof? "I asked to attend the meetings years ago. Marjorie told me my presence would constitute a conflict of interest. Now she says that was apparently a mistake."

Karl's pale blue eyes rested on her. "Marjorie has put a tremendous amount of time and effort into this trust, and taken no recompense for any of it. Are you suggesting she – or we – have failed to represent your interests?"

"No, of course not," Dori said, flushing. "I just think it would make sense for me to have a voice in future decisions, now I'm older. Especially if it's true we're facing serious financial issues going forward."

Karl turned to look across the beach to where Charlie was talking to Joe and Robert. "Do you have any specific financial training or background I should know about?"

She hadn't expected him to actually vet her qualifications. She licked her lips nervously. "Not per se. But for the last seven years I've raised my brother and paid the bills on a very tight budget. And I'm obviously familiar with the house and my family history."

"I see." He didn't sound impressed.

Annoyed, she straightened up. "Are you saying you consider Joe Gagnon more qualified for this position than I am?"

"Well, he does have a college degree and some business experience. And he's demonstrated extensive community involvement through his activities in the Chamber of Commerce, the Kiwanis, the fire department, and the Congregational Church."

She blinked. Was Joe planning to run for local office or something? How did he find the time? But then again, it was all networking, wasn't it? Would he actually want to push her out of her position just to gain more business contacts?

Karl smiled tightly at her. "I'd heard you were going back to college. Don't you think that ought to be your priority right now?"

She bristled. "I can handle both. Mr. Putney is a very busy man who doesn't even live in-state but you all seem quite keen to have him."

"My dear, Mr. Putney has resources at his disposal that you do not." Karl cleared his throat. "Perhaps you should ask yourself what it will take to establish your own life, rather than trying to wring a tenuous existence from what remains of your father's."

She felt her face flush. "I just think you should know something before you vote. Joe Gagnon has never forgiven me for not marrying him eight years ago, and he's no fan of my father's work. If he wants to be a trustee, it may be for all the wrong reasons."

Karl's brow furrowed. "I see. Thank you for letting me know." He nodded briefly at her and turned away.

Damn it. She hadn't really wanted to bring up any of that stuff. And having done it, she felt a little ashamed of it.

She walked down to the end of the dock, hoping to get a little time to compose herself, but as she got there she spied her brother and

Jenna approaching in the canoe. Jenna was paddling competently in the stern. Salinger's work in the bow was decidedly more erratic, and when he saw his sister he laid his oar down across the gunwale and waved at her.

"Hey guys," Dori said.

Jenna j-stroked closer to the dock. 'Isn't this place great?" she asked Dori. "Want to take a turn around the lake?"

"Not right now, thanks," Dori said. She turned to Salinger. "Has he talked to you about anything important?"

Salinger looked taken aback. "Like what?"

She looked back towards the house. The band was playing, so their conversation wouldn't be overheard. "I don't know. Financial stuff?"

"Nah, he mostly talked about Dad. He said they'd been working together on the next book when Dad died."

"What?"

"Yeah, it surprised me too. He said he'd been doing a lot of the research, and they'd actually collaborated on the plot."

Her dad hadn't said anything about that when he'd talked about how well his last book was going. But then, her father wasn't necessarily going to credit anyone else involved in his writing – her mother had been lucky to get any mention at all, and she had carefully edited everything he'd ever written. And Dori had been away at school, so what did she know? "That doesn't sound much like Dad. Do you remember any of it actually happening?"

Salinger shrugged. "I never paid much attention. But I don't remember ever seeing this dude at our house – do you?"

"Only at the wake."

Jenna said, "Sal, let's put this thing away and get something to eat. I'm starving!"

"Yeah, me too. Catch you later!" Salinger said.

Dori caught a whiff of cannabis as they glided past. Well of course they were hungry.

She sat at the end of the dock, gazing across the water and brooding. The lake, gently rippling in a light breeze, reflected a cloudless blue sky. It was almost as if Robert Putney had been able to order in good weather and low humidity along with the food and the music.

Karl Schreiner was right, of course. It was time she started her own life. Salinger didn't need her. Continuing to be there wouldn't help him grow up; it might even get in the way. She already made enough money she could probably rent a room in Greenfield, maybe even manage some night classes at GCC or UMass. Maybe she could even go full-time if she qualified for financial aid because she didn't have the trust hanging around her neck anymore.

And then the trustees could have the fun of paying the utilities on the house all by themselves.

It wasn't really like they were stealing her inheritance. Her father had handed it over to them with instructions to spend it mostly on him.

The dock shook as someone with a heavy tread approached. She turned to look and resisted a momentary impulse to jump off the dock and swim for it. Instead she scrambled to her feet.

Joe's face was locked in an angry scowl. "Karl Schreiner just asked me if it's true I've never forgiven you for not marrying me!"

"I had to explain to him why you are not a suitable candidate."

"Pretty tacky way to do it, don't you think?"

She felt a twinge of conscience – but just a twinge. "It's the truth."

"I'm still the better candidate."

"What kind of twisted logic explains that?"

"You're way out of your league with these people. Especially this Putney guy." He stabbed a finger in her face. "You're a fool if you think he's looking after your interest."

"But you will?"

"Hell of a lot better than you can."

She couldn't believe his nerve. "What is it with you? Is it some kind of weird control thing? I told you I didn't want you to take it. What do I have to do, get a restraining order?"

His face turned red. "You are really bad at picking your friends, you know that? Do you think Putney is putting on this big show because he wants to help you?"

"No, but it's none of your business. It's *my* business. And I don't want you in my business. If they offer you that trusteeship, you'd better turn it down, or ...." She stopped, casting about for something to threaten him with.

"What?" It was a growl.

But she had zero leverage. She couldn't even fire him from mowing the lawn. "Or you're no friend of mine!" she said, because it was the only thing she could think of, and stalked past him.

Still furious, she just wanted to go home, but Putney and Robert intercepted her before she could get to the house.

"Dori! Dad was hoping to have a chat with you," Robert said.

"It's been challenging getting a moment alone for that," Putney said, clamping a hand down on her shoulder.

She stiffened. She was far too angry to discuss anything. "I need to use the bathroom."

"I'll come inside and wait for you," Putney said.

She glared at Robert, who at least looked a little embarrassed, and headed down the hallway he'd pointed out that first night, bypassing the half bath next to the kitchen, where the caterers were busy washing things up. There turned out to be a much more luxurious spa-style bathroom at the end of the hall. Judging from the ample supply of men's toiletries it was Robert's, but it was much cleaner and better-smelling than the one her brother had claimed for himself at home.

After availing herself of the facilities she opened the medicine cabinet, but found nothing too interesting – bug repellent, deodorant, cologne. She opened the drawers in the vanity, one by one: okay, there were the prescriptions. Effexor. Concerta. Xanax. Valtrex. If those were all Robert's, the man had some issues. Effexor was for depression or obsessive-compulsive disorder. Concerta was for Attention Deficit Disorder – Salinger had been prescribed it, but of course refused to take it because it wasn't as organic as pot, or something. Xanax was for anxiety. She'd needed some herself after that plane crash. And Valtrex was what they gave patients at the home who had herpes outbreaks.

So he wasn't as squeaky clean as he'd claimed.

She felt a twinge of guilt at invading the guy's privacy, but by bringing his father in he'd made himself an enemy combatant.

Hell, it was possible he'd been one all along.

Chapter 14

"You look a little tired," Putney commented, when she walked back out. "Let's walk down to my office," he said, and led her down the other hallway, towards the bathroom Lisa had found so impressive. "My son tells me you work pretty long hours in some pretty labor-intensive jobs."

She just followed him.

"Hopefully we can do something about that," he added. "I would hope we could improve your life significantly with better management of this trust."

A part of her longed to believe it was that easy, that this wealthy old friend of her father's really had swooped in like a fairy godmother just to make life better. But if that was all he wanted, he could have shown up a heck of a lot earlier. "Mr. Putney, I'm a little curious why my father didn't name you a trustee in the first place."

Putney's face flushed. "I think I know. Over the years I advanced a fair amount of financial support to your father because I believed in his work. I suspect he or your mother may have feared as a trustee I would be tempted to seek repayment, which would have significantly reduced the estate. But I assure you nothing could be further from my mind. I'm here simply because your father was a dear friend and an important writer, and I think it's a crime how little attention his work gets. I've already talked to the other trustees about a coordinated campaign to resurrect his literary reputation. That's why I took the liberty of bringing Dr. Davis with me. We need to get started as soon as possible."

"Then you've already been named a trustee?" Dori asked.

"Oh, I would hope that's a mere formality at this point. As I was explaining to your brother earlier, one of the ways to generate excitement about your father would be to publish something new – something the world hasn't seen yet. And I know Nat was very excited about the work he was doing before he died."

That name again. Like many a white Southern boy and quite a few dogs, her father had been named after Nathan Bedford Forrest, one of the more successful rebel generals – a former slave trader who'd later become the first grand wizard of the Ku Klux Klan. Dori didn't know if her father had dropped Nathan because that wasn't the best association for a white guy writing a novel about slavery, or because he thought Bedford Bardwell sounded more literary. Probably the latter, since he'd kept the Bedford.

"He was excited," she said. "He was sober, for one thing."

Putney grimaced. "Creative people do tend to have their demons, don't they?"

"Are you creative, Mr. Putney?"

"Please, do call me Robin. Alas, not creative in the way your father was, though of course as a journalist I have done a great deal of writing. I'd love to be able to write good fiction, but it seems my strengths are on the other side of the brain: gathering facts, doing research. Perhaps he told you we were collaborating on his last novel?"

"No, never. He did mention you quite often. But he never said anything about any collaboration. If I know Dad, he probably wouldn't have felt any amount of research really amounted to collaboration."

Putney's lips thinned. "As I recall, we had even mapped out a plot together. But no doubt like many other writers he could be quite tight-lipped about his work."

"Not to me, he wasn't."

She detected a flash of open dislike, quickly schooled into pained confusion. "I'm at a loss here, Eudora. Have I done something to offend you?"

Since he was raising the issue himself.... "Well, frankly, I can't say I appreciate the way you've barreled in here to take over my father's trust."

He drew back. "Barreled in? I'm so sorry you see it that way. My son was under the impression you would welcome my help. Apparently we both misunderstood."

"All I did was ask your son what he knew about trusts. I was hoping for his advice."

"But why settle for that, when you can have all your problems solved? And from what I hear, there are some very real problems."

"I was hoping to play a role in solving those problems myself. And thanks to you, it appears I'm going to be cut out of that yet again."

"Cut out? I don't understand."

Didn't he? "There are three people vying for two open positions, and you and the guy who mows my lawn appear to have them both wrapped up. If I hadn't casually asked your son what he knew about trusts, I wouldn't be in this position."

"Oh dear," Putney said. "You're referring to that Gagnon fellow, aren't you? I wonder if there's anything we can do to fix that. I assure you, Dori, I have no intention whatsoever of keeping you out of the process. You and your brother are both uppermost in my mind as we move forward. I will be very happy to involve you both just as much as you'd like."

Was it possible she'd misread him? "I'm going to hold you to that."

He smiled. "I wouldn't have it any other way. But first, the trust needs an infusion of capital. You must have some idea where that last manuscript can be found?"

"I'm afraid not."

His eyes narrowed. "You told my son it was in the attic."

She flushed. "Yes, but only because that's where almost everything is. It's total chaos up there."

"Then I can see there's another problem we'll have to address."

When they got back to the great room, the band members were sitting at the kitchen island eating sandwiches and the two caterers were leaning against the other counter, looking bored. "Will you need us any more today?" Samantha Rowe asked Putney. "I've left out a tray of cookies with some coffee and tea. The place is pretty much cleaned up. Your son asked us to leave the leftovers, so they're in the refrigerator."

"Once these guys are done I think you're all set," Putney said.

"Settle up with my assistant on Monday. I'll tell her you did the usual excellent job." He dug into his pocket and pulled out some bills, which he gave her. "Thank you for traveling so far."

Rowe smiled and thanked him. Dori wondered just who was paying the day's expenses. Putney's company? Putney himself?

"I'm going to head home," she told Putney, and stuck out her hand. "Thank you."

"Do at least say goodbye to my son before you go. Robert!" he yelled.

Dori followed him outside. Robert was deep in conversation with Jenna. Salinger was eating a giant cookie and watching the couple with a slightly perplexed look on his face.

"Dori says she wants to go home," Putney told Robert tersely, and walked away to join Davis, who was talking to Joe. What could they be discussing? Turf grasses in American literature?

"Leaving so soon?" Robert said.

"Yes, I've had enough."

She saw Jenna ease back towards Salinger, who handed her a stack of cookies wrapped in a napkin to stash in her giant cotton handbag. Dori wouldn't have minded loading up herself if she could be sure no one would see her. Instead she grabbed a single cookie and took a bite. She hadn't actually gotten around to eating much of anything and she was hungry.

"You still seem kind of upset," Robert said in a low voice.

"I just wish I'd never mentioned the trust to you."

He gave her an apologetic grimace. "I know Dad's a very charge-ahead kind of guy. But he really can help."

Perhaps Robert believed that. Perhaps his dad believed it too. Maybe – just maybe – it was even true. She stared across the deck, to where Putney had joined Joe and Davis. Putney clapped a hand on Joe's back, producing a flash of irritation on Joe's face.

Perhaps she was transferring her anger from where it really belonged. Because Joe Gagnon was the one who was trying to usurp her as a trustee in full knowledge she didn't want him to.

At home she drank a cup of coffee and changed into old clothes. Then she headed up into the attic with a flashlight.

The sun had been low in the sky, but it was still stiflingly hot up there. The large attic space was dimly lit by two old hanging incandescent bulbs that threw a weak yellow light, and harder to stand up in than she'd remembered. It smelled like wood and dust and old books, with a trace of mustiness under it that seemed like something new. She walked the full length, just in case she'd recognize the box she needed immediately, but of course it could not be that easy. Sweat trickled down her face and front as she doubled back and began counting boxes, bending down to open a few here and there. Some were labeled in compulsive detail in shaky script that probably belonged to one of the Friends; others gave no clue to their contents.

Near the tiny window under the roof gable on the other end she discovered a leak darkening the roof. Damn. The box underneath it was stained black with water and mold and she sneezed as she opened it up. She was relieved to find just a bunch of old, mildewed snow suits. She pried the disintegrating box up as far up off the floor as she could, but she couldn't see any stains beneath it. The leak couldn't be too bad yet, then, especially considering how much rain they'd had earlier in the week. Could it have been an ice dam? But that would have dried by now, wouldn't it? She propped the remains of the box back in place so it could continue absorbing any drips. She supposed she'd better get a big old soup pot up here, and maybe a tarp.

Of course, that would be evidence that she'd known about the leak and hadn't told anybody.

So far this little expedition wasn't going at all well. A new roof on this old house might well trump college tuition.

She carefully picked her way back down the cobwebbed attic stairs into the small half-bedroom at the end of the hall, the one that had always held a crib until Harper had graduated to a twin bed crammed in next to her tiny dresser. The Friends had boxed away her collection of ragged Barbie dolls, replaced her beloved Barbie comforter with an antique quilt, and edited the stuffed animals down to the most picturesque. They'd also framed a couple of Harper's better school drawings along with her last school photograph and arranged them on the wall with an explanatory plaque calculated to produce a pang for the poor little girl who'd died so young. Dori tried hard not to notice; her own reaction to this display was always something closer to rage.

Downstairs and in the master bedroom down the hall, the phone rang.

She ignored it and walked into all the rooms on the second floor in turn, checking for water stains on the ceiling. With the exception of Salinger's tiny, still jam-packed room, there was dust on every surface and trailing wisps of spider webs festooned the ceilings. Dori hadn't been in some of these rooms since the Christmas open house. It was a little shocking to remember how large it was. Really, it was ridiculous only one person lived in it.

She didn't see any water stains on any of the ceilings, not even in the closets. Perhaps she could keep the leak to herself for a bit.

She went downstairs, trying to shake the feeling her mother was watching her and shaking her head in disappointment. Her mother had loved this house.

Sorry, Mama, she thought. I'll get to it eventually. Probably.

There was a message waiting.

Marjorie's voice was all honey. "Eudora, dear, I assumed you'd want to know the result of tonight's meeting. I hope you understand it's no reflection at all on you, but given the challenges we face we decided Robert Putney and Joe Gagnon were the best candidates, and I am very pleased to say that both accepted. Please do call me back, dear, so I can tell you more about it."

Chapter 15

Energized by fury, Dori went to the large drawer in the butler's pantry to pull out every flashlight. The one she'd used to get up in the attic had dimmed to nothing quickly. None of those left had a strong beam; she'd need some new batteries. Maybe she should get one of those LED flashlights; Janet at work had told her they were amazing. After her shift she would stop at Home Depot and get that, some contractor bags, maybe even a work light.

Guessing the total on that purchase made her hesitate, though. And what really mattered was the manuscript, and maybe any notes about it her father had left. It could take her months to clean out the whole attic. Putney wouldn't move that slowly.

She tried to think back, to just after the crash. She'd put together her father's pages and notes a week or so after the funeral – she had even skimmed through the later pages just in case they'd said anything about crashing a plane into the sea with a family aboard. Then she'd stashed them in her own bedroom, meaning to sort through them when she could. Had Robert Putney said anything to her about it back then, at the wake? All she remembered was thinking his offer to help seemed easy, glib, compared to the awkwardness she was getting from virtually everyone other than the clergymen and Karl Schreiner.

That had been such a long, painful day, retained in her memory as a series of vivid snapshots: the caskets all lined up in a row; Salinger's white face; Ruth crying; Joe's mother offering a strained condolence; Marjorie insisting Dori's mother would have wanted them to use the good china; the long kitchen table loaded with food brought by mourners.

Eventually her dad's agent had called and asked how many pages she'd found. He had been disappointed with her answer. If all she had found was seven or eight chapters, there wasn't really enough of anything to sell, even with all the current renewed interest. Unless, perhaps, there was an outline? Something they could hire a ghost writer to finish?

"Dad would hate that," she'd said.

"Yes, of course," the agent had replied, and never mentioned it again.

She should call him up and ask him if her dad had mentioned collaborating with Robert Putney. But all these media people knew each other, didn't they? What if the agent was eager to get Putney involved?

After the first anniversary of the crash, she'd tried actually reading her father's manuscript from the beginning, but hadn't gotten far. It was a family saga, and every time the narrator – a man who appeared to have a lot in common with her father – reflected on his all-consuming love for his wife or his children, she had wanted to throw the pages across the room. Ultimately she'd stuck it all in a box with some other items of her father's and put it in the attic. And this was after the Friends had already come through and done their set dressing, so the attic was already crammed.

So where the hell had she put that box?

She hadn't liked going into the attic back then any more than she did now. So she probably would have stowed it as close to the attic steps as possible, right?

Someone rapped on the kitchen door.

She opened it and there was Joe Gagnon, with a cardboard box of his own.

She glared at him.

He held out the box. "This is a copy of everything. The next meeting is tomorrow afternoon, two o'clock, up at the camp, before Putney goes back to New York. Marjorie is supposed to let you know."

She considered giving him the silent treatment, but that didn't seem very practical. "She just left a message and didn't say a thing about it."

"Well, now you know."

"I work until two. I'd be late."

"So come late."

"They asked you to deliver this to me?"

"No. The trustees don't know you have this. I haven't actually read most of it myself, yet. Too busy printing all this crap out. Salinger told me you don't have a working computer anymore. Is that true? Not even a smart phone?"

There were stacks of paper. "Joe, there's no way I can read all this by tomorrow."

"Then just skim it. The stuff on top is what Putney gave us right after the meeting. His strategic plan."

"He had a strategic plan ready to go before he even got selected?"

"This guy probably has a strategic plan for going to the bathroom. Are you going to try to make it?"

She sighed. "I'll come if I can."

"If you don't, I'll be happy to fill you in."

She stared coldly at him. If he thought this would make up for what he'd done to her, he was nuts.

He rolled his eyes at her. "Whatever," he said, and left.

She called the grocery store. "Do you think I could get off work at one instead of two tomorrow?"

The night manager sighed. "You do realize Sunday is the busiest day of the week?"

"I know, I'm sorry, but I've had some family business come up at the last minute."

"You've only been here a month. You want to risk your job over one hour?"

Was he threatening to fire her? Small as it was, that additional check made a big difference. "No, I guess not."

She took a shower and went to bed with the box of papers. Putney's strategic plan included a media campaign to promote the upcoming Bedford Bardwell Days, tie it into the thirtieth anniversary of the publication of "Tea and Slavery," and announce the sale of Bedford Bardwell's papers to the Putney Lewis Library at Brooke College.

He'd made a deal to sell her father's papers? Dori had been getting phone calls from archives around the country for the last

seven years -- though not so many lately – and had always re-
ferred them to the trustees. Besides, didn't this contradict explicit
instructions in her father's will?

Once past the strategic plan, the paperwork got more tedious.
There were lots of repetitive financial reports that didn't mean
much to her, and minutes of past meetings – also repetitive, as if
whoever took notes followed a template that seldom varied. A
recent audit was more interesting. The summary report included
notes such as "Cash management procedures need updating to
conform to generally accepted accounting practices for nonprofit
operations;" "Income has consistently fallen short of projec-
tions;" and "There is significant potential for tax liability due to
unclear separation between the trust's nonprofit operations and
occasional disbursements to two private beneficiaries." That
would be her and Salinger. Also ominous was the final note, "The
current reserve fund is insufficient to guarantee continued operations beyond six weeks in the case of an emergency; ideally, such
a fund maintains at least a three-month reserve."

Obviously this was not a situation that would be helped by a
leaking roof.

The front end manager on Sunday wasn't the same person she'd
spoken to on the phone. Dori worked all morning with grim effi-
ciency. She scowled when offered a break at 1:30.

"Something the matter?" her manager asked.

"I'm off at two anyway."

"Go ahead now, then, if you want. We're not that busy."

Dori wished she hadn't asked the night before and painted
herself as difficult. Now she could actually make it to the meeting
on time if she didn't go home first, change her clothes, or eat.

Robert was the one who opened the door after she rang the bell.
"Dori!"

"I just got off work," she said breathlessly. "Where are they?"

"They're out on the deck. They haven't even started their
meeting yet. You want something to drink?"

"Do you have some iced tea or something?"

"Yep," he said, and pulled a bottle out for her. "Unless you'd prefer another half beer?"

She smiled. "Better not. Thanks." She walked out back. Six heads turned in her direction: the five trustees and Arthur Churchill Davis. Joe smiled. Marjorie looked confused.

Putney betrayed no consternation, if he was feeling any. "Dori, how wonderful that you could join us. Will Salinger be coming, too?"

"Did you ask him?"

Putney turned to Marjorie, who said, "I didn't get a call back from either of them, actually. How did you learn about it, Dori?"

Dori ignored her. "What did I miss?" she asked, and looked pointedly at Davis. "Did you elect a sixth trustee?"

"Of course not," Putney said. "Arthur is here to present the proposal for Brooke College's purchase of your father's papers. Shall we get started? We're all set up inside."

After that slick PowerPoint presentation, complete with music and video pans of beautifully drawn artist's renderings, Dori almost felt that not only her father's papers but also her firstborn child belonged in the Bedford Bardwell Archive at the Putney Lewis Library at Brooke College.

"Impressive as always, Arthur. Does anyone have any questions?" Putney asked.

Marjorie looked confused. "It's all very lovely, but I don't understand why we're even discussing this. The will is quite explicit on this issue."

"Yes, it is," Putney said. "Nat wanted his papers available to scholars in his house. Unfortunately, the house is not capable of supporting a collection in anything approaching appropriate archival storage that could be open to the public, and there's no sign it ever will be. Given that reality, housing his papers in the appropriate academic library setting would seem to honor the spirit if not the letter of his will – and preserve them against loss."

"But we've all been working under the assumption that the house was ultimately meant to house this collection," Marjorie said. "Is that not so?" She appealed to Karl and Charlie.

Karl nodded but looked thoughtful.

Charlie frowned. "It was the original idea."

"Granted," Putney said. "But seven years later you still have no feasible financial backing in place to make that happen. I believe – correct me if I'm wrong, Dori – that your father's papers are currently stuffed in cardboard boxes in the attic?"

Dori said nothing.

"What's more," he added, "the home is still being used primarily as a private residence. That hardly makes it available as a site for an active literary collection. It also raises serious questions about the nonprofit status of The Friends of the Bedford Bardwell House."

Marjorie drew herself up. "The Friends have put enormous time and effort into preserving the home as a historic site of great literary importance. There's plenty of room in the house to establish a research library. All we need is appropriate funding."

"Exactly," Putney said. "Funding. Funding you don't have, and have no prospect of getting, unless you sell these papers."

Charlie coughed gently. "I think many of us were hoping with the recent change in the make-up of the trustees...."

Putney and Davis exchanged knowing glances; perhaps they had already discussed this likely response. "Let's get something straight right away," Putney said. "I'm willing to do a great deal for this trust, especially in the area of media attention, but I'm not here to bail you out. I'm here to refocus and re-energize your efforts. Brooke College has made a generous financial offer for this collection – one that will bring funding for the trust back up to a level that will allow the Bedford Bardwell House to continue to attract visitors for at least another generation."

Charlie cleared his throat. "I can see the value of selling the papers. However, I don't see that this leaves us with any particular reason to continue to fund the Bedford Bardwell House, given that it has not proven to be self-supporting. Why not sell the house, disburse remaining funds to the heirs, and call it a day? Eudora could use that money right now; we all know she's hoping to go back to school. And Salinger ... well, Salinger could probably live off his portion for quite some time."

Marjorie looked shocked. "Are you suggesting we abandon the

Bedford Bardwell House as a community landmark?"

"Yes, that's exactly what I'm suggesting," Charlie said. "Unless we can find new owners who are excited about it, which seems unlikely."

Marjorie said, "That house stands as a testament to the genius of Bedford and Ellen Bardwell and the tragic loss of six lives! Even if the collection goes, that important purpose remains."

Putney said, "I agree with Marjorie. And I believe if we focus on that goal, we can achieve it. The problem is you're trying to serve two purposes at the same time and doing neither well."

Dori knew where this was going. "You want me and my brother out."

Charlie folded his arms. "The will explicitly provides an interest in the house -- as part of the estate – to be divided among the Bardwell's surviving children. And right now the house and papers are the most valuable part of it."

"As I said," Putney repeated, "You're trying to serve two purposes at the same time and doing neither well. I propose that selling this collection now would allow us to settle a reasonable amount on Dori and Salinger, and refocus on what was clearly the primary goal of the trust: preserving the legacy of Bedford Bardwell."

Nobody spoke for a moment.

It was a stroke of genius, Dori thought. Everyone got something: he got his hands on her dad's papers as well as prestige for his library; Marjorie got to keep her precious show house; the trustees achieved financial solvency for their problematic trust; Salinger got some money to stave off adulthood a bit longer; and she – well, at least she got the freedom to go. Even her father got something – another shot at lasting literary fame.

So why did she feel as if Putney had just made an end run around everybody?

"Shall we vote?" Putney said.

Joe, speaking up for the first time, said, "On what?"

Putney's response was slow and clear, as if he thought Joe might be having a little trouble keeping up. "On moving ahead with the proposal to sell the papers to Brooke College."

"How can we vote on that?" Joe said. "You haven't even given us an amount. It's also not clear what exactly is included in the sale."

There was a short silence. Dr. Davis cleared his throat. "It would be in line with the usual value placed on such collections, of course, pending the successful completion of an inventory of the papers. And the sale would simply consist of all manuscripts, notes, and correspondence, since at Mr. Putney's request we did not include the copyrights, though we would certainly love to have them. I would expect the final amount without those to fall somewhere between one and one-point-two million dollars."

That sounded like a fortune to Dori. Judging from the look on Marjorie's face she thought so, too. Charlie seemed less impressed. Karl was impassive.

Joe said, "But how do we know that's the best price we can get?"

Davis and Putney looked at each other and said nothing.

Joe said, "Wouldn't it make more sense to open this up to competitive bidding?"

"It would have five, six, seven years ago," Davis said. "I don't think you'd find a great deal of interest out there right now."

"I had a call from Emory a few weeks ago," Dori said. "And the University of Georgia a little further back."

Davis took a deep breath and folded his hands with a kind of preternatural calm. "A competitive bidding process would require an inventory, which could take weeks, maybe even months. I thought there was something of an issue of immediate financial solvency?"

Dori felt a twinge of nausea. "I'm sorry. Did I miss something earlier?"

Charlie said, "I'm with Joe. Assuming we agree we want to sell the papers, we have the fiduciary responsibility to seek the best price possible. Anything else might leave us open to charges of inside dealing, especially given the obvious pre-existing relationship between one of our trustees and the institution in question. Indeed, Mr. Putney, I believe you should recuse yourself from any vote on this particular matter."

Putney's face turned red.

Davis coughed. "I could use a break," he said. "Anyone else?"

Dori followed the group out, praying there would be some food involved. Most scattered towards the various bathrooms. Davis and Putney headed directly towards the back deck. She headed for the kitchen. Unfortunately there was no sign of snacks being provided.

Joe was behind her. "You okay?"

"I'm fine."

"You look a little washed out."

She was willing to bet Lisa never looked washed out. "I'm hungry."

Joe opened the refrigerator, even though it wasn't his. "Ugh. Day-old sushi. Here's some of that cheese dip. How's that?"

"Fine."

He pulled out the leftover dip, then started opening cabinets, hunting for a box of crackers and soon finding one. "Here," he said, putting it all in front of her.

She was a little alarmed at the way he had just helped himself to someone else's food. She also wished he wasn't being nice to her. But more than anything she wanted something to eat. She dug in hungrily.

"So what do you think about selling the papers?" he said.

She shrugged. "I guess I'm...." She stopped. All his helpfulness could still be part of some elaborate game.

"What?" he said, taking a cracker and spreading it with cheese.

She shook her head. "Nothing. Thank you for getting me something to eat."

Robert came in from out on the deck. "Wow. It's not often I get to see my dad so pissed off. What did you do to him?"

Joe said, "Maybe he's easily pissed off."

Robert grinned. "Oh, he is. When you're the big kahuna, things tend to go your way. It's the kind of thing a person can get used to." He reached for a cracker and dug it into the cheese dip. "What are you doing after the meeting?" he asked Dori.

She glanced at Joe. He looked away, clearly annoyed. "Taking a shower. Why?" she said. "You want to do something?"

"With you? Always. Anything. Including that shower."

She glanced back at Joe's averted face and saw the way his jaw clenched. Back in the day she'd tried to avoid provoking that particular sign of stormy weather. "How about a movie?" she asked Robert.

Joe shot her a disgusted look and stalked back down the hall towards Putney's office. Dori was surprised to once again feel a tiny, uncomfortable thread of shame working its way through her overall sense of victory.

Why? What did she care what Joe thought? If anything, she ought to be pleased at having successfully annoyed him.

Robert tilted his head at her. "Do you really want to go, or did you just say that to bug him?"

"I'm not that Machiavellian," she said, and helped herself to more dip. Actually, though, Machiavellian was exactly what she was being. She looked on any date with Robert as reconnaissance. Bugging Joe was just a bonus.

By the time Putney and Davis came back in, Marjorie and Karl had joined them at the counter and the dip was nearly gone.

"Arthur is going to head home," Putney said. "There's not much point in his staying at this point. He's a busy man with things to do."

"I'll just get my laptop," Davis said, and went down the hall.

"We all have things to do," Karl said. "How much longer is this going to take?"

"Not long," Putney said. "Let's get going."

Dori followed the group back down the hall. Davis gave them short, grim nods as he passed them by with his bag.

Joe and Charlie were already in the room, their postures echoing each other: two sets of folded arms, two sets of crossed legs.

"I think we should table further discussion of the papers until the next meeting," Putney said. "Let's move on to the next agenda item."

"Why table it?" Joe said. "Why not start seeking competitive bids?"

"Arthur said we'd need to do an inventory of the papers first.

That was something he was willing to make part of a letter of intent, but in an actual bidding situation he tells me any organization will require more complete information, including a complete inventory."

Joe said, "Then perhaps we should start on that."

Putney said, "I believe it would take money we don't have right now.

Joe said, "I wouldn't mind working on it myself on a voluntary basis. Assuming Dori wouldn't mind having me in the house. Would you mind, Dori?"

He knew damned well she would. She glared at him.

Putney said, "Goodness, Joe, you're awfully ambitious for a brand new trustee. Didn't you already volunteer to reduce the mowing to cost?"

Charlie spoke up. "That was a requirement of taking the trusteeship, Mr. Putney. Like the rest of us, Joe is not allowed to profit from his role here."

Putney regarded him coolly. "I believe you've had a number of billable hours, though, haven't you?"

Charlie just smiled. "As lawyer for the estate I am allowed to claim costs, but I haven't claimed any for trustee meetings, just for the legal work I've had to do outside of meetings. I will grant you, however, this is an unusually complex trust. I warned Nat the costs associated with it would be far higher than most."

"I'm sure you did," Putney said, finally provoking a frown in return.

Dori said, "There's no need for Joe to get involved. I'll do an inventory myself."

Putney said, "Please don't take offense, Dori, but as a family member you may have your own interests that don't align with the trust's. For example, there may be certain papers you would just as soon never see the light of day."

Karl said, "Any papers that objectionable we might all wish to keep out of the public eye. Why don't we have Joe and Dori work together on this one?"

Dori stared at Karl. He of all people should understand her objections to that.

"Fine," Putney said, clearly annoyed. "If that's the best we can do. Any objections?"

Dori felt her face flush hot. What could she say that wouldn't make her look unreasonable?

"I can get an intern or somebody to help, too," Putney said. "But let's move on for now." He passed out a sheet of paper. "Here's a detailed media promotion plan for the upcoming Bedford Bardwell Days. I'll be the point person on this. Dori, this will involve some interviews for you. There may be other trustees contacted as well – especially you, Marjorie. I assume that's acceptable? We want to drum up as much interest as we can."

Marjorie looked alarmed. "What are we supposed to say?"

"It doesn't really matter," Putney said. "Any publicity is good publicity. The goal is to build interest and attendance that will help us generate new fundraising revenue. Don't hold back any interesting details. For example, feel free to mention the crash."

They all stared at him.

"Look, I'm sorry," he said. "I know it sounds ghoulish, but it could make good press."

Dori said, "Should we also mention it was your plane?"

Four heads swiveled in surprise between her and Putney.

He gave her a chilly smile. "If you wish. At this point anything is fair game."

Dori was suddenly conscious that she was sitting in a small room with a powerful man.

The other trustees looked a bit taken aback, too.

Putney laughed. "Oh for God's sake, people, don't look so worried. Someday you'll look back and realize that this was the exact point everything turned around."

Chapter 16

Robert picked her up at four thirty. She'd had a chance to shower and change and wonder just what the hell she was doing. Who did she think she was, Mata Hari? She ought to be up in the attic looking for that manuscript, not dating a guy just to find out more about his father.

On the other hand, wasn't that exactly what he'd done to her?

At least being away meant Joe couldn't get in the house to inventory anything. She assumed she still retained at least that last element of control: if she didn't open the door, it remained locked.

Though she had an uncomfortable feeling Putney would soon get around that, too.

What the hell was Joe's agenda, anyway? She was grateful he'd managed to derail the sale of the papers – if only because it had clearly annoyed Robert Putney – but was he actually trying to help her, or was he just doing anything he could to piss her off? There wouldn't be anybody to network with in the attic, except her.

Her and a leaking roof she hadn't told anyone about.

"You're awfully quiet," Robert said, as they drove the long curves of the road to Greenfield.

She was supposed to get *him* talking, not the other way around. "Sorry. I was wondering about your dad. What was he like when you were growing up?"

Robert's expression tightened. "Like most dads, I imagine. But away more than most. My parents have always done a lot of traveling. I went away to boarding school, too. Why?"

"So you weren't close?"

"Oh, close enough. Dad can be a little overpowering. He's a really smart, capable guy, you know, and he always expected us to be the same. I'm afraid he was never entirely satisfied with my efforts. My sister's the brilliant one."

"Just one sister?"

"Yeah, she's it. Two years older. Helene. She just got her doctorate in ancient Chinese literature. Can you get a little more obscure? I think it might be her own way of avoiding the family business."

"Then she doesn't plan to be a journalist?"

"Nah. She'll probably just do her brilliant thing in academia and maybe serve on the board when she's a little older."

"So you're on the board?"

"Not yet." Robert sighed. "Can't say I really look forward to it. Putney Publishing may seem like a huge, modern corporation, but at its core it's really a family business, and it can get pretty weird." He glanced at her. "You could probably find all this stuff out with a Google search, you know."

"Oh. I'll look it up next time I'm at the library."

The car actually slowed a little. "At the library? What do you mean? You don't have a computer? A smart phone? Nothing?"

"Nope. Not anymore."

"Not even email?"

"Yeah, but I don't use it much. I'm not sure I even remember the current password. Last time I tried it, it was wrong."

"God. How do you even function? It's like you're Amish or something."

Just poor, she thought, but didn't say, because it probably wasn't just that. She had plenty of equally low-paid colleagues who still managed to have the latest phones. She wasn't sure how they pulled it off. Some of them were married, or didn't have cars.

"What do you want to see?" he said. "Pick a chick flick if you want, I won't mind."

"Whatever gets me in the mood?"

He gave her an aggrieved look. "Do you really think that's all I care about?"

She grinned. "Yeah, at this point I'd have to say that's my operating theory."

He shook his head, but looked amused. "Then why are you here?"

"I don't know. I do think you're fun to hang out with."

"Perhaps you're attracted to me despite your better judgment." He waggled his eyebrows at her. When she merely smiled, he sighed. "Or maybe you just want a free movie."

She felt a twinge of guilt. She should definitely try to pay her share tonight, though she hoped he'd refuse. "I'd just like to get to know you better. What would you say motivates you the most in life, other than the ladies?"

He scowled. "That sounded a little too much like Dad."

"But I'm serious. What do you care about? What matters to you?"

He looked uncomfortable. "I care about my job. I'm proud to be a journalist. I like doing my part to protect democracy. What's left of it."

"You think you're protecting democracy in Jasper?"

"Oh, hell yes. Believe me, if nobody pays attention, people will get up to all sorts of mischief."

"Like what?"

"Oh, you know. Put a hand into the public till ... use their positions to do favors for themselves or their friends and family. Stick it to their enemies. Cover up abuses. Does the drunken teenage party at the state trooper's house result in any arrests, or is it hushed up? Did the superintendent of schools find a way to pad his retirement at the taxpayer's expense? Did the assessor undervalue the houses of her political allies? Why was the zoning code strictly enforced here and quickly waived there? That kind of thing."

She looked over with interest. "So Jasper is a hotbed of corruption?"

"No, it isn't. But that's only because they know we're watching. There are towns all over America where nobody pays attention anymore. And you could argue there aren't enough people paying enough attention at the national level either. They let people say whatever they want all day long on television, but they almost never do their homework. They don't follow the money."

"Huh," she said. She hadn't subscribed to a newspaper in years; it was an expense she couldn't justify. "But isn't your Dad's company part of that?"

Robert's forehead creased. "He's not involved in the day-to-day management of any of the news outlets at this point. He's in charge of the whole corporation."

"So what motivates *him*?"

He looked over at her. "Why do you ask?"

"I'm trying to understand why he'd want to go to so much trouble with this trust."

"I already told you, he's always been into history and literature. And your dad was a friend."

"Okay, but he's been dead for seven years. Why now?"

Robert looked uncomfortable. "I don't know exactly what motivates my father. But I know he's very good at what he does. Once he sets out to do something, it gets done. That's what he's known for."

"It can't be the money," Dori said. "Right? This trust has got to be really small potatoes to someone like him, isn't it?"

"I'm not privy to my parents' finances. But I would assume you're correct."

She decided not to mention Ruth's theory about preventing a lawsuit. "Maybe it's about the power?"

Robert looked taken aback. "Excuse me?"

"What is power if not the ability to make things happen? To get things done?"

Robert shook his head. "That makes my father sound like some sort of evil megalomaniac. Even if he were, why would he go out of his way just to exercise a little power related to a deceased author in some backwoods town in the hills of western Massachusetts?"

"That's what I'm trying to figure out. I didn't say the things he gets done are *bad*," Dori said. "Just that, you know, maybe he really enjoys having the power to do them."

Robert shook his head and pulled into the parking lot of the movie theater. "You don't go out on a lot of dates, do you?"

"Oh. No," Dori said, embarrassed. "I don't. Sorry."

The movie they settled on turned out to be a fairly entertaining comedy. Robert had an easy laugh that she couldn't help enjoying, and over Chinese food afterwards they discovered they shared a fondness for rude parodies. She watched him as he recalled favorite scenes and acted them out, terrible accents and all, and felt a little guilty about her primary motivation for being there. It would be great if Robert could just be a friend. Then she could just enjoy spending time with him without wondering how she was going to make it clear that no, she really didn't want to have sex with him even though he had shown her a good time.

The conversation flagged a bit on the drive home, and as they took the turn down into Jasper the tension thickened. "Well, I have an early morning tomorrow," she said, hoping the message would be clear.

"I know," he said simply, and pulled into the circular driveway that led under the kitchen portico. He gave her an unnervingly intense look. "Shall we try this again?"

She stared in surprise. "You want to?"

"I enjoyed it. Didn't you?"

"Yeah. But..."

"But what?"

"I'm sure you were hoping for a much *better* time."

That earned her warm smile. "Actually, this makes for an interesting change of pace. Maybe I shouldn't always be in such a rush to get to the end of the story. It's nice simply to have funny, intelligent company."

"Well, I think so, too."

"You seem more interested in getting under the surface of things than most of the women I date. It's kind of exhilarating. You seem to want to know the real me."

She felt yet another twinge of guilt at how he'd interpreted her efforts at probing Putney family dynamics.

"I'm interested in getting to know who *you* really are, too," he added.

She laughed weakly. "Maybe you should save your questions for that story."

"Story?"

"About the Bedford Bardwell Days?"

"Oh." He grimaced. "I can't write that one myself anymore.

We'll get someone else on the staff to handle it."

"Why not you?"

"Because we're friends. And there's the connection with my father. It wouldn't be kosher."

"Oh," Dori said. "I'm sorry to hear that."

"I'm sure it will turn out well anyway. And we can be friends regardless, right?"

"Of course."

"Good. It's nice to know you're not just putting up with me for the potential publicity. I'll call you later in the week."

She forced a smile and a wave as he drove off. No, she wasn't just putting up with him for the potential publicity. She was putting up with him to try to figure out what his dad was up to.

Chapter 17

Dori went inside, kicked off her shoes, and poured herself a tall glass of water. The Chinese food had left her feeling parched. The old answering machine was blinking: three messages. It was only eight o'clock, but she was exhausted. It felt like she hadn't had any break at all over the weekend, and in the morning the marathon would start all over again.

She gulped cold water and stared resentfully at the blinking number, trying to decide whether she had the fortitude to ignore it all night. Then the phone rang, and she jumped.

Not for the first time, she wished she had caller ID like everyone else on the planet. "Hello?" she said.

"Hi, it's Joe. I see you're finally home."

"Oh my God! Are you stalking me?"

"Yeah, of course. I've got nothing else to do. Look. This guy Putney. Don't you think he seems really eager to get his hands on those papers?"

"Yes."

"Is there something in particular he's looking for?"

She hesitated. "Maybe."

"Well? What is it?"

She didn't say anything. How did she know she could trust Joe? He was probably the last person she should trust.

"Look," he said. "I'm trying to help you here."

"So you say."

He sighed. "Well, whatever it is, I suggest you find it and put it away before he gets his hands on it. I don't trust this guy."

Did Joe think she was some kind of idiot? "I don't trust him either. I'm having a hard time trusting *anybody* right now."

"Well, personally I think Charlie and Karl are playing it straight. That's the reputation they have in town, and I haven't yet seen anything to contradict that. Marjorie may just be a nut-case, but she does seem to have it in for you. Putney, though – did you say that was his plane?"

"Yeah."

"Do you think ... I mean, would he have actually...?" For once in his life, Joe sounded uncertain.

The phones in the house were original to it, so they not only had no caller ID, there was also no way to pace around the room. She leaned her forehead against the old wallpaper, then turned her back to the wall and slid down it until she was sitting on the kitchen floor. "I don't see how. He was in New York. The plane was in Turners Falls. Dad called him up and asked if he could borrow it on pretty short notice. The crash report blamed weather conditions and pilot error. Nothing mechanical."

"Well, I'm glad it wasn't suspicious. It would be pretty freaky to think someone you know could be capable of that."

"It would also be a very expensive way to knock somebody off," Dori said. "He lost his airplane."

"I'm sure it was insured."

"Yes, but it turned out my father didn't have the right kind of credentials to be flying it. Nobody got anything is my understanding."

"So you never got any settlement from the crash?"

Was his interest in all this possibly financial? "Why does it matter?"

"Well ... maybe he thinks you could still come after him with a lawsuit. Especially if he let an unqualified pilot fly his plane."

If that were true, wouldn't he risk sparking a lawsuit just by showing up in her life the first place? "Ruth did say I should sue him."

"If Ruth and I have both thought of it, I'm sure his lawyers have." His tone turned sour. "Maybe he's trying a spot of prevention. How is Ruth, anyway?"

"Not so good at the moment."

"I'm sorry to hear."

Dori didn't say anything. Joe had never been a fan of Ruth, even in high school. She could still remember him in senior year, after a party, telling her Ruth was seriously messed up. Which Dori couldn't dispute – Ruth had gotten pretty reckless both with recreational substances and with guys. Joe couldn't understand why Dori was still close with her. Dori couldn't understand why she shouldn't cut her friend some slack: it was senior year, Ruth's father was dead, and a lot of people in town were giving her grief. And Ruth was her best friend.

"I thought *I* was your best friend," he'd said.

"You're my boyfriend. I can't pick out a prom dress with you."

"Why not?"

"Like you even want to go shopping! You'd probably say let's get it in the thrift shop."

"It could save you a ton of money."

She'd shaken her head. "You just don't get it. You don't get it because you're not a girl."

"Okay, fine," he'd said. "Just don't get all pissed off when I tell you the reason you don't get something is that you're not a guy."

He never had said that, though. No, he'd told her she was a spoiled, heartless, self-centered baby who wouldn't recognize true love if it slapped her in the face.

"Was there anything else?" she asked.

"Why are you so opposed to letting me help you with those papers?"

"You know why."

"You don't have a lot of time on this. Putney sent out an email tonight saying he's got an intern coming up later this week to help. He's hoping you can put her up in one of the bedrooms so the trust won't get stuck with a hotel bill. Charlie reminded him the trust can't assume any expenses without a vote. Putney said he expects you'll agree to put her up, but if you won't, he will."

He actually thought she'd be willing to house one of his minions under her own roof? "Are you serious? I'm supposed to put this person up?"

"Maybe it's all part of the plan. When you say no, which any reasonable person would do, he'll just use that as another example why the house should not remain a private residence."

Dori stood silently, thinking about it. Joe could be right. But if he was, what did that mean? Should she instead accept the presence of a Putney spy under her own roof?

Joe cleared his throat and continued, "His office also arranged a couple of interviews for you. He said he didn't know your email so he left messages on your answering machine."

Dori thought of that blinking light in the other room with loathing. "I don't really have any easy access to email at the moment."

"You're kidding."

She sighed. She'd already had quite enough tech-shaming for one day.

"I could help you set that up, at least," he said.

Why was it such a big fucking deal to everybody?

"Eu?" he said.

Her eyes widened. Back in the old days it had been his own pet nickname for her, as in *Hey Eu*. "Don't," she said, almost choking.

"There's nothing wrong with letting someone help you."

Oh hell yes there was. "I have to go," she said, and hung up.

Chapter 18

The next day when she went to get Mrs. Frankowski ready for lunch, she discovered the old woman slumped in her chair.

"Mrs. Frankowski? Mrs. Frankowski?" Dori asked, shaking the old woman's bony shoulder.

"Ahh," Mrs. Frankowski muttered. "Muh!"

Dori squatted down in front of her chair, trying to get a good look at her face. "Say something to me. What day is it?"

"Gahm snuh," the old woman mumbled. "Muh." One side of her face hung down, and spittle was trailing from her lips. Dori pressed the help button the old lady hadn't pressed even though it was sitting in her lap.

Another CNA, Janet, stuck her head in the door. "You got this?" she asked Dori.

"No, I don't," Dori said. "Call the nurse. And an ambulance. Possible stroke."

The nurse arrived and took Dori's place in front of the chair so she could take vitals. "Any idea when this happened?" she asked.

The patient stared up at her with one big eye and one droopy eye.

Dori said, "After breakfast I gave Mrs. Frankowski her shower and got her dressed. She wanted to sit in the chair and read for a while. That was at least an hour ago."

The nurse shook her head. "It's too bad. I thought she had some hope of getting back home someday."

Dori had been taught never to talk that way in front of a patient. "They've got that new drug now, don't they?" she said. "She might recover just fine."

The nurse gave her a skeptical glance. "Uh huh. Oh, here they are."

They stood back to let the ambulance attendants in. Dori once again explained how she'd found her. Bonnie came and stood in the doorway with her arms crossed and watched the proceedings. "How's it look?" she asked in a low voice.

The ambulance guy shrugged.

Dori had been through this sort of thing a number of times already – she'd found patients who had outright died, for that matter – but this one was hitting her harder than most. "You get better now, Mrs. Frankowski!" she cried, as they wheeled the patient out of the room. Then she burst into tears. Bonnie closed the door to the hall and wrapped her up in a hug.

Dori tried to stop crying, but the tears just wouldn't let up. Every time she thought she was finished, they'd break out again.

She could tell Bonnie was getting restless. "Honey, I've got to go call the family, let them know what happened." She opened the door, and hollered "Antoine!" In a moment, the long-time CNA who usually handled Kevin came in.

Bonnie closed the door behind him. "Antoine, do me a favor and take Dori here to my office so she can chill out for a little. Get her a cup of coffee, okay? And Dori, try not to let any of the residents see you freaking out on your way over. We don't need any more flapping around than we've already got."

Dori nodded and wiped her eyes. She blew her nose and followed Antoine out into the hallway, keeping her head down and avoiding eye contact, picking her way between all the wheelchairs and walkers in the corridor. Ambulance visits tended to bring out a crowd.

"Who'd they take?" an old man asked.

"Elsie," another said. "You know, the one with the purple robe."

"She's lucky," another one said, then added, more loudly, "I wish they'd take me. I've had enough. I want to go home now! When are they going to take me?"

Antoine was a tall, impeccably neat African American of middle age who had a quiet, gentle way with the residents, and with her, too, but it sometimes came with a price: Antoine was a deacon in his church and often felt called to witness to his Lord and Savior.

"I don't know if bringing you this coffee is really doing you any favors," he said, handing her a cup. "Sister Dori, would you mind if I offered a quick prayer?"

"I'm pretty sure Mrs. Frankowski was Jewish," she said.

He smiled. "It's more for you than for her, but I know she won't mind."

She acquiesced with a shrug. She'd learned long ago it was a lot faster to go along with a determined proselytizer.

He put his hand on her head. "Lord, bless this hardworking young lady and help her with her grief and her fatigue." He paused. "Am I right, sister Dori? Are you tired?"

Dori nodded and started crying again. Oh God, yes, she was tired.

"Lord, give her strength and courage to persist in all her daily struggles, large and small, and please help Mrs. Frankowski with hers. And if it be your will at this time, Lord, we ask you to take Mrs. Frankowski into your loving embrace, to the place where there is no pain or fear, only joy and release. In Jesus' name we pray…" He paused, waiting.

Dori refused to say it, so he supplied the "Amen."

"Thank you," she said. She appreciated the simple human comfort of Antoine's hand on her head even if she didn't rejoice in his prayer. She touched old people all day as part of her job, of course, but it was not the same as having someone reach out to touch her.

He said, "It can be really hard when our favorite residents are suddenly taken from us. Are you going to be all right, now? Can I get you anything else?"

"I'm fine. Thank you, Antoine." She squeezed his hand, returning the favor just in case his skin was lonely, too.

He patted her head. "It will be all right. One way or the other, it will all be all right in the end. The Lord will see to that! You take care now, young lady."

She nodded, again fighting tears, and he left her alone.

He was right about the coffee. It tasted as if it had been made the day before and marinated in Styrofoam all night. Dori sat slumped in one of the office chairs, forcing it down as if it were medicine.

Bonnie bustled in. "What a morning!"

Dori couldn't quite speak past the lump in her throat, so she just nodded.

"What the hell happened to you? I know you liked her, but there's no way you were crying that much over a ninety-six-year-old lady having a stroke. You've seen worse. It's not like she's your grandma."

"I never met my grandma!" Dori said, and suddenly she was crying again.

"Oh, Lord, girl." Bonnie sighed and regarded her appraisingly. "I think you just hit the wall. I can't see sending you out there again. Why don't you take the afternoon off? Take a nap or something. Try to relax. We'll see you again in the morning."

Dori thought of protesting; she needed the hours left on her shift. But she couldn't face the thought of going out there and trying to act cheerful for the rest of the day. "Okay. Thank you."

Dori drove back towards Jasper, stopping only long enough to buy some batteries. She had left the message light blinking all night. Let Putney sweat about his precious schedule.

But she suspected she was sweating a lot more about it than he ever would.

On impulse, she took the turn up to the ledges, and eventually pulled up into the empty parking lot. It was hot and humid, not exactly good hiking weather, but the house would only be worse. She picked out a shady spot under one of the gnarled old pines that had somehow rooted themselves into the broad stone of the ledges and took some deep breaths. There wasn't much of a view today; haze obscured the valley below and turned the mountains that ran north and west blue and lavender and grey. Straight overhead the sky seemed relatively clear, though. She watched a hawk turn lazy circles and listened to bees buzzing in the bushes.

She knew nothing about any relations beyond her parents. No grandparents. No aunts or uncles, no cousins. There were a few family friends she'd called aunt and uncle, but eventually she'd learned those were just honorary titles, and none of them had stayed in touch – except for Marjorie. When it came to actual family there were simply her two parents and all those brothers and sisters, who had always seemed like more than enough.

Until it was just her and Salinger.

Really, she had shown a stunning lack of curiosity about her own parents until it was too late. Why was that? Had her parents conspired to hide their pasts? Or had she simply suffered from a normal youthful certainty that nothing about her parents' lives before her own arrival could possibly be that interesting?

The answers might be in those papers. Or in the manuscript Putney wanted so badly. All of which she might well lose forever Thursday.

But in this heat, that attic might kill her.

Well, there was only one way to find out.

Chapter 19

It was so hot Dori thought she might throw up. She'd taken a jug of ice water up and was sure she'd sweated it out already. But she had also come upon a box that looked promising. It had a more miscellaneous than usual collection of paper and things in it, which was more typical of her packing style than the Friends'. It included a stack of condolence cards held together by a decaying rubber band, so it was definitely post-crash. She lugged the whole box downstairs to Harper's bedroom, and from there down to the old TV room off the kitchen, which was also one of the coolest rooms of the house, because it shared a north wall with her bedroom, which faced north and was shaded by a huge pine.

She was pulling the first items out of it when somebody knocked on the kitchen door.

Shit. She stuffed it all back in and shoved the box into the corner in front of the bookshelves. Then she draped a throw over it for good measure.

She opened the door and Ruth stood there. "What the hell happened to you?" Ruth said. "Didn't you get my message?"

"Oh! No, I thought those were from someone else." Dori said. "I thought you were in the hospital."

"They released me yesterday. The insurance company has decided I am no longer a threat to myself."

"Is the insurance company right?"

Ruth's wide grin reminded Dori of a skull. "Guess we'll find out. Can I come in?"

She stood back to let Ruth pass. "Your mom asked me to leave you alone."

"Why should you pay any attention to her if I don't? God, it's hot in here! Can't you at least afford a window air conditioner?"

"I was just going to have some iced tea. You want some?"

"Yeah, sure," Ruth said and slumped onto one of the old chairs at the kitchen table. "But you always make it too sweet."

Dori didn't fully succeed in stifling her irritation. "You want water instead?"

"No, tea is fine." Dori handed her a glass and then poured herself one. Dori drank her own down in huge gulps, then poured another and sat down.

"This would better with some vodka in it," Ruth said.

"I see you're all rehabilitated."

Ruth grinned. "That was a joke. Sort of. Not really. Seriously, Dori, you look like a drowned rat."

"I was up in the attic."

"On a day like this?"

"I was looking for something."

"What's so important?"

Dori took a deep breath. She had to say it: "One of these days you're going to take too many of the wrong kind and you really will kill yourself."

"Yeah, I know, and then I'll be sorry!" Ruth cackled. "What are ya gonna do, right? So have you seen any more of the lovely Robert Putney-Lewis?"

"I actually have," Dori said. "Did you know *Robert the Dick* is his unofficial local nickname?"

Ruth winced. "I don't suppose it's because it's just so glorious?"

If so, Joe wouldn't have been so eager to share, would he? But then again, maybe he hadn't known. "I don't mind Robert. I think we're friends now. It's his dad I could do without." She explained what had transpired with Robert's father and the trust, avoiding any mention of the manuscript. She also told her about Joe's call to the nursing home and wasn't disappointed when Ruth's eyes widened.

"I can't believe him!" Ruth said. "You must feel really..."

"Infuriated?"

"Unless this is his way of insisting you notice him again. Is that possible?"

Was it? "I don't see how, He has this very pretty young girlfriend. She gets her pubes waxed."

Ruth whooped and demanded to know how Dori knew that,

which led to a discussion of the skinny dipping, Robert's natural assets, and waxing.

Ruth declared waxing a misogynistic, porn-inspired tool of oppression, especially of naturally hairy women like her. But she'd also had it done on occasion and admitted she'd consider doing it again for the right guy. Dori thought it was just another bizarre new way to try to get women to spend money. That, and she couldn't help wondering why guys got so turned on by a woman looking prepubescent. "Don't you think it's kind of creepy?" she asked. "Like they're into children?"

Ruth shrugged. "I think they just like to see the parts better. Guys are very visual. You should have skinny-dipped, too. Let him see what he's missing."

"I didn't think the comparison was going to do me any favors."

"Did *Joe* go skinny-dipping?"

"No."

"Maybe he didn't think the comparison was going to do *him* any favors, either."

Dori laughed.

Ruth said, "You both have Puritan tendencies. And he sure knows how to hold a grudge. Remember that time I dumped a beer on him? He never forgave me."

Dori smiled despite herself. Ruth was right, that was probably the exact turning point.

Ruth shook her head. "And by the way. Your dad. What a *putz*. Didn't he realize he was putting together one of the most complicated estate trusts of all time?"

"It's not the usual thing?"

"Hell, no. Usually there's one person in charge, and that's only until the kids are thirty or so – theoretically mature enough not to screw it up."

"I don't think it was put together for us as much as Dad's own everlasting literary fame."

"Even so, it's weird," Ruth said. "Expensive, too, I would think. Why don't you try to find out?"

"Maybe I'll add it to my list."

Ruth raised her eyebrows. "Busy, are we?"

"I do have to work for a living," Dori said, with some heat.

"Yes, darling, I know that. What are you doing home right now, anyway? I only stopped by because I saw your car."

"I freaked out at work," Dori said. "Bonnie sent me home." She explained about Mrs. Frankowski, then added, "I guess I'm feeling a little strung out."

Ruth shifted uncomfortably in her chair. She *had* gone a remarkably long time without switching the conversation back to her. But Ruth said, "Anything I can do to help?"

Joe had said *you've got to let somebody help you.*

And Ruth was her oldest friend.

"Yeah, actually," she said, hoping she wouldn't regret it. "Maybe you could help me sort through this box?"

"Is that what you were looking for?" Ruth asked, twenty minutes later, as Dori sat on the floor with a slender manuscript in her lap, intently skimming pages.

"I don't know. Maybe." She was lying. It was definitely the manuscript. For some reason Dori suddenly felt protective of that fact. A stray line caught her eye, "Her nostrils flared in that way they always did when tears were imminent, and he braced himself." This was the end of chapter seven, when the protagonist's tearful wife announced she was leaving him because of his drinking and walked out the door. And that was all there was.

It could not possibly be the intended ending of a book. There were only 152 manuscript pages. But it seemed he had never gotten past that point. Dori frowned, suddenly wondering if her mother had ever made a similar ultimatum.

"What about the computer he was writing it on? Maybe there's more of it that hadn't been printed out yet."

"Salinger used it until it died. It's been sitting in the attic since then." She held up an old-fashioned floppy disk that had been bundled with the manuscript. Her father had learned the hard way to keep regular back-ups. "You can see how old it was."

"I bet someone like Putney could still get some highly paid techie to get into it. Actually, I'm sure there are still places you can pay to get stuff off of those. Like when you have old movies and things you want transferred."

Ruth *still* hadn't turned the conversation back to herself. It might be a record. Dori said, "If it hasn't melted or something from the heat. You're kind of into this, aren't you?"

Ruth huffed. "It's just ... the nerve of that guy swooping in like that! I can't stand those people! They think they can do whatever they want. I went to school with the sons and daughters of way too many of them."

Maybe that explained it. "So you wouldn't want to go out with Robert Jr. after all?"

Ruth shook her finger. "I didn't say that. When the pickings are this slim, I may just go out with anyone who bathes regularly. But he only had eyes for you."

And Lisa, and the caterers, and Jenna. "He might have liked you better if you hadn't kept bringing up how rich he was."

"What are you talking about?"

"Wiping his ass with hundred dollar bills? That sounded pretty hostile."

Ruth's eyes widened. "I said that? Out loud?"

"You sure did."

Her cheeks flushed. "I don't remember."

Dori raised her eyebrows meaningfully. It was hardly the first time.

"Okay, maybe I do need to cut back," Ruth said. She took a swig of tea and glared at it. "But not tonight. Seriously, you've got nothing?"

"Nothing," Dori said.

"Well, I've got to go. Come with?"

To watch her go drink? "Sorry, but I've got to get this stuff straightened up before Putney's intern shows up."

Ruth stood up and swung her purse over her bony shoulder. "You're really going to let a complete stranger stay in your house?"

"I haven't decided," Dori said. "But don't they say keep your friends close, but your enemies closer?"

"I doubt that was supposed to mean you had to keep them under your own roof," Ruth said. "In the same place where you sleep. I'd call that taking it a little too far."

"Oh, you know what?" Dori said. "I'll put any intern who shows up in the master bedroom! I can't be accused of being unhospitable, but it's about as far as it gets from my bedroom, and it's hot as hell up there. They'll be begging for a motel after just one night."

"But able to sneak around all they want while you're at work," Ruth pointed out.

Dori looked down at the manuscript. Ruth was right. How could she keep it safe?

Chapter 20

She hadn't driven out there in years, so she hadn't seen the professionally carved and painted sign at the road that said *Joseph Gagnon Landscaping LLC* and promised "Beautiful landscapes designed, installed & maintained." In the acre of land that sat next to the old house, rows of burlap-balled trees and bushes erupted neatly from mounds of wood chips. In the front few rows smaller plants bloomed prettily. A large plastic tunnel house stood next to the old barn, its doors propped open with cinderblocks.

This had just been a big old weedy lawn backed by a small apple orchard when she and Joe were in high school. He was always saying *I just have to mow the lawn first.*

The house looked as if it had recently been repainted in the exact same sunny yellow with white trim it had always been. Mrs. Gagnon's old overgrown azaleas had been ripped out or trimmed back, and the foundation beds reshaped to be larger and more flowing. The combination of shrubbery, grasses, and flowers looked lush and healthy, exactly as they should if a landscaper wanted to prove he had some talent.

All this from the guy who had once raged against the petty values of the bourgeoisie.

She sat in the car at the end of the driveway for a moment. Her heart was hammering at the step she was taking. Finally, she climbed the short stairs to the porch she had once known so well – also newly painted, she noticed – and rang the doorbell. She held the manila folder with its rubber-banded manuscript tucked against her.

Nothing happened, other than a calico cat suddenly appearing in the living room window and staring at her. Not a cat she remembered, though there had always been a cat or two around the Gagnon house.

She knocked. And rang the doorbell.

Still nothing.

Was he perhaps ignoring her intentionally? That was his pickup truck in the driveway, wasn't it? She peered around the side and that was when she heard the *bam bam bam bam* of what sounded almost like gunshots – but apparently were not, since the woman and children getting out of a car in the driveway of the house across the street didn't look the slightest bit worried. They waved in the typical friendly Jasper way, so she waved back.

As she took the steps down from the porch, there came the whine of a saw or something like it. Construction, then. She guessed the sounds might be coming from the barn, a large building left over from the days long before Joe and Dori were born when this had been a farmhouse surrounded by acres in cultivation.

She walked down the gravel driveway, counting one more *Joseph Gagnon Landscaping LLC* pick-up truck plus a large trailer, a small back-hoe, and other specialized equipment parked behind the house. Old leaves and grass clippings sat in great mounds beyond them. As she grew closer to the barn she began to pick up what sounded like a Red Sox game on the radio. Could be Joe.

She peered inside from the open barn door, noticing lawn equipment, detached snow plows, a workbench and neatly-organized tools. The red bicycle she remembered from their high school days leaned against a wall, draped in spider webs. She and Joe had once biked together across much of the local terrain. Where was her bike, anyway? She hadn't used it since she'd inherited the family's minivan, since replaced with her smaller Subaru.

She jumped as another loud burst of hammering interrupted the summer sound of baseball, but she still didn't see anybody. Whoever it was must be in the loft.

She looked around one more time, put her parcel down on the neat workbench, and climbed the ladder as quietly as she could, not sure whether it was Joe up there or someone else. The old wood creaked and groaned, but she expected the radio would cover it. As her eyes rose above the floor, the forest of studs surprised her, subdividing a large loft that had once been crammed with discarded furniture and old clothing. She and Joe had often used a certain cozy nook behind an old dresser for trysts.

There was no sign of that old dresser, but there was Joe, in jeans and no shirt, fitting a long piece of wood to the edge of a large opening that looked as if it had been recently cut into the wall. The late summer afternoon light bisected his body into fields of white glare and dark shadow and for a long moment she just watched him work.

He was definitely more muscled than he had been in high school.

Apparently satisfied with his placement of the board, he used a power tool of some kind to nail it into place: *Bam! Bam! Bam! Bam!*

She winced. Shouldn't he be wearing hearing protection?

"Joe?" she said, into the ringing aftermath.

He turned and stared, tool half raised in his hand, and said nothing.

"Is this a bad time?"

He blinked and carefully laid the tool down. "Sorry. How can I help you?" he said. The game on the radio went to a break, and a beer commercial swelled.

He sounded awfully formal. Which was perhaps to be expected after the way she'd been treating him. "Sorry to bother you when you're busy. I'll come back another time." Except that, of course, she wouldn't.

She quickly backed down the ladder and retrieved the manuscript she'd left on a workbench.

But he was calling down, "Hey! Wait a minute!" so she stopped and waited as he half-slid down the ladder.

"You surprised me, that's all," he said. "This is a perfectly fine time, other than me being a stinking mess." He brushed some sawdust off the light curls on his chest, then pulled leather gloves off his hands and stuffed them in a tool belt hung low on his hips. He left his hands there, thumbs hooked into the belt on either side of his waist, standing tall – legs spread apart, stomach sucked in, pectorals bulging.

Was he just possibly *showing off?*

"What are you doing up there?" she asked.

"I'm converting the loft into an apartment. It'll either be a place for some of my seasonal workers to stay, or the source of a little extra income."

A little extra income. She tried to imagine ever sounding so airy about it.

"What's that?" he said, with a tilt of his head to indicate the envelope in her hands.

"I thought about what you said. It's something I don't want anyone to find when they start going through Dad's papers. Do you think you could keep it here? Quietly?"

"What is it?" He held out his hand.

After a moment of hesitation, she handed it to him. "It's the manuscript for the book Dad was working on when he died. Robert Putney keeps asking about it and claiming he was collaborating on it, but I don't think that's true. At any rate, I don't want him to have it. At least not yet."

Joe opened the folder and stared down at it. "Even if removing it might reduce the value of those papers?"

"If Putney's already claiming he was collaborating on this book, he might try to claim it's his, or at least half his. He might even try to publish it."

Joe's eyes lifted to hers. "Yes. But publishing it might make you a ton of money."

She shook her head. Sure, she could use it, but she wasn't willing to even fantasize about it. "It's not even close to finished. Dad's agent told me years ago that there was nothing there worth publishing yet. What if it's put out there and everyone says it's crap, because it is? You know how much Dad's reputation mattered to him." She grimaced a little. But why did it matter to *her*? *Did* it matter to her?

He had opened it to the first page and was already reading. "Do you mind if I read it?"

Joe had always been a reader, but that surprised her. "You don't like his stuff."

"I like it better than I used to. Well, except for that third one. That was a real stink bomb. I think it helps to read them when you're a little older. Also, when you're looking for insights into an ex-girlfriend's otherwise inexplicable behavior."

She felt herself flush. "Like not marrying you right out of high school?"

"I already said you were right about that. I'm talking about how you've let yourself get so stuck. It's like you're in that Faulkner story we had to read in English class. Next thing you know the townsfolk will find your long silvery hair on the pillow next to some missing guy's skeleton." He smirked. "Robert Jr.'s, preferably."

Bastard. "All right, give it back. I'll see if Ruth will take it."

He lifted it up beyond her reach. Once she realized what he was doing, she dropped her hands, unwilling to play that game. He said, "Come on. You want to give it to a drunk to keep safe? I won't read it if you don't want me to."

"I don't care whether you read it. I just..." She stopped.

"What?"

"I just wish you wouldn't be such an asshole!"

He laughed. "I'll try, but if I think you need me to be an asshole, I'm going to be an asshole. Do you want to come in and have some lemonade or something? See, I'm trying to be nice. You could be nice yourself and say yes."

"Wouldn't I be taking you away from your work?"

"Eh, it'll wait. We're not supposed to get any rain until tomorrow night."

Rain? The damp box in the attic flashed into her mind. "How much are we supposed to get?"

"It's a pretty big system." He blinked. "Why do you care? Are you taking Robert Jr. on a picnic?"

How long had she thought they could actually go before the next downpour? It was high summer, after all. She looked back down the road and the way she had come.

"Dori?"

"There's kind of a leak."

He stared in the same direction she had. "In your car?"

"No, at the house."

"The house?" His voice rose. "How long have you known about this?"

"Since I went up in the attic earlier today to look for this. It's pretty small. I couldn't even find any stains on the ceiling underneath it."

But he was off and running. "Why would you even think of keeping something like that to yourself? What if the ceiling fell down? What if it started an electrical fire? The whole house could go up, *bam*, like that!" He raised his hands in the air as if to mime a conflagration, the flapping manuscript a part of it.

Surely his level of alarm was way out of proportion? When had Joe become such a hall monitor? "Okay, well, I just told you. You're a trustee. Now you know." And no way was she taking any lemonade from him! She'd grab the manuscript back if she were tall enough to reach it. She turned and stalked back to her car, wishing she hadn't come.

He stood in the driveway, watching her as she took off down the road.

The roof was going to be the final nail in the coffin of her finances. She might as well forget about getting any help from the trust with college tuition any time soon. Not that she'd ever really believed that was going to happen anyway. She had gotten too stupid to dive back into a competitive university setting and hope to pass calculus.

After she got out of her car at home, she saw Joe's pick-up turn onto the driveway behind her. She waited. Had he come to help, or to berate her further?

He hopped down from his truck. He'd put a t-shirt on, and was carrying a big flashlight. "Show me the leak," he said.

She took him up to the attic. For once, it was nice to not have someone complain about the lack of air conditioning the moment he walked in the house. The sun was nearly down and the attic had cooled to something a bit more survivable than it had been earlier.

As she leaned in next to him as he poked through the damp, mildewing collection of snow suits, she noticed he was pretty pungent. It triggered memories of their long mutual exploration, during their high school years, of what bodies could do.

If he didn't officially belong to Lisa the hairless water nymph, she could imagine bumping up against him, just to see what would happen. Just to see if there was any of the old spark left.

"Why do you even have all these old things?" he complained, killing that thought dead. God, he could be such a nag! He always had been, really, only before it had been about the oligarchs instead of her.

"They don't want me to throw out any of their stuff. Maybe they're planning to do a 'Check out the poor dead children's winter wear' exhibit someday."

There was just enough light from the lonely bare bulb charged with lighting the whole attic for her to see the flash of pity on his face. "Doesn't it get to you?" he asked. "Living in the middle of all these reminders?"

She swallowed. She didn't trust herself to speak of it. Besides, didn't he live in his dead mother's house? She cleared her throat, and said, "What do you think about the leak?"

He stood up carefully – he'd already knocked his head once. "I think we protect this area tonight, and get a roofer out tomorrow to give the board an estimate, maybe tarp the roof if he can. I know a guy. But with a slate roof..."

"...it'll be expensive," she concluded grimly.

He swept his light around the jumble of boxes and bags in the attic and scowled. "I don't know about this, honestly. The cash flow situation of the trust is pretty alarming. Could be we really should have sold those papers for whatever Brooke College was willing to give us. Could be I should have kept my big mouth shut."

"Could be, but I sure enjoyed watching Mr. Putney get pissed off."

He shook his head, but he looked amused.

She said, "So there's a way to protect this?"

"I have a trash can in the back of the truck. And a tarp. Wait here. I'll be right back."

"Thank you."

"No problem," he said, and squeezed her arm before he headed for the door.

Had that been just a friendly squeeze? Or had he just possibly been checking for a spark himself?

If so, it apparently hadn't amounted to much, since he didn't look back as he made his way to the stairs and down.

Didn't matter anyway, she told herself. There was still Lisa. Why would any healthy young man want Dori when he could have a beautiful young woman with neither inhibitions nor pubic hair?

When Joe returned she helped move the soggy box of winter wear out of the way and spread a big blue tarp. He put an old plastic can that had clearly been in use to hold cut grass in the middle of it. "Hopefully that will catch it," he said. "If you can, come up and check it when it's raining. You might need to shift it. I'll let the other trustees know what's going on."

"Okay. Thanks."

He'd also brought up a big contractor's bag, and proceeded to stuff the old snow suits and sodden cardboard into it. He sneezed, probably from the mold and dust.

"Bless you," she said.

He just smiled tightly and headed down the stairs with the bag, so she followed him, stopping to turn off the weak attic lights. He headed on out of the kitchen door to his truck and tossed the bag into the back of it. "I'll throw it in my dumpster," he said. "I think you're set for the night."

"I am. Thank you." She could feel a blush blooming on her face. "You want some iced tea?"

"Yours? Always. But I'd better save it for another time. I need to put my tools away and make some calls."

"I'm sorry."

"I told you I wanted us to be friends, didn't I?" He gave her a smile that looked more like a grimace. "I meant it." He leaned down, pecked her quickly on the cheek, and practically ran to get into his pick-up again.

She watched him navigate the long drive to the road and take off, then touched her cheek where he'd kissed it. Clearly, he'd been anxious to get away. But no one had forced him to kiss her cheek. Had that been an old friend kiss, or had he also been curious about a spark?

And, if so, had he felt it?

She had. Her heart was still hammering.

Lisa, she reminded herself. So it didn't matter, not really. Probably.

Chapter 21

"Why me?" Dori said. Bonnie had assigned her Kevin again. "He sexually harasses me, you know."

"Sweetheart," Bonnie said, "If you couldn't deal with a little sexual harassment from these old goats, you would have quit years ago."

"But he's not an old enough goat! He knows exactly what he's doing! It's gross."

"Janet can help you get him out of the room today. Maybe he's just getting stir-crazy. Or maybe you want that landscaping job after all."

Dori looked at her, but Bonnie was staring down at some paperwork. She'd heard Bonnie make remarks like that to other workers, but never to her before. Maybe she was mad about giving her that raise. "What about that pressure ulcer?" Dori said. "You looked at it, right?"

Bonnie's smile was chilly. "See, that's why continuity of care is important. You're watching out for your patient."

"He's not my patient. He's Antoine's patient."

"Antoine isn't here anymore. Kevin is *your* patient now. But if that pressure ulcer gets much worse, we'll send him to the hospital for treatment, and maybe we won't take him back. I don't think this is the best spot for him anyway."

Dori felt just a tad queasy as she walked down the hall to Kevin's room. As much as she disliked the man, she also knew their facility represented the closest thing to home for him.

Janet was a full-figured African American woman who worked hard and stayed pretty cheerful for someone who was convinced 9/11 was perpetrated by the U.S. government, genetically-modified foods were slowly killing everyone on the planet, and FEMA had a network of secret mass graves dug in every town for reasons Dori had never quite gotten clear. She walked into Kevin's room, grinning broadly, and said, "Good morning, Dori! And how you feeling today, Mr. Mackelroy? Ready to get out of this room for a little fresh air?"

Kevin rolled his eyes. "You call that fresh air? So I can watch the old turnips in their wheelchairs doze to Karen Carpenter? I don't think so."

During his catheter cleaning Dori had already rejected his inevitable proposal that she give him a blow job. Now she said, "You can always put your earphones in if you don't want to listen to whatever they're listening to."

He sighed heavily, stuck in his ear buds, and turned the volume on his player high enough that she could clearly hear the tinny sound of heavy metal playing. It hardly seemed worth telling him that it wasn't good for his ears at that volume. They appeared likely to outlast the rest of him. Or they could go at any moment. MS was unpredictable.

At least the noise provided her and Janet with cover for a conversation. "What happened to Antoine?" Dori asked.

Janet didn't say anything. They were methodically working their way through the steps required to get a patient like Kevin harnessed, hoisted, and safely moved from bed to chair. When she'd first started this job the deliberate pace of these transfers had frustrated Dori no end. Janet and other more experienced aides had taught her the importance of pacing herself – not just because it reduced the potential for accidents or injuries, but because it would keep her from being given more patients to care for than she could safely handle – at least in theory. It also meant when they were short-staffed, there were things that just didn't get done. Like getting Kevin out of bed.

"Janet?" Dori asked.

Janet kept silent, seemingly focused on the placement of straps.

Dori said, "Is he all right?"

Janet gave her a long appraising look. "You really want to know?"

"Yes."

"And can you keep it to yourself?"

"Of course."

Janet worked her lips, clearly considering. "All right. I'll tell you. The other night he was giving his cousin a ride down to Springfield when the state police stopped them. They asked if they could search the car, and of course Antoine said yes because show me a black man anywhere who's stupid enough to say no to that. Turned out his no-account cousin he was doing a favor for had a whole bag of weed on him that he'd stashed under his seat. So they arrested them both and charged them with possession with intent to sell. And they confiscated his car!"

"His *car?*" Dori said, in disbelief. "But why take Antoine's car, if it was the cousin who was doing it?"

"Why not? They get a free car out of it! And a chance to ruin another black man!"

Dori had always tended to discount Janet's theories about black men and the law, if only because she was so prone to conspiracy theories in general, but charging a man like Antoine seemed crazy. More than once, during a shared break, Antoine had earnestly explained to her that alcohol was the devil's drink, and pills weren't any better. Better to get high on Jesus instead!

She also couldn't help remembering her recent trip with one of Travis's joints stashed in her glove box. She'd given her brother a ride plenty of times. Who knew how much he was carrying on him? "My brother is a total pothead."

"But he's white, right? He'll be fine. Unless he sass a cop, or find some brother to drive around with, and then God help him."

"He does have dreadlocks," Dori said, doubtfully.

Janet guffawed. "For real? Is his hair the same color as yours? *That* I want to see." She snorted. "I still don't think you got anything to worry about."

"So is Antoine in jail?"

"Oh, no, no. Antoine's momma was more than willing to bail him out. She wouldn't know what to do without him."

"So if he's out, why isn't he here?"

"The old fool told Bonnie the truth about why he wasn't here the other day. And that was the end of that."

Dori stopped turning the handle that worked the hoist and stared at her in disbelief.

"Don't leave the man dangling now!" Janet said, and Dori started turning again while Janet steadied Kevin's bulk, guiding it towards the chair. After a quick check to make sure they would not be overheard, she added, "Bonnie may seem like she just loves you and she's looking out for you. Don't you believe it! Not for a minute. Don't matter what color you are, she'll cut you loose the minute she smells any little hint of trouble."

"What if we talked to the owner?" Dori said.

"Did you just listen to a word I said? If you need this job, don't say another word about Antoine. Maybe if he wins his trial, they'll let him sneak back, all quiet like. I can't imagine why he'd want to come back, except it's so damned hard to get a decent-paying job. 'Course it will be a hundred times harder if he doesn't get off. Or decides to take a plea, just to get the thing over with."

"Why would he do that?"

"Honey, people do that all the time. When you got to choose between, say, some fine and probation or some jury that might just look at you and decide you belong in prison with all the other black men? And meanwhile you're waiting and missing days at work while they delay and delay just to screw with you? At least Antoine has a real lawyer of his own. Not everyone can afford that."

Dori kept turning the wheel until Kevin's butt had firmly landed in the chair, then helped Janet with all the straps involved.

His music was still blasting, but Janet lowered her voice. "This world is a cruel, cruel place. I mean, look around you." She waited while Dori tucked Kevin's catheter out of harm's way and covered it in a blanket. "Certain folks get downright hateful, but you can see why, can't you? Would you want to end up like this?"

"No," Dori said. "Hell, no."

"And who knows who we'll get taking care of us? I used to think maybe it wouldn't be so bad if it was someone like Antoine. I sure wish he'd shut up with his holy rolling, but the man is good and gentle. You can just see it in him. It's a damned shame." She raised her voice and leaned down into Kevin's face with a big smile. "All right now, Mr. Mackelroy. Next stop, the TV Lounge!"

The next afternoon, when the chimes of the old doorbell rang, Dori opened the creaking big door to look up at a slim young black woman whose stylish braided extensions cascaded artistically all the way to her waist. A chic outfit and three-inch heels contributed to the whole tall, regal thing she had going and made Dori feel like even more of a frump than usual.

But it also all looked very high maintenance, which was pretty much what she'd been hoping for.

"Eudora Bardwell?" the woman said.

"Hi," Dori said. "Are you the intern? I'm Dori." She held out her hand.

The young woman gave her a brittle smile and shook her hand firmly. "Dori. I'm Maya Davis. I was told you might be willing to put me up while I help you catalog your father's papers?"

"Yep, come on in. I set up the master bedroom for you. Clean sheets and everything."

As soon as she stepped inside the door, Davis stopped dead and said, "Whoa, wait a minute! There's no air conditioning?"

Ha! Bingo. "Afraid not."

"Even in the bedrooms?"

Dori kept her voice sweet. "Why, sorry, no. I did put a big old fan in the window, though. You just might want to turn it off if it starts to pour or something." The rain Joe had promised was definitely looming in heavy clouds over the mountains to the west.

Davis stared up the grand staircase. "And it's on the second floor?" It was clear she understood the concept of heat rising.

"Yep. The room with the balcony." Technically, there was also a screened-in sleeping porch at the end of the upstairs hallway, over the carport, but the floor was rotten and it wouldn't be safe in a thunderstorm. "My parents always said this was where the rest of the country came to escape the heat. But then again, they were from the South."

"Well, I'm from Vermont, and I grew up with air conditioning."

Vermont? It was not a state known for its racial diversity. The coincidence seemed a bit strong. "You said your name was Davis?"

"Yes," she said, with a little roll of her eyes. "Yes, Arthur Churchill Davis is my dad. Yes, I'm sure that's how I got this gig."

She wasn't even trying to pretend this wasn't an inside job. "So are you actually an archivist or something?"

"No, but I've done some work in our college archives, and I got a crash course in how to inventory before I left. And I can always call the archivist if I have any questions."

Dori was glad she'd already stowed the manuscript. She just hoped nothing else too important was there to be found. "I'll be at work most of the day tomorrow, but you're welcome to dig in without me." Thunder rumbled in the distance. "Do you want to grab your luggage before that storm arrives?"

Maya smiled. "No offense, Dori, but I don't care how much they're paying me, I'm not going to try to sleep in *this*."

How much *were* they paying her?

"Is there a decent motel nearby?" Davis asked.

Dori had never really had to think about that before. "There are a couple of bed and breakfasts. There are a bunch of motels on the traffic circle in Greenfield, about fifteen minutes down the trail. And some little places in the other directions, towards Charlemont. But I think Mr. Putney said he could put you up if I couldn't. They have air conditioning." Why hadn't he just done that from the beginning? Maybe he was afraid his son would try to bed Maya Davis, too? Or maybe he already had? "Robert Jr. is living there, but they appear to have plenty of room."

Maya didn't react to the mention of Robert Jr., so apparently there was no history there. Instead she fished a device out of her giant handbag and said, "That's a little close to the glorious Putney family for my taste. Excuse me a moment while I line something up."

"I'll be back that way," Dori said, pointing, and headed back down the hall to the kitchen. Even though she had gotten exactly what she wanted, she felt a little put out. For one thing, she really *had* cleaned the master bedroom and the upstairs bathroom. For another, she wanted to pump Maya Davis for details about her father and Robert Putney.

And for another, it would be someone to hang out with. Work had been taxing. And after spending time with both Ruth and Joe the day before, she was feeling lonelier than usual at the thought of another muggy night alone.

The next morning, Maya arrived just before Dori was heading out to work. She complained bitterly of the uncivilized starting time. Dori made her promise she would be there at 3:30 when she got home, and left her the key so she could get out for lunch if she needed to.

Which meant when Dori got home from work that afternoon, she had to knock on her own kitchen door. It was an odd sensation.

"Hey, I made an extra key so you don't have to worry about getting locked out," Maya said, handing her back her key. "Hope you don't mind."

"No," Dori said. It would save her the trouble. Of course, it also meant Putney had a way in any time he wanted it. "Everything okay here?"

"Hot as hell, but fine other than that. So you're a nurse, huh?" It was a common assumption when people saw her in her scrubs.

"An aide." Kevin had been as obnoxious as ever, and they had been under-staffed as usual.

"Someone left a message about an interview," Maya told her.

"Great," she muttered. Just what she needed.

"Hey, interviews are good," Maya said. "More publicity means more book sales, which means more royalties."

Dori pushed the play back button on the message machine. A woman with a terrifyingly sophisticated European accent of some kind wanted to set up a time to talk to her, preferably at the house.

"Oh, I know her," Maya said. "Or her stuff, anyway. She's pretty famous. But you don't have to do it here, you know. Get her to take you out for a meal. She can expense it."

Had Maya noticed how pathetic her store of food was? Or did she just want more time alone in the house? "Doesn't seem like I'll be able to help you very much at this rate," Dori said.

"Is Putney paying you to help me?"

"No."

"Then who the fuck cares? I'd just as soon have more billable hours myself. Just take care of yourself. You look tired. Look, I bought some cookies. Some milk, too. Help yourself."

"Oh!" They were the fancy bakery kind. "Don't mind if I do," Dori said. "Thank you." She was more than happy to be bribed, if that was what Maya was doing.

"I'll just be in the study," Maya said. "I already ate my share of those."

"You don't look like you ever eat anything." In fact, Maya bordered on skinny. Maybe she had an eating disorder? It would be reassuring to know there was some chink in all that perfection.

Maya stopped at the doorway. "I just stop when I'm full. I call it the "Dessert First Diet." I should trademark that before somebody uses it, right? Too bad I have, like, zero credentials as a dietician. If you know of anyone who wants to co-author a diet book, let me know!"

The cookie was delicious. Dori chewed and swallowed and felt endorphins releasing or not releasing or whatever it was that made people feel better. She poured a small glass of milk, grabbed another cookie, and went into the study, where Maya was digging in an old file cabinet. "So you work in publishing?" she asked.

"I guess," Maya said. "Putney gives me odd jobs to do here and there. I just graduated and I'm still deciding whether I want to go to grad school or just dive in to what I really want to do, which is make documentaries."

She sounded as airy about that as Joe sounded about extra income from an apartment. "Well, good luck," Dori said, instead of the "must be nice" at the tip of her tongue. A bad case of pure envy made the cookies suddenly feel heavy in her stomach.

Chapter 22

Maya had already left for the night when the reporter, Angelika Schweitzer, arrived. Dori didn't ask her where she'd developed her accent, afraid it would immediately brand her as a rube. Schweitzer was wearing the kind of wispy, organic, naturally-dyed cotton clothing Dori only ever saw in the windows of boutiques she couldn't afford. She almost never saw it at thrift shops, either. Probably it fell apart before it could get there.

After a quick tour of the house and some friendly chit chat, they ended up in the parlor, which was still fairly tidy from her prep for the last Friends meeting. Schweitzer asked permission to record the interview, which Dori gave her, watching a little nervously as the woman played with something on her tablet and then laid it on the sofa between them.

"Tell me about your father," Schweitzer said. Though, really, it sounded like *fahtuh*. All her w's also came out as v's.

"What would you like to know about him?" Dori said. Intellectual-sounding accent or not, surely the woman had done some homework?

"What was your relationship with him like?" *Vhat vas.* Really, she sounded like the stereotype of a Freudian psychotherapist. Did it perhaps help her get people to spill their guts?

Damned if Dori was going to do any of *that.* "Well, he was my dad."

The woman waited, head cocked attentively, big dangly earrings swinging.

Dori willed herself to stop staring at them and look Ms. Schweitzer in the eye. "I mean, I loved him. But it could get a little tense at times."

"I believe you were just nineteen when he died?"

"Eighteen. Almost nineteen."

"Still in the years of the teenage rebellion, perhaps?" It was offered in a wry, understanding sort of way.

Had she been? "I was away at college. I don't know about any teenage rebellion. I guess I used to give him some attitude from time to time."

"Attitude? About?"

Should she say? "Well, he drank. Not at the end, but before that. I'm sure you know. Everyone did." It had been mentioned in all the obituaries.

"And how did that make you feel?"

Wasn't that a really banal question? "The way any kid would feel in that situation, I imagine," Dori said. "Anxious, I suppose. Disappointed."

Schweitzer waited, but Dori didn't add anything.

"And what did you think of your father's writing?"

Oh, God. Not that. "I pretty much tried to stay out of it," Dori said. "You know writers." Too late it occurred to her she was, in fact, talking to one.

"Do *you* write?"

"No." Not anymore. For a while, in childhood, it had been her career goal. Watching her father had cured her of it.

"The way you say that sounds a little, I don't know...." The woman waited.

Dori smiled and refused to fill in the blank.

"Angry?" Schweitzer finally suggested. "Disapproving?"

"Well. You know," Dori finally said. "Everything revolved around his writing. Here we were, a house bursting with children, and we had to be quiet so he could write. Plus, he wanted approval from everyone all the time. Every time he wrote a new scene, he seemed to need some applause. And maybe I was too young for it, but I just didn't personally like a lot of it."

Schweitzer's eyes widened. "You didn't like *Tea and Slavery*?"

That would be a scandalous pronouncement, wouldn't it? "I wouldn't go that far. I think it's a good book. I mean, everybody likes that book. He wrote that one before I was old enough to read. I just didn't like the others much. Getting through them felt like a chore. Especially after hearing or seeing parts of them multiple times."

"You read drafts of your father's work?" Schweitzer looked genuinely intrigued.

"Of the last one I did." He'd gone through so many drafts. It had never really worked. "Yes. It got old."

"Too close to home, perhaps?"

Dori blinked. "It wasn't that. Mostly I just thought it was kind of dull. And kind of…" She hesitated. She didn't dare say what she really thought: Self-indulgent. Pretentious. Boring.

Schweitzer pressed her. "Kind of…?"

"I don't know," she said, instead of the truth. "I was still just a kid! Given my druthers I was reading Harry Potter and "The Lord of the Rings" and Sarah Dessen and Jane Austen. I mean, I'm just not his target audience. I'm not into stuff that's Literary with a capital L." She said it with a touch of defiance. Her dad's favored audience had always been whoever would write the review for *The New York Times*. Much to his grief.

"The critics didn't care for the last two books, either. It must have been difficult for your father, after achieving such success with his first book."

"No doubt," Dori said.

"But you were there. You would know."

She was not going to rat out her father at his most drunken and self-pitying. She just smiled.

Schweitzer gave her an impatient look. "And how do you feel about him crashing that plane?"

Dori felt her face flush.

"Some anger, yes?" Schweitzer said.

"How could I not? That was practically my entire family."

"It was a terrible tragedy."

"Yes."

"Did you suspect he was drinking?"

At the time, she had. "The report said he wasn't," Dori said. "Apparently he just flew into the ocean."

"You suspect suicide?"

"No. I think it was just completely sober bad flying."

"And after that, you continued to live here, with your younger brother, I believe? I have been trying to reach him, and not having much luck."

"He can be a little hard to track down." Dori would just as soon it stayed that way. "This was our home. We didn't have any place else to go."

"Not to any of the extended family?"

"There is none. Dad's parents died when he was young. Mom was a foster child."

Schweitzer looked through her notes. "Actually, your mother's parents live in South Georgia. Your grandfather is a retired air force officer."

Dori went still. She had *grandparents?*

"They did tell me they had never met any of you children," Schweitzer added.

"I didn't even know they existed," Dori said. She got up and walked around the room, before she realized how weird that must look and stopped. "Are you sure?"

"Yes."

Dori stood, staring down at her. "Do you want something to drink?" she asked, mostly so she could get herself out of the room.

"No, but you go ahead if you need to," the woman said, and followed Dori into the kitchen with her tablet held out in front of her. "Have you ever even been to Georgia?"

Dori heaved the old refrigerator open and grabbed the iced tea pitcher. "I don't think I've ever been south of New Jersey."

"I see," Schweitzer said, with a tone that suggested disapproval. "Well, let's move on. How was your relationship with your mother?"

In the week that followed, Dori wondered why she hadn't asked Schweitzer for her grandparents' phone number. Then again, she hated phoning people she knew, let alone people she didn't.

Every time she thought about calling the reporter up and asking – for Schweitzer had left her a card – Dori told herself that her grandparents had never called her, either. It wasn't as if she was that hard to find. A letter to the publisher, or even directory assistance in Jasper could have gotten the call through. They were the only Bardwells in town. They didn't even have an unlisted number.

Each afternoon when Dori got home, Maya would complain about the heat. The study was slowly filling up with piles of paper. Some, it turned out, had come from the attic, since she'd already gone through his office files.

"You went up there?" Dori said, a little shocked. She couldn't imagine Maya and her high heels up on those stairs or in that heat bath.

"First thing in the morning while it was still cool. I don't have a death wish."

"Have you found that manuscript Mr. Putney wants?" Dori still wasn't absolutely certain another, longer version didn't exist.

"Not so far. It's all from the three published novels, as far as I can tell. He wasn't exactly the most organized guy."

"No, he wasn't," Dori said. That was why she was still a little worried.

Ruth called. "Guess what I did last night!" Her voice was so full of excitement Dori assumed it would be about a guy.

"What?"

"I attended my third AA meeting!"

"Really? That's great!"

"Yep."

"So it's going well?"

"You wouldn't believe some of the people I see there. Too bad I can't tell you who they are."

"I'm so proud of you."

"I thought you would be. I have a sponsor now, too, but I hereby commission you to be my official cheering section."

"*Yay*," Dori said, happy to oblige. "Seriously, Ruth. That's wonderful."

"So how about some pizza tonight?"

Dori hesitated, if only because for once she wasn't hungry. Maya had been bringing in lunches and snacks and always urged Dori to help herself to the leftovers. That afternoon she had come home to hummus and pita chips. The night before they'd even gone out to dinner at the diner together. "I have an expense account," Maya had explained. "Might as well use it, right?"

Dori wasn't sure whether Maya felt the need to surround herself with food at all times, was trying to grease the skids for herself, or was taking a sneaking sort of pity on her. She hoped it wasn't the latter, but she wasn't too proud to go along if it was. Also, she enjoyed Maya's company more than she'd expected.

But of course Ruth wasn't really asking her to go because of the food. "Sure," she said. "What time?"

In the study, Maya was tapping away on her laptop.

"I'm going to take a shower and then go meet a friend for some pizza," Dori said. That struck her as kind of rude, so she added, "You can join us if you'd like." She hadn't asked Ruth for permission, but she didn't think she needed it. She knew Ruth would be curious about Maya.

How would Anthony react to a black woman in his place? One of the chefs at the diner had shot them a dark look, though Dori supposed it might have been because of her own behavior the last time she was there.

Maya said, "Thanks, but that's okay. I'm almost done with this pile, and then I have a date with a shower and a nice video in my lovely air-conditioned room."

"I'll say goodnight, then," Dori said.

"Yep. See you tomorrow," Maya said, and waved her off.

Dori drove away, thinking that it was nice having someone else in the house. Was it stupid to think Maya was becoming a friend?

Probably.

She picked up Ruth and told her about inviting Maya. "You wouldn't have minded, would you?"

"Nope," Ruth said. "Because now you can't get mad at me if Joe shows up."

Dori's stomach flip-flopped. "What do you mean?"

"I ran into him after the meeting. It was in his church, I guess, or maybe they just hire him to trim the shrubbery. Anyway, he was being unusually pleasant to me, and he was obviously concerned about you ... so, I told him we might be there tonight."

"Then you didn't really invite him." She let out a breath.

"I said he'd be welcome to join us, but I didn't know if you were even going to be available yet. But it would be a sign of interest, wouldn't it, if he shows up anyway? With so little to go on?" She raised her eyebrows.

The whole thing had a certain flavor of high school to it. Early, early high school, before she and Joe had even started going out. "Are you forgetting Lisa?"

"I don't know Lisa from a hole in the wall. Is *he* forgetting her? That's the question."

Chapter 23

Joe was not at Anthony's, however, and Joe was nothing if not punctual. Dori relaxed but also felt a twinge of disappointment. She watched Ruth spar with Anthony over their order. Was it flirting? It clearly made Anthony happy. It couldn't really be about the possibility of free food, because Ruth seldom ate any of it. And she clearly didn't really want Anthony. She liked him, though. They liked each other. They liked whatever it was they were doing.

How could someone who could wring so much pleasure from a simple transaction like ordering a slice of pizza ever want to kill herself?

"So how's your appetite these days?" she asked Ruth, as they waited in the booth for their slices to appear.

"Kind of crazy," Ruth said. "I can't believe how much I'm craving sugar! I'm going to get fat."

"You could stand to gain a few pounds."

"Yeah, the doctor told me that, too." Ruth had ordered a root beer instead of her usual diet soda. "She said I need to start worrying about my liver, my kidneys, my pancreas, all that crap."

The bells on Anthony's door rattled, and in walked Joe.

"Well, lookee there," Ruth said, with a grin.

He looked their way, flushed a little, put his order in, and walked over. "Mind if I join you?" he asked.

"Have a seat," Ruth said, with a merry look at Dori.

Ruth had probably strategically left her handbag in the way, but perhaps he would have chosen Dori's side of the booth anyway.

"Hi," he said to her.

"Hi," she said back. "Where's Lisa?"

"In class. She's studying to be an EMT."

"Yes, I heard," Dori said. "That's brave of her."

"Kind of runs in the family," he said. "She tried to become a firefighter, too, but I think all the gear was a bit more than she really wanted to handle. Her dad wasn't exactly keen on it, either."

"The gear?" Ruth asked.

"All that stuff we wear when we turn out. It's really heavy. And then on top of that you have to deal with these heavy, hard-to-control hoses. Brute strength matters. EMT's don't have to gear up in quite as much stuff or drag hoses and ladders around."

Dori said, "They have to lift and move some awfully heavy patients."

He said, "Yeah. I guess you'd know about that."

Dori said, "You must be proud of her." Ruth kicked her under the table.

He just looked at her. "So where's Robert Putney-Lewis this fine evening?"

"I have no idea."

"You're not going out anymore?"

"We were never 'going out.'"

"You didn't enjoy the movie he took you to?"

"Oh, I did. I had a great time, actually."

Anthony brought Joe his slices. He looked a little skeptically at Joe, but didn't say anything.

Ruth said, "My prediction is that Robert will never end up with Dori no matter how good a time he shows her."

"Excuse me?" Dori said.

Ruth said, "I've been reading about alcoholic families. Dori's the eldest child. Worse, the eldest daughter. People like you make up the bulk of all the nurses in this country, did you know that? Joe, the secret to winning Dori's heart is probably to drink too much, tell her you love her with your breath full of booze, and then pass out. Make her put you to bed, make her clear up your vomit. Break some promises. She'll feel as if she's known you all her life."

Dori said, "Those are the last things anybody should do! I hate every last one of them!"

"She *has* known me all my life," Joe said.

"You say you hate them," Ruth said to Dori, ignoring Joe, "but they also feel completely normal to you. Look at who you've kept as your best friend. Look at what you do for a living. And back in the day, when you fell for Joe? He was just another grungy pothead."

"I was not!" Joe protested.

"He really wasn't," Dori said, though it was true he was the one who had introduced the occasional joint into their relationship. "A pothead, I mean. He *was* kind of grungy." She smiled.

Ruth nodded. "And you loved that."

Dori didn't disagree.

Joe looked at her, his brow wrinkled. "You *liked* the grungy thing?"

"Better than this Republican lawn guy thing you have going," Dori said. "Not that it matters what *I* think. I'm sure Lisa approves."

He stared down at her for a long moment, then turned back to his soda. "You must like young Robert's hair."

She smiled. Robert's hair was long, but beautifully styled. "He does have beautiful hair. I wish *I* had his hair."

"There's nothing wrong with your hair," Joe said, and Ruth raised her eyebrows meaningfully at Dori, who had experienced a pathetic little thrill but gave her friend a small scowl in return. That had been a very *Joe* way of putting it – that there was nothing wrong, not that there was something right. She wondered if he'd ever managed to sweet-talk anybody.

Maybe clients with really big lawns.

Ruth said, "Beautiful hair is also not going to be enough for Dori, because Robert is not tormented by anything. He wouldn't fit her imago." Dori recognized an older relationship theory Ruth had liked to entertain, back when she'd been trying to figure out why her own boyfriends were always such complete disasters. Clearly she hadn't seen Robert's medicine cabinet. Too bad she couldn't tell them about it without betraying her own snooping.

"Also, Robert's a slut," Ruth said. "And your dad was very loyal to your mom, wasn't he? It's not just alcoholism, it's also what we grow up with. Dori is going to fall for someone who's monogamous, but so tortured by failure he can't stop drinking.

Though I suppose it's possible she'd settle for a guy just being chronically ill."

Dori huffed her disapproval. "These things are not cast in stone. You're the eldest daughter of an alcoholic, too. I don't see you dying to nurse anybody."

"I'm an only child, so I get my pick of all the dysfunctional family roles. I prefer to be the over-achieving, anxiety-ridden second-generation alcoholic."

There was pained silence. "Who's in recovery," Dori said. She'd done some reading about alcoholism and codependency herself, over the years, though she'd never gotten up the courage to go to a meeting.

"Yes, in recovery!" Ruth lifted her root beer. "To three whole days of sobriety!" There was a sarcastic edge there.

"It's great," Dori said. "You're saving your life."

"That's right, I am," Ruth said. "I'm saving my life, one fucking day at a time."

Joe traded a concerned look with Dori, which warmed her as much as anything he'd said or done that night. Sometimes she just needed somebody else to be as freaked out at things as she was.

Into the awkward silence that followed, Ruth asked, "So how did that interview go? Do you know she tried to talk to me? Where's she from, anyway?"

"Austria," Joe said.

Dori turned to him in surprise. "You met her?"

"Briefly, on the phone," he said. "It was kind of a strange conversation. Among other things, she asked if you had ever said or done anything someone might classify as racist."

"Racist?" Dori said, shocked.

Ruth leaned forward. "Did she say why she was asking that?"

"No," Joe said. "I told her no, of course."

Ruth said, "You should have asked her why she was asking that."

Joe said, "I was just surprised to get the question."

Dori ran back over her interview in her own mind. She didn't remember race even coming up. It had just been poking and prying into her relationship with her family. Dori felt tired just thinking about it. "She did say she might have some follow-up questions after she talked to some other people."

Joe said, "Well, tell her you're not racist."

"No, don't," Ruth said. "Then she'll be sure you are."

"I'm not worried," Dori said. Unless... had she said anything she shouldn't have to Maya? But Maya didn't strike her as the kind of person who would rat her out if she did. Then again, she didn't really know Maya. And she was working for Putney.

As was Schweitzer.

Later that night, the phone rang. Schweitzer indeed had some follow-up questions.

"Is it true you offered to wear blackface for the Bedford Bardwell Days?"

Oh.

Fuck.

There it was.

Where the hell would she have heard about that? Marjorie? Dori's heart began to thump.

She considered denying she had said it.

But she *had* said it. There was no getting around that. And in a room full of people. "Yes, I do remember saying that. It was a joke. Not a very good one, obviously."

"It was supposed to be funny?" The reporter wasn't bothering to hide her skepticism. "You were joking about blackface?"

"The thing is, they didn't want a bounce house."

"A what?"

"A bounce house. One of those inflatable houses kids play in. For the carnival. They said it wouldn't fit historically. Which is a little nuts, you know. This house isn't even forty years old. It's just a replica."

"What does that have to do with blackface?"

"Well, if they wanted to make everything fit with the era of *Tea and Slavery*, wouldn't they need some slaves? I mean, wasn't that kind of the whole point of the novel?"

"So you were trying to raise their consciousness?"

"I wouldn't give myself that much credit," Dori said. "I was irritated. Here's this shrine to my dad's everlasting genius at writing a book about slavery, and there was a bunch of white women who wanted to tastefully pretend both slavery AND bounce houses have never happened."

There was a silence. "Are you suggesting slavery and inflatable children's carnival equipment are somehow comparable?"

What? "No, I am not. Of course not!"

There was a little "humph" sort of noise from the line, and then Schweitzer said, "I haven't noticed much diversity in this area. Do you actually know any people of color?"

How did Schweitzer define "know"? Dori said, "I've worked with a number of African American colleagues. And there was a black guy in our school when I was growing up." She didn't add that Steven, who had a mild case of cerebral palsy that had left one side of his body less developed than the other, had been adopted by two white people. He'd gone off to college to be an engineer and she hadn't seen him since. "I also went to NYU for nearly a year. So I have certainly experienced more diverse environments than this." She thought about mentioning Maya Davis or her father, but that would probably sound like she was throwing in every single African American she'd ever met out of sheer desperation.

"I guess that covers it, then. Thank you."

"That's all?"

"Yes, I'd say I have plenty."

"When is this going to be published?" Dori asked.

"That's not up to me," Schweitzer said. "And obviously I'm still writing it. I could email you a link when it comes out, if you'd like to give me your email address."

"That's all right," Dori said. "I'm sure I'll hear something."

"Yes, I'm sure you will." *Veel*. It sounded grim.

Chapter 24

On the Saturday before the Bedford Bardwell Days weekend, the Friends showed up to begin their housecleaning. Marjorie gave a gratifying shriek at seeing Maya's piles of papers all over the study floor. Maya herself had gone home to Vermont and her beloved air conditioning for the weekend.

"Well, this obviously isn't acceptable!" Marjorie said. "Our visitors are going to want to see where your father wrote his books."

"On the antique typewriter?" Dori said. "If you can pretend he wrote on that thing, can't you just as easily pretend he loved to type surrounded by piles of papers?"

With age, the lines in Marjorie's thin face were getting so deep they almost looked painful when she frowned like that. She sighed, and folded her arms, staring at the disorder. "We'll need to box it up and put it away."

"Absolutely not," Dori said, and enjoyed the way Marjorie's eyes widened. "You know why we're doing this. Mr. Putney's intern has a complex organizational system going here, and it's going to be shot to hell if we start moving stuff." She wasn't sure if that was true or not, but it sounded good. "If you want to suspend the cataloging that badly, it would be best to take it up with the board."

It earned her a withering glance. "We don't have time for that, Eudora, as you well know. Very well. We'll just have to keep everyone to the front of the house this year. We'll tell them this back area is in need of repair. Just like the roof." She blew out a disgusted breath. "That tarp is hideous! We can only hope it might bring us some more significant capital contributions this year." She closed the door on the room. "We'll just rope off this whole wing."

Dori decided she should have tried something like that earlier.

It would have been so nice not to have to dodge strangers wandering into her living area during past events.

"By the way," Marjorie said, in parting, "I heard that the article in *The Recorder* will run Thursday."

"Oh, good." She told her what she'd heard from Maya, via Putney, that Schweitzer's article was scheduled to appear in the Sunday magazine of his Boston paper the next morning. Dori didn't know anyone who actually read that paper, so her fear of what might be coming had calmed a bit.

"All this coverage! Such lovely exposure for us," Marjorie said. "I just hope we'll have enough refreshments for everyone."

Dori worked the Sunday shift at the grocery store, as usual. A few fat Sunday editions of Putney's paper crossed her register, but nobody said anything to her about it. When she got off shift she bought a paper for herself and took it out to the car.

It wasn't the cover story in the magazine, thankfully. But there was a big spread inside. The headline read "Bedford Bardwell's surviving daughter struggles with an unwieldy legacy."

A full page was taken up by a photograph Dori could have wished were more flattering. She was sitting on the front steps of the house, looking like a lost waif. The caption said, "Eudora Bardwell works 50 hours a week as a Certified Nursing Assistant and grocery clerk."

The article itself was well written and depressingly accurate in assessing the financial straits both Dori and the Bedford Bardwell House were in. The blackface comment had been used as a striking introduction – and a callout – but the context was explained much as Dori had explained it. From there the article focused more on conjectures about why the Bardwells had left the South and why they had built a replica of a plantation house. Schweitzer wrote it might have had less to do with the racial politics of *Tea and Slavery* than it did with family dysfunction, noting that although Bedford Bardwell had been an orphan, the official story that Ellen Bardwell had been a foster child was a lie even her own children had been told.

On the last page, there was a picture of her grandparents standing in front of a tree hung with Spanish moss, as well as an old picture of her mother and father, much younger and all dressed up for the Pulitzer Prize ceremony.

Dori held the picture of her grandparents up closer, frustrated by the papers' relatively poor print quality, trying to discern traces of her mother in either face. There was something in the curve of the man's nose and in the shape of the woman's face, perhaps. But the woman in the photograph was so tightly permed and made up, it was hard to relate her to her own mother's casual pony tail and natural freckles. The man looked grim and unyielding; there was perhaps a slight similarity to the fierce set her mother's mouth could take on when someone was misbehaving.

She had worried over nothing, really. She didn't see anything that could do her any real harm. The only mention of the upcoming Bedford Bardwell Days was pretty badly buried, though. Marjorie would be disappointed.

Chapter 25

The next morning when Dori went in to get her day's assignments, Bonnie was sitting at her desk reading something intently on her computer.

"Good morning," Dori said. "I still have Kevin?"

Bonnie looked up. "No, no Kevin. I'm afraid we're going to have to let you go."

Dori felt her stomach drop. "What? Why?"

"I've been getting phone calls all morning!" As if on cue, her phone began to ring again. Bonnie checked the number, shook her head in disgust, and ignored it.

"I don't understand."

"From reporters! They're asking me whether you have a history of racial insensitivity."

Dori felt her skin go cold. "I hope you told them I don't."

"I told them the truth, which is that I didn't know what they were talking about. But I see on the Internet you said something about wearing blackface? It's everywhere!" Bonnie gestured at the screen. There was the picture of Dori dwarfed by the house. She could see the word "blackface" but most of the type wasn't legible from her distance. She also recognized the cover of *Tea and Slavery*.

Dori stared at the screen as the word "everywhere" echoed in her mind. She was quite used to people telling her that stuff she didn't know about was "everywhere." They usually said it in a pitying or even accusatory sort of way, as if she had intentionally set out to be ignorant.

And now *she* was the one who was everywhere.

"It was a just dumb joke I said in a meeting weeks ago. A stupid, stupid joke. I never expected it to show up everywhere."

"Well, it has, and I'm afraid it leaves me no choice."

"Bonnie, I need this job. And you're understaffed! And I'm

good at it!" She took a deep breath and tried to calm down. This couldn't really be happening. "How can you fire me, when I haven't done anything wrong?"

Bonnie's expression darkened. "If you read the employee handbook we gave you when we hired you, you might have noticed you are explicitly prohibited from engaging in any conduct that might reflect poorly on the facility. And this certainly qualifies. Not to mention I don't have all day to fend off reporters."

Dori just stood for a moment, struck dumb, as the cold reality of the situation finally sank in. Janet had warned her, hadn't she? "Just like Antoine," she said bitterly. "How many years did he work for you? How many years have I worked for you?"

Bonnie flushed. She stood up and said, "I'll accompany you while you clear out your locker. We'll mail you your final check." She pointed her chin at the door.

Dori didn't move. "Don't I get any severance?"

"No."

"Unemployment?"

"It's not designed to cover situations where you've violated policy. But it's up to the state to decide that, if you apply."

"Will you give me a good reference, at least?"

The expression on Bonnie's face shifted to a kind of skeptical pity. "If you get someone to actually offer you a job, I'd be willing to vouch for you as a hard worker and capable nurse's aide. I'm not going to speak to anything else."

"But you know I'm not racist! You know, Bonnie!"

The phone started ringing. Bonnie glared at it, then at her. "I don't know anything," she said. "You act like you can barely find two pennies to rub together, but it turns out you live in a mansion! Seriously. What you people get up to on your own time always amazes me."

Back in her car, a trembling Dori sat the contents of her locker down on the passenger seat. It didn't amount to much, just a change of everything for when she got excessively peed, pooped, or vomited on in the course of her duties. She started the car and blasted the AC on high for the noise as well as the cooling, and finally let herself start crying in big hacking sobs.

She hadn't even been able to say goodbye to any of her colleagues or patients. Bonnie had hustled her to her locker and then out the door.

Eventually her attention shifted from crying to snot management. There had to be tissue somewhere in her handbag, but she gave up and used the sleeve of her tunic instead. It wasn't as if she would need it for work anytime soon.

It hadn't even been a good job. Everyone seemed to think it was beneath her. Even Joe, who mowed lawns for a living. The pay was terrible and the work was hard. But she'd felt useful there. And valued.

Before this.

She'd never actually been fired from a job before. How was she going to keep gas in the car and her insurance paid – and the utilities? What would she do for health insurance? Was the grocery store going to fire her, too? She probably ought to stop there and find out, but she wasn't due there until the next afternoon, typically her longest day as she went from one shift to the other. Maybe she shouldn't give them any ideas.

And if she drove home, Maya would be there – the one person in Jasper who would be most justified in taking deep personal offense at what she'd said. What if she decided Dori was an awful racist, too?

Perhaps that was why, when she finally headed for home, she took the turn to Joe's place instead.

She parked on the street in front. She could see him in the driveway, consulting with a couple of men who looked Hispanic. Joe noticed her car, and held up a quick finger to her: wait.

The men finished their discussion with Joe, got in the truck, and drove off. There was mowing equipment in the back, so it was fairly obvious what for. Joe stayed where he was, pulling a device out of his pocket and looking down at it.

Did he expect her to keep waiting? She got out of the car and walked to him, her pristine nursing shoes crunching in the gravel.

He looked up from his device and shook his head at her. "Blackface? Really?"

She stopped dead, then turned to go. Why had she hoped for

anything other than more judgment from him, of all people?

More than anything she wanted her mother, but that obviously wasn't going to happen. Where could she find any kind of support? Would Ruth be home? Would Ruth be able to contain her disgust?

But then his hand was on her shoulder, and Joe was saying, "Hey!" and then "Are you crying?" The answer must have been obvious, because he pulled her into a hug. "Oh jeez, Eudora. You always did have a big mouth."

She cried and hiccupped into his *Joseph Gagnon Landscaping LLC* polo shirt while he patted her back. After a while, she was conscious of him guiding them both back towards the house, up the porch steps, through the front door, and into the house, which didn't appear to have changed much from their high school days. He sat her down at the same old chair at the same old yellow kitchen table they'd shared so many times when his mother was alive. "Cup of coffee?" he asked. "Or maybe a shot of something? Or both?"

"Coffee." She grabbed a napkin from the old napkin holder and blew her nose.

He set to work with a coffee maker, which also looked very old, though it might have just been stained.

The calico cat from her last visit jumped up on the table and meowed for attention.

"Shoo!" Joe yelled, and the cat jumped down and flounced off. He said, "That's my fault. Mom would kill me if she saw the way I let her jump up there."

"Is she new?" Dori asked.

"New to you. Betty. Mom got her a couple of years before...." He stopped. "Before I came back home."

The Gagnons had always had cats and the Bardwells had always had dogs, but after the slow and horrifyingly expensive death of her father's beloved chocolate lab General, Dori hadn't dared to take in any other animals. "I just got fired," she said.

He looked over from his gathering of mugs and other coffee-serving paraphernalia. "From the nursing home?"

"Yeah. I don't know about the grocery store yet." She should probably tell him she didn't take it with milk and sugar anymore. On the other hand, maybe she could use a little extra sweetness and light.

"Neither of those jobs is irreplaceable," he said.

"They might be for me. Now that everyone thinks I'm some kind of racist."

He grimaced sympathetically. "So you saw the news this morning."

"It was on the TV, too?" She slumped a little more. "God!"

The coffeemaker started hissing and dripping. Joe leaned against the counter and looked down at her. "Who could resist a story like that? Bedford Bardwell's only surviving daughter makes blackface joke. It's literary and political without requiring anyone to actually, you know, read a book."

She wrapped her arms around herself and dropped her head onto the table.

The edge was really rather grimy, wasn't it?

A large hand patted her head. "These things fade away as fast as they blow up. You might even be better off, in the long run."

That brought her head up. "Better off? How's that?"

"Apparently *Tea and Slavery* has already jumped into the #1 spot at Amazon. That should pay for a roof repair, at least, if it lasts."

Her father would have been happy to hear about strong sales again. But would he have been willing to have his daughter labeled a racist to get it there?

Maybe.

Joe said, "Look, worst case scenario, I'll hire you. The work is hard, but the pay isn't bad. I'm just not sure how much satisfaction you'll find in landscaping compared to, you know, wiping butts and emptying bedpans."

He ignored her glare and put a tall mug of coffee in front of her, then a little jug of milk, a sugar bowl full of hard lumps because it clearly hadn't been used in a while, and a spoon. He grabbed his own mug of black coffee and sat down across from her. "I do wonder what the hell you were thinking, though, telling a reporter something like that."

"I didn't tell her!" She decided to take token amounts of milk and sugar, mostly because she hadn't stopped him from setting it all out. "It came up during the follow-up. She asked me to confirm it. Someone had already told her. That must be why she asked you about the racial stuff. I explained to her I had said it as a joke, and that's how she reported. I didn't think it would be smart to lie about whether I'd said it, given that plenty of people could have heard it."

"Including Marjorie?"

"Yeah."

They sat in a silence for a moment.

Joe said, "Why does she hate you?"

"I don't know if she hates me. She just wants her own way. She wants to *neutralize* me." She sipped her coffee. Token or not, the milk and sugar were comforting. "Sometimes I think she expected us to look on her as a replacement for Mama, or something, and we just didn't."

He grunted. "Could be. She doesn't have any children of her own."

"Thank God," Dori said, before realizing it was mean and might well apply to her someday. "Though maybe having children would have made her nicer." It hadn't made her father less drunk, though, had it?

Or maybe it had. Maybe he would have ended up in a ditch in his twenties if he hadn't had a family.

Silence fell for a bit. She drank coffee and looked around. It was a bit less cluttered than it had been when Mrs. Gagnon was alive, because there were no trays of baked goods waiting for a hungry teenage boy and his girlfriend to consume them. The effect was tidy, but it also seemed to her just about every surface could use a good scrubbing.

Joe drank his coffee and watched her. "This was a smart place to come. I doubt anyone will think to find you here."

"You think they're looking?"

"I don't know. I would imagine some reporters might be interested in hearing something from you about now. Your father was so private it probably makes the story more enticing. You mean to tell me you haven't heard from young Robert yet?"

"I don't know. I haven't been home yet."

"I guess not having a phone with you can be good in some ways," he said. "Look. I have some advice. I took a course in public relations in college. If anyone from the press approaches you, politely tell them you'll be making a statement soon. And then, if they keep asking questions, just walk away. Whatever you do, don't say 'No comment.' That always makes you sound guilty."

Her heart began to thump again. "You think I'll have to make a statement?" She'd escaped her local notoriety for that infamous "no" to Joe's proposal by going away to college. The plane crash had brought a buzz of national media attention down on them, but she'd been insulated from it by her own shock and grief, as well as the efforts of people like Charlie and Marjorie. She and Salinger had never had to say a word to the media themselves – they'd merely had to accept all those condolences at the funeral.

Joe said, "You're going to want to make an apology, obviously. But you want to get it right, and you want to keep it from becoming a free-for-all. So ... just stall them until we can get everything set up. Or stay hidden. You're welcome to stay here, if you want."

"Who's 'we'?"

"The trustees."

"Oh." Right. He was doing this in his capacity as a trustee.

"Meanwhile, I recommend you don't look at anything. No news on TV, no Internet. It'll just make you feel bad."

She'd have to go to the library to check the internet anyway. For a wild moment she wondered if they might bar her from the public library, too. "I wonder what Maya Davis thinks about all this."

He winced. "She's at the house?"

"Probably." Once she'd had her own key, Maya had stopped arriving before Dori left for work.

"Well. Like I said, you're welcome to stay here." His phone pinged and he looked at it. "They've just called an emergency board meeting for tonight."

"Do I have to go?"

"You can't. It's an executive session to deal with the 'crisis.'" He gave her a pinched smile. "I'm afraid I really need to get back to work if I'm going to make that. But you can hang out here, if you want. Take a nap, even." He nodded at the cat that was sitting and staring at them. "Betty will be happy to keep you company."

Dori got up and put her cup in the sink, giving it a rinse as she always had in the past. The old porcelain sink was stained and held dirty breakfast dishes. The old linoleum floor was a bit sticky, too. It was kind of reassuring to see Joe didn't have every aspect of his life in perfect condition. She was tempted to stay and clean for him, but that was surely too much like being a girlfriend. She leaned down to pet the cat, but the cat shied away, and Dori was in no mood to cope with feline rejection on top of everything else. "Thanks, but I'll go. And thank you for the coffee. I really just needed someone to talk to."

"Anytime. I'll let you know what happens tonight."

"Thanks. Say hi to Lisa for me," she said, and pecked him on the cheek.

"Okay." His smile was bemused.

Chapter 26

She drove past two television satellite vans parked on the road in front of her house, sped down the long driveway, parked next to Maya's car, and rushed into the kitchen to a ringing phone that stopped before she could get there. The ancient answering machine had 12 messages on it and was blinking "memory full."

The first two were from reporters, one local, one in Georgia. She stopped the playback when the third was yet another reporter.

It took her a while to find Maya, who wasn't responding to calls of "Hello?" Dori found her on the floor in front of the old sofa in her dad's study, various manuscript pages arranged around her. Tinny music could be heard leaking from her earbuds.

"Hi!" Dori yelled.

Maya jumped, then took her earbuds out and gave her a startlingly huge grin. "Why, Mizz Dori! Does mistress wan' me get the big ol' fan, try and keep her cooooool in this awfa' heat?"

Dori decided she should probably just go sit in her room and accept her life was going to be shit for days, months, maybe even years. "You saw the news."

"Did you really say that?"

"Yes. It was a joke. A bad, stupid, horrible joke."

"I'll say." Maya smirked. "I tried to use it as an excuse to get out of this sweat lodge, but Dad said your original point was 'inelegantly put, but not unwarranted.'"

Maya's father had defended her?

"He also said you probably don't know shit about blackface. Not that he put it exactly like that."

What was to know? "It's white people in black make-up," Dori said. *Duh.*

"Oh, no, no, girl. Are you telling me you've never heard of minstrel shows? You really *don't* know shit." Maya pulled out her phone and found something on it. "Here. Watch this."

Dori dropped onto the sofa. In the video, a white woman and a white man in blackface performed a routine that highlighted all the ways in which the supposedly black man was stupid and lazy. They even made jokes about him being a monkey. Dori peered down at it, surprised to see genuinely black musicians behind him. How could they stand to participate? She couldn't stand it and she wasn't even black. "Okay, that's just awful," she said, and handed it back. "You're right, I had no idea it was that bad." She dropped her head back on the sofa and stared at the ceiling. The paint up there was beginning to peel. Was the flat roof leaking, too? "They're all like that?"

"No, but you get the idea."

"So I'm screwed."

"You are," Maya agreed, just as the phone started ringing again. "It's been doing that all morning." She leafed through the pile of papers in her lap, frowning. "Maybe this is generational karma for the way your father stored his shit."

Dori rolled her head towards her. "Yeah, there were regular crises when he couldn't find important things. Mom was pretty good at figuring it out, if it existed in the real world. They'd bring me in when he couldn't find it on the computer." She'd actually been pretty handy with them once upon a time. It felt so long ago.

Maya said, "So why haven't you published a book?"

Dori squinted at her. "Because I haven't written one?"

Maya shook her head. "You're the only surviving daughter of Bedford Bardwell and it's never even occurred to you to write one? You have no idea how easy that makes it! There are writers who would *kill* to be you. Hell, any agent worth his salt would find you a ghost writer to write a book *for* you. Are you telling me his agent never even asked?"

"You think they'd hire a ghost writer for the racist girl?"

"Oh, hell, yes. That just makes people more curious. In fact, this could be what you write about. Call it *BLACKFACE*. In capital letters. There. Remember I told you that when you get your huge advance."

"I don't want to be a writer," Dori said. "Writers are assholes."

"That title might work, too."

Dori laughed. "You want some iced tea?"

"The real stuff, not that powdered shit? And sweet?"

Could anyone possibly be more high-maintenance? But Dori's mother would have appreciated Maya's standards. "The real stuff. And sweet."

"Then yes, please."

When Dori returned with two tall glasses already beaded with condensation, Maya joined her on the old sofa. "Oh, yeah. You know how to make it right," she said, after gulping half of it down. "Thank you." She put her glass down and turned to face Dori directly. Her back was straight and tall, and Dori straightened too, sensing something formal was about to happen.

Maya said, "Dori, it seems to me you need an official black friend."

Dori stared at her a moment, then let a nervous laugh out.

Maya said, "And I am available."

Was she serious, or was this some kind of set-up? Dori looked from Maya's face down to the iced tea still gripped in her hands. What the hell was she supposed to say? "That's cool," she hazarded.

"Your official black friend," Maya said, as if it were important to clarify that.

"I don't think I understand."

"It's a professional position. It means I have to get something out of it, too." Maya raised her eyebrows, as if waiting for an answer.

For a hysterical moment, she wondered if Maya might just be trying to entrap her in yet another awful racial faux-pas. Was she miked? Was there a hidden camera somewhere? She cast a few pointless looks around the room. "I just got fired. I don't have any money to hire a 'professional' black friend if I even wanted to, which I can't say I do, because frankly that sounds really, really weird."

Maya grinned. "It *is* weird, isn't it? But my dad has built a very good life out of being the official black friend of people who are rich as fuck."

Like Robert Putney, presumably. Dori had assumed there was

probably some sort of quid pro quo involved, at the very least benefiting Brooke College. "He calls it being their official black friend?"

"Oh hell no. Well, maybe a little behind their backs, when he's had a glass or two. But if you ever say I told you that, I'll deny it."

Apparently there was no secret taping under way, then. Then again, people were always filming things and then editing them to make them say whatever they wanted. And Maya had been smart enough not to say it in a room full of people. "I really just don't have anything to offer you. Unless this is about my dad's papers again."

She stiffened. *Was* it? Had Maya perhaps been sent specifically to make that attempt? Had this whole thing been a set-up?

"I know you don't have money," Maya said. "You're like some poor little princess whose fortune is tied up in India, or something. But the potential is there. And you've got something I need more than money – you've got a story that's genuinely newsworthy."

"God!" Dori said. "Like I need more of that!"

"But you do, girlfriend. Right now, only one side of the story is getting out there. Here you are, this sweet little white girl who made one stupid remark that's been taken out of context and suddenly her life is turned upside down. People will just eat up the true story of how you found yourself in this situation. Remember how I told you I want to make documentaries?"

Dori's suspicion of being set up only deepened.

Maya said, "I thought this situation was already interesting before this happened. Here you are, living the desperate life of the working poor in this crumbling mansion, the only survivor of a famously reclusive American novelist..."

"I have a brother!"

"Okay, here you are, you and your brother, living a hardscrabble life in this..."

"He doesn't live here anymore."

Maya glared at her.

"Seriously," Dori said. "It's not that interesting. It's just pathetic."

"That's where you're wrong." Maya deepened her voice. "After having such a father, and being raised in liberal New England, how did Eudora Bardwell turn out to be a notorious racist?"

"Hey!"

She kept her announcer's voice going: "See how the tortured politics of race in America can have unexpected, life-altering consequences!" She grinned. "You see? Now it's more interesting. For literary types, anyway."

"Only because I'm suddenly this awful, notorious racist!"

"Yes, exactly!" Maya said. "That's your new reality. But you can have a hand in shaping that, too, you know. You can change the narrative with some help from your new official black friend. Will you at least think about it?"

Joe had promised her it would die down quickly. "Anything I do might just make it worse."

"Girl, I've known you for what? A week and a half? I already know you're not a racist. At least not any more than the average clueless white girl is. But the world out there, it doesn't know. And it never will if you don't get the word out. Every time they look you up, there you'll be, making that same stupid blackface joke."

Dori looked down at Maya's phone on the table, thinking of the awful video she'd just watched. She had never thought of herself as clueless about race, but her confidence was shaken.

Maya said, "This is not all on you, anyway. Nobody would care what you said if your white father hadn't written the most famous book about the evils of slavery. But then he left the South and raised his big white family in a big white house in what might just be the whitest little corner of New England, and he never even once took you back home to visit, and he even lied about your family. And personally I just really want to know: What the fuck was up with that?"

Dori had begun to wonder that herself. "I don't want to smear my dad's reputation."

"It's not smearing," Maya said. "It's just the truth. My Dad is an expert in your dad, you know. He talks about him over the dinner table all the time. And he doesn't know the answer to any of those questions, and he doesn't go try to find out because he's an English professor and to them if it's not in some text some-where it might as well not even exist. But wouldn't you like to know? Because I think it's pretty fucking weird."

Dori looked at her. Could Maya really be any kind of friend to her, even an "official" one? She existed on a completely different plane – one with ample money and connections and education, never mind the racial divide. And it could still be part of a set-up. "Have you discussed this with your father and Mr. Putney?"

Maya scowled. "I told my dad about it. As always, he told me everybody and his brother thinks they can make documentaries and I'd be better off using this little job as a springboard to a better one at one of Putney's operations."

If it was a lie it was perfectly delivered to lull Dori's suspicions.

"Speaking of assholes," Maya added.

Dori couldn't help a smile. "My number one focus has to be to find a new job. I have bills to pay."

"I understand that," Maya said. "Let me see what I can come up with."

How could she expect to "come up with" something? Dori sat there, nursing her tea-and-half-melted ice cubes, while Maya re-turned to her sorting.

The optics of the scene suddenly struck Dori as regrettable. Here she was, a white woman, collapsed on the sofa drinking iced tea, while the black woman worked. "Do you want me to help?"

Maya gave her an appraising look. "I'm getting paid for this, and you're not. And honestly, you don't really look like you're up for much of anything right now. If you want to just hang out, though, I'll probably have some questions as I go along."

Dori nodded and leaned back, blinking back tears. Both Joe and Maya had responded to her with more kindness than she had expected. Probably more than she deserved. They might both have other agendas at work, too, of course, but at this point she was grateful for any mercies.

That was when the doorbell rang.

Chapter 27

Hours later, Dori felt as if she were turning into some kind of statue. She sat there on the old sofa in her father's study, while Maya left once again to deal with someone at the front door. Maya hadn't waited to be formally accepted as official black friend – she'd simply started answering the door when Dori had shown no inclination to do so. Maya had also disconnected the phone. And ordered pizza to be delivered for dinner. And paid for it.

If she was also handing out her card and explaining she was working on a documentary about Bedford Bardwell's legacy and would be releasing news about it soon – which she was – that wasn't enough to make Dori stop her.

Maya appeared in the doorway. "There's some guy called Joe Gagnon who tells me he's your friend?"

"Oh. Yeah, he is," Dori said. "You can let him in."

Joe picked his way through the paper stacks and stood over her. "How are you?" he asked.

Was it not obvious? But perhaps it was, because then he sat down and took her hand. She exchanged a quick look with Maya, who raised her eyebrows in obvious interest. Dori realized she needed to make introductions, but the doorbell rang again. Maya rolled her eyes and left.

Joe said, "I see she didn't beat you up."

"No, she's been great."

The board, he told her, had decided it was time for her and Salinger to leave, so the house could be devoted to the purpose her father had imagined for it. They would each receive a settlement of some kind for their interest in it, which would be determined after a market appraisal was done, and they'd have time and if necessary some additional funds to make the transition; this was just the official notice. "Unofficially, Charlie wanted me to let you know you could fight this, though the cost of doing that would eat away at any money you might get out of it."

"I'm not going to fight it," Dori said wearily. It was what she'd wanted all along, really. And Salinger was already gone.

They also wanted Dori to give an official statement to the press the next day. A publicist had already drafted one for her. He pulled a folded-up paper from his pocket and unfolded it before handing it over to her. "Officially, you have the right to suggest changes to the wording. Unofficially, the board wants you to just read it, refuse to take any questions, and disappear for a while."

She stared down at it, stung by the idea she should just "disappear." Especially as spoken by him.

He put a hand on her shoulder. "It's not as bad as it sounds. Putney has given you a pretty generous travel stipend to go lay low for the next two weeks while we get this stuff sorted out." He pulled an envelope out of his other shirt pocket, took out the letter in it, unfolded it, and put it in her hand. It was a credit card and something headed "Letter of Understanding." Joe said, "This allows you up to two hundred dollars a day for two weeks. If necessary, it will be extended, but Putney says that should be enough time for things to die down. There's a spending limit on it, so don't try to go over. He's charging these as travel expenses associated with an editorial project. In return you need to agree to write a personal essay or at least sit for a second interview upon your return. If you write it and they publish it you will also be paid for the article." He sat back. "It's not a bad deal."

She laid both items on the coffee table in front of her. "He got me fired!"

"He had no way of knowing what you'd said, or that it would end up in the article and then go viral."

"Are you sure about that?"

"He said he doesn't interfere with editorial. I don't know. Maybe it's true, maybe it's not. But he could hardly have known ahead of time you'd said that about wearing blackface."

She closed her eyes. No. Unless Marjorie had told him.

He grabbed her hand again and squeezed it. "You're going to be all right in the end. This will *all* pass."

She nodded, and sighed, then pulled her hand free so she could read the statement they'd prepared for her. It was short and impersonal, a statement of apology without any excuses or even any explanation. She said, "I didn't realize how awful what I said was. I bet a lot of people don't. Shouldn't I try to explain?"

"No," he said. "Anything you say right now, in the middle of all this heightened attention, has the potential to get used against you. It will sound like you're trying to make excuses. The publicist said it's better to just take your medicine as quickly as possible and get it over with. Maybe in that article, after things have cooled down a bit, and you can really weigh your words..."

They didn't trust her to say the right thing. With good reason, obviously. The anxious sense of shame she'd been feeling all day congealed into nausea. She looked away, taking a long, trembling breath to try to settle her stomach.

He put a hand on her upper arm and rubbed it comfortingly. "Where can you go?" he asked.

He hadn't offered his own house this time. "No idea. Besides, I have a shift tomorrow afternoon."

"Are you sure?"

Actually, no. She got up and went to the kitchen, where she kept the number she needed, plugged in the phone, and called the grocery store.

No, in fact, they did not want her for her shift the next day. She wasn't fired, but she also wouldn't be scheduled for any hours for a while. "I tried to leave a message, but your machine was full," the manager said. "It's nothing personal. We just want you and everyone else to be safe. You understand that, right?"

"Safe?" she asked, her eyes turning to Joe, who had followed her into the kitchen. Night had fallen, and he was closing the café curtains she usually left open.

There was a pause on the other end. "You've been getting some death threats?"

"I *have*?" She'd heard of such things happening to people who'd landed in some kind of infamy – like that dentist who'd killed a beloved African lion so he could hang its head on his wall – but she couldn't believe anyone thought her offense actually rose to that level.

She hung up the phone and stood there, looking at Joe. "Death threats?" Had he known about that? But he didn't look surprised.

"It's bluster," he said. "Putney said it's very common. People think they can say whatever they want on social media, because it's so anonymous. And you're a young woman, which tends to bring out the worst trolls. It's best not to even look. Definitely never engage. And these people almost never actually do anything."

"Almost never?" She leaned against the wall. "I don't have any idea where to go."

"How about Georgia?" Maya said, from the doorway.

They both turned and stared at her.

"Let's go find your people," she said. "That reporter did, after all. I'll drive – if you let me film it."

"Are you insane?" Joe said.

Dori realized she still hadn't made any introductions. "Sorry. Maya Davis, Joe Gagnon. He's a board member, so he already knows about your project here. He's a landscaper." For once she said it without being snide.

He offered his hand, and Maya shook it rather formally. "Dori said you're Professor Davis's daughter?"

"Yes." Maya said. "I'm also a documentary filmmaker."

Joe lifted his chin. "Oh, yeah? What documentaries have you made?"

Maya's chin rose, too. "This will be my first."

Dori said, "Maya has been really helpful."

Joe shot a concerned look at Dori. "Is she already filming?"

Maya said, "I just got my first footage out front. That's some crazy shit out there. I'd also love to get some of you two, if you don't mind. You have an interesting kind of energy going on."

In the appalled silence that followed, the doorbell rang. Maya sighed. "I'll get it." She turned to go, but paused long enough to say, "I'd just like to point out I am more than earning my keep here."

They both listened to her heels clack down the hallway towards the front door.

Joe said, "Why would you even consider taking part in a documentary? That's the kind of thing that got you into this mess in the first place."

"I want to meet my grandparents."

"So go meet them on your own. Look, you can stay at my place tonight if you want. We'll figure out a place for you to go. And at least that way you'll have someone with you."

Because of those death threats that almost never resulted in anything? Or was he just trying to keep her from making things worse with Maya? She was grateful in either case, but some devil made her ask, "What would Lisa think?"

He flushed. "I'm not married to her, you know." His phone suddenly blasted a different tone than the simple ping she'd heard earlier, a measure or two from a popular love song.

Perfect timing. "You can get that," she said sweetly.

"It can wait." His flush deepened, and he turned off his phone.

Dori said, "I'm actually very interested in Maya's proposal. I enjoy hanging out with her." Meeting her new-found grandparents also seemed a lot less scary with someone else along.

"She works for Putney."

"She doesn't like him any more than I do."

"She's on his payroll."

He didn't get it. How could he? He didn't know Maya. She just hoped she did.

She'd need to pack. For two weeks, or for one week with a laundromat visit in the middle? Summer was surely even hotter in the South. She turned toward her bedroom, calculating, and noticed that down the hall Maya had her arms flung out and her body planted in the doorway, effectively blocking entrance to someone. She couldn't hear the conversation, but Maya's body language suggested some irritation.

Joe put a hand on her arm. "If your relatives haven't shown any interest in you in all this time, what are the chances you're going to actually enjoy meeting them now?" She recalled him once saying his dad's parents had disappeared from his life almost as fast as his dad had. "And even if you want to go, that doesn't mean you should do it with some girl you barely know who wants to film the whole thing. Who, again, is working for Putney."

She looked up at him. "So am I, if I use that debit card. I don't think she's much more of a fan than I am, though." She lowered her voice. "Did you tell anyone about the manuscript?"

"No! Why, did you?"

"No!" Dori went to the refrigerator and poured him a glass of iced tea without asking him if he wanted any. "Here."

He took it and drank it down. "Thank you." He put the glass in the sink. "Where did you put that debit card? You should put it in your wallet before you forget it, or lose it."

He was a nag, Joe was. But he was a nag who meant well. She headed back to her dad's study, but Maya turned and asked her, "Do you want me to let in Ruth Moscatiello and Robert Putney-Lewis?" She bugged her eyes a little at that name.

Dori exchanged a quick glance with Joe. "Yeah, they can come in."

Joe scowled. Maya didn't look thrilled either.

Ruth walked in and gave her a hug. Robert hung back, exchanging cold stares with Joe.

"Are you here as a friend or as a reporter?" Joe asked.

"Friend," Robert said. "Though I'd be happy to do an interview if Dori were willing."

"Nope," Dori said. "I only have enough iced tea for one of you, but I'm making more. Come on back to the kitchen."

Chapter 28

Later that night, as they sat laughing in the ratty old TV room, it struck Dori she hadn't actually had a group of people she could call friends in her house since high school. Robert Jr. and Maya had shared anecdotes about his dad that made them all laugh, and Ruth some funny stories about the psych ward. Joe had told a couple of horror stories about unreasonable clients. She'd shared the time one of her male patients had disappeared while her back was turned, only to be found naked, except for his shoes and socks, waltzing by himself in the empty dining room. In telling it she'd suddenly gotten tearful, but Robert had leapt into that awkward moment with another funny tale.

Robert had also gone out at one point to get donuts and coffee at a local gas station. The doorbell ringing had stopped. Perhaps the formal announcement about the next day's press conference satisfied the reporters, or maybe it was already too late even for reporters. She couldn't be *that* important.

She ought to call it a night, too, she knew. She hadn't packed for a trip to Georgia. She hadn't listened to the messages that had filled her answering machine. She hadn't spent any time memorizing her bland "statement." She hadn't even thought about what she might need to do before hopping in a car and disappearing for two weeks.

Joe's phone sang a love song yet again and he frowned and left the room briefly. Not long after, the doorbell rang, and he stood up. "That'll be Lisa," he said, and left to get it.

He reappeared with Lisa and introduced her to everyone she hadn't already met. He didn't introduce her as his girlfriend, but Lisa wrapped an arm around his waist, making it clear enough. Maya shook Lisa's hand and then looked a question at Dori. Dori just smiled – until Lisa emptied her shopping bag and plopped a large bag of chips, a container of dip, and a six-pack of beer down on the old wooden chest that served as a coffee table.

Right in front of Ruth.

"Go for it!" Lisa cried, and sat herself down cross-legged on the floor in front of it all.

Nobody moved. Everyone watched Ruth, who'd gone a little pale and was staring fixedly at the beer.

Lisa took a bottle and held it out to Dori. "Joe said you were all here being supportive, so I figured I'd join you. Rough day, huh?"

Dori looked at Joe, who winced apologetically at her. She shook her head to the proffered beer. "That's really sweet of you, Lisa, but I think it's a little late for us to start partying now. Can I take a rain check?"

Lisa said, "I have a little weed on me, if you'd prefer that."

Maya stood up abruptly. "Wow, I need to go get some sleep. Nice to meet you all. Dori, I'll see you in the morning. We're on for the road trip?"

"Yes," Dori said.

Joe looked sharply at her but said nothing. He hadn't resumed his seat, which left him looming over his girlfriend. "Lisa, we should let Dori get some sleep."

Dori couldn't see the look Lisa gave him, but she could see her turn back and look straight at Robert as she said, "Or we could take this elsewhere."

He smiled at her, but said nothing. "Want an escort?" He asked Maya.

"No thanks," she said. "Good night!" she said more generally, and there were general cries of "good night" and "nice to meet you."

"I'll see you out," Joe said to Maya as she passed him by, not offering her any choice in the matter. "Is that your car next to Dori's?"

"Yeah," she said warily, and they left the room.

Lisa's face was still pink. "Sorry. I guess my timing sucks. If Joe had answered my *first* call..."

Dori said, "I think as a board member he's had his hands full. It hasn't just been a rough day for me."

Ruth said, "You don't actually seem all that traumatized to me."

What, were they competing, now, to see whose life could get more traumatic? But perhaps Ruth was right. At some point during the evening Dori's misery and shame had faded and she had begun to enjoy herself. "It's been nice having company," she said. Maybe she shouldn't have rained on Lisa's party. Part of her wished they could all stay there all night, distracting her from any further thought of what she had done. And it wasn't Lisa's fault she didn't know about Ruth's drinking.

"What did Maya mean by road trip?" Robert asked. Dori looked at him. The whole evening might have all been officially off the record, but he was still a reporter.

"It's a long story," Dori said, and stood up. "But I think your dad already knows about it." Maya had already arranged to get excused from archiving for a couple of weeks.

He grimaced and got up. Lisa and Ruth rose as well. Lisa looked wistfully down at her unopened chips, dip, and six-pack. "Take it with you," Dori suggested. "We'll try this again someday. Just a little earlier, okay?"

Lisa's "Oh, okay – thanks" struck her as tinged with just a bit of contempt. The young woman re-bagged her booty and headed out, followed closely by Robert. He offered Dori a sardonic salute as he passed.

Did Lisa think she was patronizing her? Being a party pooper? But Dori couldn't really bring herself to care.

Ruth waited for the others to clear out to give her a tight hug. "Here's where I'm supposed to tell you to take it one day at a time. Or put it in the hands of a higher power. Or whatever bullshit works for you."

Dori chuckled. "Thanks."

"Just be glad I didn't knock that little bimbo over the head and steal her beer. At least not yet. She'd better not linger too long in the parking lot."

"She works with the state police, if that helps any," Dori said.

"Oh, God. It does!" Ruth said. "Maybe that's why she doesn't mind carrying in past a bunch of cops." She leaned in and lowered her voice. "Do you trust Maya?"

Dori shrugged. "I like her."

Ruth made a face. "Well, good luck. Call me when you get a chance."

Dori nodded and saw her out. Joe and Maya were still conversing next to Maya's car in the thin silvery light cast by the old outside fixture and the kitchen windows above the café curtains. He gestured to Ruth to join them. Robert and Lisa's cars were already headed down the long driveway. The outside was a little cooler than the house, but still muggy, and the hum of cicadas was loud enough to drown out their conversation.

Should she go see what the hell they were discussing so intently? But she suddenly longed for solitude just as fervently as she had enjoyed the company earlier. She closed the door on her now empty house and locked it, surveying the kitchen. Should she make another batch of tea, or was it pointless, given her travel plans? Still, she might need to offer some hospitality to someone in the morning, and tea was pretty much all she had. It seemed unlikely she could get to a market before the next day's insanity commenced. So she started the kettle boiling, set up the big old glass pitcher her mother had taught her to brew tea in, and plugged the answering machine back in, deciding she'd get through the messages at the same time.

She had deleted two messages from reporters when she heard a hard knocking at the kitchen door.

Her heart started thumping. It was probably just a very determined reporter, she told herself, rather than someone who wanted her dead, but when she pulled aside the curtain over the door's window she saw it was Joe, looking at her with some exasperation. When she opened it, he said, "Why'd you lock me out?" His truck was the only vehicle left, she saw. Someone's rear lights were turning onto Main Street.

"I thought you were leaving."

"I'm not leaving you here by yourself. Don't you know how easy it would be to break into this house?"

She peered towards the now-empty road. The TV vans and police cars had gone and the place did suddenly seem very dark and isolated. "Is this about the death threats? The ones you told me I shouldn't worry about?"

"Yep. Do you want me to stay here, or do you want to come to my place?

Why were those the only two choices? "I could use my handy-dandy new debit card and go stay in a motel."

"Yes, you could. I'll just see you safely there, if you don't mind."

She probably should mind, but who was she kidding? He had that gruff thing going she had learned, years earlier, to associate with Joe being protective, and it brought a lump to her throat. In the house, the tea kettle started shrieking, so she backed up, letting him follow her in.

Dealing with the kettle gave her time to get her voice under control. "I appreciate the offer, Joe, I really do, but I need to get ready for tomorrow, and that's going to take a while. I don't want to keep you up all night."

"Then tell me how I can help."

It was a kind offer, especially from someone who looked pretty tired. His beard was far beyond a five o'clock shadow and he looked days overdue for his Republican hair trim. "Could you listen to the rest of these messages and delete any I don't need to do something about?"

"Sure."

"I'll just get some sugar into this while it's still hot." She took the canister down from its shelf. The sugar supply was dipping significantly. She hadn't made this many pitchers of tea in a long time.

He played the next message. This time it was a voice and a name she recognized immediately from the CBS Evening News. The national news. CBS was the only station that came in well without cable, so it was the one she had watched in recent years, when she watched at all.

Those big names she saw on camera actually got on the phone themselves to try to wheedle interviews?

"You said you need to pack?" Joe said. Probably he'd noticed the way she'd stopped her stirring to listen in horror.

"Yes."

"So go pack. I'll let you know when I'm done here."

She left the tea to finish brewing and went.

Chapter 29

She dragged her suitcase out from under the guest bed she'd begun to use even before she'd moved back home permanently. Flannery, who'd had to room with Carson, had eagerly made Dori's old bedroom hers once Dori went away to college. Dori had no desire to take it back from her dead sister. It would have entailed negotiations with the Friends. It would mean coping with the heat of the second floor. And it would require thinking about Flannery more than she could bear.

All the bedrooms except Salinger's were like that.

Her parents had always called the room she was using now part of "the modern wing," along with the large kitchen and the TV room, as well as her dad's study. She'd once asked her mother why they called it that when it had been built at exactly the same time as the rest of the house. "Because that's what it would be if the house were older," she'd said, as if that explained it.

It had never bothered her to sleep alone on the ground floor before, but tonight it occurred to her that her windows could be easily breached, especially since she'd need to leave them open if she didn't want the heat to be unbearable. It would also require little effort to break the glass in the kitchen door, or in the French doors that led from her father's study to the patio. There were still wires on them from an old security system that she could not remember ever actually working, though. Maybe they would serve as a deterrent.

She picked through her clothing, looking for stuff that was not too warm and not too ratty. She didn't lack for cut-off shorts and old t-shirts, but finding something presentable that wasn't a uniform, didn't need laundering, and might pass muster with her mysterious grandparents was trickier.

Down the hall, she could hear messages beginning and being quickly deleted. Joe was being efficient. He always had been. It was an admirable quality, at least when it wasn't being applied to sweeping her out of his life.

She'd only managed to pack the basics when she heard his heavy tread coming down the hall. He stood in the doorway and said, "There weren't any messages you really needed to respond to. Have you heard from Salinger?"

"No. I guess I'll try calling Jenna's place in the morning."

"I'll take care of that for you. He got a debit card, too, so I'm sure he'll be happy to see me. What are you going to wear for the press conference?"

Wear? She stared at him, dumbstruck. Yes, she'd known she was supposed to read a statement. Yet somehow it had not occurred to her she was going to actually be on camera.

He walked into the room, looking curiously about him as he did. She hadn't personalized it all that much, just hung some favorite art she'd borrowed from other rooms and stacked it with books. He said, "A dress, maybe?"

She shoved hangers aside so she could get a little deeper into her closet. "My old prom dress won't do, that's for sure."

He walked over and peered into the closet. "You still have it?"

"Kind of pathetic, right?" She flipped through hangers. A lot of what she had hanging were nursing tunics. She wouldn't need those in Georgia, not unless she decided to stay there and get a job.

Maybe she should, if Georgia proved more hospitable than Western Massachusetts.

"Why are you sleeping down here?" he asked.

"It's cooler." It also had a bigger bed, and she had hoped, incorrectly for the most part, to still have a sex life after returning to Jasper.

Ah, there it was. She pulled out the sedate little black dress she'd stuffed at the very end. "How about this?"

He grimaced. "Isn't that the one you wore to my mom's funeral?"

Oh, so he *had* seen her there. She'd certainly avoided any receiving lines, but she'd liked Mrs. Gagnon too much to skip her funeral just to spite Joe. "Yes. And *my* mom's." Staring at it critically, she realized she had no memory at all of making the purchase. Perhaps Marjorie had just shown up with it. If so, it was another thing she'd never thanked her for. "I'd better make sure it still fits."

"You don't look like you've put on an ounce," Joe said. It wasn't said with any admiration, but he didn't sound critical, at least.

She smiled politely. She hadn't gained weight, but she knew she was out of shape compared to Lisa.

He cleared his throat. "I'm sorry I wasn't there for you, Eu. When they died." He was staring at the dress, but he let his eyes meet hers briefly.

She felt her heart skip a beat and settle into a hard pounding that unnerved her, maybe even pissed her off. She was really too strung out by everything else that had happened to add unexpected intimacy from him on top of it. Especially when something in his eyes made her suddenly quite certain all it would take was a touch to set off something even more intimate. She strove to keep her voice from betraying how rattled she was. "Well, you're here now. I appreciate it."

The moment stretched between them. Then it snapped, hard, when he added, "I suppose wearing that dress might make them feel sorry for you."

Had he always been so good at saying exactly the wrong thing? "Or maybe they'll think I'm trying to manipulate them into feeling sorry for me." She turned away from him.

He seemed oblivious to her irritation. "They might also simply conclude you don't have any money to buy a new dress."

"Which would be just another way to make them feel sorry for me. Right? But nobody is going to notice it's the same dress. Who notices stuff like that? And the only reason I don't have another is I haven't had any occasion to go get one. They're only five bucks at the thrift store. I can afford that."

"The thrift store? I'm glad you've finally learned the wisdom of my ways!"

She sighed. "I'd better try it on, just to be sure." She looked at him and waited.

It took a moment, but he got the message. He pointed at the hall. "I'll be out there." He closed the door behind him and then called, "You didn't used to be so shy!"

"You didn't use to date women who wax their hoo-hahs!" she retorted, and heard him chuckle.

The dress still fit, but it *was* tighter – tight enough that getting the zipper all the way up in the back risked catching some skin. She needed help. But if she showed him her bare back, he might interpret that as permission to make a move.

And what if he did?

Was that why Lisa had shown up at the house so late? Had she sensed how things might be going?

She stared at herself in the mirror. What kind of a woman was she, to even consider it?

But why did Lisa deserve her loyalty? "We're not married," he'd said earlier, when she'd advocated for Lisa against herself, and suddenly she felt a terrible ruthlessness settling in. He was right, they weren't married.

Also, Lisa was a ninny.

She opened the door and turned her back to him. "Can you zip it up for me?"

She heard his sharp intake of breath, felt him raise the zipper carefully, and then nothing. Apparently he was going to behave himself.

But then his hands were resting on her hips, almost circling her waist, and she could feel his hot breath on her bare neck. She let her head fall back, baring her neck to his lips, and then she turned into his hungry mouth.

And then it was all about getting out of the dress she'd just gotten into.

They lay together in her bed, hands clasped between them. There had been a gallant attempt at post-coital spooning, but it was just too hot.

"I've missed you," he said.

"I've missed you, too." She turned her nose into his shoulder and nuzzled it briefly. "I think you've expanded your repertoire."

He chuckled. "You have, too, if I'm remembering correctly."

Was their entire love life so vague a memory? Just how busy had he been in the interim? Irked, she stood up and grabbed her robe off the back of the door. "I should go take a shower."

"Can I join you?" he asked.

She looked at him, a lovely naked man spread out across her bed, gazing at her with something that looked an awful lot like unfiltered affection.

They'd never shared a shower before. They'd never had her whole house to themselves before. It was a little astonishing to realize they were now adults and could, in fact, do whatever they wanted with each other and no parents anywhere would be able to raise an objection. "Yeah, okay," she said, and lifted her robe to flash her bare ass at him as she sashayed out the door.

"I'm going to be useless tomorrow," she said later, as they settled back into her bed for what promised to be no more than a couple of hours of sleep. "I hope Maya is getting some sleep."

He sat up. "You're still going?"

She sat up, too, roused to battle by his tone. "Why wouldn't I?"

"Hello?" he said, hand signaling between them.

It was reassuring that he seemed to feel what had passed between them was significant enough to require a major change in plans. But what did he think, that one – okay, two – bouts of love-making had settled everything between them?

Her heart began to race. Was he going to freak out when she rebuffed him? "This was really great," she said, echoing his hand signal. "I *loved* this. But I'd still like to meet my grandparents. And the board still wants me to disappear for a while, don't they? And what are you planning to do – dump Lisa retroactively?"

He scowled and looked off into the distance. "I wouldn't be the least bit surprised if she's in bed with Robert Putney-Lewis as we speak. She'd do anything to get in that summer house again. That's probably why she showed up here tonight."

"I thought she was acting pretty possessive of you. And even if she is in bed with him, you can't assume she is. That would be rude."

"Rude!"

"Yeah, rude."

He shook his head. "I think this situation has moved beyond etiquette, Miss Bardwell."

"You *are* cheating on her, you know. Who knew you could be so *bad?*" She hit him gently in the arm with a fist. "And as much as I might appreciate having some company in the dog house, your transgression hasn't been made public yet. We might be able to save *your* reputation."

His brows drew together. If he was suddenly thinking about the possible ramifications of blatantly cheating on the fire chief's daughter in a small town, that was probably a good thing. She added, "Leaving your truck parked outside the house all night probably wasn't the best idea."

"I was just protecting you," he said. "Death threats, remember? I didn't know this was going to happen."

"Right. The thought never crossed your mind."

He smirked.

She said, "So how good are you at pretending outraged innocence when somebody suggests it?" He hadn't been very gifted at lying back in the day.

He sighed.

They weren't going to get any sleep at all, were they? She yawned and slid down flat on the bed again. He echoed her yawn and then did the same, until they were shoulder to shoulder.

She said, "So here's the plan. I go away for two weeks, and you use the time to dump Lisa."

He stared up at the ceiling. "If she's upset about it, her father's going to kill me. Mind you, I don't think she will be. But you never really know."

"Tell me about it," Dori said, with an edge.

He said nothing. Apparently he had no desire to open up further discussion of their break, and she let it go. She said, "I recommend the time-honored technique of all weenie men everywhere: Make it so obvious you're just not into her anymore that she dumps you first." It had certainly been the preferred method of her two short-lived college boyfriends. "You were already kind of starting that, weren't you?"

"Yeah," he admitted.

She smiled wickedly. "Of course, it's not too late to change your mind. She is lovely."

He rolled over on top of her, pinning her. "You've always been the one for me, and you know it. I imprinted on you at a young age, like a stupid baby duck or something."

"Thanks!" But she knew what he meant. It did feel involuntary.

He added, "As a sex partner, I mean, not like you're my mother. *That* would be weird." He kissed her, and she kissed him back.

It was hard not to feel all was right with the world again just because they were doing this, even though she knew she shouldn't.

He said, "Do me a favor. Don't let me screw this up this time."

She stared back, her focus shifting from one intense hazel eye to the other. How the hell was she supposed to do that?

"I'm putting you in charge," he said. "When it's time for the relationship to move along to the next stage, you just say so."

"Are you kidding me?" she protested. "That'll never work. You would hate that. We'll work things out together, like normal people do."

"So you agree – we're together? That's official?"

"Unofficially official. You still have to tell Lisa. But, yes. Yes."

He kissed her again, and didn't stop.

Not that she wanted him to. Yeah, there wasn't going to be any sleep at all. She was going to be exhausted the next day. Walking might just be a little problematic, too.

Chapter 30

"What the hell is Stuckey's?" Dori asked Maya, after having seen more signs for it than she would have believed possible.

She'd pretty much slept through the first day and night of their trip. She could barely even remember reading her statement to a crowd of people while cameras clicked and whirred and lights went off in her face. She'd been so sleep-deprived and stressed at the time she had felt weirdly disconnected from reality. She'd tried to ground herself by focusing her thoughts on the man standing behind her with a discreet hand on the small of her back, but in some ways that had just contributed even more to feeling like it was all a dream.

She and Joe were back together again? Really?

"Basically, just gas stations," Maya said.

They were already hundreds of miles from home. The morning had begun with some pretty scenery in Virginia, but at some point the interstate had become one interminable flat road between forests draped in Spanish moss. Watching ripples of summer heat distort the horizon had been fascinating for about five minutes, maybe ten. That left road signs for visual entertainment, most of them promising towel outlets, fast food restaurants, retribution for sinners, something called "South of the Border," various Florida tourist attractions, and Stuckey's. Lots and lots of Stuckey's.

Maya added, "With stuff to eat. Especially pecans."

"It's peh-CAHNS, not PEE-cahns."

"Girlfriend, my parents are both from Georgia. It's PEE-cahns."

"Yeah, well, my parents were Southerners too. And that's not how they say it."

"Maybe your parents were ignorant white trash," Maya said.

Maya was clearly joking, but what if Dori's parents had been white trash? Was that why they'd been so hell-bent on building an ostentatious plantation house?

"Actually," Maya said, "I should warn you we'll be stopping over in Atlanta at some point. My mom is staying there with Big Mama – my grandmother -- this month. We usually do that every August while dad finishes whatever writing project he's working on and gets stuff set up for the fall, but this year Mom went down early."

Too late, Dori thought of everything nasty she'd said about writers. "I didn't realize your father was a writer, too."

"He's not a novelist," Maya said. "I'm sure they're the real assholes."

Dori smiled.

"Although, actually," Maya said, "what I hear is the ones who are wildly successful right away are the ones nobody can live with."

Could be. Her father had often behaved arrogantly. Of course, what came out when he was plastered was something that looked a hell of a lot more like shame. Maybe wild success followed by utter failure could do that.

Yet another road sign proclaimed the importance of stopping at something called "South of the Border." Dori asked what it was.

Maya snorted. "Ticky-tacky old-fashioned tourist trap with Pedro the god-awful stereotypical Mexican. I suppose we could still stop there and try to be ironic as hell about it or something. I just hate to give them any of my business."

"Let's not, then," Dori said. Maya would probably expect to record it. She had her phone set up on the dashboard and had actually filmed Dori answering some questions earlier that day while they drove, mostly about why she hadn't even known she had grandparents living. Dori hadn't been able to tell her much. She remembered that for a "family tree" exercise she'd tried to help Flannery with once, her mother had said, "Just tell your teacher we started fresh with this family. It was better that way."

"That's an interesting choice," Maya had said. "Especially considering your dad wrote a famous novel about the past set in what everyone assumes is a thinly disguised version of the town he grew up in."

"Maybe he was ashamed of it," Dori had replied. "Maybe his family had slaves. Or a minstrel show."

But a new thought occurred. "I wonder if Dad got death threats. Maybe moving north was their way of hiding out."

After she'd read her bland statement in front of the house and then stepped back, Charlie had accepted some questions from the assembled press. One reporter's question had mentioned "eleven threats of death or physical harm on Twitter alone." Dori had leaned back into Joe, wondering how something that sounded like cute little birds could be home to so many terroristic threats.

"Your father *did* get death threats," Maya said. She glanced over at Dori. "Enough that his publisher never forwarded anything without checking it first. There were a few when *Tea and Slavery* first came out, more when it won the Pulitzer, and then a whole lot when it was made into a movie, though most of those went to the actors, not him. How could you not know that?"

"He never said anything about it."

"Haven't you ever looked up your own dad on Wikipedia?"

"Why would I? He's my dad."

Maya shook her head. "Don't go into investigative journalism." Clearly she felt Dori was lacking in sufficient curiosity or ambition or both.

Dori was beginning to agree with her, at least in regard to her own family. How could she have known so little about it? But then again, her parents had discouraged any discussion of their history. It just wasn't done. It would have been like telling the rest of the world her father was often plastered by noon. One did not speak of such things.

Maya shifted into the left lane to pass a slow-moving truck. This was a fairly rare event; Maya was a very conservative driver. Dori was not. She often sped up to pass slowpokes in those precious few places on the curving Mohawk Trail between Greenfield and Jasper where passing was possible. Maya's careful speed on such an open road was frustrating. "You're an awfully cautious driver," she said. She thought about saying "Don't go into auto racing," but didn't.

Maya shot her a hard look. "Which one of us do you think

needs to worry more if we get pulled over?"

Dori flashed back to Janet's explanation of what had happened to Antoine. "Oh," she said.

"Mm-hmmm. It seems to me white people who get death threats never seem to end up dead, compared to black people. And plenty of black people who *don't* get them end up dead."

"Have *you* gotten death threats?" Dori asked.

"Outside of high school? No. Not yet."

Not yet. She spoke as if it were inevitable. Then what she'd said finally registered. "You got death threats in high school? You got death threats in *Vermont*?"

Maya patted her leg. "You're so clueless, sweetie, you really are. You don't think there are nasty racist yahoos in Vermont? You've never noticed anyone driving around with Confederate flags on their truck, or their motorcycle, or their shitty old car? Once I even got the classic noose in my locker. I thought, Yes! I've finally arrived! I really am black! Because, you know, when you grow up in Vermont, it's sometimes possible to forget it for five minutes at a time."

Dori just looked at her. It was the first time Maya's tone had verged into outright bitterness.

"Sorry," Maya said. "Did I scare you? I let my black anger slip for a minute there."

"It *is* kind of scary."

Maya grinned. "I love the way you just come right out and say it. No wonder you're in such big trouble."

No doubt it was why agreeing to make a documentary with Maya was potentially disastrous, too. "Do you think your dad moved to Vermont because of death threats?"

Maya gave her a quick, surprised look. "I never asked. But I doubt it. When you're an academic you pretty much go wherever you can get tenure." But she frowned uncertainly.

They drove for a while in silence. More trees draped in Spanish moss. More heat distortion above the horizon. A car full of young men passed them going fast, blowing its horn. Someone's pasty butt was plastered to the window.

"Speaking of yahoos," Maya said with a roll of her eyes. The car had Pennsylvania plates. "So what were you doing with a Putney in your house last night? I got the impression you're not a fan."

"Oh, Robert's okay. I think. He's just a local reporter."

"And international ladies' man."

Dori laughed. "Well, yeah. Did you ever...?"

"Oh, hell no. He never even tried. Maybe he doesn't like his ladies dark, or maybe my dad told him he'd cut his balls off if he came anywhere near me. He did offer to escort me out to my car, but that might have just been because he's a reporter."

But Joe had been the one to actually do it. "What did Joe want to talk to you about?"

"I think he was trying to figure out if I was up to no good." Maya smiled. "Beat his breast a little about not screwing with you. And he made me put his phone number in my contacts and vice versa, so he could keep in touch. What is up with him, anyway? I figured he was your boyfriend, at least until that girl showed up."

"He was my boyfriend in high school," Dori said. "He's a trustee of the estate, now. And a friend." She could feel her cheeks turning hot.

"More than that, I think," Maya said.

Dori couldn't help a smile, but she said nothing.

"He called last night while you were out cold."

"What? Why didn't you tell me?"

"I wanted to get on the road, and then I forgot. Anyway, you can use my phone to call him whenever you want."

"Thank you, I will. That won't use up all your minutes or something?"

Maya shook her head. "Nah. I don't know how you can even live without a cell phone?"

"I did have one for a while. But service was always spotty in Jasper, and I just don't miss it. Or didn't until now." She didn't want to tell Maya about her embarrassing level of debt. Maya seemed to have a knack for money. She had already taught her the fine art of sharing an affordable motel room, eating cheaply, and taking the rest of the day's per diem out in cash. Dori realized she might just save enough on this trip to cover a month or two of expenses when she got home.

"Poor little rich girl," Maya said. "You remind me of that crazy lady who lived out in the Hamptons next to Jackie Kennedy's place in a falling-down mansion full of cats. Here you are with all this white privilege just pouring out of you, and you don't have a clue how to use it. If Putney did set you up with that article, he was actually doing you a favor. But you probably don't even see that."

"A favor?" Dori stared at her. "No, I sure as hell don't."

"The public's attention is valuable, Dori. Valuable, and fleeting. Use it or lose it."

If Maya honestly thought Robert Putney had done Dori a favor, what did that mean for Dori's chances to come out of this documentary without even more notoriety? Wouldn't it be in Maya's best interest to drum up any scandal she could find? And wouldn't she feel completely justified in doing it, convinced she was also just doing Dori a favor? She'd already as much as said that any attention was like money in the bank, that it all but guaranteed Dori a gigantic book deal she wouldn't even have to write herself.

But Dori had agreed to this undertaking. And she really did want to meet her grandparents. And she was making a little money, too.

So, she'd just go along for the ride and see what she could learn along the way.

Why were those two old ladies shooting them looks of disgust?

Dori looked down at her t-shirt and shorts. They weren't unusually short or spattered with antisocial messages or anything. It wasn't Sunday, so nobody could expect them to be wearing their Sunday best. She looked across the little laminated restaurant table at Maya, who had dressed professionally even for travel. She was chewing a French fry and using her index finger to flick things around on her phone. Every once in a while she'd laugh and pass the phone over to share the joke. Dori got about half of them. Quite often she had no idea who the people mentioned were.

"Where have you been for the last ten years?" Maya finally

demanded. "How can you not know any of this stuff?"

"We only get one channel," Dori said. "I don't watch a lot of TV."

"And you never go to movies, either? Or rent a DVD?"

Dori shrugged. Yes, she occasionally went to a movie. Usually when Ruth was in town, though. Ruth would know what movies they should go see. "I read. There's a whole house full of books. And the library has more. My parents weren't very big fans of television. We used to rent videos, but the player died." Her parents had often stopped the cable too, especially between book contracts, or when her mom was between jobs. Sometimes she thought the only reason they ever got it back was her father's desperation to see some Southeast Conference football each fall.

"It's like you've been living in a cave," Maya said. "A muggy, un-air-conditioned cave."

"So they're really expecting us tomorrow morning?" Dori said. Maya had talked to her grandparents even before they'd left Jasper. She'd gotten them to agree to some filming. Dori had been surprised about this, until Maya explained she was paying them a "per diem – just for their trouble."

"Is it more than our per diem?" Dori had asked. Maya's, like hers, was $200 a day.

"Oh hell, no. They're taking quite a bit less. $50. Of course I don't expect them to let me film them the whole day long. They sound pretty old. They probably won't have a ton of energy. But if we're lucky we can get another day or two out of them, or at least some information to follow up on."

Dori thought it would have been nice if her grandparents had been happy simply to see her without getting paid for it, but she supposed the filming did add an intrusive element to the experience.

Sharing a motel bathroom with someone she didn't know all that well had interfered with Dori's morning routine, which was probably why she found herself camped in the cramped little bathroom stall of the diner after they'd eaten lunch.

That was where she was when two women came in and – God

help them in the foul atmosphere Dori had created – needed to use the facilities themselves.

"You go on ahead," one called kindly to the other, when she finished first. "I'll meet you outside."

"Oh, I don't mind," the other woman said. "I can't taste or smell much anymore."

Lucky for her, Dori thought weakly, tucking her feet back and sitting as quietly as she could. It was always mortifying to stink up public bathrooms.

"At least we can be fairly certain it's not just someone sitting there for hours to use her phone," the other said. "I hate that!"

"Oh, I know. That's sooooo rude. Even ruder to sit and use it at the table, though, when you have company."

Oh. That was it. The glaring ladies. They hadn't liked Maya's phone use.

"Especially when you have better company than you have any right to expect."

Wait. What?

"And that girl, what a sight. She clearly doesn't take sufficient pride in herself," one said. "She just sat there all hunched over, keeping company with that..." The woman paused, and didn't say it. She didn't need to say it. It hung there, unsaid.

"Probably just white trash," the other said.

"Or a girlfriend." They tittered.

"Seriously, though. It burns me up to see a girl so beaten down, and that other one just sits there like the queen of Sheba, dressed to the nines, using a fancy phone you just know our tax dollars probably paid for, one way or the other."

"I know. I know. But everything's so backwards these days. You never know what you're going to see."

They left.

Dori sat there with her mouth open, and not just because she was breathing through it. She'd heard people say awful things before, especially her senile patients – and Kevin – but there was something so breathtakingly casual about it that it made her wonder whether it was in fact a Southern thing. Or was it just something she'd managed to be oblivious to all her life?

Later, in the car, Maya said, "You're quiet."

"Did you see those old ladies who were glaring at us?"

"Oh, yeah," Maya said, with a roll of her eyes. "So what else is new?"

"I heard them talking in the bathroom. They wondered if I was your girlfriend, or just white trash."

Maya laughed. "Girlfriend, huh? White trash because you were sitting with me, of course. Better get used to it. Some people will think you're betraying your race when you hang out with someone outside it. And not just white people, either."

Chapter 31

"You want some privacy?" Maya said, once they had settled into their motel just off the Interstate in Valdosta for the night. "I just want to see the news, and then I can disappear for a bit if you want. A long hot shower sounds real good about now."

"No need. I'll just go outside."

"Be careful. I don't trust the kind of people who stay in these places."

"*We're* staying here."

"Yeah, but we're slumming to save money. Strange guy approaches you, you head right back in, okay? I'm not saying he's going to kidnap and torture you. He might just want to grab my phone and run for it." She pointed her chin at the phone she'd lent Dori.

"I'll be careful." Dori carried the precious device out and closed the door behind her. Mindful of Maya's warnings, she looked up and down the concrete balcony that ran the length of the second floor, but nobody was around. Down in the parking lot, an attendant was emptying bags into a dumpster. Beyond it, an array of lit signs glowed far above the road in the rosy-tinged twilight: Waffle House, McDonald's, and various motels all better known than the one they had chosen.

Joe's greeting was efficient: "Joseph Gagnon Landscaping. How can I help you?"

"Hi, it's me."

"Hey!" he said, his tone distinctly warmer. Perhaps she'd just imagined a moment's hesitation. "How are you? *Where* are you? Is that traffic I hear?"

"Yeah, a bit. We're in Valdosta. It's all arranged to go meet my grandparents tomorrow morning. How about you?"

Yes, there was definitely a hesitation. "I've had better days."

She pressed the phone closer to her ear. "What happened?"

"Lisa told me she thinks she's pregnant."

Dori opened her mouth, but couldn't think of a single thing to say.

"And it would be mine," he added, unnecessarily.

"And that's possible," Dori said, not bothering to make it sound like a question.

His voice rose. "I don't see how. I always use a condom."

She believed him. He'd used them with her, too, without a trace of awkwardness. It was clearly a habit. "But the timing..."

He sighed. "Yeah, the timing would work."

If she'd entertained any idea his attempt to starve that relationship to death had been waged in any serious way for more than a couple of weeks, she let it go. She stared out across the asphalt parking lot, past the glowing signs. Vehicles – most with their headlights on – were zooming by. How many of those people were also speeding out of someone's life?

"Dori?"

It had been a dream, what they'd shared that night. A little break in her solitary existence that wouldn't really amount to anything in the long run. "I guess you didn't tell her about us, then."

"What? Of course I did!"

She stared at the phone in surprise, then relief, then a kind of chagrin. After all, why would Joe be any gentler toward Lisa than he had been toward her? "Before or after she told you she thought she was pregnant?"

"After. We both said we had news. I made the mistake of letting her go first. I was hoping she was going to dump me and save me some trouble." He grunted in a disgusted sort of way. "That'll teach me."

"She must have been pretty upset."

"I'll say. She slapped my face!"

Dori swallowed a half-laugh at his expense, her loyalties divided by outrage on behalf of a fellow female who knew how it felt to be wronged by Joe Gagnon. She sat down on the warm concrete of the second floor balcony, leaning back against the stucco wall. "So what happens now?"

"I have no idea."

"You must have some idea."

"I really don't. Is she really pregnant? If so, does she want to be pregnant? Am I really the father? Is she going to tell her dad? Will he kill me? I have no idea."

"*Kill* you?"

"Well, hopefully not that," he said. "But he's very protective. He could probably ruin my business like *that*, if he wanted."

"And she knows it's me you're dumping her for?"

"Uh, yeah."

Great. Now the fine people of Jasper could add "stole Lisa Summers' boyfriend" to her list of offenses.

He added, "I told her it wasn't just because of you, that I just didn't think we had that much in common, but that didn't seem to help."

She just shook her head. He was such a *guy*.

"Anyway," he continued, "if she really is pregnant, and she goes forward with it, and it's mine, I'm not just walking away like my own asshole father did. You need to know that."

She was confused. "What are you saying? You'd marry her?"

"What? No! But I'd still be that kid's father. We'd have to work it out somehow. People do. It just, you know, it means you'd have to be a stepmom, and the child support would be a drain on our finances, and ... you know, holidays and big milestones would get complicated."

Wait a minute.

"Dori?" he said.

"Yeah?" Had she missed something in all that sleep deprivation?

"You can deal with that, right?"

"I'm confused. Did we...?"

"What?"

"Did we get engaged and I missed it?"

Dead silence. Then: "You agreed we were together."

"Yeah. Together. Not married!"

"Not yet. But you are thinking about it, at least, aren't you?"

"I'm still just getting used to the idea you don't hate my guts anymore!"

More silence.

"Look," she said. "I'm fine we're together again. I am, I promise! This all just seems to be moving a little fast."

"Well, yeah, obviously we're not engaged," he said. "Not officially." His tone sharpened. "But that is where we'd be headed, isn't it?"

She blinked. How was that not just another proposal?

A minivan drove up into a parking space below her and a family started getting out of it, wearily collecting their belongings. A girl who looked about ten insisted she needed her pillow, which made her younger brother insist he needed his, too, and she could hear the mother say, "Okay, so get them" with the kind of excessive calm that suggested she might be trying not to scream. The father leaned in and emerged with a slumbering toddler draped over one shoulder and at least three bags in the other hand. "Honey, can you get the door?" he said. There was not even a trace of impatience in his voice.

Unlike Joe's, when he said, "Dori?"

It wasn't that she didn't want him. "Are you going to cut me dead again if I'm not ready to do exactly what you want exactly when you want me to do it?" Her throat closed up. It still hurt like hell, even eight years and so many other losses later.

"I think I learned my lesson about that. I'm trying. I just..." His voice trailed off.

A wail arose from somewhere down below. She guessed the sleeping child had awakened and found himself in a strange new place. "What?" she asked.

His voice got higher. "Tell me you're not just messing with me."

"I've never just messed with you!" Okay, not counting certain remarks about a young Robert Putney-Lewis. But she didn't think that rose to a level that required confession.

She heard a soothing maternal "Aw, baby," from below. The crying paused and became intermittent. The other children's voices rose in a jealous clamor for attention, one that Dori, an eldest child, recognized all too well.

Joe was the only child of a mostly single mother. Was that what was going on here? Was it possible he just wouldn't be able to cope with not being the center of her universe at all times? Could she live like that?

Would it be any different than what her mother had done, endlessly catering to her father and his tortured art?

"Joe?" she said. He'd gone quiet. Maybe he was busy reviewing all her recent behavior.

"So, just to clarify," he said, "you're not messing with me about this being a relationship we can take seriously, and I shouldn't freak out just because you don't want to marry me, like, instantly."

Just to clarify? No, he was not her father. Less romantic, far more sober. Maybe that was a technique he'd learned in his business classes. "Sounds about right," she said.

"Okay. All right." He took a deep breath. "So tell me about your day." And she did.

Only after she went back in and returned the phone to Maya, who was pecking away on her laptop, and then stepped into the shower and started washing her hair did it really sink in she'd just survived her second marriage proposal from Joe Gagnon.

A complicated, backhanded marriage proposal. A horrifying mess of a marriage proposal. That she'd turned down once again.

But they were still speaking. That was surely progress of some kind.

Chapter 32

Her mother's parents lived miles off the nearest state road. Maya let her phone talk her through various turns on narrow, lightly-trafficked roads between flat fields of pine scrub and weedy horse pastures. The clay soil was less vividly red here than it had been further north, more of a pale orange. The occasional grand McMansion alternated with decrepit trailers, modest ranch houses, and old shacks with rusting metal roofs. "This looks more like Florida than Georgia," Maya said, in a tone that did not suggest that was a good thing.

"I've never been to Florida," Dori said.

"If we miss a turn that may change," Maya said, and glanced again at the map on her phone.

Dori had already read the bare facts in the article: Her mother's parents were named Judson and Alicia Steele; they lived in an unincorporated area south of Valdosta; and they had complained that her father repaid their kindness to him by making off with their only daughter.

Dori and Maya had been unable to find anything else; there was not even anything to be seen of their address via Google satellite except tree tops. On the phone, Judson had told Maya the landmark for making the turn into their driveway was two pillars of old tires that had been painted white.

"Nervous?" Maya said, as Dori sat quietly, her arms folded protectively against the black dress she'd decided to take out again for this occasion. In some vague part of her mind she felt it might make a kind of physical connection between her mother and these people, although that was ridiculous.

"I don't know what to think," Dori said. "I'm not even sure I believe they are really who they claim to be."

"Yeah, we should probably try to confirm that," Maya said. "You'd expect them to have pictures or something, right? And if they are who they claim they are, you have to wonder why your mother didn't want anything to do with them."

The phone alerted them their destination was coming up on the left. Maya made the turn onto a long, unpaved driveway that was none too smooth. They bumped along as it wound past a hammock of gaunt pines and palmetto that hid everything from the road. Dori looked at Maya and wondered if she was also thinking nobody would ever see anything back there.

The house was reassuringly ordinary, though – a well-kept stucco ranch with a large pole barn next to it, where a fairly late model Buick sedan was parked. Coleus and red geraniums rioted all along the base of the house, which was towered over by spreading live oaks trailing moss. In the only sunny spot in the yard, a few petite palms erupted from a bed of ferns.

"They know I plan to film this," Maya said, grabbing her phone and setting it up for video. "But I'll try to stay in the background. This is your reunion."

"If you say so," Dori said. Her heart had begun to pound. She got out of the car and headed for the front door just as it opened.

The woman who walked out first only hesitated for a moment. "Oh my *gaaaaaawd*, look at *youuuuuuuuuu!*" she squealed, and held out her arms for a hug, which Dori gave her. "I can't believe I finally get to meet you!" the woman said, squeezing tight. She turned to the tall man behind her. "Look, Jud! Look at that hair! There's no question in my mind, none at all!"

"Hmmph," the man said. "Eudora, is it?" He held out a hand clearly ravaged by arthritis.

Dori shook it gently. "Dori is what I usually go by."

"Nice to meet you," he said, and lifted his eyes to Maya. "Are you usually filmed everywhere you go?"

"No," Dori said, embarrassed, and gestured for Maya to join them. "This is Maya Davis. I believe you've already discussed this on the phone?"

He looked a bit taken aback. "You're the Miss Davis from Brooke College?"

"I am," Maya said, and held out her hand. "A pleasure to meet you in person, sir."

He shook it, then gestured to his companion. "My wife, Mrs.

Steele."

"Well, hello!" the older woman said, her smile turning a touch brittle. "And will you be filming *everything*?"

"No, not everything," Maya said. "As I told your husband, we can set up wherever you would like, as long as it has reasonable light. Outdoors, even."

"I see." That last comment seemed to have assuaged her in some way. "Well, come on in. Let's see what will work for you. And you can let me know if you'd rather have coffee or iced tea."

The interior of their house was dim and air-conditioned, although not as frigid as the restaurant where they'd eaten breakfast. For a mid-century house it seemed oddly stuffed with heavy dark wood antiques; not a single wall stood free of furniture, heavy, mildewed mirrors, faded portraits in gilt frames, lamps, or statuary, and there were thick Oriental carpets layered on top of the wall-to-wall carpet. The heavy curtains and dark reds and greens of the wall colors added even more weight.

The effect was suffocating.

"Did my mom grow up here?" Dori asked. It was not her mother's style at all. While Ellen Bardwell had been fond of antiques, especially from the Arts and Crafts period, she hadn't turned her nose up at any decent modern piece, either, including a number she'd rescued from the town dump and refinished. But she'd kept plenty of open space between furniture for her brood to run around in, and had always kept her walls neutral and everything well lit.

Her grandmother said, "Oh, no, not Ellen. She grew up in base housing, and then in the manse. We'll show you some pictures later." She looked around a little grimly. "We saved what we could, more than we can really fit into this little house. Perhaps you'll get some of it, now. My mother would be so thrilled to think some of it has managed to stay in the family."

"I'll wait on the patio," Mr. Steele said, and stalked off.

"And what would you like, dears?"

They chose coffee. It was clear Mrs. Steele was prepared to make a pot. They hovered in the kitchen as an awkward silence fell, watching her measure coffee with slightly shaking hands.

"Can I help with anything?" Dori asked.

"Oh, no. While this brews, let me show you about the place. You saw the living room when you came in, of course." She beckoned them out of the kitchen into a formal dining room, which was also crammed with more furniture and dishes and accessories than it could comfortably hold, then back through the kitchen and into a study or family room also ringed in antiques, but otherwise dominated by a large screen television with two well-worn contemporary recliners stationed in front of it. A table behind the recliners had a half-assembled puzzle laid out on it, as well as stacks of magazines and cheap paperback romances. They exited to a screened-in patio at the back of the house, where Mr. Steele had already sat himself at a table covered by a vinyl table cloth that looked brand new. It was already set with a creamer, sugar, mugs, plates, and a Bundt cake of some kind. While the air was warm and humid, it still felt fairly pleasant at that early hour. Outside the screen birds chirped and called and flittered back and forth from an understory of bushes under spreading live oaks.

"It's lovely!" Dori said.

"Yes, beautiful," Maya added, but Mrs. Steele had already disappeared.

"All her doing," the old man said. "Your grandmother's," he corrected himself to Dori, with a frown. "She'd spend all day gardening if I let her."

That lady reappeared with a pot of coffee, which was served round and followed by slices of the cake – a pound cake soaked in lemon sauce – and there was some conversation about the food and then some more conversation about the garden. Dori eyed Maya: What now?

"This was all so delicious, thank you. Do you mind if I start filming again?" Maya asked.

"I suppose we did agree to that," Mr. Steele said, sounding none too pleased. "I take it this location is acceptable?"

"Yes, it will do fine as long as I can move over to that side of the table," Maya said. "That way you won't appear as silhouettes. And maybe you could sit closer to each other? Since I only have one camera?"

No objection was raised, so they rearranged themselves as

Maya fiddled with her phone, which doubled as a camera. Her grandmother kept dabbing her mouth with napkins. "I sure would love an opportunity to freshen my lipstick," Mrs. Steele said. "How about you, Dori?"

"Uh, okay," Dori said.

Mrs. Steele hustled her into an avocado-green bathroom. "Let's fix you up a little, dear," she said, and proceeded to rustle in a tray full of make-up. "You're not taking full advantage of your natural beauty. God may have given you very fine features, but it's up to you to define them."

"I'm not sure how hygienic it would be to share make-up," Dori said. Some of it looked decades past any expiration date. She had put on her usual that morning – a little eyeliner, a little eye-shadow and mascara.

"Oh, I'll be careful." With shaking hands, she picked up a fat black eyeliner pencil. "Close your eyes!"

"How about I do it," Dori said quickly. "That way you can work on your own freshening up if you'd like."

Mrs. Steele looked skeptical, but handed it over. "Ellen never wore enough make-up. Wouldn't even cover her freckles. Don't be shy, now. The camera washes you out if you don't do a proper job with the make-up. I have a friend who has done a little local television and she is an expert at such matters. She also says the camera always adds twenty pounds, and she's right. She looks quite matronly on the TV. Yet no one would have the slightest idea of that if they met her in person!"

Dori wiped the eyeliner she'd been given with a tissue, and gingerly lined her upper lids.

"Why bless your heart, you're not going to ignore the lower lids?" Mrs. Steele had just outlined her lips in a startlingly red lipstick, doing a surprisingly steady job for a woman with tremors. Dori humored her by touching up the corners of her lower lids.

"And don't forget the eye shadow!" Mrs. Steele added, and started surveying her stash. "Blue to bring out your eyes?"

"How about some brown?" Dori said. "That's my usual color."

Mrs. Steele frowned. "All right. Here. I also have extra fake eyelashes if you'd like."

"Uh, better not," Dori said. "They must be getting tired of waiting for us."

"Never let anyone rush you when it comes to your appearance, that's my rule. Shall we cover your freckles?"

Did she have that many? She wasn't Salinger. "I'd rather not," Dori said firmly.

"Perhaps just a little powder then." Mrs. Steele handed her a giant bowl of it with a puff. "It will help with the lights and the humidity. You *always* want powder!"

There were no lights, Dori thought, but gamely gave each cheek a token pat of powder, realizing as she did so that this was exactly the scent she'd noticed on many old ladies who had come in to visit their failing husbands or friends.

Mrs. Steele filled in her lipstick and began to campaign for Dori to do the same. Dori negotiated her down to a salmon pink from a bright red.

"I suppose your impressive youth will make up for any omissions," the old woman said. "Sadly, that is not the case for me at all. Now, do remember to smile! It makes all the difference in the world. Nobody likes a sourpuss, not at *any* age."

Back on the patio, Maya and Mr. Steele were engaged in a lively conversation about the prospects for the Georgia Bulldogs. Dori's father had been a passionate Florida Gators fan, but she couldn't bring herself to care one way or the other. She'd never noticed her mother had, either, except in a sympathetic "there, there" sort of way.

"Who's your team, Eudora?" Steele asked.

"I don't really have one."

"Good God," he said, looking at his wife. "Are you *sure* she's related to us?"

Dori noticed Maya – after a slight widening of her eyes at their make-up – start filming. She said, "So ... what can you tell me about my mother?"

"Oh, we can tell you quite a lot about both of your parents," Steele said, and looked grimly at his wife, whose determined smile stiffened.

"Your father was my nephew," she said. "We took him in at sixteen when he was orphaned by a car accident."

Mr. Steele said, "And he repaid for our generosity by making off with his cousin, our daughter. Whom we never saw or heard from again."

Dori stared at him – he was scowling, arms folded – and then at her grandmother, who looked oddly satisfied, and finally at Maya, who just kept recording.

"Maybe you could tell me a little more about that?" Dori said, aware her voice had gone unnaturally high.

"Oh, you'd better believe we will," he said.

"Do you believe everything they told you?" Maya asked later, as they were driving back to the motel.

"I don't know what to think," Dori said. She had accepted they were indeed her grandparents – she'd seen the pictures on the wall, the photo albums, even her mother's birth certificate. They'd asked Dori to come back soon, to let them get better acquainted, and she'd told them she would try, although she wasn't sure she ever wanted to go back.

Her father, according to them, had moved into "the manse" with them – which to her and Maya's surprise had been located outside Tallahassee – in Florida, not in Georgia at all – when he was sixteen, after his father had smashed into an oncoming truck with the rest of the family in the car. Her grandfather said, "John Henry Bardwell was dead drunk, of course. A bit ironic your daddy did practically the same thing to his family, don't you think?"

"Dad wasn't drinking when that happened," Dori protested. She got disbelieving smiles from both of them.

"He'd always gotten along well with his cousin Ellen," her grandmother continued. "And apparently they began to get along much better than we realized. Then they had some sort of falling-out – I don't know what it was, but it was noticeable that Ellen didn't want anything to do with him suddenly – and while that was going on he got that girl pregnant."

Dori said, "What?"

Her grandmother barely paused. "She was such a slow girl. A real lump of a girl. Loretta Ledbetter was her name. All those

Ledbetters had a tendency to drop out of school and start drop-
ping babies almost as soon as they hit puberty. Dumb as posts,
and not all that much to look at, either. Terrible teeth. Anyway,
apparently this one took a shine to Nat. Or maybe he got drunk
and took a shine to her. Who can say? Your daddy was already
drinking too much. And then," she continued, "he just outright
refused to marry that girl. Not that we could blame him for that,
but he wouldn't even accept he might be the father. Claimed he'd
never laid a hand on her, when the truth was he probably just
couldn't remember. Or didn't want to. Never mind plenty of
other people remembered he'd been all over her at some party.
No, he refused any responsibility at all."

She looked at her husband, and he continued the story. "And
just a week or two later, that girl ended up in the river. Drowned
like a rat. Someone found her purse on the old bridge in Ellaville.
The coroner ruled it an accident, but we had our own suspicions.
By then we'd had quite enough of your daddy's drinking and ir-
responsibility, and we told him he'd have to go. What we didn't
foresee was that Ellen would go with him."

"How old were they?" Dori asked.

Her grandmother said, "He'd just turned seventeen. She was
sixteen. We never heard from them again. Apparently they got
married at some point."

Dori said. "And they were cousins." Was that even legal? Was
that why her parents had hidden out in a little town in western
Massachusetts?

"Perfectly legal," her grandfather said. "Throughout the South.
And in Massachusetts. I looked it up. Doesn't make it the smartest
thing to do. All your brothers and sisters were perfectly normal,
though, from what I read? No defects, no mental retardation. Is
that true?"

'We were fine," Dori said. Carson had been born with a cleft
palate, but she decided not to share that detail.

Maya said, "You didn't tell Ms. Schweitzer all of this, did you?"

"No," Mrs. Steele said. "It's family business."

Family business they had just allowed to be filmed in exchange
for $50.

Maya asked, "What color was that girl?"

"What girl?" her grandmother said.

"The one who drowned."

"White, of course," her grandmother said. "White trash," she clarified.

"Did Nathan Bardwell even *know* any black people?" Maya asked.

"I have no idea," her grandmother said. "Maybe before he came to us. We had black help around the house before he came, but in those days money was tight and there was nobody. Of course, I suppose since he went to the public high school and played football, he might have met some. Or maybe they met some after they ran off. God only knows where they lived, or how, before that book came out. I still can't believe he wrote that whole thing. He was no great student, I can tell you that. I wouldn't be surprised if Ellen did most of the work."

"It sure was a hatchet job on us," her grandfather said. "It's no wonder they never showed their faces here again."

Maya turned off her phone. "Would you mind if I recharged this on one of your outlets?" she'd asked.

"I don't see why not," her grandmother had said. "Would anybody like more cake?"

Chapter 33

At the motel room, which felt far more like a refuge than it had in the night before, Dori kicked off her dress shoes and flopped down on top of the riotously patterned bedspread. Chosen to hide stains well, she suspected.

If it was legal to marry your first cousin, it must not really be such a bad thing, surely? With the exception of that cleft palate and the red hair half of them had shared with their mother, they were all pretty normal.

"Do *you* think your mother wrote most of *Tea and Slavery*?" Maya asked. She changed fastidiously into flip flops – she had already aired her own dark suspicions about the carpet and linens in the room – and sat down at the little table next to the window to set up her laptop.

"No," Dori said. "She probably had a big hand in editing it. She always did. But I never saw her do anything of her own. Not that she would have had the time anyway. I suppose she might have guided him a bit. She had a way of suggesting things. Just sort of putting them out there and then praising you to high heaven if you did any of them. Maybe she did that with my dad, too, but not that I ever saw. She'd just say how'd it go today? And then he'd either say something like *you don't want to know* or talk our ears off about whatever brilliant thing he'd come up with. When she was editing him, though, things would get really tense. I wouldn't have wanted to be his editor. Once or twice I suggested things to him and he nearly bit my head off."

"Really? He showed you his work?"

"Oh yeah, sometimes. Especially if he was drunk, or Mom wasn't around."

"Was it any good?"

"Well, he could write. It wasn't necessarily anything that really grabbed me, though. That really pissed him off sometimes.

He said I had what he called 'plebeian' tastes, that I preferred popular authors and 'flash-in-the-pan' sensations. I eventually decided that was code for women authors or anyone who was selling more books than him."

"My father never shows me anything," Maya said. "But all he writes is literary criticism. I had to look up some of his work to research this project. Damn, is it dry! I don't think he ever met a word he wouldn't try to upgrade to something more obscure. I'm talking *synecdoche*. I'm talking fucking *mimesis*. And he doesn't explain them in the text, either. It's like he's just daring you to admit you don't know what they mean."

"Do *you* know what they mean?" Dori didn't.

"I do now," Maya said. "Thanks to Google! Don't quiz me, though. Hell, after reading all that stuff, I think I could probably bullshit my way through a doctorate in literature, no problem. But why would I want to do that when it would just mean bullshitting my way through a bunch of stuff nobody wants to read for the rest of my life? At least your dad's stuff gets read."

Not as much as he ever wanted. And would he still be read after all this got out? Dori stared up at the ceiling. A single strand of web hung off the sprinkler there, floating in the light breeze from the air conditioning unit. It seemed futile. There were no bugs in the room. There didn't even appear to be a spider. Maybe it was just the forlorn leavings of a former, more glorious web.

Maya said, "If that was a hatchet job on your grandparents, that would make Old Man Foote your grandfather Steele, right?"

"Foote. Steele. Both one syllable with silent e's. Both tall, thin, and mean. Sounds like a match."

"And your grandmother?"

"I guess she'd be the mother. Mamie. She wasn't so bad."

"She wasn't so good, either. Vain, silly, went along with everything her husband did. Snuck in a kindness now and then, but not in any way that really mattered."

"Well, yeah," Dori said. Had that make-up session with her grandmother been a kindness? She was a little afraid to look at the results. "Does that mean Henry was my dad?"

"Ugh," Maya said, wrinkling her nose. Critics often debated

who the true protagonist of the novel was – the slave Beulah, or Henry, the eldest son, the sensitive young white man who fell in love with Beulah, got her pregnant, and then utterly failed to rise to the occasion. It was one of those old-fashioned novels that used an omniscient point of view, dipping into characters' minds at will, so there was no clue to be taken there.

Had it been her father's way of letting himself off the hook? Did he think having to acknowledge the baby of a poor white girl in the 1980s was akin to a master having to marry a slave in the antebellum South?

But, of course, the novel *despised* Henry. It had some sympathy for him, but it still despised him.

"There's no one like my mom in that book," Dori said. "Unless Clara counts. And she's his sister." Yuck, that was even worse than cousin. At least Henry hadn't fallen in love with Clara. But he *had* lost her good opinion. The novel had ended with the epilogue of him dying ten years later, running fatalistically into battle at Shiloh, defending the institution of slavery that had cost him his child and the love of his life. Bayonetted, he lay among the other dead and dying and drowned on his own blood.

She felt a sudden chill. *Drowned.* Like Loretta.

And her family? Had he intentionally set out to drown himself ... and his wife and his kids? Not that they *had* drowned – she'd been told that it was the impact that killed them. But he might not have expected that.

Maybe he'd just done it subconsciously. But surely that was bad enough.

Maya stood up and stretched. "What I can't fucking believe is that your dad turned a dead white girl into a dead black girl and suddenly he's written the most important book about slavery since *Uncle Tom's Cabin*. Not even *Beloved* can compete with it."

Dori looked at her, feeling a little too dazed by her own conjectures to fully take that in. Also, she still hadn't read those two books and hated to admit it. "You got it all recorded?" she asked.

"Oh yeah. In fact, I'd better start downloading it and backing it up now. This stuff is fucking gold."

Dori watched as Maya sat down again, connected her phone to her laptop, and lost herself in her task. Clearly, the rest of the world – or at least that tiny slice of it that cared about American literature and its practitioners – would soon learn what they'd just learned.

Had Dori just managed to destroy her father's legacy?

And did it matter if she had?

Once Maya was done with her phone, she handed it over and said, "I know you want to call him."

Dori had already changed back into shorts and a t-shirt and didn't even wait to put on sandals before she went out to the balcony and placed the call, something she had finally learned how to do without assistance.

"Dori?" he said.

"Is this a good time?"

"Sure," he said. "I'm glad it's you."

She smiled out at the parking lot and the Waffle House sign. It was nice to be appreciated.

"I've had four clients call me up today and cancel their service," he added. "I thought this was going to be another one."

That was not quite the kind of appreciation she'd had in mind. "Because of Lisa?"

"Nobody's said, but that's my assumption. They're all friends of the Summers'."

"Well, here's hoping he doesn't have too many friends," Dori said.

"He's the fire chief. He's everybody's friend." He sighed. "How are you? How did it go with your grandparents?"

Dori could hear him cheering up as she related the day's events, even though he made obligatory sympathetic noises now and then. "You're happy I'm not crazy about them, aren't you?" she said.

There was a short silence. "Well, I'm guessing you aren't likely to move in with them any time soon. And Georgia would be a really long-distance relationship."

She smiled. "At least from here I couldn't lose you all the rest of your customers."

"It's not your fault. If the worst happens, I'll just go get a second job somewhere while I rebuild. But hopefully it won't come to that." He yawned. "Sorry. I didn't sleep well last night. As long as we're speaking of jobs, did you put in for unemployment?"

"No. What's the point?"

"I think you should."

"Bonnie told me it's not for people who violate company policy."

"Yeah, but that would be the state's judgment call. You should apply. Worst case scenario, you'll force her to deal with annoying paperwork."

"Well, if you put it that way," Dori said, without enthusiasm. She'd been enjoying not thinking about the depressing tasks that awaited her at home. "Did Salinger get his card?"

"Oh, yeah," he said. "I expect he and Jenna will be having a fine old time."

"At least she's finally getting something out of the relationship."

"At least he'll always know she loves him for who he is instead of what he can give her."

"Unless she just really, really wants a regular supply of pot without having to go get it herself."

He laughed. "Yeah, well. But never underestimate the value of having someone to talk to. Someone you really *enjoy* talking to."

"I don't." She paused, her heart so full she couldn't talk for a moment. "I don't."

Chapter 34

The next day Maya and Dori checked out of the motel and headed down the state highway to Florida, in search of that bridge in Ellaville and "the manse" and other landmarks the Steeles had told them about. Maya wanted to film them and also try to confirm the Steeles' version of events.

Maya had been hunting online most of the night, but hadn't been able to find anything that didn't simply repeat the lies her father had apparently provided in his author biography for *Tea and Slavery* – that he'd been born and raised in South Georgia, the son of poor sharecroppers who'd died young, and had met his wife, a foster child, at a July 4th dance.

"Independence Day," Dori noted. "How did Schweitzer find them with so little to go on?"

"I asked her that. She said she didn't take your father's word for it, she was persistent, and she was lucky. Your mother really was from South Georgia – she was born while your grandfather was stationed at Moody Air Force Base. And that's pretty close to where they live now. So she just started calling every Steele in the area. If your grandparents hadn't moved back up there she would have hit a dead end, because your father never said a word about Florida. I'm just glad they didn't say anything to her about this Loretta business. If it's true, I've got myself a genuine scoop!"

"I guess actually being from Florida explains Dad's thing for the Gators," Dori said. "But wouldn't you expect someone who knew him to say something about it?"

"Literary authors who aren't insanely rich or actors or something are never that well known," Maya said. "And the kind of people who might recognize authors are usually not the kind of people who harass celebrities. Besides, they didn't even have the Internet in those days."

Dori wished they still didn't. The night before she'd asked

Maya if they were still talking about her.

"Oh, it's dying down," Maya had told her. "You're not on the trending list anymore. Of course that's not really a good thing if you want to cash in on this."

"I don't!"

"You are young in the ways of the world," Maya said, in a falsetto, and smirked a little. At Dori's inquiring look she'd said, "*Pride and Prejudice*, the BBC version written by Fay Weldon."

"Darcy in a wet shirt?"

"No. Nothing so vulgar and un-Austen-like. Not that I mind that sort of thing, generally speaking. Hey, we could stream it tonight. Are you up for some Austen?"

Dori absolutely was. Nobody ever got thrown off bridges in Jane Austen novels.

She and Maya had sat on one of the beds with Maya's laptop across their knees, eating take-out Chinese. "How did you even know about this version?" Dori had asked. "I think it's older than we are."

"My mom is fucking insane for Jane Austen," Maya said. "We probably have every version of everything Austen ever created."

Dori had squinted at her. "Your mom isn't white, is she?"

"What? No! You think only white people can love Jane Austen?" It was possibly the most offended Maya had ever looked.

Oops. "Sorry. I never really thought about it before. I love her, but Dad always said it was romantic claptrap of the poor suffering upper classes." He'd put on a mocking English accent when he said it, too."

Maya scowled. "Asshole. Maybe he *did* throw that girl in the river."

They stared down at the Suwannee as it flowed placidly beneath them, the color of strong tea. "Definitely deep enough to drown in," Maya said.

And definitely private enough to murder someone, Dori thought. They were standing on an old rusted bridge that had been roped off from the decaying road that led up to it. Trees were beginning to grow out of the old concrete. Vines had covered over an adjacent abandoned restaurant. "How would she even get out here? It's in the middle of nowhere."

"Maybe she hitch-hiked," Maya said. "Or maybe it's close to her place." They had passed some sandy dirt driveways, an old shack or two, a lonely gas station, and the entrance to a state park, but for the most part the area was dominated by gaunt pines, dense stands of palmetto, and pasture.

"Or maybe someone drove her." Would her father have had access to a car?

"There was a lot of suspicion of her father at the time," Maya said. "Apparently that family was the subject of numerous domestic calls. He was quoted as saying he hadn't drowned her sisters when they got knocked up, so why would he drown her?"

"Did they ever name my father as a suspect?"

"No. The web page that talked about her dad said there were rumors that any of several high school students might have gotten her pregnant," Maya said. "There were also rumors she would do anything a guy wanted for twenty bucks."

"Couldn't they just test and figure out who the father was?"

"They didn't have DNA analysis in those days. A blood test might have ruled people in or out, but apparently nobody ever made your father take one. Also, she'd been in the water for a while before she was found. I suppose it might have made it difficult."

Dori sighed, looking down at the swirling brown water. Maybe Loretta had needed money badly enough to sell herself. Or maybe that thing about the twenty bucks had just been a mean high school rumor.

She tried to imagine her father hoisting a pregnant girl over the rusty iron rail, and failed.

As waspish as her father could get behind people's backs, she'd never seen him be cruel to anyone's face – at least not about things unrelated to their taste in literature or boyfriends. In public, he'd never so much as berated a waiter. He wasn't even a mean drunk – he was a morose, self-pitying one. He'd never raised a hand to any of them, and seldom yelled. "I really don't think my dad would throw a girl off a bridge," she said.

But she could see him being haunted by a drowned girl. Especially if he really *had* gotten her pregnant, or thought he might have.

Maya was staring up the river at an abandoned railway trestle, her expression remote. She was probably thinking that nobody ever thought their loved ones could do any of the bad things they actually did.

They got back in the car and drove on to the small town of Jeffersonville, which sat sunbaked and sleepy on either side of the state road. Maya's phone talked them to the address the Steeles had given for "the manse."

"Wow," Maya said.

Dori stared. It was a nearly perfect match to their house in Jasper. She'd noticed the similarity in pictures her grandmother had showed her, but it had been harder to take in the exact scale in photographs. Mrs. Steele told her it had been the manor home of a large sugar and cotton plantation, but the land had been sold off after the Civil War. It did look older than the Jasper house, and a bit better kept – there were stone planters cascading with flowers on either side of the front door – and it sat much closer to the street. It had also, clearly, been converted to offices – there were small tasteful signs for a law firm, a dentist, and an insurance agency. The lot it sat on was relatively tiny, though, closely bordered on both sides by doctors' offices of much more recent construction.

"Want to go in?" Maya asked. "I'm going to film this in any case, but it will be more interesting if I can get you reacting to it."

Dori got out of the car and looked up at the second floor balcony. It had petunias and vines spilling out of three evenly-spaced planter boxes. The only time her house had anything hanging from that balcony was during Bedford Bardwell Days, when the old ladies hung patriotic bunting.

She pulled open the front door – it was a lot less sticky than hers – and walked into the grand foyer.

There was a table with another floral display – this one silk – and a number of business flyers. There was a small rack of brass mailboxes on the wall; apparently the house also had apartments on the second floor. A lower, false ceiling sported vents for the central air conditioning that was very much in evidence. A glass door where the door to their parlor had once been led to a law office. Dori walked down the hall towards the kitchen. There she found another glass door for an insurance agency that had claimed the area in her house that was her father's study. A solid door greeted her at the entrance to what she knew as the kitchen. "Please use the patients' entrance off the parking lot," a sign on it said.

"So what do you think of this place?" Maya asked, filming.

Dori shrugged. "It makes more sense to carve it up this way than to try to keep it going as a single home. Unless someone's got tons of money to spend on utilities and upkeep. I sure like the air conditioning."

"It doesn't bother you to see it this way? Would you do this with *your* house?"

"It was never my house. If it were my house I would have sold it by now. It's the Bedford Bardwell House." She gave the recording phone a grim smile and shouldered past Maya.

She wanted out.

Chapter 35

She ended up sitting on a bench in the shade of a big live oak because Maya hadn't followed her out and Maya was the one
driving.

"Where were you?" Dori asked, when she finally showed up.

"Canvassing the folks to see if they knew your dad or your
mom or Loretta Ledbetter. And I hit pay dirt. We're going to eat
lunch with a guy who knew your dad. He doesn't want to be recorded – typical lawyer – but he wants to meet you."

He wanted to meet her? Dori thought of every stereotype of
Southern vengeance she'd ever encountered, but then reminded
herself the man was a lawyer. Not likely to come to lunch with a
shotgun. Maybe a lawsuit. "What's his name?"

"Samuel Chestnut."

That sounded almost antique. "What do we do between now
and then?"

"Library. Maybe they've got a stash of old newspapers or mi-
crofiche or something and we can find some more details about
Loretta Ledbetter. And they'll probably know who the history
mavens in town are."

Maya was giving her an education in persistence. For once, she
had an idea of her own. "What about the police?"

"What about them?" There was an edge to Maya's tone.

"We could ask to see the case file."

"That would be pointless."

"Why?"

"Those aren't public."

"They aren't?" People in detective novels and television
shows were always getting their hands on case files. Of course,
they also had a convenient way of becoming intimate with actual
detectives. "Maybe we could see if someone who worked the case
retired and wants to chat over a cup of coffee."

Maya didn't look up from her smart phone. "If you want to track that down on your own, feel free."

It was the first time she'd ever heard Maya turn down a challenge, but it only took her a moment to figure it out. "Because you're black?"

Maya raised her eyebrows at her in obvious exasperation. "Sandra Bland ended up dead after a road stop because some cop thought she took the wrong tone with him. And I happen to know I'm not really the best at maintaining the right tone."

"Sandra Bland?"

"Oh my God!" Maya said. "Seriously! You need to be better informed. You just do."

"Sorry."

Maya shook her head in disgust, and the silence was tense for the two minutes it took to get to the library and park in the shade of another huge live oak. The library looked like something built in the Carnegie era and proved to be both beautiful and cramped inside.

The neat, middle-aged woman at the desk took them to a set of old file cabinets in a back room and said, "This is actually kept by the Historical Society. You can take file folders out and make copies of anything you want, but we do charge for those. Just please make sure you put everything back the way you found it."

Maya asked her, "Did you know Bedford Bardwell?"

"The author?" The clerk looked startled. "How would I know him?"

Maya said, "He lived here."

Dori added, "You would have known him as Nathan Bardwell. Or Nat."

"Bedford Bardwell lived here?" the woman said. "That would have been well before my time. I thought he hailed from Georgia."

Dori said, "That's just what he told people."

"Huh. Well, I'm from Ohio," the woman said. "So I'm afraid I wouldn't have known him in any case. I'll ask around for you, if you want."

"That would be great," Maya said, and handed over a few of

her cards.

Later, at the small restaurant in the middle of town, Samuel Chestnut greeted them both cordially, then gave Dori a long, assessing look. "You take after your mother more than your father," he said. "And it's not just the hair."

She smiled politely. "You knew them both?" Chestnut was a tall, thin man with longish grey hair, in a light grey suit that hung on him loosely. To her eye he looked a lot older than her parents, but they hadn't had a chance to age over the last seven years.

"I did." He urged them to order a good meal. "My treat," he said. "It's an unexpected pleasure to meet the daughter of my old friends."

After the waitress took their orders, he told Dori, "Your father and I used to sit in the back of English class together and ridicule poor Mrs. Sumter. In hindsight, she was probably doing her job at least as well as the others, but we just couldn't resist. She used to wear these awful support stockings rolled up to her thighs we could see when she bent over to get into her bag. And she had an absolute mania for *Gone with the Wind*. Your father mentioned it as often as he could, just to throw her off track."

"Did she make you read it?" Dori asked. She'd never gotten around to that one, either.

"Oh. No. I think she realized that would have been a lost cause. Have you seen the size of that thing? Your father read it, though. I recall he said it was romantic claptrap about the problems of the upper class."

Dori exchanged a small smile with Maya, who said, "A slave-owning upper class."

"Yes, indeed," he said, and tilted his head at her. "How did you come to be involved in this project, Miss Davis?"

"I'm the daughter of an eminent Bedford Bardwell scholar," Maya said. "And I'm a documentary filmmaker, as I believe I mentioned earlier."

"Yes, you gave me your card," he said. "Yet you can't be more than – what? – twenty-five?"

"Twenty-one," she said.

Dori eyed her with some consternation. Maya was even

younger than she'd realized.

"You're very accomplished for such a young lady," Chestnut said, with a smile. "And you, Dori? I read you're a CNA?"

She really would have preferred him to skip over her career, such as it was. "I was until recently."

"Yes, I saw your little faux-pas has blown up," he said. "Were you fired?"

"Yes."

He grunted in commiseration. "Wish I could help you with that, but my practice is confined to Florida. Not that I could do much about it here. Employment is very much at-will down in this state."

Maya said, "Mr. Chestnut, what we are most interested in at the moment is an allegation made by Dori's grandparents that Bedford Bardwell murdered a young woman named Loretta Ledbetter because she was carrying his child."

"*What?* Murdered?" He sat back and stared at her, clearly astonished. Then he looked at Dori. "I don't believe that for a minute. Why on earth would you even ask such a thing?"

"Um," Dori said. "Because I'd like to know whether it's true."

Maya added, "You must admit there are some interesting parallels with *Tea and Slavery*."

"It was a suicide in *Tea and Slavery*. And Loretta wasn't an enslaved person. She wasn't even black. She was just one more Ledbetter girl getting knocked up in her sophomore year."

"By my father?" Dori asked.

He frowned. "My dear. Were you not fond of your father?"

"Of course I was." She could feel her face flushing. "But now this accusation has been made, now that it's out there, I'd like to know whether it's true."

"It's 'out there'?" he said, and narrowed his eyes at Maya. "I've never heard it before."

Maya said, "What makes you so sure it's not true?"

"Nat was no murderer," Chestnut said. "He was a decent young man. At least when he...." He stopped.

"When he?" Maya prodded.

Chestnut sighed. "It's no secret your father didn't handle alcohol very well. But in that article you said he'd gotten a handle on that, finally?"

"Yes. He'd been sober for about six months when he died," she said.

"I'm sorry," Chestnut said. "It must have been quite difficult for you. The dying *and* the drinking."

"Yeah, it was." Though in some ways her dad's sobriety had been more difficult to handle than his drinking. She had gotten used to him being passed out early instead of awake and alert. And there had been more tension between him and her mother about things like money, not less. She had been quite relieved to go off to college.

Chestnut laced his long hands together and stared at them for a moment. "Honestly? I believe you never really know what otherwise kind and respectable people are capable of when they think their way of life is at stake. Sometimes they may think there's some profit in it and they won't get caught, or they may get carried away by carnal desire, or addiction. But I know your father had a conscience. And he had nothing to gain from Loretta dying at that point. And even if she had suggested that was his child – and I hadn't heard that at all – he had no particular reason to believe it was true. I'm afraid Loretta was widely known for sleeping around. She was a very good-natured girl, but slow-witted. She would do anything for a little male affection, and many young men – probably older ones, too – took advantage of that. I suppose she might also have taken a look at the manse and assumed your father could be her meal ticket. And I don't think there would have been any way of knowing whose child it really was until the child was born."

"But it could have been his," Maya said, her tone flat.

Chestnut shot an embarrassed look at Dori. "I won't say it's impossible. He was a healthy young man. But he was also hung up on Ellen. That was obvious to anyone who knew them."

"If Loretta slept around so much and my father insisted he wasn't the father, why would my grandfather throw him out of the house over it?" Dori asked.

Their lunches arrived and conversation waited until their

server had left them alone again.

Chestnut held up a long finger, signaling for them to wait, and assembled his po-boy sandwich of fried shrimp. She and Maya had both ordered the fried catfish; she could see Maya's eyes closing in appreciation of the hushpuppy that had come with it. She picked up her own and inhaled reverently. It took her right back to her mother's table and the tense scramble among her brother and sisters to get their fair share of the good stuff.

"He was probably just looking for any excuse," he said, after a good swallow. "The Steeles couldn't afford to keep that old building up. They sold it just a year later. I suspect the man's military pension wasn't nearly as comfortable as he'd expected, and maybe it cost a lot more to live in there than they'd counted on. He might have resented having his wife's nephew to feed on top of all that. Or he might have noticed how well he got on with his daughter. Your dad didn't make it easy, either."

"He didn't?" Dori said.

"Keep in mind Steele was military. An officer. He expected things to be done a certain way. But Nat wouldn't cut his hair. Wore the same jeans day after day. Wouldn't attend church. Skipped class whenever he felt like it. Smoked cigarettes. Got suspended a couple of times. Worked some dodgy jobs for some dodgy people. My mother once told me he was an angry young man, probably still grieving his family. All I knew was he was a lot of fun to hang out with. He always had a way with words. I was surprised to see he'd published a book, but I was not surprised it was a good one."

Dori said, "So people around here did know about that."

"Oh, sure. The Arts Council tried to invite him to come down for a celebration of his work a couple of times, through his publisher, but he never answered. I don't think he wanted anything to do with us. What else were we to conclude when he made up that whole life story? I sent him a letter myself, after I read the book. Never heard a word back. I sure was surprised to see the picture of your house in that article. Why the hell would he build it just like that place he hated?"

"I wish I knew that, too," Dori said. "Do you own it now?"

"Oh, no, no. We rent the office, that's all."

Maya had been eating steadily. Now she put down her fork. "Mr. Chestnut, did you ever see Nathan Bardwell with any people of color?"

Chestnut rested his eyes on her for a moment before he spoke. "I'm sure he worked with African Americans in some of his jobs," he said. "And the school was integrated. Not so much in our academic classes, though. And there was never much crossing of racial lines, at least not socially. Nat did play football, though, before he got kicked off the team over the last suspension. That was *very* integrated. Even our coach was black."

"Do you think Loretta would have committed suicide?" Dori asked.

He looked out the window as if he were looking back in time. "I didn't know her that well. I have always wondered what made them so sure she wasn't just climbing on that old bridge and fell in."

"Why would she go climb that thing all alone?" Maya said, not bothering to hide her skepticism.

"Who says she was alone?" he said. "Maybe someone was with her and ran off, afraid to admit they'd watched her drown. Maybe they were afraid they'd be accused of drowning her."

"And how would she have gotten out there?" Maya asked. "It's in the middle of nowhere."

"Not really. The Ledbetters still live out that way. It wouldn't have been that far for her. And plenty of folks could have given her a ride."

"Like my dad? Did he have a car?" Dori asked.

Chestnut took a big bite of his sandwich and chewed for a while, looking at her. Finally, he wiped his mouth and said, "He had a motorcycle."

Another surprise. Her father had had a motorcycle? He'd forbidden them to so much as ride as a passenger on one.

Just as he'd lectured them about wearing lifejackets. And about knowing how to swim.

Maybe it was a good sign he'd never lectured them about not throwing people off bridges.

"What if Loretta had threatened to tell Ellen she was having his baby?" Maya asked.

Chestnut leaned back and gave her an appraising look. "You have a financial interest in stirring something up here, Miss Davis, don't you? What if this is actually nothing more than two bitter old people defaming a man who is no longer around to defend himself?"

"What if this sheds new light on a book widely regarded as an American classic?" Maya countered. "Which everyone currently believes to actually be about slavery," she added.

"You don't think it had anything useful to say on the matter?" Chestnut said. "I found it profoundly moving."

"I think its authenticity is deeply in question," Maya said. "The more I hear, the more I think Bedford Bardwell gussied up a tale about a poor dumb white girl whose death haunted him by pasting a thin veneer of something with more social significance on top of it and presto-change-o! Suddenly it's a fucking American classic!"

Chestnut regarded her for a long moment. Dori began to wonder if it was simply a lawyerly habit, to allow him to organize his thoughts. "You may have a point," he finally said. "Nobody in this country cares about poor, uneducated white people. We even call them *white trash*. It's as if we've all decided they have no excuse at all for their poverty. I don't know. Maybe Nat knew his book would be more marketable among the reading classes if the victim was a beautiful, dignified black slave. Maybe he also thought it would be more successful if he moved the setting from Florida to Georgia, because most people think Florida consists of Disney World and some beaches. I'm sure we are all guilty of being drawn to what we want to believe. If you want to believe *Tea and Slavery* is yet another fraud perpetrated on the black community, I suppose I can understand that. But I believe you'd be letting your own prejudices blind you to the value of a beautiful book about the human condition."

Maya pursed her lips and looked down at her plate for a moment. "Maybe I'd like to see some other beautiful books about the human condition get a little more air. Some that aren't written by white people. Some that might actually be about an authentic black experience."

Chestnut tilted his head at her. "I find it curious, then, that you're focusing yet more attention on this white author. But I'm also afraid I can't discuss this further at the moment, as I need to get back to the office. Please don't worry about the bill – they will charge this lunch to my account. Do order some dessert if you'd like – I recommend the pecan pie, which your waistlines will be able to handle much better than mine." He stood up and offered a handshake to each of them. "It was a real pleasure to meet the daughter of an old friend, Dori. And I look forward to seeing your documentary, Miss Davis. You all take care now."

"Are you all right?" Dori asked Maya, who was staring after him with a fierce frown on her face.

"I'm fine," she said. "You?"

"Shall we take him up on the pecan pie? Which, by the way, he pronounced *my* way."

"Oh hell yes let's have the pie," Maya said. "Though you *both* pronounce it wrong. And then let's plan out the rest of the day." They sat down, but Maya continued to watch as Chestnut crossed the street and walked toward his office.

She was also unusually subdued about the pie, which was indeed delicious.

Chapter 36

"The thing is," Maya said abruptly that evening, as they were settling into a new cheap motel off Interstate 75, "I have to work with what I've got. I don't have anything this juicy about a black author. I mean, I was thinking about doing a documentary about how the New York literary establishment screwed over Zora Neale Hurston, but Alice Walker kind of already did that. Plus, the more I learned about it, the more I could see how she might have brought it on herself, because she made shit up and she was a freaking loony tune about segregation. I also have my doubts how many people ever read her for pleasure. That dialect of hers, it's almost like reading Shakespeare. Your dad's book at least has some hope of being read outside of school."

"Not as much as you might think," Dori said, and explained about her father's declining royalties in recent years.

"Well, I'm sure they're good right now, thanks to that little joke of yours. And this documentary will help, too, if it gets out." She sounded less confident than usual.

"What if the Steeles are lying?" Dori said. "Is it fair to even give them an airing?"

"They're just the Steeles now? Not your grandparents?"

Dori shrugged. What made someone a grandparent, anyway? It had occurred to her even Marjorie had functioned more like a relative to her – if an awful one – than either of the Steeles.

Maya sighed. "We still don't know it's *not* true. There's still a drowned girl. And that's still suggesting something about where your dad got his story."

She had been quieter than usual all afternoon, as they stopped by various landmarks to film footage: the town, the high school, the river again. Even so, she'd asked everyone they saw if they remembered Nat Bardwell or Ellen Steele or Loretta Ledbetter. Nobody had been particularly forthcoming. A few admitted to vague memories, but no one had been willing to be recorded, except for one voluble fellow who, they'd soon realized, knew absolutely nothing.

On their way from the river, just as Samuel Chestnut had said, they found the Ledbetters' address of record. Confederate battle flag stickers decorated each side of their rusty old mailbox. A sandy drive disappeared into thick undergrowth, where a hulking old oak had a "TRESPASSERS WILL BE SHOT" sign on it.

"Oh, hell, no," Maya said, and Dori was vastly relieved Maya wasn't going to just power through that. She still stayed long enough to film the mailbox and the sign, though. While she was doing that, Dori realized a hill of vines fairly close to the road was actually growing over an abandoned car. Maya got that shot, too.

At that moment, however, she was scowling fiercely at her computer.

Dori said, "Mr. Chestnut's thing about focusing on a white guy is bugging you, isn't it?"

Maya looked up. "Some footage I didn't get is bugging me more. But yeah, it is. I don't know why. What the fuck do I care what some old white guy in a cracker town thinks about my project? I don't need his permission and I sure as hell don't need his approval!"

But perhaps she had gotten used to having it anyway, Dori thought. She said, "When you're done, can I call Joe?"

"You really should take some of that money you're saving and get yourself a phone."

"I can't take on new expenses right now. I don't even have a job."

"I keep you telling you, girl – all you have to do is take this opportunity and run with it." Maya shook her head in exasperation as she watched something on her laptop.

Dori supposed she had already taken a step towards what Maya had suggested. She'd come along, hadn't she? She was even enjoying certain aspects of it. But she also felt bad about it. "Airing your dirty laundry is vulgar," her mother had said many times. She would not have been happy about this project at all.

"Hi, this is Joe Gagnon of Joseph Gagnon Landscaping. I can't answer your call right now. Please leave a message and I'll get back to you as soon as I can."

Dori stared down at the phone in her hand, then out at the partially lit sign of their motel glowing in the warm, breezy night as traffic continued up and down the road and the nearby interstate. This was the fifth call to Joe that had gone to messages. She'd already left a couple. She'd even called his old landline number, but it was no longer in service.

A mosquito whined in her ear, so she slapped at it and headed back into the room.

She and Maya had gone out for a light supper at a Waffle House and watched a little more Jane Austen. Maya was already asleep.

Dori put the phone down on the bedside table between them – Maya also used her phone as an alarm clock – and changed into her sleeping t-shirt.

Why wasn't he picking up her calls? Had he had second thoughts about Lisa? Or about her? Had his phone run out of charge or fallen in a toilet or slipped out of a pocket? Maya had assured her all sorts of things could happen to phones, which made the thought of spending good money on one even scarier.

She got under the sheet and punched down the too-lofty motel pillow as best she could, then stared up at the little red light in the smoke alarm. The Steeles had asked about her mother, and about the house, but they hadn't actually asked her much about herself. They hadn't shown any curiosity about Salinger, either. Maybe they thought they'd already read all about them in the article. Of course, she had also kept them busy with questions.

She had a standing invitation to go back, though, "any time." There was that. It hadn't been addressed to Maya, just to her. So that was familial. They hadn't shown her a guest room, though – or any of the bedrooms.

She turned over in the motel bed, thankful for the refuge, but also aware she was depending on Maya for transportation and Robert Putney for expenses.

Joe had told her she had a home with him if she wanted it. And she did. She just wasn't sure how long it could last, or that it was a smart move. But she wanted it anyway.

But did she still have it?

What was that music? Dori woke in the dark and heard Maya muttering "Fuck!" as she tried to answer her phone.

Was it Joe? What time was it? She peered at the alarm clock on the bedside table between their two beds. 4:23 am. Her heart began to beat hard. Nobody called at that time about anything good.

But it wasn't Joe, apparently, because Maya said, "Mama?" and then listened, and asked, "But she's going to be okay, isn't she?"

Dori decided to go to the bathroom and give her some privacy.

She sat on the toilet in the blindingly bright bathroom and wondered what she would do if Maya suddenly had to leave. Maya was her transportation. Maya was also the one who seemed to know what she was doing.

The night before they'd discussed their plans for the day – getting more footage Maya needed, seeing if they could get a Ledbetter to meet them in a more public setting, then trying to set up another session with the Steeles to confirm or deny what they'd learned in Florida.

Would the per diem be enough to pay for motel, meals, and a rental car of her own? Dori doubted it.

"Bad news?" she said, when she came out and found Maya sitting stock still in bed, her hands on her mouth.

"Big Mama's in the hospital," Maya said, sounding a bit dazed. "She had a heart attack."

"Do you need to go?" Dori asked.

"Yeah," Maya said, and then her face contorted. "Mama said this might be it! Just like that! How can that be? She's never even had a heart problem that we know of! She's only sixty-seven! She's not even *fat!*" She began to cry, which turned into great big anguished sobs.

"I'm sorry," Dori said, and rubbed her back. "I'm really sorry."

Clearly, Maya loved her grandmother without reservation. Dori felt a stab of pure envy. Who could she ever feel that uncomplicated a connection to? Joe, perhaps, someday – if he ever picked up the phone again. Maybe Ruth. Maybe her brother. But it was hard to imagine.

A short time later Maya came out of the bathroom, as immaculately put together as usual except that her eyes were still red from crying. "Dori, I know we talked about you coming to Atlanta with me at some point, but it's going to be insane. Everybody loves Big Mama and it's a big family and they're all going to be converging on that house and totally freaking out. But I don't want to tell you to wait for me here, either, because I have no idea how long this will take."

"How much do you think it would cost for me to rent a car?"

Maya sighed shakily, smoothing a hand back over her braids and looking around the room absently. Dori had completed her own packing and piled all of Maya's belongings in one place to make it easier for her. "I don't know. And you can't rent a car with this debit card. They'll need to put a hold on it that's more than we're allowed per day. Do you have your own credit card? You could use the cash you've saved to make up any difference when the bill comes. Or you could just call Putney and tell him why you need a higher limit."

"I won't have a phone, either," Dori said, just realizing it. There was no way she was asking Putney for more money. She realized she was beginning to breathe too fast and took a long, deep breath to calm herself. She'd managed to survive without her parents for seven years. She could handle this.

She just hadn't expected to have to do it so far away from her car or anyone she knew.

Maya zipped up her suitcase. "Worst case scenario, you go to Atlanta with me and we get you on a plane or a bus back home. I'm sure they've given up staking out the house by now. It's not like you're Kim Kardashian."

Whoever that was.

"Your grandparents also said you were welcome any time, right?" Maya said. "That's another option. I could drop you there on my way up. Maybe you could find out more about your parents. But I would understand if you don't want to do that."

Dori stared at the wall, considering it. It wasn't her idea of a good time. But they *were* her grandparents. And, at least in theory, that was why she'd come along on this little adventure in the first place.

Chapter 37

"Oh, we're *sooooo glaaaaad* to see you again!" Her grandmother's voice stretched into a high-pitched squeal again. She hugged Dori tight and turned her attention to Maya. "Do you have time for a cup of coffee and a piece of cake?"

"Thank you, but I really need to run." Maya gave them both apologetic smiles – the one for Dori looked a shade more sincere – and got back in her car. Dori watched it bump its way down the driveway and mentally repeated her new mantra: *I'm an adult. I can handle this.*

"Her grandmother had a heart attack?" Mrs. Steele said, shepherding Dori into the dim house. "How horrible!"

"Yes, she's very upset."

"How sweet she's so close to her grandma," Mrs. Steele said. "That's something I'd love to have with you, even after all this time."

"Me, too," Dori said, honestly enough.

"Now, it has been an awfully long time since we had anybody to stay, so I'm afraid I'm still working on the guest room. Let's have some coffee, and then maybe you can help me get some more stuff out of there so I can make up the bed."

Dori still hadn't seen any sign of her grandfather. "Where is...?" Dori hesitated. What should she call him?

"Your granddaddy went to the commissary. We're not used to feeding three!" It was said gaily and yet Dori sensed an edge.

"I can help with that. Maybe I could take you out to dinner." It wasn't as if she'd be racking up a motel bill that night.

"Don't be silly. You're our granddaughter. And from what we read in that article, you're not exactly sitting flush yourself."

"No," Dori said. "I'm going to have to find a job pretty fast when I go home." Joe, of course, had said she could work for him. But that was before they'd had sex. And before that second marriage proposal she'd refused. And before he'd stopped picking up the phone. He hadn't picked up that morning, either, before they left the motel, or in the car as they approached her grandparents, when she'd tried one last time.

Maybe it had just taken him a little longer to get angry and dump her than it had the first time?

Well, she'd survive. The whole idea of being back with him kind of felt like a dream anyway.

Not anything she'd really begun to count on yet.

Maya had promised to let him know where she was if he ever did call. Dori eyed the old avocado green telephone on her grandmother's kitchen wall, which was wall-papered in a bilious yellow and green pattern that surely dated back decades. "Do you mind if I make a phone call?" she asked. And could she get any privacy for what might be a rather unpleasant conversation?

"Of course not. But perhaps you could wait until we've drunk our coffee?" Her grandmother picked up the tray, once again arranged nicely.

Dori followed her back to the porch, where she found the rest of the Bundt cake they'd begun during their last visit waiting.

"I hope you don't mind I didn't bake you a new one," Mrs. Steele said. "You were just here, really, and we haven't finished it yet."

"Of course not. Why waste a perfectly good cake?"

Her grandmother smiled. "I can tell we're going to get along just fine. Now, before he gets home – tell me all about your mother. Was she happy in her marriage? She certainly had a lot of children with him. They didn't become Catholic or anything, did they?"

"What? No. We weren't anything. I think they just wanted a big family."

"Goodness. I wonder why."

Perhaps it was because they were building themselves a family from scratch, Dori thought, but didn't say. "Did you know Loretta Ledbetter?"

That earned her a snort. "I knew her mother, Mary Sue. Such a trashy family. Mary Sue started popping out babies when she was just fifteen, just like her sisters, and I guess the next generation saw no reason to break from tradition."

Dori frowned. "So, Loretta's father was...?"

"Oh, Lord knows who Loretta's real father was. Ledbetter was Mary Sue's last name, but she also eventually shacked up with one of her Ledbetter cousins." She shrugged a little. "It's possible that was Loretta's actual daddy. The folks in that little hollow are known for bad teeth and inbreeding."

Dori grimaced. By Mrs. Steele's account, she was inbred, too.

The old woman perhaps realized what she'd just suggested, for she hastily added, "You seem perfectly lovely to me, Eudora. It couldn't have been easy, losing your parents so early."

"No. It wasn't." Dori wanted to ask why they hadn't stepped forward at that point, but couldn't quite gather her nerve to do it directly. "So you knew about it when they died."

"Well, of course. It was national news. Imagine finding out you've lost your only daughter that way! Your granddaddy said we'd lost her a long time before that, but a mother never gives up hope."

Dori took a deep breath. "Why didn't you, um, try to get in touch with us?"

"Oh. Well." The old woman clasped her hands together at her wrinkled neck. "Your granddaddy positively refused. Why on earth would I want to go through all that heartache all over again, he said. You'd be complete strangers, taught all your life that we were awful people."

"We didn't even know you existed."

Her grandmother's mouth twisted. "I don't know if that's better or worse. *Thou shalt honor thy father and thy mother.* Have you even been baptized?"

Dori was vague on what exactly that entailed. "I don't think so."

Her grandmother put a hand up to her own cheek. "Fortunately, it's never too late! Well, unless you're dead. Your poor little brothers and sisters. Shall we go work on the guest room?"

Dori blinked, not able or perhaps even willing to follow her grandmother's train of thought. Religion was not often spoken of among the people she knew in Jasper. Even the Community Church people kept their "John 3:16" and "Jesus is the reason for the season" signs out of sight until holidays came around. Joe, a Congregationalist, had often struck Dori as a bit furtive in his practice, and she wasn't sure whether he had just humored his mother or truly found solace in it. Was he continuing to attend out of faith or stubbornness or because it was good for business? Ruth had ridiculed the Catholic Church she'd grown up in with both glee and bitterness. Whenever the subject had come up at home Dori's father had pronounced religion the opiate of the masses, which Dori only later in school learned was Marx's idea, not his. Her mother had simply told them it wasn't polite to mock other people's beliefs.

The hall to the Steeles' guest room was down a narrow hall made even narrower by its sculpted green carpet and green-and-gold wallpaper in a tiny geometric pattern. They turned left into a room stacked nearly to the ceiling with boxes, baskets, and large bric-a-brac. A tarnished brass coat rack. An old treadmill. A giant gilt-edged mirror leaning up against an old roll-top desk. A narrow lane on either side allowed access to the bed, which was covered in boxes and bags. Tendrils of dusty spider web hung from the ceiling and festooned the walls.

"Maybe I could just sleep on a sofa," Dori said. "I could even find a motel. I really don't mind."

"Oh, it's a perfectly good bed once we get it uncovered," Mrs. Steele said. "I've already moved some of it, but my back is not the strongest."

"Where do you want me to put it?" Dori asked.

"That's the tricky part," her grandmother confessed. "All our storage is pretty full up. But we could start stacking along the wall in the hall. It will give me an incentive to get some of it out to the thrift store."

"Maybe we should just take it to the thrift store today," Dori said. "I'll help you."

Mrs. Steele gasped. "Without even going through it? You may want some of this, you know! There may be valuable antiques in these boxes!"

"Okay, hallway," Dori said, and picked up a dusty box. This revealed the existence of a few dead roaches on the old white cotton chenille bedspread, lying on their backs with their legs in the air.

"Oh my. I can see I'll have plenty of laundry to do!" Mrs. Steele said, and quickly plucked them up using tissues she pulled out of her pocket. "We do have an exterminator here once a month, but I believe these creatures sometimes come in with the groceries."

Dori began to think harder about catching that bus. It wasn't that she was terrified of insects. Joe's lifelong passion for plants had extended to fascination for the bugs on them, so she had developed a tolerance for insects – in their natural habitat. Not where she was supposed to sleep.

Her grandmother had gotten a filthy feather duster and was attacking the spider webs she could reach, which thankfully included the ones directly over the bed. When Dori returned for another box, she said, "You know, some of these are your mother's clothes. They might fit you."

She'd kept them all these years? "Wouldn't they be from … what? The seventies? The eighties?"

Mrs. Steele looked off into the distance, her expression vague. "Reagan was President. Padded shoulders, I remember that. I've cut them out of my favorite outfits. I have a whole drawer full of shoulder pads in different fabrics, just in case they come back in! I'm afraid I have a hard time throwing anything out. It drives your granddaddy crazy."

"I really could help you pack up some stuff for the thrift store, or even the dump, if you'd like," Dori offered. "We could take it there this afternoon."

"The dump! Oh my goodness!" the old lady said, and actually started breathing fast. "No, dear, no. I'd have to go through everything first. Who knows what treasures might be tucked into these boxes? Why, we could be throwing out your inheritance!"

Dori didn't see how people living like this would have anything much to leave, and if so why they would choose to leave it to her. "Wouldn't Uncle Vern be your heir?"

"Oh. Well. We think he's probably passed by now."

Dori blinked. "Probably?" There were pictures of Ellen and Vern hanging in the dining room, and they were both all over the albums. Neither Steele had said a word about this apparent second loss when she and Maya were there the first time. Her grandmother clasped those gnarled hands in front of her throat again. "It's not something we like to talk about. Certainly not with someone like your Miss Davis. You see, Vernon was in the Air Force for a while, just like his daddy. But he hurt his back in a training accident. They put him on painkillers, and, well, it all fell apart from there. We discovered he was stealing from us to support his drug habit. My jewelry, which should have been Ellen's, or yours? He took every good piece I had. He even stole your granddaddy's identity. That was a nightmare of many years' duration, let me tell you. We told him he was out of the will because we were afraid he might murder us for whatever we had left. Not that we ever got around to making a will. There didn't seem to be much point at the time. And that was the last we saw of him. It's been – oh, at least ten years since we heard a word about him. So I believe that leaves you and your brother. There won't be much money. But I believe there *are* some valuable heirlooms. A lot of this furniture is antique, you know."

"I see," Dori said. "I'm sorry about your son."

Really, her grandparents appeared to have some of the worst luck in the world with their own children.

She took the last box out to the hall. One wall was completely lined with old boxes, but the bed was finally clear.

When she turned back, her grandmother had pulled the sheets and coverlet off the bed and wadded them up in her arms. The mattress pad she left in place looked old, but not stained. "I'll just get this into the washer!" she said.

"Can I make that phone call now?" Dori asked.

"Why, of course. But first, let me show you how to work the machine. It's a little cranky. We're on well water here, you know."

Apparently she expected Dori to stay for a while. Also, she seemed to feel that washing clothes was far more complicated than Dori did.

In a utility room crammed with yet more stuff – including a vast array of bug extermination products – they slowly filled the iron-stained tub of the washing machine and, when it was full, poured in detergent. "Next, I always add a little ammonia," her grandmother said, but as she reached for it a door slammed open. "That will be your granddaddy!" she said, and apparently decided the ammonia and the full tub of laundry could wait, for she scurried out of the room. "Hello, dear!" she cried loudly. "Guess who's here!"

Dori caught a glimpse of her grandfather headed for the kitchen with plastic bags of groceries. "There's more in the trunk!" she heard him say gruffly, and she followed her grandmother out through a narrow alley that provided passage through a garage just as crammed with boxes and large items as the guest room had been.

There wasn't much left: toilet paper, paper towels and a couple of bags of sodas. Dori took those, since they were the heavy ones, and headed for the kitchen, where Mr. Steele was putting stuff away.

"Hi," she said.

"Hello," he said. "Welcome back. I hope you appreciate that I went to the commissary on a Saturday for you. And how long will we have the pleasure of your company this time?"

"Just a couple of days, probably. I need to get a bus schedule."

"So your fancy documentary filmmaker dumped you off here. You're not planning to keep filming us, are you?"

"No, sir," Dori said. "Maya's grandmother had a heart attack. Naturally, she needed to go."

"Naturally," he said, with a little smile, as if she were being naïve to believe it. "Put one of those in the refrigerator. No doubt you'll be wanting some later."

Dori was not a fan of soda, especially not of the grape and orange flavors he'd purchased. "I hope you didn't get that just for me."

"Alicia told me to get it. I told her it was a waste of good money, but she insisted. Ellen loved grape soda, she said. Never mind that you are clearly not Ellen." He said it with a roll of his eyes he didn't bother to hide from his wife, who had just walked into the kitchen. Apparently she had stowed the paper goods somewhere else.

"I didn't know that about my mom," Dori said. "There must be all sorts of things I don't know about her."

He harrumphed.

Mrs. Steele said, "The laundry's going. I guess I'd better start lunch!"

"I could take you both out if you'd like," Dori said.

Her grandfather raised his eyebrows. "Could you? And just how do you propose we get there?"

Huh? "I suppose I would be depending on you to drive. And to pick the place. I don't know this area at all." She was already feeling the lack of Maya's phone rather keenly.

He said, "There's nowhere decent to eat around here. Alicia will scrape something together. She always does. Now, if you'll excuse me. I didn't get to read my paper this morning." He paused at the doorway. "I'll take another cup of coffee when you're ready," he told his wife.

He left, and this time it was her grandmother who rolled her eyes. She poured some of the coffee she'd prepared earlier in a mug and stuck it in a microwave for sixty seconds. They stood there, silently, watching the seconds count down. Her grandmother stopped it just before the timer could sound. "Here. Could you?" She pointed her chin in the direction her husband had gone.

Mr. Steele was sitting in his recliner, with the paper held open in front of him. The TV was quietly warning of coming economic chaos and how to survive it by investing in gold. Dori said, "Here's your coffee."

"Microwaved it, did she?" he said, but he took it from her and took a sip. "She thinks I don't notice these small acts of insubordination."

"Is there another phone around here somewhere?" Dori asked. She'd really prefer not to get officially dumped where he could listen in.

He put the paper down on his lap. "Why?"

"I need to call my boyfriend."

"Don't tell me," he said, and sighed. "You live with this boyfriend."

"No, sir."

"Just a boyfriend, not a fiancé?"

"Just a boyfriend." Perhaps not even that anymore, but she was hardly going to go into it with him. She waited, but he offered no assistance. "Is there some reason you don't *want* me to call my boyfriend?"

"You just got here," he pointed out. "It just seems odd, that's all."

"Yes, sir. That's true. But if I can't make any phone calls, I won't be staying long at all."

He raised his eyebrows in surprise. "That would break your grandmother's heart." He didn't say it as if he wanted her to feel guilty. It was more like an observation of fact. Perhaps even a point of satisfaction.

Dori waited, but he said nothing more, just smiled thinly, picked up his newspaper, shook it out and resumed his reading.

Was this some kind of weird-ass military thing?

She went back into the kitchen. "Is there another phone?" she asked her grandmother.

The old woman looked up from the oven broiler. She was bent over, watching it intently, her hands braced on her thighs. She made a sour face in the direction of the den and lowered her voice. "He'll fall asleep after lunch. You can try then." She went back to staring into the oven. "I hope you like tuna fish with melted cheese on top."

"It sounds delicious."

That earned her a smile. "Perhaps you could set the table out on the patio?" her grandmother said. She pointed at a tray where she had gathered placemats, cutlery, dishes, and a bowl of potato chips.

Dori took it out. Her grandfather didn't look up as she passed through the den to the patio. It was hot and humid, even in the shade provided. Cicadas hummed loudly in the yard. A lizard on the screen bobbed his head and skittered away. She could not catch so much as a glimpse of any other house. She couldn't see the road, either, but she did hear a solitary car pass by.

It had been a long, thinly settled drive in from the state road. They hadn't passed many gas stations or convenience stores along the way that she could remember. How long would she have to walk if she needed to get out of there on her own?

During lunch she decided there was little point in putting off the questions she and Maya had wanted to ask. Perhaps her grandfather would be only too happy to drive her to the closest town if she irritated him enough. "Maya and I were wondering what exactly made you so sure my father killed Loretta Ledbetter."

He finished chewing his mouthful of sandwich, watching her the whole time. He held up a finger. "One, she ended up in the river right after she told him she was pregnant."

"According to what we learned, any number of men might have been the father."

"You went to Jeffersonville?" her grandmother asked eagerly. "Did you see the manse?"

"I did. It looked nice."

"For an office building," her grandfather said. "How the mighty have fallen! Your grandmother's attachment to that godforsaken money pit cost us what could have been a much more comfortable retirement."

"*My* attachment!" her grandmother said. "As if you didn't want to move there yourself! As if we ever do *anything* you don't want to do!"

He stared coldly at her.

She dropped her gaze to her plate and picked up and ate a single potato chip.

He turned his gaze back to Dori and lifted another finger. "Two. A few nights before they found that girl's body in the river, your father came home soaking wet on his motorcycle. *What happened to you?* I asked him. *Got caught in a storm*, he said. But he wasn't just wet. He was *drenched*. Had to leave his shoes outside. And he was shivering, even though it was August and hot as Hades. Went right up to the bath, didn't come down until the next day."

He lifted a third finger. "Three. Sheriff came looking for him a week later. He wasn't at home that evening." A fourth finger went up. "Four. When I told him he had to go, he didn't even put up an argument."

"Maybe it was an accident," Dori said. "Maybe she fell in and he tried to save her and couldn't."

"I suppose nobody wants to think their own father is capable of murder." Her grandfather leaned back and wove his long knobby fingers together across his narrow chest. He spread his large hand out, all five fingers extended. "Five. That book of his."

"But Beulah wasn't murdered. She committed suicide."

"Convenient, if that's what you want everybody to think actually happened to the girl you got pregnant. We *are* talking about the man who went on to kill our daughter and most of our grandchildren. And even if it *was* suicide, wasn't that his fault, too? I actually take comfort in my perception he *did* feel guilty about Loretta. I hope it tortured him. I hope it dogged him all the way to hell."

Silence fell.

He stood up. "I believe it's time for my afternoon nap. I just hope I can get to sleep. It pains me greatly to be forced to relive that time of our life." He gave her a parting glare.

They watched him go. "He'll be out cold in ten minutes," her grandmother said. "I mixed some Benadryl into his grape soda."

Dori stared. The old lady smiled. "A woman needs a little peace once in a while. You'll be able to make your phone call without any trouble. Just help me with the dishes first."

Chapter 38

Her grandmother switched the laundry over to the dryer, poured herself a glass of something from a decanter and went into the other room to watch a reality crime show. Maybe that was where she'd gotten that Benadryl idea.

There was still no answer on Joe's phone.

Dori tried Ruth's number. Maybe she could tell her something.

Ruth said, "Oh my God! You haven't heard? He's in the hospital. With smoke inhalation."

"What? Since when?"

"Well, since the fire. It was just... wait a minute, I'm not sure." Dori heard her call, "Thursday night, Mom? The fire at the Manners' farm?" She lowered her voice. "Yeah, two days ago. How long do they keep people in for smoke inhalation?"

"I have no idea!" Dori said. She could hear the hysteria in her own voice. "He hasn't been picking up his phone."

"Well, maybe it melted," Ruth said. "Or maybe he can't talk. Maybe he's on oxygen or something. But most likely the battery ran out and he doesn't have his charger."

"Why didn't you call me?"

"How the hell was I supposed to do that?"

Dori shook her head. "Look, you have to help me. I need to get there. But I'm somewhere in South Georgia at my grandparents' house and I don't even know where the nearest airport is. I'm also not sure these people will give me a ride."

"What happened to Maya?"

"Her grandmother had a heart attack. She had to go."

"Oh. Well, give me your address and I'll look it up."

What *was* the address? Dori scanned the kitchen counter and found some mail. She gave the address to Ruth.

"Oh, that's easy," Ruth said, and directed her to the Valdosta Regional Airport and even offered to pick her up at the other end.

"Now I just have to figure out how to get to the airport," Dori said.

"Call a cab," Ruth said, and read off two numbers for her. "Do you have cash?"

"Yeah," Dori said. She had quite a stash, actually.

"Call them now. Take any flight to Atlanta if you can't get all the way to Hartford. Once you're there you'll have a lot more options. You could fly to Boston, Albany, whatever. It doesn't matter to me. I can come get you."

"Thanks, Ruth. I appreciate it. Do you have the hospital number handy too, by any chance?"

First, she called a cab company. They said they could be there in about twenty minutes.

Next, she called the hospital. Joe had been transferred, they told her. He was at Patriot General in Boston.

"Boston? Why?" Dori asked.

"He's in the burn center," she was told. "Do you want the number?"

"Yes, please."

This time she was told his condition was listed as serious but stable.

Dori took a deep breath. "Can I talk to him?"

"I'll try to put you through," the woman said, sounding doubtful. And, indeed, the phone just rang and rang. Dori let it do so for an obnoxiously long time, but finally hung up.

"Is everything all right, dear?" her grandmother said. She was in the doorway of the den. "You're making an awful lot of phone calls."

"I'm sorry. I just found out my boyfriend is in the hospital. I have to go."

"Goodness! I was hoping we'd have much more time together!"

"I know. I'm very sorry." Except she wasn't. Mixed in with concern for Joe was rather a lot of gratitude for the excuse he was giving her to go.

Her grandmother had clasped her hands in front of her again.

"He won't be safe to drive anywhere, not for a few hours yet. If he even agrees to take you. And I'm afraid I never got a license. Perhaps you could wait until tomorrow? We can work on him gradually that way."

"It's all right. There's a taxi on the way."

Her grandmother's eyes widened. "Oh. I see. Well. Is there anything I can get you for your trip? Perhaps a snack?"

"Thanks, no. I'd better get my suitcase. Would you like me to get those boxes back on the bed for you?"

Mrs. Steele's mouth worked for a bit before she nodded. "Well, yes. Yes, if you don't mind. He'll make such a fuss if they're left there."

So Dori put the boxes back. By the time she was on the last one the cab was outside blowing its horn. "I'm sorry," she said. "The cab's here. Thank you for your hospitality!"

"We should wake your grandfather, let him say goodbye." But she didn't sound at all certain.

"Just tell him I said thanks for the hospitality." She gave her a quick hug, then ran out with her suitcase and hopped in the cab. She waved goodbye from the back window.

She could not imagine any circumstance that would make her want to go back.

In line at the small airport, Dori realized if Joe was in Boston, it wasn't smart to fly to Bradley and waste all that time getting her car and driving to the other end of the state. She turned to the relatively harmless looking woman behind her in line for tickets who had her smart phone in her hand and asked, "Is it possible I could use your phone to call somebody real quick?"

"Oh my!" the lady said, taken aback. "Well... I assume it's a domestic call?"

"Massachusetts," Dori said.

The woman looked her over and looked at her luggage, and said, "I suppose as long as you can do it right here in front of me." She unlocked her phone and handed it over. Dori dialed Ruth, whose "hello?" sounded wary.

"Joe's been transferred to Boston. Patriot General," she told her. "Maybe I should go straight there instead of Hartford."

"Boston? Jesus," Ruth said. "Yes, go straight there. I'll get you at Logan and take you to the hospital. Can I call you back at this number if I need to?"

"No, it belongs to a nice lady in line with me." She smiled at the lady, who gave her a tense smile in return.

"Well, find yourself another nice lady when you're sure what flight you'll be coming in on, and let me know."

"I will. Thanks, Ruth." She handed the phone over to the woman. "Sorry. I'm trying to get up to my boyfriend."

"I heard you say burn unit. I'm a nurse. Did they tell you how bad his burns are?"

"Apparently it's just smoke inhalation. I don't understand why they transferred him all the way across the state for that."

"I'm sure they just want him to be in the best hands," the woman said, and patted Dori's hand. "I wish you the best. I really do."

Something about the woman's pity made Dori's stomach drop. "But it's just smoke inhalation."

That earned her a kind smile and another pat on the hand. "I'm sure your support will mean the world to him. Look, they're ready for you." She gently pushed Dori towards the counter. "This young lady needs to get where she's going as quickly as possible," she said. "It's a medical emergency."

Dori's heart began to thump. Was this woman suggesting Joe could actually *die?*

Chapter 39

It was nearly 10pm when she and Ruth finally arrived at the burn center. She'd called the hospital again before getting on the plane to Logan, to find out if she could visit him even though she'd be getting in so late. This time she'd been put through to a nurse, who'd sounded thrilled that she was coming.

At the nurse's station, one said, "We've been trying to find you!" and another added, "He was so happy to hear you were coming."

"Then he can talk?" Dori said.

"Oh, no, I'm sorry, he's been intubated all along. He was writing notes. He went on ventilation this afternoon, so I'm afraid he's sedated now. You can still see him, though. He may hear you, but he won't be able to respond."

Dori's stomach clenched into an even harder knot. "He's getting worse?"

The nurses glanced at each other. "The doctor will discuss that with you in the morning, but it's very common. Sometimes we just need to make sure they can't cough their tubes out. Do you want to see him?"

"Yes, please," Dori said. Ruth looked pale, but nodded, too.

They had to suit up before they could go on the ward. The smells Dori had long associated with patient care – antiseptics, lotions, plastics, piss, and shit – were mixed in rather more than usual with the tang of blood and the sickly sweet odor of decaying flesh. And someone, somewhere was moaning in real pain, not just confusion.

"I think I'm going to be sick," Ruth whispered. She did look green behind her mask.

"Go back and wait in the waiting room," Dori told her.

Ruth nodded and ran.

In his room, Joe lay still, a tube in his mouth held in place with two ties around his head, and a gastric line in his nose, and more connections running from chest and finger and arm. His lips were bandaged and his ears looked a bit ravaged, but he still looked like Joe. Not unrecognizably swollen, which the woman at the airport had warned her was possible.

At least his chest was rising and falling steadily. A little too steadily.

"It's okay, you can touch him," the nurse said. "The only external burns he has are on his head. Just watch out for the IV lines." She started checking various readings from various pieces of equipment.

Dori reached under the layers of thin blanket to grab a limp, warm hand, wishing she didn't have to wear gloves. "Hi, Joe. Sweetheart. Sorry it took me so long to get here. I didn't hear what happened until this morning." She squeezed, but there was no response.

"He left you a note," the nurse said, and pointed with her chin at his bedside table. Along with a couple of magazines, there was a sheet of paper folded in thirds with a big "DORI" written on it.

She unfolded it and read.

Eu, I'm sorry I couldn't hold them off until you got here, but I guess breathing is kind of a priority. Thank you so much for coming. You'll have to tell me all about your trip when I can actually listen.

I have a favor to ask. If you get a chance, my phone is in my truck, wherever that is. Maybe still at the fire station. The nurses have my keys. If you can get the phone to Alonzo Rodriguez, he can try to keep my customers happy (or you can, but he knows what is needed). The social worker has left some documents in my file that will help you act on my behalf.

If by some small chance I don't make it (but don't worry, I will) please tell your friend Robert Jr. I have some questions about how this happened. 1) I didn't have any training for search and rescue, I'm just a hose man. 2) Summers was the only other guy in there with me. Said it was a "training opportunity." 3) Seems to me I got knocked off the line. Maybe I'm just paranoid. They told me I was confused. But if he did this because of Lisa, he's a menace. (So be careful!)

See you soon. Love you with all my heart. So want to have a life with you,
   Joe

The nurse said, "You okay?"

Dori nodded *yes*, but she was reeling on many counts. Joe thought Chief Summers had tried to *kill* him?

"Did anyone read this?" she asked.

"No, it's addressed to you. Should we have?"

"Was he confused?" He sounded so lucid.

"Probably best to discuss that with the doctor tomorrow."

That was still hours away. "Can I stay here?" she asked.

"It's not really allowed. Most people prefer to stretch out in the waiting room, if they don't have anywhere to go. It might be a good idea to get some good rest and come back in the morning. You look pretty tired."

That she was. It seemed unreal to her she'd started out at 4:30 that morning in Florida with Maya, spent a couple of nightmarish hours with her grandparents in Georgia, and somehow ended up in a Boston hospital on the same day. "I don't want to miss the doctor," Dori said.

"You won't, unless we suddenly get some new admissions."

Dori stared down at Joe, rubbing his unresponsive hand. He looked so defenseless. "He doesn't have anybody but me."

The nurse smiled and looked down at her device. "Actually, a man he works with came by earlier this evening. A Mr. Rodriguez?"

"Oh! Good. Did he get keys?"

She looked down again. "Yes. Mr. Gagnon had left instructions to give them to him. Unfortunately, he was already sedated when Mr. Rodriguez got here." She looked down at her tablet. "He's had phone calls, too, but of course he couldn't talk. And a church sent flowers, but I'm afraid they're not allowed here. He also got something from his department." She nodded over at a small shiny Mylar balloon arrangement that said *GET WELL SOON!*

A pretty incongruous gift if the chief had tried to kill him.

The nurse said, "It's quite a drive from out your way?"

"Yeah, it's at least a couple of hours," Dori said, not adding that

Boston's traffic would intimidate the average Jasper resident. It certainly intimidated her. She was thankful for Ruth, who knew Boston streets well after her years in law school.

She stared down at Joe's beautiful long eyelashes as she caressed his hand.

The nurse watched for a moment and appeared to come to a decision. "If you want to sleep in the chair, I'll get you a blanket. But you should probably tell your friend."

"Oh, thank you!" Dori said. "I won't be any trouble, I promise."

Dori woke to sustained light and bustle. It had been a long, noisy night of people coming in to check on Joe, as well as noisy traffic in the hall outside. She'd almost begun to envy Joe his sedation.

She stayed as she was for a while, watching between cracked eyelids as a woman efficiently suctioned Joe's breathing tube. She was trying to figure out if what she was hearing was normal or not when the woman said, "You must be the girlfriend."

"Yes," Dori said, and sat up and stretched her shoulders back. "Dori. How's he doing?"

"Marissa. Best to discuss that with the doctor."

Dori sat up straighter. "Is it bad?"

Marissa shook her head, but repeated "Best to discuss it with the doctor."

Were all these people just slavishly obeying the rules, or did they figure bad news should be left to someone at a higher pay grade? "When will the doctor be here?"

Marissa looked up something on her tablet. "There's a broncho scheduled for 9:30, but he usually pops in earlier to see how patients are doing."

Dori looked up at the clock. It was just past seven in the morning.

"Take a shower if you want," Marissa said. "I doubt he'll show up before eight."

"I'm a CNA," Dori said. "I could give him a sponge bath if you want. And make the bed."

That earned her a smile. "Ask the charge nurse at the desk. I doubt anyone would object."

As Dori had already discovered the night before, just sitting there next to an unconscious guy was a bit maddening. She'd sat and told Joe that Alonzo had his keys. She'd told him how flattered she was he trusted her with his affairs. But Joe, of course, had not responded in the slightest way.

She hadn't included that she was pretty freaked out about his theory about the chief, or that all this was adding rather a lot of pressure to what was essentially a four-day-old relationship.

That wouldn't be kind. Or true, even. They had a much longer history, if the first round counted.

But would she have trusted him as much as he appeared to trust her? Did he really trust her, or was it simply that he had nobody else? What if having nobody else was such a strong force bringing them together that it disguised other ways in which they would *not* be good for each other?

Was that what had happened with her parents? If she'd been her mother, she'd have wanted any opportunity to get out of that house, too.

Technically, of course, her parents had had a successful marriage. At least until its end.

"You've done this before," a voice said, and Dori looked up from where she was drying Joe's long, pale leg to see an older man she hoped was the long-awaited doctor smiling at her from the door.

"Yes." She covered up Joe's leg and stepped back. "Certified for it, even."

"Eudora Bardwell, I believe? I'm Dr. Halloran."

"You can call me Dori." They shook hands, hers gloved and his not. Did he realize he'd just gotten contaminated? But he immediately went over and washed his hands at the sink.

He was well into middle age and had a prominent belly. Not for the first time, Dori wondered why so few health professionals seemed to work at staying healthy. But then, perhaps they understood better than most that everyone was going to go somehow, someday. "I'm sorry it took me so long to get here," she said.

"It can be challenging to make arrangements when a patient gets transferred." He gave her a sympathetic smile.

"I was traveling down south, actually. I didn't hear a word about it until the middle of yesterday."

"Ah," he said. That earned her a look she couldn't quite interpret. Didn't he believe her?

"They keep telling me I have to ask 'the doctor' about his prognosis," she said, not bothering to hide her exasperation.

"Well, let's see how he's doing this morning. Normally I'd ask you to step out, but since you're *certified*." There was a gentle mocking there. He began a quick examination, listening, palpating, and checking various vitals. Then he stopped and folded the tablet in his arms against his chest. "Mr. Gagnon has a lot going for him. He's young and healthy and has no significant external burns. Now that you're here, we're glad to see he'll have some family support, too. He did have some CO exposure, but that's pretty much cleared by now and doesn't seem to have affected him greatly, though issues can take a while to show up. His airway injury is pretty serious, however. Unfortunately, there's really no predicting how any given patient with this condition will progress. What we're dealing with right now is edema...." He stopped. "You know what that is?"

"Swelling," she said.

"Yes. Edema, resulting in some fluid build-up, sloughing of the cells that line his airway along with some of the soot that got down there, bronchospasm. He's been on 100% oxygen since the EMTs got to him, and that will continue. *If* we can keep his airways clear and avoid infection, he should be fine in a couple of weeks. Three at most."

She'd expected to hear something more like three days. "That long?"

"Well, every patient is different. Maybe he'll breeze through this in less time. Again, this is assuming no infection, no seriously obstructed airways. I know it can be challenging to take that much time from your other obligations, especially this far from home." He reached out and briefly squeezed her hand. "And of course, he won't be conscious for most of this. That doesn't mean he might not be aware at some level that he has you here. So we do encourage families to stay if they can. Talk to him, touch him. It can make a difference." He put the tablet down on a bed table and started pecking away at it.

"Time isn't the problem," Dori said. She had plenty to spare at the moment. "I guess I just didn't realize how serious it was."

The doctor didn't look up from what he was doing. "How long have you two been together?"

She released a startled little laugh as she realized how ridiculous the answer was going to sound. "Since Monday night." At his look of surprise, she added, "But we were also together in high school. I've known him since kindergarten."

"Nice guy?"

She nodded, then added, "Yes," since he was looking down at his tablet. "Most of the time."

"Most young women want a guy who's nice *all* of the time." There was a mild reproof there.

"He's fine. He's a lot more mature now than he was at eighteen."

The doctor grunted, a noncommittal noise that suggested to Dori he was still a bit concerned. "He certainly trusts you. Once he heard you were on your way he made arrangements with the social worker to give you durable power of attorney, medical proxy, even made a simple will and named you the beneficiary. He seemed especially vehement about the death benefit the state gives on-call firemen. He didn't want any proceeds to go to his ex-girlfriend."

"Death benefit?" Why would the doctor even mention that?

"Five hundred thousand dollars to wife or surviving child," he said. "You're not going to qualify for a relationship that began Monday. His ex-girlfriend wouldn't either. Unless it was actually a common law marriage?"

"No," she said. "But their child...."

"He has a child?" he said, clearly surprised. She could see him racking up more doubt about Joe's character.

"No. At least, not yet. She told him she was pregnant this week. We don't know if it's true."

That earned her another grunt. Nothing she'd said so far was helping Joe's case, was it? She said, "He told me he was going to support that child and share custody with her if she went ahead and had it. But she didn't necessarily know that ... and she's also the fire chief's daughter."

He lowered the tablet to one hand and stared at her. "You know, that's interesting. Because usually injured firefighters get *a lot* more support than this from their department. We thought perhaps it was because he hadn't been doing it for very long. Either that or he was unpopular for some reason. The distance can be a challenge too, of course."

"In the note he left me he said he hadn't been trained for what he was doing there yet. And the fire chief took him in there, and he thinks he got —" How had Joe put it? She pulled the note out of her pocket and checked. "Knocked off the line." She wasn't sure what that meant. She held out the note.

He read it, and perhaps reread it, since she was sure he read faster than the time he spent staring down at it. "He believes the fire chief might have tried to murder him."

It sounded crazy. "He does say maybe he was just confused."

"They said he was, at the ER. It's a common symptom of CO poisoning. Then again, if he was babbling about someone trying to murder him, they might have just assumed he was." He sighed. "You Bardwells do seem to attract some bad luck, don't you?"

She took a step back. What did that have to do with Joe? Though knowing who she was perhaps explained the weird look earlier. Did he also know about her recent notoriety?

"You *are* the daughter of Bedford Bardwell, aren't you?"

"I don't see how that can possibly be relevant here."

He gave her a tight smile. "Well, I enjoyed *Tea and Slavery,* and I'm sorry about your family. We won't have a murder if your young man doesn't die, so let's focus on that. Why don't you finish up here, and then when we come back you can go get a cup of coffee while we do this bronchoscopy."

"I'm not squeamish. I could stay."

"No, you can't." he said. "*I'm* squeamish about sticking things down people's airways when their loved ones are watching."

Chapter 40

Later, when Dori thought about the two weeks she spent with Joe in the burn unit, she would see it as a kind of enforced retreat in which she could put aside concerns about how to make her way in the world or what other people thought of her.

But the world had kept intruding, too.

The third day, Ruth had shown up with Robert Jr., a combination Dori hadn't expected. Over coffee in the cafeteria, they'd caught her up on the state of Joseph Gagnon Landscaping LLC, which was not particularly good. On the plus side, Alonzo Rodriguez had managed to keep the lawns of the clients it retained mowed, but he wasn't sure how to make payroll at the end of the week. And a couple more of Joe's clients had dropped him.

Robert told her he'd started digging into the story of the fire. "I've heard a rumor he panicked in there," he said. "Which is not something you usually hear in a situation like this. Usually what you'll hear is that someone got 'disoriented'. A firefighter *can* panic, especially if he's lost and running out of air. But to have his comrades actually *call it* that? That seems a bit harsh. Especially when they're all volunteers to begin with."

He wanted to know anything Dori knew about how Joe had come to be injured or why he might have an enemy. She told him about his break-up with Lisa, though she decided she'd better not share the part about Lisa saying she was pregnant. For all she knew, that might get Joe's house burnt down, and it wasn't really her secret to reveal. She also decided she'd better not share the note Joe had written, at least not unless Joe took a turn for the worse. She did tell Robert what Joe had said about lacking the training for what he'd been doing at the fire.

When the discussion about Joe's situation petered out, Dori said, "So you two drove all the way over here together?"

"It's only a couple of hours away," Ruth said, but it seemed to Dori that she looked a little pink.

"I wasn't sure you'd talk to me if I came on my own," Robert said, which appeared to deflate Ruth a bit. "Would you have?"

"Oh heck, yes," Dori said. "It's pretty boring in there."

He laughed. "That's flattering."

"Don't you have a writing assignment to do for this guy's ruthless media magnate father?" Ruth said.

Robert said, "Hey!" but there wasn't any heat in it.

Ruth continued, "Maybe you should use all this boring time to get started on that. Or come back with us, use that Power of Attorney to fix Joe's payroll, and grab your car. If what you say is true, he'll never even notice you've been gone."

Dori felt a shiver of panic down her insides. "They think even patients in comas can tell when their family is around."

"Are you sure you're not just afraid to set foot back in Jasper?" Ruth said. "I know how that feels. You have to push through it."

Dori said, "I'm not afraid. I just don't feel I should leave." But even as she said it, she began to wonder if Ruth was right.

Later, as she sat with Joe and his relentlessly pumping lungs, she began to wonder if she was shirking her true responsibilities.

She rubbed moisturizer on his arms for the second time that day, mostly because it felt like a kind of interaction. "Should I go?" she asked him, and held her hands over bicep and triceps as if she could hear his answer through his skin. But there was nothing, just the mechanical whoosh of his chest being pushed out and pulled back in.

A state police detective arrived on the fourth day. He asked Dori questions and took Joe's note as evidence.

Too late, it occurred to her that if something went wrong and Joe died, that had been the last word she'd ever have from him. She should have made a copy. She bought a notebook and a pen in the gift shop and wrote down the one line she had read again and again: "So want to have a life with you."

Maya arrived later that same morning. Dori had asked Ruth to let her know what was happening.

She looked tired. Her grandmother had died of her heart attack and had just been buried just two days earlier. "Oh my God," she said, "There was so much wailing and carrying on at that funeral! I'm from Vermont. I don't care what color you are, you don't fucking *wail* in Vermont."

"I'm so sorry, Maya," Dori said.

"She had high blood pressure, but other than that she seemed completely healthy. Do you know African American women die of heart disease 30% more often than white women? And women in general are almost twice as likely to die of a first heart attack as men?"

"No, I didn't know that. How's *your* blood pressure?"

"Probably pretty fucking high at the moment! I'm still fucking pissed off about it!"

"Want me to borrow a cuff and check it?"

Maya drew back. "You know how?"

"Yeah, of course."

Maya's blood pressure was 128/90. "That's pretty high for someone your age," Dori said. "You should probably keep an eye on it. But it could just be because you're fucking pissed off."

Maya snorted.

Dori said, "You aren't heading towards Jasper, by any chance?"

"Yeah, I am. Putney wants me to finish that inventory. You want to come with?"

"Yes, please." Dori had begun to think maybe it just took her a ridiculously long time to get used to any new idea. "I have to do some stuff for Joe's business, and I might as well get my car." She went over to the sink to wash her hands, then grabbed Joe's hand in both of hers. She rubbed her thumb across his chilly palm and wondered if he was cold. At least he wasn't shivering. Maybe she'd tell the nurse he seemed cool before she left. "I should be back tonight. Tomorrow at the latest."

There was no response, of course. She brushed his hair back. She'd stopped wearing those sweaty nitrile gloves with him. Nobody was getting on her case about it, either.

Maya stood next to her and looked down. "Does his helplessness make you love him more, or less?"

Dori squinted at her. What kind of question was that?

Maya said, "I was so shocked to see Big Mama lying in a hospital bed. It was like the whole world had gone wrong. But it also made me feel very protective, like she was a baby who needed to be taken care of. That's a different kind of love, but very powerful. But with a man? Women get turned on by a tough guy who can protect them, not the other way round, don't you think?"

Dori leaned down towards Joe's ear. "Don't worry, I still think you're a tough guy."

There might be an element of truth to what Maya said, but she knew it would make Joe insane to think that.

She stopped at the nurses' station to return the blood pressure cuff. "I'm going to go home for the afternoon. I've got some stuff I need to take care of."

"Good," the nurses told her. "You need a break. How can we reach you if we need to?"

Dori gave them Maya's number.

Maya shook her head. "You *really* need your own phone."

"I know," Dori said. She had finally gotten used to that idea, too. Which was a bit ironic, because cell phones weren't allowed on the burn unit.

Chapter 41

They stopped at a strip mall in Leominster and Dori finally bought a low-end smart phone and thirty days of cellular service. She used it to call Alonzo Rodriguez, and they arranged to meet at Joe's place later that day.

Rodriguez turned out to be a tall, muscled, darkly attractive man who – at least to Dori's eye – filled Maya's recent description of a tough guy rather well. However, when he gave Maya an admiring once-over she responded with a death stare.

He just grinned and showed them Joe's office in his dining room and the manila envelope of cash and checks he'd been collecting from customers.

"Will we be able to pay the men this Friday?" he asked. "I thought I'd use the cash if I had to, but that's not the way he does it."

"Do you know how much they're due?" Dori asked.

"Well, I know their *hours*," he said. He pulled a grubby notebook out of his back pocket and tore off a page for her. "And I know their rates. I'm not sure about the withholding."

Damn it. Joe *would* be so upstanding he actually paid his laborers on the books. "I'll try to figure it out," she said. "How about I'll leave them right here, signed, and you can come in and get them and give them out when he usually does – Friday after work? If I can't figure it out, I'll put cash in envelopes for them, and he'll just have to adjust it later."

"That works," he said. His phone pinged and he looked down at it. "If you don't need me anymore, the crew is waiting."

Maya said, "How does she get back in here?"

"Oh yeah," he said. He grabbed a key off a pegboard rack on the wall. There was a whole row of keys, with keychains, each neatly labeled. "Here," he said, and handed it over. "Let me know if you run into any problems." He winked at Maya and left.

Maya huffed. "As if I'd ever go out with a guy who mows lawns for a living!" she said. "No offense."

Dori raised her eyebrows. "Right now you're hanging out with someone who used to wipe butts for a living."

"Yeah, okay, I wouldn't marry you, either."

Dori grinned and looked around the dining room/office. The old table and chairs were still there, pushed off to the side instead of centered under the old light fixture. It wasn't a beautiful use of space, but it was very orderly.

Maya said, "Is Joe as much of a raving tight-ass as that pegboard suggests?"

"I don't know. Maybe. Ask me after I figure out what to do for his payroll. When do you think the credit union will close?"

"Look it up on your phone, girlfriend," Maya said. "You can do that now, remember?"

Maya drove them to her house, which still had a large blue tarp over a section of the roof. There were no reporters in evidence anywhere. Dori didn't even go in, just got in her car and raced to the credit union in Greenfield before it closed. There, the clerk called the hospital to verify one of the witnesses, then added her to Joe's accounts, lips pursed a bit in suspicion, though that faded when Dori promptly deposited his accumulated checks and cash.

Since the credit union was close to the grocery store, she stopped by just in case they'd thought of assigning her any hours anytime soon. They hadn't. She explained she was in the middle of a hospital vigil and the shift manager smiled a little too kindly and said she should just call when she was available again, and then they'd "see."

It didn't sound encouraging. Perhaps it was past time to file that unemployment claim. Though her assignment from Putney counted as work, she supposed. So maybe not.

Back in Joe's dining room-slash-office she sat down and tried to figure out how he did his payroll. His house was very quiet when she was the only one in it, and she jumped nervously when the air conditioner installed high on the dining room wall suddenly kicked in. Alonzo had shown her Joe's secret password stash, not that she needed it, since his computer wasn't locked and his browser automatically plugged in everything she needed.

That didn't mean Dori had the slightest idea how to use Quick-Books.

She called Maya for help.

"Google it," Maya said. "Or do a search on YouTube. Sometimes the videos are the most helpful."

Dori said. "At this rate I'm going to be here all night!"

"So you'll be there all night," Maya said. "At least he has air conditioning." She gave a pained sigh. "This place isn't any more comfortable for having been closed up for days."

"I was really hoping to get back to the hospital tonight."

"What do you think your guy would want? His employees to get paid or another foot massage he doesn't know he's getting?"

Even if Joe were somehow being heartened by the physical contact at some level, the answer was obvious in all the paperwork he'd managed to get done before they knocked him out.

"I'll bring you over some pizza when I'm done here," Maya said. "You figure out how to do those checks in the meantime. Because I'd sure as fuck rather watch more Jane Austen than try to figure out your boyfriend's accounting."

Dori called the hospital – Joe was fine. In fact, they were going to start weaning him off the respirator the next day. "Don't get too excited," the nurse told her. "That can take days."

"Will he be awake during it?"

"He'll be sedated until we're sure he's breathing well on his own."

"All right. I'm going to stay here tonight, then. I've got to figure out how to pay his employees. I could probably stand to do some laundry, too."

That earned her a chuckle. "You might want to bring a change of clothes for him, too. He *will* be going home one of these days."

That idea was both thrilling and a little nerve-inducing. Would they still get along in the same room, at the same time, when they were both awake?

Dori succeeded in getting the checks set up in Joe's accounting system, complete with withholding. What she couldn't figure out was how to print the damned things. She decided she'd let Maya help her with that, and went upstairs to see if she could find a change of clothes for Joe. His bedroom was stiflingly hot with no air conditioner in evidence, and looked virtually unchanged from his high school days, complete with the same old Che Guevara poster and a John Deere calendar from 2006. It was also layered in dust. It finally occurred to her he was probably using the master bedroom, so she walked down the hall.

Yep. She smelled Joe the moment she opened the door, at least in part because of the overflowing laundry hamper next to it.

His mother's room had always been almost Shaker in its simplicity, with a white chenille bedspread and heavy but simple oak furnishings, its only splashes of color coming from the books she tended to pile everywhere, and an old crazy quilt she'd kept neatly folded on a quilt rack at the end of her bed. Joe hadn't changed much about it, except that the crazy quilt was in a jumble at the foot of his unmade bed, and the piles of books had changed from romances and women's fiction to nonfiction – politics, economics, business, horticulture – plus a few mysteries and a few literary titles.

She lay down on his bed nose first and inhaled his scent unpolluted by hospital lotions. Then she turned on her back, remembering how their dog General had loved to roll in stinky old animal carcasses in the woods, and stared up at the old ceiling.

How recently had Joe had sex with Lisa here? And on these very sheets, probably, because they were not particularly clean. She inhaled, but there was no particular tang. Nothing strong enough to drown out the dirty laundry, anyway. Nothing that suggested a new life had begun here.

Could she be a good stepmother to Joe and Lisa's kid? But she had years of experience taking care of multitudes of people she wasn't related to. So that shouldn't be a problem.

She turned on her side. On the bedside table sat her father's manuscript, not even in its manila envelope.

So he'd been reading it. Did Lisa know about it? What if Maya had come up here and seen this? Would she have realized what it was? Would she have felt betrayed by Dori?

Was Dori betraying her by not revealing it?

But what did Maya care? She was just doing a job for Robert Putney.

And Dori sharing an unfinished first draft with a man who wanted to claim it as partly his would be betraying her father.

Right?

After meeting her grandparents, she had much more sympathy for her father. For her mother, too. Who *wouldn't* have fled that couple, given half a chance? And despite being homeless teenagers with nobody looking out for them, they'd made a go of it, even achieving fame and fortune, if only temporarily.

It made her feel pretty unaccomplished in comparison.

The doorbell rang. Maya with the pizza, probably.

Dori grabbed the manuscript and stuffed it under Joe's bed – despite the cat hair and dust bunnies, torn condom wrapper and lone sock already in residence there – and bounded down the stairs.

But it wasn't Maya.

Chapter 42

He was a tall man. Tall and broad and smiling, with heavily silvered curls and a neat silver mustache. A good looking man.

The SUV parked in front said "Fire Chief." She took an involuntary step back.

"Hi there," he said, and held out a hand. "I'm Lionel Summers, Chief of the Jasper Fire Department. I heard there was someone in the house, and hoped Joe was home. You must be...?"

"Hi. Dori." Who had told him someone was in the house? She looked across the street, but the driveway was as empty as it had been since her arrival.

Perhaps someone driving by.

"Is Joe home?" Summers said. "We've been worried sick about him."

The smile and the eye contact never lapsed. He didn't seem like a guy who was lying. But what did she know?

"He's still in the hospital. I'm just here to take care of a little business for him." She smiled politely even as her gut tightened at the memory of Joe's written warning to be careful.

"But he's going to be all right?" the man said.

Every social instinct her mother had ever drilled into her was screaming at her to volunteer information, but as far as she knew this guy had tried to kill her boyfriend. "So far so good," she said.

Let the lack of detail annoy someone else for a change.

"We weren't sure he could have visitors yet."

That was surely an outright lie. She gave him a tense smile. "Well, I'll tell him you were asking about him." She used as final a tone as she could manage.

He lowered his voice. "Perhaps we could talk." He looked past her into the house, clearly suggesting they could do it indoors.

No way was she letting that man in. She patted her pocket to make sure she had the key on her and stepped out, pulling the door shut behind her. She gestured at the wicker chairs on the front porch, took one herself, and smiled in invitation. "What would you like to talk about?"

He sat down, his rigid smile finally betraying some tension. "Poor Joe had some pretty bad luck on his first interior attack. I feel just terrible about it. It obviously took us longer than I would have preferred to get him out of there."

"He was in there with you, I believe?" she said.

He gave her a sharp look. "Yes. I thought it would be a good training opportunity for him." He shook his head. "You just never know."

"Yeah, I guess not." Would they ever know if he'd tried to kill him?

Summers coughed slightly. "Anyway, we raised some funds to help him out with his lost work days." He pulled an envelope out of his pocket and handed it over.

"Oh. I'm sure he'll appreciate that." She took it and smiled. "Is there anything else?"

"Well." He looked down at his lap, spreading large hands across his thighs. "A state police detective came around to ask some questions about the fire. Did he talk to you folks, too?"

Was there any way to avoid answering such a direct question? "Do they think it was a suspicious fire?"

"There hasn't been a determination on that yet." He looked out across the street, where a car was pulling into the driveway. A woman got out and stared a bit at the two of them sitting on Joe's front porch, but was quickly distracted when her two kids exited, too. They all went in. There was no friendly wave this time.

"I was away," Dori said. "In fact, I didn't know Joe was in the hospital for nearly two full days."

"Oh. Sorry. He still had Lisa listed as his emergency contact with us." He coughed. "I guess she didn't feel the need to keep you informed."

"It would have been difficult for her to reach me anyway. How is she?" Did he even know about the pregnancy? Did he care if he didn't, at this point? "Joe told me she was pregnant."

His face reddened. "Yes. She told us, too. But now she says she got it wrong. This whole thing!" He shook his head. "You can imagine a father's feelings."

What was he saying? Part of her longed to ask "So you thought you'd try to kill him?" Instead, she said, "Joe was anticipating child support and shared custody, so I expect he'll be relieved to hear he's off the hook. Maybe a little disappointed, too."

Summers stared at her for a moment, then stood up. "Well. I'd better get going." Although he towered over her, he seemed somehow diminished. "Please make sure he gets that check. It was a pleasure to meet you, Dori." He stuck out his hand.

She shook it because she couldn't think of anything else to do, smiled politely, and sat there for some time after he drove off, pondering the conversation. She opened the envelope and peeked at the check. It was for a couple thousand dollars, drawn on the department's account.

Was this something she should tell the state police about? She still had the detective's card in her wallet.

But Maya pulled up at that moment, and walked up to the porch, pizza box in hand.

She was a much more welcome visitor.

"So do we get to watch *Persuasion* tonight?" Maya asked, between mouthfuls of a slice of mushroom pizza at Joe's kitchen table. Dori was eating hers even as she gathered two glasses of water and a roll of paper towels.

"If you could just help me print out the checks," Dori said. "It keeps telling me it *has* printed them, but nothing happens."

"Is the printer on?"

Dori scowled.

Maya said, "It can't be that hard. It really can't."

"I look forward to you showing me how not hard it is."

Maya chewed and looked around the kitchen. "This kitchen looks like 1920 got a couple of 1980 appliances plugged into it. He doesn't even have a dishwasher."

Her house and Joe's were both weirdly frozen in time that way, but hers was mostly ersatz while his was genuine. "His mother didn't have a lot of money to spare. I think it's kind of charmingly retro, myself."

Judging from the look on her face, Maya did not think it was any kind of charming anything. "And now you've seen boy-friend's accounts? Nothing to make you run screaming away?"

"He's doing better than I am. But he also has more debt and expenses. My guess is that it could get scary if he can't get back on his feet fairly soon."

Summers' check would surely help, but she wasn't sure about depositing it. Couldn't that conceivably signal acceptance of something that Joe might not want to accept?

The doorbell rang again.

This time it was the neighbor. She had a pet carrier with her. "Hi, I'm Mattie! I saw folks in the house. Joe's finally home?"

"No, I'm sorry, he'll be in the hospital a while longer. I'm his, um, girlfriend. Dori."

"Oh, yeah? My husband went to school with you and Joe. You remember Ralph Murchison?"

"Oh, yeah, Ralph," Dori said, and smiled. Ralph had spent his school years afflicting most of his teachers and then had surprised everyone by going into teaching himself. "Funny guy."

"The thing is, we've both kind of lost our sense of humor about this cat. I guess she's nervous or something because she pees just about anywhere. Could be a vet thing, but I'm afraid our budget doesn't stretch to taking other people's cats to the vet."

Dori said, "No, of course not. I'll figure something out." She grimaced a little, wondering what it could be.

"We'd be happy to come over every day and feed her and change the litter," Mattie said. "I just can't take any more peeing. I thought about just stowing her over here anyway, but I didn't want to do that without letting someone know."

"You have a key?" Dori said.

"Oh, we've had each other's keys for years."

Maya came up behind her and Mattie's eyes widened. "I'm sorry. You have company." Her eyes shifted back to Dori's a bit anxiously.

Dori introduced Maya as the daughter of a professor at Brooke College, which Maya quickly amended. "I'm also a documentary filmmaker." She pulled out a card and handed it over.

Continuing doubt flitted across Mattie's face, but the insistent meows coming from the carrier at her feet seemed to erase it. "So, anyway, here's Betty. If you could just wait a sec I'll send the kids over with the food and the litter pan."

Dori said. "If you *could* come in and take care of her while we're gone, that would great, because I have to go back tomorrow. Maybe we could also exchange phone numbers? That way you can reach me at the hospital if you need to."

Mattie obligingly pulled out her phone – she was much better at adding a contact than Dori was – then dashed back across the quiet street.

Maya sighed. "She's wondering why there's a black girl in Joe's house and whether this means armed gangs and crack ho's will follow."

"Maybe we should invite her to watch Jane Austen with us. That will calm her fears."

"No. Just no."

A few moments later they took delivery of litter box and cat food, met the kids, who offered enthusiastic advice about what Betty did and didn't appreciate, and then their mother herded them out and they closed the door on it all. The house rang with silence until it was broken by a long and plaintive meow.

"Hey, welcome home, Betty," Dori said. She opened the carrier and the cat bolted out and ran up the stairs in a flash of fur.

"Let's heat up the pizza," Maya said, and turned back to the kitchen.

"I'll do it," Dori said, a little worried about what Joe might have in his oven. "Why don't you try to get the printer to print while I do it?"

The oven was disgusting. The walls were layered in grease and the racks dripped with brown bits of charred food. On the plus side, this suggested Joe actually used it sometimes, unless perhaps his mother had lost interest in cleaning it at the end of her life and it had sat that way, entombed in grease, ever since.

She noticed he had a toaster oven, which was also grimy, but not nearly as bad, and set two slices to heat up in it.

In the dining room a printer whirred into action, so she went to watch eight paychecks spit out. They looked so real. It was really that easy? It made getting paid seem much less magical.

Maya said, "You were sending it to One Note."

"What the hell is that?"

"Nothing worth explaining. I reset the default, so you shouldn't have that problem again."

"Thank you," Dori said. She leaned against the doorway between kitchen and dining room and looked around. Even here, the wood floor needed scrubbing. There were spider webs on the ceiling. "This house needs a good cleaning."

"Don't *you* do it," Maya said. "It's *his* house. Next thing you know you'll be cooking and cleaning and raising his children, and then you'll be old, and then you'll die."

"Maybe that's not such a terrible thing." Especially the getting old part. Her parents and four of her siblings hadn't gotten to do it.

Maya closed her eyes as if she were seeking patience. "You said they were going to pay you off for your portion of the house. Use that money to go finish your degree. Do something with your life."

"Right. They'll probably hold campus protests if I step foot in a classroom."

"No, that's already old news. If you don't want to go to school, write a book. At least get a deal to have a ghost writer write a book, while you've still got enough notoriety to make them want you. It's too bad you can't find that manuscript."

Dori immediately pictured it, sitting upstairs in the litter under Joe's bed. "Dad wouldn't have wanted anyone to see that one. Not ever. It was an incomplete first draft. For a writer that's like going out in public with your underwear showing and a whole roll of toilet paper trailing behind you."

"Yeah, for a writer who's alive. Your dad is dead. No more toilet paper required." Her eyes narrowed. "Did you hide it?"

Another direct question she sure as hell didn't want to answer. Fortunately, she smelled something that made a useful distraction: burning pizza. She snatched out the two slices. There was a little char. "You don't mind a little carbon, right?" She transferred them to the kitchen table. "Should I put more slices in?"

"One more for me, maybe," Maya said. "You didn't answer my question."

"Why do you care? Did he offer you a big finder's fee or something?"

Maya grinned. "There you go. You're getting better at figuring out how that guy works!"

"You know why he wants it? He claims he was collaborating on it with my father, and he knows my father isn't here to say that's a lie. He wants his name on a bestselling novel. He tried to write one once and it was a dismal failure. But with my dad's name on it as co-author, he's pretty much guaranteed a spot on the New York Times Best Seller's List."

"So?" Maya said, and blew on the end of her slice. "Your half of that would still make you and your brother a nice little pot of money."

"No, it would make the *trust* money. They can spend that however they want. Maybe they'll give some to us, maybe they won't. And Putney's a trustee."

"Oh." Maya crossed her arms. "But so is Joe, right?"

"Yes. But God only knows what they are getting up to while he's out of commission. Probably selling those papers off to the Putney Lewis Library for a very reasonable price."

"Nope, not that. I haven't finished the inventory yet. And he was fine with me going off with you. Honestly, I think you're being a little paranoid."

"Am I? Maybe he's hoping your documentary will get rid of me once and for all."

Maya stared at her, slice drooping in her hand. "We know that ain't gonna happen."

Dori stood up, her own slice forgotten, to make her point. "Suppose he gets his hands on it, gets to edit your footage however he wants? At best, I look pathetic. At worst, I look... pathetic." She sat down. "I mean, I *am* pathetic. I know that. You can't edit around that. But that doesn't mean I have to like that being broadcast to the whole world! Or my dad suddenly looking like a possible murderer. And Robert Putney would *love* that, because then *Tea and Slavery* would get another burst of notoriety

– and then the next one, the one he claims is partly his, will have a good boost out of the gate. If he can just find it and get it finished."

Maya said, "Why the hell would he go to all that trouble? You're forgetting, people like Putney always get their way eventually. He'll sue you for that manuscript if he has to."

"He can't sue me for something I don't have," Dori said. "Maybe it got thrown out with the wet stuff after that roof leak. Maybe Salinger used it for toilet paper one day when were out. How the hell do I know?"

She couldn't believe how enthusiastically she was lying. But if anything, Maya was looking more suspicious.

"Come on," Dori said, grabbing the not-burned second set of slices out of the toaster oven. "Let's take these in the other room and watch some Jane Austen."

"I'd like to be one of her heroines," Dori said, when it was all over. "All they ever have to do is tuck some lace and put up with their relatives. They don't have to work. They don't have to cook. They don't even have to reheat pizza."

"Which they never get to eat," Maya said. "And they have to find the right husband or end up eating gruel in a garret for the rest of their lives, or being some pathetic Aunt Somebody. And neither of us would have had those lives anyway. We'd be the ones cooking and cleaning for them. Or worse. I'd probably be off on some plantation, cutting cane and getting raped by the master."

Oh, yeah. There was that. Dori could definitely imagine herself emptying chamber pots. "Do you want to sleep over?" she asked Maya.

"Why, are you scared to sleep here alone?"

"No. Just figured I could save you some cash."

Maya smiled. "Nah, I think I'll go. It's too late to cancel my reservation. Whatever happened to that cat?"

Good question. Dori hoped she hadn't spent the evening peeing on Joe's bed. "I'd better go up and look for her."

Maya picked up the bag of cat food still sitting by the front door and shook it. "Here, kitty, kitty!"

They waited.

"She must have been really traumatized," Dori said.

"Children will do that to you," Maya said. "I'll help you find her before I go." She started climbing the stairs, calling "Here, kitty, kitty!" She paused to say, "If Joe has a can of tuna anywhere, now would be a good time to open it."

Dori headed for the kitchen, until it occurred to her one of the most obvious places to look for a cat was under a bed. By the time she'd followed Maya into Joe's room, Maya was already on her knees. "There she is," she said, in a coaxing voice. "Come on, girl-friend! No one's going to hurt you." Then she stopped dead for a moment, and pulled out the manuscript. She looked down at it. "What is this?" Her tone had gone completely flat.

"I don't know," Dori said. It was a pathetic attempt.

Maya read out loud:

Surely she knew that he would do anything for her, anything at all. That she was the center of his life and the balm of his existence – sadly, though, not the only balm he ever sought. For even he was be-ginning to consider the possibility that he had been drinking too much.

She held it up for Dori to see. "This is it, isn't it?"

Dori said nothing. What could she say?

·"Eudora Bardwell, you lied to me!"

Dori said, "I refuse to let Putney get his hands on this. Don't I get to keep anything from my parents?"

"Yes, of course, but not this. This is important literary shit," Maya said. "My father would *kill* to get a look at this. Not to men-tion it's also worth a thousand bucks to me personally."

A thousand? Damn. "Then I'll pay you a thousand bucks to keep your mouth shut about it."

"I don't want your money that I know you don't have! I can't believe you lied to me!"

"I didn't want to fight about it. And I didn't want that bastard Putney to steal it. And I don't want my father exposed to any more ridicule than he's already faced."

"Dori, your father is DEAD." She shook her head. "MY father the Bardwell critic is ALIVE. As are YOU. And for fuck's sake, Dori! That cat could have peed on it while we were watching a fucking Jane Austen video! I may not be a trained archivist, but I can tell you that you're being really, really, really irresponsible here."

"You're right, I'll take better care of it." She held out her hand. "But it's still mine."

Maya pulled it closer to her chest and glared at her.

Was Dori literally going to have to fight her for it? Maya was taller and wearing potentially deadly shoes.

"What do I have to do?" Dori said. *Call the cops* was on the tip of her tongue, but she had a feeling that would be unforgivable.

Maya stared down at her. "You know what? I'll keep this quiet on one condition."

"What?"

"You have to finish it. You have to finish writing this novel."

Dori stared at her in disbelief. "I'm not a writer. And I'm not my father."

"So study his work and pretend you are – the *Tea and Slavery* version of your father, not the arrogant self-pitying fucking bullshit version who wrote the other books. Finish it. And when you get your nice big fat advance, then you can pay me my thousand bucks. No, make it two thousand."

"The minute I try to do anything with it, Putney will find out about it."

"Yes, but if he finds out about a book finished by the daughter of the author, he's going to have a hard time making his own claim stick, won't he? This is the perfect way out, don't you see?"

No, Dori did not see.

Maya said, "So, here's the deal. I want to see a finished manuscript no later than six months from today. Your finished draft. And for fuck's sake make a copy of this thing, and put the original away somewhere safe. Watertight. Fireproof. Bug proof. Low humidity. You hear me?"

"I can't just sit down and write a book the way my dad would have!"

"Who said it would be easy? But if you don't do it, I'll tell Putney you have it, and he'll sic his lawyers on you. He'll probably try that anyway, but he won't know for certain you have it unless I tell him."

"I bet you think you're doing me a big favor with this," Dori said bitterly.

"I am. A huge favor. Do we have an agreement?"

Dori glared at her. Maya glared back.

"Fine," Dori said.

"Say it."

"Yes, we have an agreement. I'll try to finish the damned book."

"You will finish it. There is no try." Maya handed it over. "Good night."

And she left.

Dori sat down on Joe's bed. Maya had taken full advantage of that opportunity to push her exactly where she hadn't wanted to go. Of course, it was her own damned fault for not hiding the manuscript better.

Betty picked that moment to finally come out from under the bed and meow. She hopped up on the bed and looked expectantly at her. Dori rubbed her ears. The calico rolled on her back, inviting more attention to the soft white fur of her belly, and Dori gave it, enjoying the loud purrs.

Taking care of Joe in the hospital would be so much more rewarding if he could purr to let her know he appreciated her ministrations. Or smile. Squeeze her hand. Anything.

"Sorry I'm not there with you," she said to the empty room and the man who wasn't in it.

She looked down at the manuscript. "Sorry you're not here, too," she said to the father who was never coming home.

Chapter 43

Joe was weaned off the respirator quickly, though not so quickly that Dori didn't wish she had stayed at the house a little longer and cleaned it up instead of sitting at his bedside reading her new photocopy of her father's manuscript over and over and brooding about what the hell she could do with it. It was better than *The Buried Prince*, but that wasn't saying much.

Also, it appeared to be the story of a marriage at the breaking point. How the hell was Dori supposed to write about that? Where had her father expected to go with it?

Towards sobriety? Towards a happy ever after? But how likely was that? *Tea and Slavery* had ended with the deaths of the heroine and then the hero. *The Measured Marriage* had ended in a flop house. *The Buried Prince* had ended with – crap, yet another drowning. Somehow she'd forgotten.

Once Joe was conscious again, after the sweetness of having him squeeze her hand back, and that first, tentative kiss on his healing lips, and the joy of hearing his painfully hoarse voice, she also faced an unfortunate truth: Joe was not a good patient. And Dori knew patients. Joe didn't rise to the level of Kevin, but he was still pretty awful.

He was shocked by how long he'd been out, and frustrated at the continued shortness of breath that made their walks down the corridor necessarily slow and short. He complained that his mind was fuzzy, his lungs were shot, his legs were weak, the food was bad, the ward was loud, and his business was going down the toilet while he was trapped there. It didn't help that Chief Summers had taken to calling and asking for him. He also had a short, awkward visit from a couple of older ladies at his church, who spoke fondly of his mother, told stories of him as a little boy, and then spoke warmly of the concern shown by their dear friend Lionel Summers. Joe was steaming by the time they left.

Dori had brought a tablet she'd found in his office so he could check in on his virtual life. She had him take her through his accounts, and they were able to determine that no, he was not in any immediate danger of going bankrupt. Yes, he was probably going to have a bad year. If the winter lacked snow and thus snow plowing, another source of income would be required. But it wouldn't have to be anything unrealistic. And that wasn't even including any income she might start earning.

Not too long after that they were shuffling down the hall when one of the swollen burn patients in his bloody, oozing dressings was wheeled by. Dori told Joe what she had learned from the nurses – that each day they took the burn patients in to have their burns scraped clean – which promoted healing but was also sheer torture, so much so that even heavily sedated patients still felt it.

After that he stopped complaining about every single thing quite as much.

But he still complained.

The state police detective showed up to interview each of them again, separately. With Dori, he simply listened to her story again, asked her how sure she was about some of it, and took notes. He also took pictures of the check Summers had given her.

"Should Joe deposit it?" she asked him.

"I don't see why not," he said. "Let me know if it bounces or anything."

According to Joe the same detective had pushed back hard on everything Joe told him. Was he certain he'd been knocked off the line? (Yes.) Had he seen Summers push him? (No.) Was it possible something had fallen from the ceiling? (Maybe.) Had Summers told him it was a training opportunity? (Yes, he had. He'd told everyone.) Did he have any reason to believe Summers knew his daughter was his beneficiary? (He was the fire chief!)

"He made me feel like I was the bad guy!" Joe said, and coughed. He was still getting oxygen and nebulizer treatments.

When Dr. Halloran dropped by later that morning, he said Joe had stabilized, and if he could handle a full day without oxygen he could go home – but he'd need to get his outpatient therapy, keep up the nebulizer treatments, and keep a rescue inhaler with him at all times. His breathing would get better over time. Probably.

"*Probably?*" Joe said. He looked horrified, which Dori thought was understandable.

"Here's the thing," the doctor said, "It varies tremendously from patient to patient. You're going to need to try to stay away from irritants. No smoke of any kind, including wood fires. You're in landscaping, right? Wear a good quality air mask when you're dealing with fine particles of anything – fertilizer, grass, dirt, sand, pollen, anything. Obviously, I don't recommend fire-fighting again anytime soon."

Joe didn't answer. He was blinking hard.

The doctor looked over at Dori. "Frustration and anger and depression are very common at this stage of recovery," he said. He looked at Joe. "Let's see what we can do to help you with that, too."

"I just want to go home!"

"And you will, probably tomorrow or the next day. But I don't think you're going to want to drive out here every day, so we need to make sure you can survive whatever quality of outpatient therapy you get out your way."

"Every day?" Joe said. "Every DAY?"

"Mr. Gagnon, we didn't nurse you back to health just to lose you to an asthma attack or pneumonia," the doctor said. "Your airways suffered a serious injury. It's going to take time to recover. I'll check in with you tomorrow."

When he left, Joe lay back, staring at the ceiling. He had tears in his eyes. And he did not want to talk about it.

On the drive home Joe watched her navigate Boston traffic for the six minutes it took to get onto I-93. She noted some white knuckling and ghost braking, though he managed to avoid saying anything out loud.

He'd never been in a car she was driving before. She'd been his passenger many times, as he'd often driven them in his mother's old car once he had a license.

He'd been driving that night of the prom, too. That had certainly been an awkward ride home. But he'd gotten her there, and he wasn't the kind to abandon his date somewhere, no matter how bitterly she had embarrassed and disappointed him.

Perhaps that was why, even in that sullen silence, she had never imagined they wouldn't share another conversation for eight years.

She had downloaded the same app Maya used for navigating, even though she'd studied the directions and they were not complicated. She just found it comforting to have a voice brightly warning her when a turn or an exit was coming up.

"These things don't always work in the hills," Joe said. "And sometimes they'll lead you dead wrong."

"I studied the route ahead of time. It's not hard. I just like the way it gives me a little heads up before I have to do something."

He frowned and settled back into his seat. "Did you get any of that writing done yet?"

"No." He knew that. Had either of her parents nagged as much as he did? Not in front of the children, she didn't think. In fact, her mother struck her as one of the most complaisant wives in history. Or maybe she'd just hidden it all from the kids. Certainly her father's manuscript was obsessed with the idea of a beloved wife who was about to throw in the towel.

But how could her mother have gone anywhere? Once the youngest were in school she'd worked part-time here and there. Nothing that could have supported all those children.

And if Dori grew dependent on Joe and his business, couldn't the same thing happen to her?

Perhaps neither of them should depend on it. There was at least a possibility he would continue to suffer breathing difficulties for the rest of his life – breathing difficulties only aggravated by what he did for a living.

For the moment, they had agreed she would stay with him while he was recuperating, and beyond if she felt comfortable. Putney's debit card was still, miraculously, giving her $200 a day, and she was still saving most of it. She already had a security deposit to put down on a place if she needed it.

Earlier, she'd told him, "You have to promise you won't get mad if I decide I need to move out once you're feeling better."

He'd stared at her for a long moment. "I'd be worried," he said. "I suppose I might be angry, too. But I don't want you to feel trapped. So ... okay. I promise. I'll handle it."

"Good." It came out clipped.

"You're worried I'm going to pull another eight-year hissy fit the first time we have a serious disagreement."

"Yep."

"I'm not the same guy I was eight years ago. I don't have to have every single thing go my way anymore. I'll probably still *try* to make it go my way. I haven't changed *that* much. But I don't want to be an asshole. I really don't. Assholes die alone."

"Lots of people die alone," she said, remembering some of her patients. "It's not always because they are awful. Sometimes they're just the last ones left."

Was that why she felt so bound to him now – that he had no one else? That they were both orphans? Salinger was still alive, so someone else shared some of her memories of the family they'd grown up in, but Salinger was about as dependable as a moth. And Joe also had many shared memories of their childhoods, their parents, their growing up.

What if it was what Ruth had suggested, that the daughters of alcoholics felt compelled to take care of people? If that was the subconscious dynamic going on here, what would happen when and if Joe was back to perfect health?

She glanced over from the traffic on I-93. Joe had fallen asleep. Some of the skin on his ears and lips and around his mouth was a new and fragile pink, mottling his normal tan. His hair was long and unkempt, and the beard he hadn't gotten around to shaving off yet was scruffy.

But oh, he was beautiful.

Chapter 44

The first couple of days felt like playing house, interrupted by drives over to the hospital in Greenfield for follow-up respiratory therapy. She cleaned and scrubbed and vacuumed and cooked and washed up. They watched television together, and she gently nagged him to do his nebulizer treatments, and in the rush of energy he'd have after them they'd often fool around, which was lovely. The rest of the time he slept a lot.

The third day her debit card from Putney no longer worked. She called Maya, who she'd been avoiding because of their fight over the manuscript. "Did your card cut off, too?"

"No, because I'm still working," Maya said. "What are you doing?"

"Taking care of Joe."

"Not what he's paying you to do, girlfriend. He carried it longer than the original agreement, didn't he? There aren't any reporters asking around anymore, anyway. You could come home."

"I guess I owe him that article, then. Or an interview."

"Better write your own. You're too fucking honest in interviews."

"I know – but what should I write?"

"Can't help you there. I've got enough of my own work to do." There was more than a hint of impatience there.

Dori had been starting and deleting openings to the article for days. The more she'd tried to think of what to write, the more tangled up she'd get in imagining potential disaster scenarios. She said, "If I write about Loretta Ledbetter, that's going to scoop your documentary."

"Oh." Maya sighed. "Yeah, please don't. You could write about your grandparents, though. That's already out there."

"I can't write about them. Not truthfully. It would make them look like terrible people."

"You don't think they're terrible?"

Dori said, "Well, maybe, but who am I to say they're terrible? Maybe they're doing the best they can and that just isn't very good. I don't see any point in hurting their feelings." Her grandmother's, anyway.

"Your father sure as fuck didn't worry about hurting their feelings."

"But I think he kind of did. He changed the names. He changed the location. And the time. He called it fiction. A lot of it probably even was."

Was *that* why her father's later books were bad? Had he run out of material?

Maya said, "I don't think he did all that to protect them. I think it was to protect *him*."

"Maybe I could write about blackface."

Silence on the other end, then: "I seem to recall recommending that in the first place."

Dori said, "I could write about how I came to understand just how insensitive that joke was."

There was a grunt. "Maybe."

"Which would have to include writing about you, because you're the one who enlightened me."

There was an even longer silence.

"Ha, see!" Dori said. "It's not such a great thing to contemplate when it's *you* being written about!"

"No, I'll take the publicity. I need it. You just better make me look damned good."

"I can do that."

"And not a word about the official black friend thing. Dad would kill me."

"Of course not," Dori said. She felt a little flutter of nervousness. "Is that still how you see it? As official?"

"Oh hell no," Maya said. "If it was official, do you think I would have given you back that fucking manuscript? Are you working on that, at least?"

"I'm thinking about it."

"Thinking ain't writing."

"You want to come for dinner?"

"Joe won't mind?"

"No, of course not."

But perhaps Joe did. He got quieter and quieter the more Dori and Maya chattered over the proper way to cook string beans and whether mayonnaise should have anything to do with it, why "ma'am" shouldn't be considered an insult, how to rank various Jane Austen videos, and what a menace Dori's grandmother was with the Benadryl.

"I'm going to go up to bed," he finally said. "I'm tired. It was nice to see you, Maya." He gave Dori a peck on the cheek. His face was grey.

"You need another treatment," Dori called after him.

He didn't answer, just plodded slowly up the stairs.

What was going on?

Maya twisted her mouth disapprovingly. "Don't hook yourself up with a guy who's jealous of you having friends. That never ends well."

"Maybe he's really just tired," Dori said. "He tires easily."

"Doesn't sound like much fun."

"He's still healing. Breathing is something we take for granted, you know?" She pushed around the remains of her dinner. In addition to the string beans, she'd made ham and biscuits. She was becoming her mother.

Maya asked, "How's his work going?"

"I'm not sure, honestly. His crew still goes out every day. But he seems pretty anxious about it." Depressed, too, she thought, but didn't say. She was pretty sure Joe wouldn't appreciate her talking about it.

The next day Joe called the state police detective and put the phone on speaker so she could hear it, too. What was going on with the case? Nothing, he was told. They'd learned Summers had asked permission to use the old farmhouse in a training drill and he had then, belatedly, admitted to setting the fire himself – he claimed he hadn't at first because he was worried about getting blamed for Joe's injury. But the case for attempted homicide was still completely circumstantial. The prosecutor had deemed there wasn't enough there to persuade a jury beyond a reasonable doubt. If they came across something more definitive they would, of course, take it up again.

"So he just gets off?" Joe said. It seemed to Dori there was something broken in his voice.

The detective said he might get somewhere with a civil suit charging negligence, or he might not. "You should probably think about how your neighbors might react," he warned him. "The taxpayers are the ones who'd be on the hook to pay damages. And you should talk to a lawyer about it if you're thinking of doing that. At least you've got some time to see what your damages are, whether it's medical bills or loss of income. I'd document all of it if I were you."

They'd both sat there, a little stunned, when the conversation was over. She put a hand over his and squeezed it. "You all right?"

He pulled free of her clasp. "I'm going to take a walk."

"I'll come with you."

"I'd really rather be alone."

"Do you have your inhaler?"

He pulled it out of his pocket and waved it in the air in disgust. "Of course I do. Can I go *anywhere* without it?"

"Just don't do anything crazy."

"I don't have enough breath to do anything crazy!"

She went up to the bedroom and watched as he slowly paced the border of his property, though she lost sight of him among the gnarled apple trees in the north corner. Then he moved back to the gravel driveway and seemed to take inventory of his big equipment. Several times he bent and coughed. Then he went into the barn.

She stood at the window petting Betty, who was flopped over her shoulder. Dori listened to the cat's contented purrs and watched and waited.

And waited.

All right, that was enough waiting.

She heard it from the bottom of the stairs, the awkward hiccup-ping sound of a man weeping. And then a fit of coughing. And then more weeping.

Should she go to him? He obviously didn't want to be seen. But what was she there for if not for moments like this?

He had obviously heard her climbing up, since she found him trying to clean his face on his shirt.

He was in the furthest corner of the room, close to where that old dresser had been back in the days when the loft had been a crowded storage space.

She sat down next to him. "We used to have a good time back here, didn't we?" she said.

He sighed, and coughed, and shook his head. "I wish I'd never laid eyes on Lisa Summers! I thought I'd come back home and build a future out of what my mother left me. And now it's all gone to hell. Honestly, I don't even want to see these people any more. I wish I could leave this fucking town and never come back. I really do."

Unlike Joe, Dori had always felt like an outsider in Jasper. "Then let's go."

He shook his head. "I can't. Not without starting all over from scratch. Everything I have is locked up in this house and this busi-ness."

"You can't sell it?"

"Not for anything close to what it's worth to me. Not yet." He sighed. "I really thought I had it figured out. It seemed clear to me you can't ever get ahead in this country unless you own some-thing yourself. Even if you have to build it yourself. But I hadn't accounted for how a business like this one can go south in a sec-ond if you cross the wrong person. I knew Lisa's dad was going to be protective, but I thought, so what? I'm a good guy. He won't ever have any reason to bother me."

She squeezed his hand. There was no point in suggesting he might have been a little gentler in letting Lisa down. It probably wouldn't have made any difference anyway.

"But now ... I tell you what," he said. "The only people who can *really* do whatever they want in life are people like Putney –

or Summers, with his goddamn smile and his glad hand."

Her old Marxist boyfriend was back. But she didn't feel like celebrating.

He took some deep breaths, and some deep coughs. "Dori, you shouldn't let yourself get stuck here. You need to go finish that college degree! You need a decent career. You stay here, you might end up just like my mother did, trying to keep things together without any help from a man who can't support his own family."

"You're not your dad."

"What if I never really get back on my feet?"

"You're already back on your feet! Joe, you just walked the property and then you climbed up here!"

"Like an eighty-year-old man."

"It won't always be like that."

"It won't matter if I don't have any clients."

"Did you lose another one today?"

"No."

"Have you lost any more this week?"

"No."

Dori suddenly realized she sounded just like her mother, talking down whatever recent hysterical complaint one of the children had brought her. Had her mother had to do this for her father, too? What had she done when the hysteria was warranted?

They sat quietly for a moment.

"Maybe we should call those people whose lawns haven't been mowed for them for the last two weeks. Could be they've had a change of heart by now."

"I don't want them back. They're Summers' cronies!"

She sighed.

"I know, I know," he said, and sighed. "Mom would tell me apparently I just need to feel sorry for myself and to let her know when I was done."

She smiled. "Don't you just hate that? I was just thinking about my mom, too."

"Seriously, though. What if I can't ever breathe properly again?"

"You could get a desk job. You have the degree, you have the skills. We'll figure something out," Dori said. "Our parents scraped a living out of some pretty rough times. You and me, we're already experts at it."

Chapter 45

Perhaps because she finally understood how much pressure Joe was feeling, Dori got to work more seriously at something besides homemaking. She borrowed his computer to get herself a new email address and contacted Robert Putney to suggest the article idea and ask for a specific page count and deadline.

He tersely passed her on to an editor, who asked for 1,000 words and gave her a deadline at the end of the week.

Less than a week? Dori was a little panicked. She was also too embarrassed to ask what it paid, if anything. She'd used or withdrawn over $4,000 from Putney's debit card, which seemed like more than enough for 1,000 words. Maya said that was chump change to Putney, but it seemed like a heck of lot of free money to Dori.

It seemed like less after she'd tried six different lead paragraphs and found herself struggling to say anything about blackface that couldn't conceivably be interpreted as racist by someone.

Joe left her to it all morning, staying busy with his crew for a bit and then with phone calls upstairs. Only after she heard the hum and hiss of the nebulizer upstairs did she realize they'd missed a scheduled treatment.

She went upstairs to where he was sitting on the old bed, reclining on a pile of pillows against the slatted wooden headboard, bare feet crossed in front of him, eyes shut. A cold front had come through the night before, so they'd turned off the air conditioners and opened the windows. Sheer curtains softly lifted and fell.

His eyes opened when she crawled up next to him on the other side. "You okay?" she asked.

He nodded and squeezed her hand. The pump hummed and the mist hissed. It was strangely intimate, the way illness could shrink a life down to one room, to a pair of lungs seeking a breath, to a hand in your hand.

"How's it going?" he asked her, when the medicine was gone and he could put the mask aside.

"I suck."

"That's what you always said in school before you got a hundred on a test or an A on a paper."

"That was school. This is reality. I'm sorry I forgot to nag you to do your treatment."

"Yeah, I think I need to try to keep to the schedule a little better myself. Couldn't figure out why I was feeling so crappy."

"And now?"

He pointed to his straining jeans. "I think I may be developing a Pavlovian reaction to the sound of the nebulizer. At least when you're around."

"You're not the only one," she said, and took off her shirt.

Sex with a breathless young man required a measured pace, they'd already discovered. But it also turned out that wasn't such a bad thing.

Later, after lunch, she was struggling with her explanation of the history of blackface when it occurred to her some research would help, especially if she could find that minstrel show video Maya had shown her. Her first instinct was to go to the library. Then she realized Joe's computer had internet access. So she did a search for "blackface."

And that was when her name first came up.

There was the original article about her, and a bunch of opinion pieces by other people reacting to it, most of them arguing about *Tea and Slavery* and authenticity and the peculiar blindness of white privilege, some explaining what blackface was, and others reporting about the storm of condemnation it had caused, or the effect on Bedford Bardwell's sales. Her heart thumped as she read so many casual assumptions she was either racist or ignorant or stupid.

It made her wish she could open up her own skin, step out of her body, and leave it behind, starting over fresh as someone else. In fact, for the first time, it occurred to her the most immediate advantage of marrying Joe might be the opportunity to go through the rest of her life as Dori Gagnon instead of Eudora Bardwell.

At the bottom of the search results page was a link to Twitter posts with #BardwellBlackface in them.

Her father must be turning over in his watery grave. #Bard-wellBlackface

So much white privilege, so little understanding. #BardwellBlack-face

#BardwellBlackface Stupid racist bitch, paint blackface on her, rape her, stab her ugly heart.

Just shows what white-ass bullshit mythology Tea & Slavery is. #TheRealBedfordBardwell #BardwellBlackface

#BardwellBlackface Don't blame Bedford Bardwell for his stupid racist brat. Too bad she wasn't in that plane.

And more. Hundreds more. Rape and murder were shockingly common threats. There were also some racists holding her up as a hero of the white race. She read and read. Every time she reached the end, more tweets would load. Every once in a while one would strike her as particularly hurtful.

Went to school with that bitch. Total snob. Not surprised she's racist too. #BardwellBlackface

She and that fucking coward @GagnonLandscaping deserve each other. #BardwellBlackface

Ugly inside, ugly outside. Nobody in this town likes her. #Bard-wellBlackface

It didn't help that someone had been posting racist taunts as @EudoraBardwell, complete with links to blackface videos. Each one had generated outraged, murderous responses, though she also noticed a few responses saying things like "This is not the real Eudora Bardwell, you fucking idiots." They were from @DocumentingDavis.

"How do u know?" someone responded.

"Sitting at lunch with her right now. No twitter account. No phone. Clueless not racist."

"You eat with that racist bitch? What the fuck is UR problem?"

"Fucking idiots like you."

Dori flashed back to those meals on the road when Maya's fingers had been tapping away. It didn't seem even the least bit rude anymore.

She crept upstairs. Joe had fallen asleep. Good. He had enough to deal with already, and she had a feeling he hadn't checked in on @GagnonLandscaping for a while.

She called Maya. "Can I come over?"

"Girlfriend, it's your house."

"Nobody's hanging around waiting for me to show up, are they?"

Maya told her to wait a minute. Then she said, "Nope. All clear. Why, is someone bothering you?"

"I looked up my name online. I saw the tweets."

There was a long silence. "Are you okay?"

"Not really. I mean, I knew it was bad. But not that it was THAT bad."

"Maybe you shouldn't be driving. You want me to come get you?"

"No. I can drive."

And she could. It was a reassuringly normal thing to do. She'd left a note for Joe, and drove the mile or so to the Bedford Bardwell House. How many of the people in the houses she passed had Twitter accounts? And if that was what was happening on Twitter, what were they saying at the fire house, or the churches, or the general store?

"You look a little pale," Maya told her. "Which is to say even paler than usual."

"I feel like I've been kicked in the stomach by a million little feet. Not such a big deal individually, but when you add them up..."

"I've actually been researching this problem," Maya said. "You're not the first person it's happened to. What you need to do is start replacing all that bad shit with your own good shit. You can probably get it done in less than a year. You need to start doing it anyway to help sell your book. The fortunate thing is that bad shit sells, too. So really it's a win-win."

"It doesn't feel like a win-win!" Dori said. "Maybe I'd rather just run away to Peru." Maybe Joe would like to go with her.

"They *do* have the Internet in Peru."

"The Klondike, then. The Arctic. Wyoming."

Maya handed her an old envelope. "Forget all that for a minute. What do you think of this?"

On the back of a telephone bill envelope, her father had written:

Drunk realizes asshole boss fucking his wife
Royal bender
Wakes in jail
Kicked out of house
Tries to enlist boss's wife
She doesn't care
Sobers up out of sheer rage
Living in car
Starts campaign to ruin boss's life
Belatedly realizes this ruins his own family's life
Gets shit together so he can help them
Traumatized wife wants no help
Gives it surreptitiously
Finally figures out that's what love is
Sets ex up with a good man
They're happy
Finally, he can start drinking again

"Sounds like an outline, doesn't it?" Maya said. "Does it fit what you have so far?"

Dori stared down at it. "Yes. But I can't write that!"

"Yeah, I know. Who'd want to write that as the ending of their own father's book? You think you have bad press now!"

"You know what? Let me just give the manuscript to you. You get your finder's fee. I'll start mowing lawns."

"Or you could change it to a happy ending. All you'd really have to do is say, 'Finally, he can start drinking again. But he doesn't. The end.' That would be happier."

"Dad never wrote happy endings."

"Yeah, but you see, it's your book, too. People will say, oh isn't it sweet, she saved her daddy the drunk."

"Maya, you are the most cynical nice person I know."

She smirked. "I found something else you're going to love."

Dori followed her into her dad's office, which was stacked with at least a dozen document boxes, though there were a still a few stacks of loose papers.

Maya said, "Remember you told me Putney tried to write a novel and it was a miserable failure?"

"Yeah."

"See this shelf?" She pointed.

"Oh my God, is that it?" Dori said, and pulled it out. It was a fat hardcover with a bright red jacket and a giant metallic gold title: "TABLOID," though "ROBERT PUTNEY" was in type almost as big. As soon as she opened it, a stack of folded papers fell out.

Maya said, "Careful, that's what's important."

Dori bent down and picked them up. They were print-outs of an email conversation between BedfordBardwell1970@aol.com and r.putney@putneypublishing.com.

Ran into your agent today, Nat, and he said you have a new one in progress. Excited to hear you are back in the saddle. Would love to hear more about it.

Hi, Robin. It's about the damage alcoholism wreaks on a good marriage. We'll see how it goes.

Sounds a little bleak. Hope all is well.

Ha. We're fine. I hope. It's possible sobriety can wreak a little damage, too.

Well, we would love to see you both soon. We'll be up in June.

Think I'd better focus on the work and the family for a while. But I'll keep it in mind.

What's your setting?

Contemporary this time. A town like this one.

Dori looked up at Maya. "That doesn't sound like collaborating to me."

"I know." Maya said, "There are a couple of other exchanges in there that make it even clearer. He was printing them out and keeping them all in that novel behind him on the shelf. Maybe he didn't trust Putney any more than you do."

"Have you found any records of money loaned or given to him by Putney?"

Maya said, "I've found check stubs, but they are for your mom. They say editorial. Read the next batch."

Hey, Nat, I have an idea for your book. What if your MC drinks because of sexual abuse by a relative when he was a kid and then he finds out his stupor left his own kids at risk from a sexual predator? That could up the ante, right? Maybe even lead to some bloodshed? Punch things up a bit? You should be thinking of that next movie deal at this point in your career.

Robin, I'm grateful for all you have done for us, but please don't suggest specific plot ideas to me. If I had been planning to write something like that before, I couldn't now, not without leaving myself open to the charge that I'm using your idea.

Understood. But as I know I've mentioned before, there are worse things than collaborating on a project together. I've got the deep pockets and connections to promote the hell out of anything we come up with. And you do *need a success.*

Thanks, Robin, but that's not how I work. You could ask Ellen if she'd like to collaborate on a novel. She'd probably be more amenable to that kind of thing. And she's a damned fine editor, if you pay attention to what she says. I'm certainly planning to listen better this time.

I'll keep it in mind. But you should keep my proposal in mind, too. I hear your eldest is at NYU. It only gets more expensive from here.

She's on scholarship. Dori's our star pupil. She can do whatever she sets her mind to. But thanks again for your interest.

Dori sat down on the old sofa and reread that last message.

"You're fixating on the last bit, aren't you?" Maya said.

Dori nodded, blinking back tears.

"It surprised me," Maya said. "If you don't mind me saying so. You haven't really struck me as the most confident person I ever met."

"I didn't know he thought that about me," Dori said, and swallowed hard. "Maybe he was just saying it."

"He never said anything like that to your face?"

She shrugged. "Yeah, but it was always kind of sarcastic. Like *look at Miss Goody-Two-Shoes with her Fancy A's.* 'Real artists take chances. Real artists break the rules.' That's what he always told me. Besides, you learn not to take anything a drunk tells you too much to heart."

"And your mom?"

"Oh, mom was always supportive. But she was my mom. She was supportive of dad, too, no matter how bad he got. So ... there was not that much credibility there, really. It's really nice to see him writing that, but did he even know me? I'm not sure he did."

"He was your father, Dori. Maybe you were just more confident back then."

She had been, of course. She hadn't lost most of her family yet. She hadn't gotten so far off track. Or fired. Or hated. She'd already gotten dumped by the man she loved, but that by itself wouldn't have amounted to so much, not at that point in her life. But it all added up. The erosion of one's self confidence was a cumulative process.

Maybe it was like alcoholism and you had to hit bottom before you could start building it back.

Had she hit bottom yet?

God, she hoped so.

Maya took the sheets from Dori and started laying them out on the coffee table. "So, I think we need to document these before I catalog them."

"What do you mean?"

"Copies. Location. Dates. So it can't fucking disappear. Because here's direct evidence any collaborating Putney thinks he was doing with your dad is purely in his own mind. You have your phone? We both take pictures, the record ought to be safe."

Dori cocked her head. "You're finally buying my theory?"

"Putney's asked me about emails and that manuscript in every conversation we've had about this job. That level of persistence … and then this? I think maybe you're right."

Dori looked around the room. "How much longer do you think you'll be doing this?"

Maya said, "I'm almost done. I expect to finish boxing things up tomorrow. But now that I know what he did with that book, I'm thinking I should check all these damned books." She sighed, which Dori could understand. There were a lot of bookshelves, and a lot of books.

"Some of them are up in the attic, actually," Dori said. "The Friends didn't think all of Dad's books looked appropriately literary."

Maya's eyes widened. "What? How many books?"

"I don't know. Three or four boxes. Or five. Or six. Basically, all the paperbacks."

Maya sighed. "Maybe you'd better make that two days."

"Don't finish up without letting me know," Dori said. "I have an idea. For the novel."

Maya held her hand up. "I don't want to hear about it yet. Go sit your butt down and *write it.*"

Chapter 46

The idea was to finish her dad's novel by alternating his manuscript – finished by her according to his outline – with the point of view of the man's daughter. She could do that. She could probably even find a happier ending for it without totally undermining her father's intentions. She went home and copied his back-of-the-envelope outline with lots of space between elements, and started filling it in with the daughter's story.

Yeah, she could definitely do that. In some ways it would be like writing one of the old parodies she'd excelled at in high school, just not funny. Or not funny in the same way. She wrote a few pages in the daughter's voice just to see if her confidence was unwarranted. But it came easily. And it felt good. But of course, that was how her father usually felt, too, when he was drafting, no matter how bad it was.

She put the novel aside and went back to her assignment. If she thought of it as free publicity for the novel, maybe it wouldn't feel so impossible. Maya kept insisting even bad press was better than no press.

Her stomach clenched, not believing that for a second. She decided she would literally show it to everybody she cared about before she submitted it. They were the people who had already stood by her. They would tell her if she was making a terrible mistake.

Her editor approved her piece, after asking for some revisions that did improve it. And Joe had been an earlier, pickier reader, questioning a few of her rhetorical decisions, and pushing her towards some points she might not have had the nerve to attempt otherwise.

After telling her it was scheduled to run the next day with the headline she'd requested, the editor also warned her. "You may get most of your blowback from the alt-right this time, meaning the neo-Nazis, and they can be pretty brutal."

More brutal than what she'd already seen? Really?

She'd run an earlier draft past Maya and even Dr. Davis, asking them both to please try to react as if they didn't know her. Dr. Davis told her the reasoning and the history were sound and he hoped it would educate people. Maya said it was pretty good considering it was written while white, but it probably wouldn't satisfy everybody.

But it had completely escaped Dori she might instead outrage a whole bunch of white people. She asked the editor, "You really think I'll get more blowback than I did the first time?"

There was a small sigh on the other end of the line. "Honestly, there's no predicting. Depends on how much it gets read and shared. But in terms of sheer malice? I would expect it to be ugly. Not on our site – we moderate. But on Twitter? You probably shouldn't even look."

"Well, I'm kind of an old hand at that," Dori said. She still didn't understand Twitter. Maya loved it. Maya had helped her get the fake Eudora Bardwell shut down and helped her start up her own verified account, but Dori hardly ever looked in on it – the only people she followed on it were Maya, Maya's father, Gagnon Landscaping LLC, Robert Putney-Lewis, and the town of Jasper, mostly because she'd discovered it would post notices about recycling pick-ups.

When Joe put out the light that night, she said, "The editor told me it's probably going to start up all over again."

"What is?"

"The nasty stuff. You know, like death threats on Twitter."

"Oh. Well, it's just bullshit. The nasty ones are a bunch of losers sitting alone somewhere on their stupid devices. It's not like the literary world will feel they need to rebuke you as a matter of duty this time."

"You think that's what that was?" The ones that had stuck in her mind hadn't struck her as particularly literary.

"If you're lucky, this time some of them will just notice how well you can write."

She was silent.

"You can, you know. You always could."

"The family business." The one she had long blamed for destroying her family.

"Why do you keep resisting it? All my mom could leave me was this house and this barn. All your parents could leave you was a name that's still worth something in literary circles. You might as well get whatever advantage you can out of it. How do you think the people at the top get all *their* power and money? Most of them inherit it."

"Yeah, but that isn't fair."

"You're right. It isn't. It isn't fair, but it's how it is. Life isn't fair."

She clutched his hand. He was still in a pretty dark place.

Later that night Joe rolled over and must have realized she was lying there wide awake. "Can't sleep?"

"Nope." She could literally feel her abdominals tightening against the tweets to come the next morning as if they had physical mass. "I think it's worse now that I understand what will happen."

"Was it really so bad last time? I seem to recall having sex three times in one night."

She snorted gently. "That *was* a pretty effective distraction." She rolled on her side to face him. "Why, are you offering?"

They stared at each other in the moonlit dark. And then he yawned.

She chuckled. "It wasn't my plan to wake you up in the middle of the night. Go back to sleep. You can distract me tomorrow."

He reached over and clamped his hand on her ass and pulled her towards him. "Nope. Don't worry. I got this."

The next morning, there it was, right on the lead page of the online version of the paper:

THE STUPID WHITE GIRL'S GUIDE TO BLACKFACE
My father, Bedford Bardwell – a white man born and raised in Florida, although he claimed to be from Georgia – wrote what at least

*one white critic called "the greatest American novel about slavery."
Thirty years later, living in the same small 99% white town in Massachusetts where he and my white mother raised their six white
children, I told a blackface joke that went viral.*

*How did that happen? The way I suspect it happens to most stupid
white people who make blackface jokes.*

*I thought I knew what blackface was. I didn't. I thought it was
white people putting on black make-up. And that was just enough, I
figured, to shock the 100% white lady volunteers at the monthly
meeting of the Friends of the Bedford Bardwell House who were annoying me with their genteel avoidance of slavery. And bounce
houses.*

Yes, I was that immature.

*And also that ignorant. I had no idea of the full racial connota-
tions of the blackface joke I made. Maybe whoever decided it was
worth sharing that bad joke with a reporter didn't know, either, or
maybe she did. In any case, my joke got reported, and then it got
shared thousands of times, and my life would never be the same.*

*I'm pretty sure the white boss who fired me over it also had no
idea how bad it was. She just knew how irritating the reporters' phone
calls were. I finally began to get schooled in what I'd done wrong
when I went home and an African American friend generously decided to fill me in instead of writing me off.*

*Maya Davis is a talented documentary film-maker and part-time
archivist who was organizing my father's papers at the time. She
pulled up an old black and white minstrel show comedy routine on
her iPhone and told me to watch it.*

*There on her screen I saw a nicely dressed white woman, in the
straight role, performing opposite a white man in grotesque blackface. There was nothing realistic looking about his make-up. Eyes
and mouth were left white in big circles with ridiculously large pro-
portions. He was dressed in a clownish suit and he made just about
every joke possible about how lazy, cowardly, and stupid he was. The
white lady casually called him "stupid," and he didn't so much as
wince. Neither did the actual black musicians seated behind him.*

*I later discovered this was actually a scene from the movie 'Yes,
Sir, Mr. Bones,' about a boy learning about minstrelsy from a bunch*

of retired performers. So it's not really a primary source from the era of blackface, which predates moving pictures. (During real minstrel shows, it's also highly unlikely white and black performers would ever appear together on stage.) Yet it's striking that in 1951 this scene was still considered filmable:

White woman: Now all I want you to do is meet me at the zoo in the morning at nine o'clock.

White man in blackface: With the rest of the monkeys?

White woman: With the rest of the monkeys.

White man in blackface: I'll bring my grandpa with me.

Turns out, if you want vicious racial stereotypes to really have some staying power, you make them part of your popular culture. Did you ever wonder how Jim Crow got to be the name given to segregationist laws in the South? It's because of a blackface character, Jim Crow, who appeared in minstrel shows all over the country. Zip Coon was another one. The mammy originated there, too. The dandy, the over-sexed Jezebel, the shuffling uncle who'd do anything for the master – these stereotypical figures all blossomed to life in minstrel shows that were popular all over the country, including the Northeast, before, during, and after the Civil War.

The uncle figure, in fact, originated in traveling shows that ripped off Harriett Beecher Stowe's popular "Uncle Tom's Cabin," often while changing its abolitionist message to something that was proslavery. (That has also left us with an unfair impression of the actual Uncle Tom character, who was a heroic figure.)

Minstrel shows were so dominant a form of entertainment in their day that some African American troupes took their own shows on the road – and even wore blackface for them!

Some African American critics have accused my father of essentially wearing blackface as a novelist in his portrayal of Beulah, the enslaved protagonist of "Tea and Slavery." There may be more truth to that than they could know, as a future documentary from Maya Davis will show. And yet it's surely also an inevitable risk for any white author who writes characters of color.

Despite the risks, I can't help but feel segregation in fiction is as harmful as segregation in real life, not just the old Jim Crow kind, but the default segregation of where we live, where we go to school, who shows up in what way in the history books, who gets called in for an interview, who gets the job, who gets a decent mortgage rate, who gets valuable tax breaks, who gets published, who's more likely to get arrested and put in prison or shot, who gets slotted into what congressional district, and … well, you get the idea.

The disadvantages of poverty are significant for whites, too, but it's been shown over and over again it's a lot harder to escape them if you're black. And some of that is because of the vicious stereotypes we Americans honed in those minstrel shows and still carry with us today, often without any idea where they originated.

Those who've felt the sting of those stereotypes in their daily life understood why my blackface joke was completely out of line. Those who've studied the history of racial politics in America also knew.

And now, finally, I get it, too.

So here's my advice. It's very simple, really: Are you white? Then don't tell blackface jokes.

The comments under the article were mostly kind, but of course the paper would have moderated out the bad ones. "Don't even look at Twitter," Joe said. "I'll check it later in case there's anything important."

"Fine," she said. She had decided she was willing to wait years, really.

"It would be kind of like Natalie Cole and Nat King Cole singing 'Unforgettable' together," she explained on the phone to her father's agent the next day. She didn't add what she was privately thinking – if Nat King Cole was a drunk who'd never finished the song, and Natalie Cole didn't know what the hell she was doing.

"I like it," he said. She'd been planning to screw up her courage and call him about her idea for finishing her dad's novel, but he'd called her first, to congratulate her on her piece. "Send me the first three – no, better make it four – chapters and an outline."

"It might take me a while. I just started working on it."

There was a slight pause. "You don't have any experience at this, right?" he said. "You realize you're probably going to require some pretty heavy coaching. We might even need to bring a ghost writer on board. Is that something you could live with?"

She had expected that question, and wrestled with her stubbornness. "Yes."

"Good," the man said. "In that case, I'm sure we can get a deal."

Chapter 47

Dori moved the stuff she wanted to keep from her home to Joe's house, stacking most of it in his old bedroom and attic since they were still treating the arrangement as a temporary measure. Repairs and renovations were soon to begin at the Bedford Bardwell House, financed by the sale of his papers to the Putney Lewis Library at Brooke College. The trustees were waiting for an appraisal and the first post-scandal royalty check to determine how much they would settle on Salinger and Dori for giving up their interest in the house. It had been agreed each of them would also receive ten percent of royalties from the estate for the life of the copyright. This, Dori knew, and hoped Salinger would understand, might really seem like something at first, but would likely dwindle to very little in time.

Joe still insisted she should use that money – and the astonishingly large advance her agent had won her for her and the estate for her novel based on her father's manuscript – which also hadn't begun to be paid yet – to go back to school and get her degree. Now that Joe knew she was taking her writing seriously and gingerly building an online presence – blogging, tweeting, and slowly replacing Eudora Bardwell, Blackface Idiot with Eudora Bardwell, Reformed Blackface Idiot – he'd started sending her every version of "Don't Quit Your Day Job" he could find. There were plenty.

Her agent had already warned she'd need to keep writing steadily if she ever hoped to make a real living from it, even with the built-in advantage of her name. The good news, as he saw it, was that the best parts of the manuscript she'd submitted so far were the ones she'd written in her own voice rather than trying to imitate her father's. In fact, he wanted a proposal for another novel as soon as she'd finished the current one.

Dori was making steady progress, but it wasn't easy. She often fantasized about going back to working with patients. She enjoyed writing more than she expected, but she also felt she could only stand working away in that quiet room upstairs for about three or four hours a day before it began to feel claustrophobic. She also hated the feeling that trailed her through all her waking hours that there was always something more she could and should be doing. If she went away to get a degree, she thought perhaps it should be in nursing or pharmacy or occupational therapy, not English. Something with work hours that ended when you left the place. Writing then could simply be something extra, like Joe's apartment in the barn, which he'd begun to work on again.

Sometimes, when he'd left dishes in the sink or gotten on her case about something, she would fantasize about living in that apartment herself.

He was an encouraging but critical reader, particularly useful at telling her when the parts she'd written for the male protagonist didn't sound believably male or, as she finished her father's half, enough like Bedford Bardwell. Her agent was a lot less picky, she told him once, frustrated.

"He knows it will sell no matter how mediocre it is," Joe said. "For him, this book is probably just a gimmick. I want you to blow them away."

It sounded violent. He was still angry about the fire, still convinced Summers had tried to kill him. The more time they spent together, the more she realized Joe was angry about a lot of things, from his disappearing father and struggling mother and the cancer that had taken her life, to the old boy network in town and a rigged national economy. He was even angry at God, something she'd been spared by not believing in the first place. It was all understandable to her, and Joe didn't erupt very often, but it still made her a little nervous to live with that slow burn.

One day when he was complaining bitterly about something, she said, "Do you want a drink?"

He just looked at her. "Seriously? You want me to have a drink?"

It was what her mother had often said, she realized. What both parents had often said. "No," she said. "No, not really."

Angry or not, she felt he was more present with her, more truly himself, than anyone ever had been before, including his younger self. Certainly not her parents, with all their secrets from the children, though perhaps – she hoped – not from each other.

When it came to the writing, she told Joe, he probably shouldn't encourage her. What if she actually started to believe she had talent? How much better might her father's life had been if he'd been forced to relegate his writing to hobby status, and make a normal living fixing motorcycles or something? And what nerve did she have, trying to pretend to be a writer herself, without all those years of sweat and tears and rejections that were supposed to go along with it? She was cheating, really.

That was, in fact, what most of the nasty tweets about her were saying now.

But she'd also already experienced enough gratification at the words that blossomed under her fingers to realize how seductive it was. She understood far better than before why her father had refused to give up for so long. There was also something about typing over his work in progress that had forced her to appreciate his abilities more than she had before.

But some of the gratification she felt simply came from beating Robert Putney at his own game. Shortly after the papers – complete with that partial manuscript (Maya had gotten her finder's fee after all) – had gone up to Vermont, Dr. Arthur Churchill Davis had published a scholarly article on that last incomplete work, including the full text of it, the emails with Putney, and the outline her father had left.

To Maya's delight, he'd also quoted from his daughter's successful YouTube series called "Searching for Bedford Bardwell," which was receiving plenty of media coverage and probably contributing more to Dori's rehabilitation than anything she'd done herself, even if there was way more commentary on her awful make-up during that discussion with her grandparents than she would like.

Maya was in talks about doing a longer piece for PBS, though she was holding out while she tried to tack on funding for a documentary about heart disease in women of color that they seemed a lot less excited about.

Dori was thinking of asking her to collaborate on a book proposal about their travels, because she couldn't help thinking that, once again, the story had ended up being a predominantly white one, and maybe there was no way to fix that without getting Maya's side of the story in there, right out of Maya's mouth. Maybe the two of them should go back down for a couple of weeks and hunt up Maya's roots instead of Dori's. Or maybe that whole growing-up-black-in-Vermont thing deserved a little more attention. But that would have to be Maya's book, not hers.

Joe's landscaping business was doing better by the time leaf season came along, although some of his old customers never returned. But she suspected he would never feel the same about Jasper. He had quietly walked away from his church, the Kiwanis, and the Fire Department, even though Lionel Summers had announced his retirement as fire chief and Robert said it might have had something to do with Joe's injury. Joe had not only refused to attend the retirement dinner, he said he had no intention of working with any of those guys ever again.

"They probably only knew what Summers told them," she said.

"Not one of them came to me on his own," he said. "It was easier for them to believe whatever he told them. And even if I did panic" – for he knew that was indeed the story around town – "why does that deserve their ridicule? They're treating it like some sort of hazing I failed! To hell with them!"

She supposed it didn't really matter, unless of course his house caught on fire someday.

Dori began driving their social life, partly out of a sense that if she didn't, Joe would end up in an even darker place. She organized meals with the neighbors or Joe's employees, as well as visits with Maya. She even had Charlie Perrault and Marjorie Haight over for dinner and offered them a long-overdue thank you for all their help when her parents died and since. It made Marjorie tear up a little. Dori also tried to get her to admit she'd been the one to talk about the blackface joke with the reporter, but Marjorie simply looked pained and said, "That reporter probably spoke to a few of the ladies there that night, my dear. Why does it even matter?"

It mattered to Dori. But there were so many things about her parents and other people that she would never know. Perhaps it was best to let them all go.

Somewhat to Dori's surprise, their social calendar also began to include quite a few double dates with Ruth and Robert Jr. Those two were spending a lot of time together, but not making much of it.

"Why are you keeping it so unofficial?" Dori asked Ruth one unusually warm night late in October when the two of them were sitting at the end of the dock at the Putneys' lake.

Ruth looked back towards the shore and lowered her voice. "Because I think he's a sex addict. He says he can control it, but I think that's bullshit. I told him he should find a twelve-step group."

"They have groups for that?" It sounded like the perfect way to hook up with other sex addicts.

"They do. But he claims it's not an addiction. That he really loves sex, but he can stop anytime he wants. But he's also got a lot of shame about it. You'd think that might be a clue. So I expect he'll be on to the next woman soon, if he isn't already. He slept with Lisa, you know."

Dori stared her surprise.

"Yeah," Ruth said. "Right after the fire. That was before we got together. He said he was pumping her for information." She snorted.

"That must have cheered up Lisa quite a lot." She hadn't been heard from at all, though Dori knew she was still around.

"Oh, yeah. She got to sleep in the summer house! He took her to a fancy party down in New York, too. No wonder she suddenly wasn't pregnant anymore. He thinks he did Joe a big favor, though he says it was really for you."

Dori looked back to where Robert and Joe were lounging in

the Adirondack chairs with their beers, happily critiquing the current candidates for President. An interest in politics was at least one thing they had in common.

Robert, clearly, was capable of some Machiavellian moves himself. She felt a moment's pity for Lisa.

A brief moment.

She frowned at Ruth. "If you don't trust him, how can you do it?" She thought of that bottle of Valtrex in his bathroom. Of course, for all she knew Ruth had a bottle of her own.

"Oh, I'm just enjoying it while it lasts. He really is very good in bed, you know. Five stars to Robert the Dick. And how are *you* doing?" Ruth raised her eyebrows and smiled invitingly.

Dori said, "I have no complaints." And she didn't, not in that regard.

"Are you sure?" Ruth asked.

It was much harder to get anything past Ruth when she was sober. "He keeps saying I should go away to college, finish my degree."

"Good for him."

"I'm twenty-seven. If I graduate in three years, I'll be thirty."

Ruth frowned. "And if you don't get a degree, someday you'll be fifty and you'll still have no degree."

"Okay, but what if I still can't decide what I want to be when I grow up?"

"Go to school. It will give you the tools to figure it out." Ruth was still studying for the bar exam. She hadn't quite passed the first time.

Dori looked out at the lake. "Neither of my parents went to college. They did all right."

"Yeah, and look at them now."

Dori breathed in sharply. As if college could have saved her parents.

And now, apparently, it was supposed to save her.

Chapter 48

It started snowing early and hard, so Joe was getting a nice income from plowing driveways. But New England winters were unpredictable, so he also asked the trustees to let him sell a truckload of Christmas trees in front of the Bedford Bardwell House – a much better location than his own place – with a percentage of profits going to the trust. That was how Dori found herself in three layers of clothing next to a not-terribly-effective warming fire in her old driveway on a moderately cold December night, waiting for a young family to decide which tree was for them. It couldn't be easy to do in the early winter dark, using only what light shone from the LED strings around the enclosure Joe had set up in the front yard.

If they ever did this again, they'd need better lighting.

Would Dori even be here then? Home on break, perhaps, if she went back to school, as Joe kept urging her to do.

"It's lopsided," the mother said about one the father had pulled out and stood up, so the group moved further down the row of leaning trees.

Everything is lopsided, Dori felt like telling her. Nothing is perfect. Not even those trees, lovingly shaped for years on some hillside by a local tree farmer.

Joe ducked out of his little trailer with a hot cocoa for her. They were taking turns thawing out. "More tough customers?" he asked. The last couple had maintained a disdainful air from the beginning and left empty-handed, loudly discussing the better options they'd likely find in Greenfield.

"I don't think so. But I have a feeling they're going to take a while." She sipped her cocoa and leaned discreetly against him. He slid an arm down behind her back and squeezed her butt.

The two boys wanted the biggest one, but their little sister was lobbying for a scraggly apartment-sized fir she apparently saw as some kind of rescue tree. The wife and husband were grimly debating whether the bigger tree would even fit in their house. "How about something a little smaller?" the mother said to the boys, as if she needed their permission.

Dori's parents had always used the same old plastic tree. It was just cheaper.

"How many kids do you want?" she asked.

He looked down at her. "I don't know. One of each seems kind of ideal. If it works out that way. You?"

"More than one. Have a couple, and see how it goes. None of this only child crap."

He gave a startled laugh. "Am I that screwed up?"

"No. I just don't want any kid of ours to be all alone in the hospital someday because he has no relations."

"So you think Salinger would show up if you ended up alone in the hospital?"

Good question. "Eventually, if I was there long enough." He'd probably try to bring her some weed. It was his customary hostess gift every time they had him and Jenna over for dinner. When they'd told him thanks, but that wasn't really their thing, he'd instead brought it cooked into brownies, and failed to tell them until they'd each eaten one.

Joe said, "I'm not sure he's the kind of uncle I'd want my kids to hang out with."

"Supervised visits," she said.

"We're getting ahead of ourselves anyway," he said.

Were they?

When she thought about all the marriages she'd ever seen in real life, rather than in fiction – which tended to end with the wedding – she was forced to conclude marriage was a horrifying crapshoot. She loved Joe, but he had some worrisome tendencies. Their relationship would never be all hearts and flowers. It would never be any kind of love she'd ever imagined as a girl. It was dangerous, maybe even stupid. It was her mother belting herself and her children into a small plane under lowering skies because her husband believed he could fly.

She looked up at a veil of thinly moonlit clouds. But wasn't Joe as grounded as any anyone could be? He literally dug holes and planted things in them for a living.

She faced him and her heart began to thump. "I don't want to go away to college."

He stared down at her for a moment. "You don't think that would be the smart thing to do?"

"Yes, but I don't want to do it. Not unless you come with me."

"You know I can't do that. Not yet. Maybe in a year or two."

"Exactly. So maybe I'll do some courses at GCC. Or online. But I don't want to waste any more time. I think we should get married. And then in another year or two, if we haven't killed each other yet, I think we should have kids."

He laughed, and then he bent down a little and searched her eyes. "You're sure?"

"As sure as I can be."

He looked uncertain again at that.

Dori said, "Remember when you told me you were putting me in charge? I said that would never work, but I've changed my mind. Let's get married, Joe. Marry me."

He grinned broadly, but he also folded his arms and drew back a little. "I used to fantasize you'd come crawling back to me on your knees and beg me to marry you after all. This would be in front of a crowd, of course – and I'd look down at you for this long dramatic moment ... and then I'd tell you to go to hell."

His tone was affectionate, but those words! "You seriously have some anger issues."

"Yeah, I know." He drained his cup. "You done with that?" He held out his hand for her cup.

She gulped the last swallow down and handed it over. "I'm not crawling, and they're not even paying attention," she said. "But if you're going to tell me to go to hell, you might as well go ahead and get it over with."

"You thought I might actually do that?" He tossed the cups in the trash bin and then came back and lifted her right off the ground in a hug. "Of course I'll marry you. How many times have I already asked?" He put her back down and they kissed, and kept kissing.

But someone was coughing. "Excuse me," a disgruntled voice

said. "We'd like to buy this tree, if you don't mind."

They leapt apart. "Sorry!" Dori said.

"We just got engaged," Joe said. "That'll be forty bucks. Would you like me to give it a clean cut?"

"Yes, please," the man said, and handed the cash over. "And congratulations."

His wife said to her, "Yes, congratulations." She turned to check on her trailing offspring. "Kids, would you stop looking at the trees! This is the one! We've got it! At last." She rolled her eyes at Dori.

Joe man-handled the tree into a rack and took his chain saw to it. Dori always found it loud and a little terrifying. Someone could get hurt with that thing.

"At last," she echoed. And she smiled.

A personal note

Reader, I need you.

If you got this far, I hope you enjoyed this book. And if you did, I have a favor to ask, because my ability to continue writing and publishing depends on me gaining more readers. Could you do any one of the following for me? I would so appreciate it.

Review it on Amazon, or wherever you purchased it.

Review it or rate it on Goodreads or Library Thing.

Follow me on Amazon or BookBub.

Join my mailing list (get missing scenes and other freebies!) or check out my web site and blog.

Tell your friends, book club, library, or bookseller about it.

Like or follow me on my Facebook profile, my Facebook author page, Twitter, or Pinterest.

I would love to hear from you personally and will most likely write you back. You can reach me via email at sandra-hutchison@sheerhubris.com or via snail mail sent to the publisher's address on the copyright page.

Thank you!
Sandra

Acknowledgments

This book would never have made it into your hands without the able help of many friends who provided useful information and critiqued early manuscripts for me. Ivana Addo kindly allowed me to pick her brain about patient care (and should not be held responsible for any errors I've made despite that). Lucia Nevai, Nandini Sheshadri, Rachel Vagts, Barbara Naeger, Lisa Arrington, Nancy Johnson, Ann Norman, Harry Ramble, and Amy Hughes gave me useful beta feedback in matters large and small. Lisa and Nancy were particularly kind in sharing their reactions as African American readers, so important to a white author traversing ground that doesn't really belong to her.

And, of course, this book would never have gotten to you if I had not enjoyed the support and friendship of so many others out there with my earlier books. You know who you are, but I give special thanks again to Lucia Nevai, S.M. Freedman, Tim Farrington, Jenny Milchman, and Julia Spencer-Fleming, traditionally published writers who have been generous and collegial even with someone on a different path. Likewise, I thank supportive indie colleagues, especially Mary Maddox, Tahlia Newland, S.M. Spencer, K.J. Farnsworth, Lisa Arrington, and Emelle Gamble. Thanks as well to the support of many fellow writers in Awesome Indies and the Women's Fiction Writers Association.

Thanks to my family for their patience and support, particularly my parents Alexander and Jackie, as well as Jaime DeJesus, my son Alejandro (who has had to put up with a lot of vagueness and distraction from me over the years), my brother and sister-in-law Drew and Kara Hutchison, my stepdaughter and her husband, Lourdes and Edward Sambucci, and the whole extended Hutchison and DeJesus families.

Thanks to my church family at St. John's Episcopal Church in Troy and my colleagues at Hudson Valley Community College. It still tickles me when any of you read my books and tell me so instead of running screaming away.

Thanks to the authors of two riveting books I relied on in my research: Jon Ronson's *So You've Been Publicly Shamed* and Robin Gaby Fisher's *After the Fire: A True Story of Friendship and Survival.* I am also indebted to Dr. Bruce Potenza's instructional videos from the UCSD Regional Burn Center. Once again, any errors are mine. People, I beg you: Make sure your smoke alarms are working.

Please know you are also in my heart if you have ever reviewed one of my books, shared one of my posts, showed up for an event, rated a book on Goodreads, told a friend, or helped get the word out in any other way: THANK YOU! Authors depend on you generous souls who do this far more than you realize.

About the Author

Born and raised in the Tampa Bay area, Sandra Hutchison survived a transplant to a small, snowy New England town during high school and eventually stopped sulking about it, though it's possible she's still working it out in her fiction. She currently lives in Troy, New York, where she teaches writing at Hudson Valley Community College.

She is the author of THE AWUL MESS: A LOVE STORY (2013), a semifinalist for the 2014 Amazon Breakthrough Novel Award, and THE RIBS AND THIGH BONES OF DESIRE (2014), awarded a Seal of Excellence from Awesome Indies.

Learn more at SheerHubris.com, Amazon, Facebook, Twitter, Goodreads, or Pinterest.

Sign up for her mailing list at sheerhubris.com and get access to free books, advance reading copies, and missing scenes.

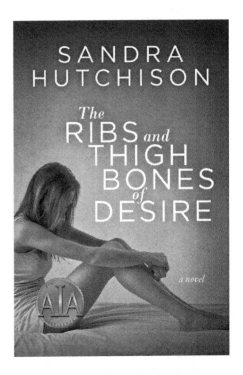

A teenage girl and a widowed physics professor risk scandal and worse when they try to help each other survive unexpected losses.

Physics professor David Asken doesn't know how he survived the plane crash that killed his wife and daughter, but he figures he must have run for it. Sixteen-year-old neighbor Molly Carmichael, who used to be the babysitter, isn't exactly eager to keep house for him while he recuperates. He's quietly planning to kill himself. She's trying to cope with her flamboyant artist mother's highly sexual art and highly sexual lifestyle, as well as her own adolescent stirrings -- but that's nothing compared to what she'll face after a drunken teen party. Will the unexpectedly tender connection that grows between man and girl help, or just make it worse?

This provocative coming-of-age novel set in a small town in 1977 asks whether there's ever a time when doing the wrong thing might be exactly right.

If you like book club fiction with unforgettable characters, mounting suspense, and a moral dilemma that will leave you thinking long after you finish, you'll love this novel Tim Farrington (THE MONK DOWNSTAIRS) calls "a gutsy, beautiful book."

Includes group discussion questions at the end.

"It's rare that a story captivates me so deeply, but David and especially Molly will live with me forever." ~ S.M. Freedman, author of THE FAITHFUL

Order it at Amazon or your favorite retailer today!

Divorced by a husband who wanted children she couldn't have, editor Mary Bellamy has left the Boston suburbs to telecommute from tiny, affordable Lawson, New Hampshire. All she wants is peace and quiet, and maybe a cat. But the unhappily-married Episcopal priest who is trying to save her heathen soul might be susceptible to more earthly temptations. And the handsome local cop who is an excellent kisser confuses her by being in favor of gay rights, but opposed to sex before marriage.

Soon Mary is keeping a scandalous secret at great cost to her own happiness. Worse, her disintegrating ex-husband threatens what little she has left. But in this witty and affectionate tale of small town life, Mary discovers the connections she's made can result not only in terrifying risks, but in unexpected blessings.

If you like small town fiction with compelling characters, page-turning suspense, some humor, some heat, and plenty of romance, you'll love THE AWFUL MESS.

"THE AWFUL MESS is a wonderful read!" -- Julia Spencer-Fleming, author of IN THE BLEAK MIDWINTER

"It renews me as a reader, to enjoy a book so much; and as a writer, see it done so well." -- Tim Farrington, author of THE MONK DOWNSTAIRS

A semifinalist for the Amazon Breakthrough Novel Award.

Order it at Amazon or your favorite retailer today!

Questions for Discussion

WARNING: CONTAINS SPOILERS!

1. Which Bardwell follies is the title referencing?
2. We only see Dori's parents through her memories. How does her perception of them change? Does yours change? How good a job of parenting do you think they did, on balance?
3. There are a number of deeds that are suggested but never fully revealed in this novel: What really happened with Dori's father and Loretta Ledbetter? *Did* the fire chief try to kill Joe? Who ratted on Dori for her blackface joke? Why would the author withhold more definitive answers to these questions?
4. A white novelist who writes characters of color and takes on race issues necessarily does so from a position of privilege. Does this author avoid the pitfalls of that, or fall right into them? How well does Dori's piece about blackface work in this context?
5. Maya speaks for African Americans who can't help but notice their cultural history being appropriated by white authors like Bedford Bardwell. She says they drown out more authentic voices. Samuel Chestnut argues that Bardwell's novel has beautiful things to say about the human condition. Where do you come down in that debate? Where does this novel fall in that debate?
6. Dori is young, stressed out, and certainly not immune from personality defects in this novel. What are they, and does she overcome any of them?
7. Joe has some tendencies many women would find troublesome. Would you marry a man like him? Is Dori making a mistake at the end of this novel? What are their chances for a successful marriage?

8. Did Dori's mother make a mistake when she ran off with Dori's father and married him? What does the novel seem to be saying about marriage in general?

9. How does this novel portray the differences and similarities between North and South? Is it fair in doing so?

10. Dori makes a number of churlish comments about writers throughout this book but ends up a writer herself. Is she really meant to be a writer, or is this just a temporary solution to her problems?

11. Maya has a cynical yet enthusiastic view of the book business. Dori's view is just cynical. Is either view valid? What does the novel seem to be suggesting about publishing and literature?

12. Robert Putney-Lewis has both admirable and not-so-admirable traits. Why does Ruth hook up with him, and is she right about their prospects?

13. What does the novel seem to be saying about local journalism, the mainstream media, and social media?

14. Dori's naiveté and lack of access to social media may seem implausible to many readers who depend on it daily. Why would the author portray her this way?

15. Dori's experience of poverty while living in such a grand setting may seem implausible to some readers as well. Your thoughts?

16. The author has said she drew inspiration for this novel from Jane Austen's *Persuasion,* Mark Twain's *The Adventures of Huckleberry Finn,* Jon Ronsom's *So You've Been Publicly Shamed,* and the controversial release of Harper Lee's *Go Set a Watchman.* Do you see this in the final product? Can you detect other possible influences?

17. Given the list above, is there too much going on in this novel? If so, what subplots would you have dropped, and why?

38295247R00204

Made in the USA
Middletown, DE
16 December 2016